The author spent many years training to qualify as an accountant, then many years in management banging heads together, including his own. But the urge to write finally won and this is his second novel.

His first, 'The Gay Solicitor', played a little trick on the reader. The solicitor was not gay. Just light-hearted and carefree in accordance with the original meaning of the word.

No tricks this time.

By the same author

The Gay Solicitor (Vanguard Press 2006)
ISBN 978 1 84386 268 9

LIKE FATHER, NOT LIKE SON

Edward K Norris

LIKE FATHER, NOT LIKE SON

Vanguard Press

VANGUARD PAPERBACK

© Copyright 2008
Edward K Norris

The right of Edward K Norris to be identified as author of this work has been asserted by him in accordance with the Copyright, Designs and Patents Act 1988.

All Rights Reserved

No reproduction, copy or transmission of this publication may be made without written permission.
No paragraph of this publication may be reproduced, copied or transmitted save with the written permission of the publisher, or in accordance with the provisions of the Copyright Act 1956 (as amended).

Any person who commits any unauthorised act in relation to this publication may be liable to criminal prosecution and civil claims for damages.

A CIP catalogue record for this title is available from the British Library.

ISBN 978 1 84386 401 1

*Vanguard Press is an imprint of
Pegasus Elliot MacKenzie Publishers Ltd.*
www.pegasuspublishers.com

First Published in 2008

**Vanguard Press
Sheraton House Castle Park
Cambridge England**

Printed & Bound in Great Britain

Acknowledgement

I should like to commend once more Craig Battersby for his tremendous help with the computer operations.

Also his partner Trish (alter ego Leanne) for her unfailing inspiration.

"Listen, Mark!" Vince Adams got hold of his shoulders. "You've got to face the facts. There's only one way to get rid of your father."

He drew his fingers across his throat.

Mark went a little pale. "I know! I know! I've not much feeling for him, the bastard's always held me down."

He went quiet. "But that IS a bit drastic."

"Don't you want the millions that would rush through your fingers from the sale of 'Tall Trees' and its huge estate, all situated in the Surrey stockbroker belt?" Vince was mocking.

Mark thought about the luxurious country hotel and its numerous rooms and suites. Facilities, solarium, steam room, gymnasium, swimming pool, even tennis courts. Then there was the massive grounds.

'Tall Trees' sprang from an old manor house and grounds bought for a song at the end of the last war by his father's father and carefully developed over the years. It was now number one for the wealthy and famous, and, although big business, the family had kept control.

Vince was getting impatient. "Well?" he demanded, "And don't tell me again you'll think about it. My backers will get tired."

Mark said curiously, "Who are your backers?"

"That's not for you to know. Obviously they are big enough or they wouldn't be interested. Come on!" he said forcefully, "I want an answer."

Mark said at last and without enthusiasm, "OK, but I want to know when and how."

"You'll know. You'll be part of it."

"What!" Mark's voice rose in agitation.

Vince soothed him. "All we would want from you is the time and route your father will take. We will do the rest. We have experts at arranging accidents."

Mark was still indecisive so Vince pushed him before he could draw back. "Right," he said. "I'll make the arrangements and get in touch when we're ready." He raised his brows. "OK?"

Mark didn't like it but he nodded, and the deal was done.

As he left Vince's office he shrank from his decision, yet he knew there was no alternative to remaining under his father's thumb. He had never really had affection for him. His father had wanted a copy of himself, and he wasn't. They clashed in every direction.

He shook his shoulders as if to clear his mind as he drove through the gates into 'Tall Trees'. There was a board meeting to attend.

He entered the boardroom last and his father, said sarcastically, "Something keep you, Mark?"

Before he could answer his mother Helen interrupted. "Let's get on with it, Don."

Mark sat down next to his sister Janet. Alan Freeman the company Secretary sat the other side of the table, and that was the full board.

Mark was very quiet and had little to say.

"Something on your mind?" Janet asked him afterwards.

"You could say that," he said.

He was still troubled about his decision and wanted to make one last effort to persuade his father to sell, if not now, in the future.

He walked into his office and faced him.

His father didn't look pleased. "What is it, Mark?"

"I wondered if you'd give some more thought to selling... Perhaps in the future?"

"How many times have I got tell you, Mark. We are not selling now, tomorrow, or ever. Everything remains in the family." His father glared at him crossly.

Mark tried again. "I understand your view, Dad. But think what it would mean to mother and Janet. No more responsibilities. Free to do absolutely what they want. Aren't they entitled to some of the good life?"

"They consider they have the good life. YOU'RE the odd one out." His father waved his arm, his temper rising. "Get out of my office before I get annoyed."

Mark left. The die was cast... Fuck him!

In the evening he rang his current girlfriend Carol. She had lasted longer than most.

Mark could be charming, but he was also moody and his scowls had often shortened his relationships.

"Hi!" she said, "We got a date for tonight?"

"Let's snatch a meal out then go to your place, eh?"

This suited Carol. Apart from the fact Mark was one of the wealthy Addison's, his powerful aura excited her. They had been to bed a few times, and he could be hot and exciting, but he could also be dull... She wanted to find the real Mark, and intended to find out. She had glimpsed in him a touch of ruthlessness but this didn't put her off. She had a streak of that herself.

"You're on, darling," she said.

"I'll pick you up at seven."

On the dot, from her window Carol saw his red Lotus pull up outside her flat and went to the door to meet him.

They dined at one of Mark's favourite places overlooking the river, 'The Riverside', where he got a lot of respect from the staff. That was one of the things Carol liked about Mark. The way people deferred to him. She had to admit he had an air of authority... From bossing people about at 'Tall Trees', she guessed.

They finished the evening at her flat, and Carol wondered if Mark would stay the night. He had been unusually quiet at the restaurant.

They sipped drinks and Carol looked into his face and was nettled.

She said a little crossly, "I don't think you've been with me tonight, Mark. What's up?"

He suddenly realised how insensitive he'd been.

He took her hand. "Sorry, darling, I've a problem up at 'Tall Trees' and it won't go away."

"Can I help?"

" I'm afraid it's one for me personally."

He tried to cheer up. "Let's have another drink then make love."

Carol was all for this but wondered if Mark would disappoint; his frame of mind was not encouraging.

He did disappoint. Although going through all the motions and finding the right spots, she thought it was mechanical man putting on an act.

She held her peace afterwards because she knew Mark could also be superb in bed. Better luck next time, she thought.

A week went by, and Mark heard nothing from Vince, then another week, and he began to think perhaps he was having second thoughts and would come up with another plan.

Then the dreaded call came through. "We're ready. Tell us your father's itinerary for the next week. Preferably evening drives. We know his silver Mercedes."

Mark tried to put him off. "He's nothing planned that I know of."

"All right, the following week. Don't tell me he's not driving anywhere then." Vince let a little threat creep into his voice.

Mark realised Vince had sensed his cold feet, and he was in a sweat. It was now or never.

Then with a masterstroke Vince pushed Mark over the edge. "Come on, Mark. You going to be your father's boot boy all your life or are you going to reach out for the waiting millions?"

Put starkly, this was too much for Mark. "All right," he mumbled, "I'll ring you by the end of the week."

He put the phone down, strangely relieved. No looking back.

At the end of the week he rang Vince and asked him what day had been chosen.

"Better you don't know," he said. "But it will be one evening next week."

It turned out to be Wednesday, and the news came through as Mark was at his mother's house.

Donald had been fatally injured in a head-on crash with a massive articulated wagon.

The driver said he took the bend and suddenly saw a Mercedes in front of him, no lights. He didn't mention that immediately after the smash he had reached the wreckage and turned off the Mercedes' lights.

Helen was devastated and kept repeating helplessly through her tears, "I can't believe it! I can't believe it!"

Mark put his arms round his mother and tried to comfort her. "He wouldn't have known anything about it," he whispered.

But, even in this dreadful first hour of torment, he put his plans first.

"Perhaps," he suggested, "we might sell up. Get away and start a new life. Would you like that?" He gave her a long sympathetic look.

"I don't know," she answered in a dull voice. "I shall have to start a new life, that's sure." Then she burst into tears again.

There was a flurry at the door and Janet came hurtling in white faced.

Mark drew back as Janet flew to her mother, and they immediately cried in each other's arms.

He diplomatically moved to the drinks cabinet and came back with large whiskies for the three of them.

Janet took a large swallow and insisted her mother do the same. Mark needed no bidding.

To his dismay, Janet then took charge, and gave Mark a string of instructions. Who to inform. Contact the police. Advise the family solicitor. Plus a host of other duties.

She finished with a grim face. "And we want particulars of the accident. Dad was a careful driver, and one thing he would never do is drive without lights. He always switched on at the first sign of dusk. We all know that for certain, don't we?" Her eyes swept over them both defiantly.

Mark didn't like the new purposeful Janet that was emerging but knew this was not the time to mount a challenge. Perhaps she thought it was her duty to take charge, being a year older.

He would soon alter that, he thought grimly.

The next day the police arrived. They introduced themselves as Detective Inspector Lew Green and Sergeant Sally Golding. They were in plain clothes.

They were very polite, expressed their sympathy and asked the usual questions.

Was Donald in good health? Had the car been serviced? What time did he leave home? Was it a business or private trip?

Helen interrupted their routine.

"You haven't given any details of the accident." She said stiffly, "One thing I will challenge absolutely is that my husband was driving without lights." She looked at Mark and Janet for support, and Janet vigorously joined in.

"No way! He always switched on at the first signs of darkness. He had contempt for those who didn't and wasn't polite in what he called them."

The inspector looked uncomfortable. "I'm afraid we can only be guided by the evidence. The driver of the wagon stated he suddenly saw the car in front of him without lights and had no chance of avoiding him."

"He was driving a massive articulated with a big trailer and was forced to swing out to negotiate the bend." The Inspector hesitated, "He said that if he had seen the car ahead he would have slowed down because he wouldn't have had sufficient clearance."

"So what you are saying," Helen said coldly, "is that the accident was entirely due to the absence of lights on my husband's car."

The Inspector tried to be diplomatic. He said soothingly, "It is possible, Mrs Addison, your husband THOUGHT he had switched on his lights, but he hadn't."

His answer was Helen's grim face and disbelieving comment. "Impossible!"

"Are you going to investigate this, Inspector?" she challenged.

"Of course," he replied. "But I have to tell you in all honesty that with only the driver as witness, and the switched off lights in the Mercedes, our scope is limited."

The hostility of the family was obvious, and the Inspector and sergeant were glad to get out of the house.

The sergeant said mockingly, "Daddy can do no wrong."

"Seems like it," the inspector grunted.

With the departure of the police there was a momentary silence in the house then Helen said, "Looks like the police have already made up their minds."

Mark said carefully, "As they pointed out they've little to go on."

"I don't think I can accept your father was driving without lights, and he would never be careless on the road," she snapped. "You ought to know that, Mark."

Mark was trying to keep his self- control. "But the police don't have our inside knowledge."

"Well, there's nothing we can do about it, is there?" Janet interrupted.

Helen pursed her lips, "I don't know."

Mark was surprised at her comment but wisely kept his mouth shut.

Another aggravation for Helen was that the funeral had to be delayed because a post mortem had been ordered, and she couldn't understand this.

Mark explained that apart from establishing the cause of death, the police would check for any physical impediment that may have affected his father's driving.

This brought a disdainful sniff from his mother. "Sheer waste of time."

Three weeks had elapsed since Donald's death, and at last Mark got the telephone call he had been expecting from Vince. He was in his office at 'Tall Trees'.

"Well, the obstacle is removed," Vince began. "Do we get some action soon?"

"I'm already working on it, Vince. But if I rush, it will create suspicion. Just leave it with me."

Mark's confident tone reassured Vince but he thought he seemed indecisive. "Well, speed it up," he said.

Mark had been keeping close to his mother since his father's death, and was waiting for an opportunity when she was in the right mood for a good talk about selling.

The trouble was that Janet kept popping up, and she pursued the opposite course... Must keep the business going. Dad would have wanted it.

She was fast becoming a nuisance, and Mark realised he must speak to his mother soon before Janet had her thinking along exactly the same lines.

He got his opportunity when Janet was out for the day and he called on her.

They briefly exchanged embraces and Mark sat down, facing her.

"How you feeling, Mum?"

"Not brilliant. I still can't make the funeral arrangements. Blasted police!" she said. "Instead of looking into the accident all they do is get in the way."

Mark wanted to get off that subject. "I'm sure," he said smoothly, "they are working on it." He tried a small smile, "You know what government departments are like, bogged down with routine. The police are in the same boat.

"What you could do with," he suggested, "is a break away from all this. Get away from the pressure and responsibilities. Give yourself a chance to think."

"Sounds inviting," she agreed, and Mark left her feeling more satisfied.

Then an unexpected complication occurred.

David Summers appeared on the scene with a smart young woman he introduced as his daughter Barbara.

It all seemed to happen very innocently.

At a hoteliers conference David had got himself and Barbara introduced to Helen, and from then on he appeared as the kindly adviser, with Barbara, a bubbling personality, offering sympathy and charm, for which Helen at this particular time was grateful.

David was a big fair man with lots of blonde hair and an engaging smile. Barbara was a smart brunette with big brown eyes and a very friendly manner.

Helen was easy prey, and they struck up a relationship.

Mark didn't like this development at all. He had expected an open field to launch his plans and he tackled his mother immediately.

"He and his daughter are just friends," she said. She gave a sniff and said sarcastically. "They've given me more understanding and sympathy than most of those around me."

"Now then, Mum," Mark said. "You know how we all feel, but business has to go on, and much more is falling upon us now that Dad's gone."

Helen was suddenly contrite and touched Mark's arm.

"Of course, darling, I hadn't thought."

Mark seized his opportunity, "So who IS this David Summers?"

Helen hesitated. "Well I don't know his personal business."

Mark persisted. "You met him at a hoteliers conference. Does he own a hotel?"

"I really don't know, but I can tell you he's very understanding and has given me good advice."

Alarm bells began to ring in Mark's head. "Advice? In what way?"

Helen bridled. "Never you mind. I'm not going to be cross-examined."

"I'm only thinking of your interests, Mum."

She replied tartly, "Don't you forget, Mark, I'm the major shareholder in the family now; I don't expect to be dictated to."

Mark saw he'd gone too far. "Good heavens, Mum, I'm only trying to protect you."

Helen drew back and decided to give Mark the benefit of the doubt.

"All right, Mark. Let's say no more about it."

She gave him a quick kiss. "Just stop worrying about me."

Mark went hotfoot to his office and rang Vince.

"Think we might have a problem," he said, and explained what had happened.

"Give me a name," Vince said impatiently. "I'll check him out."

"David Summers, daughter Barbara."

"Doesn't ring a bell," confessed Vince. "But if he's with the big boys I'll find him."

He rang off.

It was a week before he rang Mark back, and his tone betrayed he was puzzled.

"No trace of him," he growled. "And nobody knows the name."

"He has to come from somewhere," Mark protested.

"Bloody obvious. Maybe someone's keeping a tight mouth."

"Is there an alternative?"

"Plenty! He could be a freelance. Sell on commission, but unlikely. He could represent an international group. The pickings are huge."

"Anything else?"

"Your guess is as good as mine. But one thing's certain, Mark. You've got to do some digging."

"I'll get on to it."

"Pronto, Mark!" Vince rang off.

David Summers was well aware that 'Tall Trees' with its prime piece of land in the Surrey stockbroker belt was irresistible to the big money boys and he was keeping his head cocked for a move from them.

The reason he had not been picked up in Vince's survey was simple.

He wasn't in the building industry. He was the land valuer for an international group of hotels. Their idea was to turn the estate into a huge motel with very expensive villas for the rich and celeb market.

But he was biding his time before exploding his agenda.

Helen confided her thoughts about Donald's accident to him and he immediately suggested she get a private detective on the job.

"You won't miss the money, will you?" he said with a smile, and he gave her the name of a private detective.

. And that is how Alec Donovan came to be sitting in Helen's lounge.

He was a man in his forties with a weather-beaten face, but very shrewd eyes, and he had an air of determination which Helen liked.

"So you reckon there's no way your husband would have driven without lights? How can you be so sure?" he asked her.

"Ask anyone in the family. He was obsessed. Years ago he nearly knocked over a cyclist without lights and he never forgot."

"You realise," Alec said slowly, "That what you are suggesting might amount to a conspiracy to murder. If someone switched off the lights in your husband's car after the accident there can only be one reason. To conceal that he WAS driving with lights. Did you mention your thoughts to the police?"

"They weren't interested," Helen said bitterly. "I think they thought I was in shock, and raving. To them the case was open and shut. Finish!"

Alec was thoughtful. "You realise this could be a long haul, and expensive?"

"I'm not short of money. All I ask is that you keep me informed. Say, a report every so often."

"So be it," Alec said. "I'll make a start with the articulated vehicle and the driver."

"Will you be able to get the records?"

He smiled. "Don't worry, I have my contacts."

Alec was a man who inspired confidence, and now that she had done something Helen felt as if a burden had been lifted. It had been preying on her mind that Donald's death was suspicious.

Unaware of these hovering clouds, Mark now put his thoughts to unravelling David Summers and his daughter.

He decided Barbara was the easier target and he could use a social approach. She was a very attractive girl.

He waited until their next visit then called at his mother's house.

"Ah!" he said, "I've been waiting to meet you both. My mother has mentioned you several times."

Barbara gave him a dazzling smile as he took her hand, and Mark immediately felt attracted.

Then David shook hands, and Mark found himself under the scrutiny of keen blue eyes. "So you are Mark," he said easily. "You may have a hard job living up to all your mother's praises."

"I have heard a lot about you too," Mark replied smoothly. "I wondered if you were in our business?"

He held his breath for the reply.

"Not really," David said. "But I have gathered a lot of experience in hotel management."

Mark lifted his brows and was about to shoot another question when Barbara stepped in. "Mark, never mind business, why don't you tell me about yourself?"

Mark instantly seized his opportunity.

"Come for a meal with me and we can talk."

Barbara agreed without hesitation. "Should I put on my best frock?"

Mark was sorely tempted to say 'I might prefer you without,' but discretion won.

25

"Do your worst," he said. "I'll book us tonight at my favourite restaurant overlooking the river."

He left his mother's house well satisfied and looking forward to an interesting encounter.

When he picked Barbara up in the evening he was dazzled.

He already knew she was attractive, but tonight she was positively glamorous and sexy. Her big brown eyes seemed to sparkle with devilment.

"What have you done to yourself?" he asked gaily. "I didn't realise I was escorting a femme fatale."

But Barbara was equal to Mark. "You shouldn't drive a red Lotus," she said. "An invitation to sin."

They both laughed and were instantly at ease with each other.

Barbara had her dark hair draped across one side of her face and it gave her an elfin look. Particularly when she put her head on one side and smiled.

Mark was hooked. He hadn't expected this but he couldn't neglect the desire hurtling through his veins. Business could be postponed a little, he told himself.

When they reached the Riverside restaurant Barbara was impressed.

"What a beautiful location!"

She was even more impressed with the respect Mark received from the staff, and giggled, "Are you their boss?"

"They know me."

"You kidding?" Barbara was beginning to notice the steel in Mark.

The food was first class, and with plenty to drink he was thoroughly enjoying himself. His eyes hardly left Barbara, and she encouraged him all the time. Mark was buzzing.

Then horror of horrors. Carol appeared, with a man by her side Mark had never seen, and she immediately approached their table.

"Hallo, Mark. Evening out?" she asked. She didn't sneer, but very nearly.

But Mark kept cool and said politely, "Business appointment. I'll explain later." Then he lifted his brows and murmured, "And you?"

"My brother," she replied, and sauntered off.

In fact, her escort was not her brother but an old admirer; Carol was fishing around. But she was annoyed that Mark would do the same thing and she did not consider her thinking illogical.

Mark knew she was lying as much as he was but he was also angry that she'd spoilt his evening.

"Sorry, Barbara," he apologised. "One of those things."

But Barbara was amused. "I like a man who attracts women," she said softly. "Makes me feel superior."

Mark relaxed and knew for certain there could be possibilities with Barbara.

After their meal they climbed into his red Lotus and he asked, "Where to?"

"Well," she said. "Red is my lucky colour. I reckon you should have some of the luck. Your place?"

Mark put his hand over hers. "You surprise me more every minute, Barbara."

She gave him the elfin look. "We ARE in the twenty first century."

"Aren't we just," he exclaimed. "Hold tight!"

His foot went down hard on the accelerator, and the powerful surge jolted Barbara back in her seat, but she just laughed, and was still smiling when Mark pulled up outside his flat with a big roar.

She had a good look round.

"My! You do yourself well."

"What's money for?" he said carelessly.

Then she was in his arms, and as those inviting lips opened Mark had a rush of blood.

He picked her up, swept through the bedroom door, and onto the bed.

Their clothes came off in magical time and Mark got his first view of Barbara's naked body. Her glorious breasts inflamed him, and as he pulled her tight Barbara stroked herself against him, her whole body one big movement of caress.

Mark could hardly contain himself. Barbara's lips were everywhere and when she came back to his mouth and guided him between her legs he felt ready to explode.

Somehow she had judged the moment correctly. Mark certainly hadn't. She quivered in his mouth and as if on signal they locked in ferocious rhythm.

After a little while she moved in his arms. "How did you like that?"

"Don't ask! I want to do it again."

"Let's get our breath back first, shall we." A big smile spread across her face.

In the morning, over breakfast, Mark remembered his business commitment.

"You're not really David's daughter are you?" he asked.

Her eyes sparkled in amusement, "I'm a working girl."

"But are you David's daughter?"

"What do YOU think?"

"I guess no. Now tell me," he said impatiently.

"You guess right. I'm David's PA, personal assistant. We go all over the world together. It was decided it wouldn't look right for a fifty year old to be accompanied by a girl in her twenties. So we became father and daughter."

Mark was intrigued. "You said you go all over the world together. What on earth is your business?"

"David is land valuer for an international group of companies whose interests stretch across the world."

Mark began to get a little nervous. "You mean he works solely for this one group?"

"Well I suppose really he's self-employed. But they take up nearly all his time."

"So is he here to value 'Tall Trees'?"

" 'Tall Trees' isn't for sale, is it? But David does have a social life. Like us." She added impudently, "Well not quite."

Mark grinned, but he didn't believe David would spend a lot of time cultivating his mother without good reason, and he was now certain he knew his motives.

"Well I hope I can see you a few more times before you scoot off round the globe again," he said.

"I think that can be arranged," she said cheekily.

Mark got on the phone to Vince. "Not good news," he said gloomily. "That David Summers is land valuer for an international group of companies... I got it out of his daughter... Well she's not his daughter. She's his PA."

There was silence at the other end of the phone for a moment then Vince snarled, "Fuck! So we've got competition." There was another silence then he said, "We'll have to rethink our strategy." He raised his voice, "But you keep close to this girl."

The phone went down with a bang.

"Have a nice day," Mark muttered.

A week went by, and Carol came on the line.

"You avoiding me, Mark?"

"Tied up in business, darling."

"With your business appointment at the restaurant?"

"Yes, as a matter of fact. She's the PA to a land valuer at our place. I don't suppose she'll be here much longer."

"I can think of different ways of conducting business," Carol said icily.

Mark bridled. "Come off it, Carol. You were doing the same."

"A brother doesn't count," she said loftily.

Mark didn't want to break up with Carol. He knew Barbara would not be around permanently, more like a flashing meteor, he thought. So he bit back the word that sprang to his mind. Liar!

"O K," he said, "Let's make up with another date."

"Let's," Carol agreed. And this time she was determined to doll herself up to kill the opposition. Striking while the idea was hot, she said, "Tomorrow night. 'The Riverside'."

Mark had to agree. "You're on," he said.

The next night he whistled as Carol slid into his red Lotus, gracefully displaying a long line of leg.

"You look the part tonight, darling," he said. "I hope that dress doesn't fall off."

"You mean DOES fall off," she said. "Well, like they say, there's a time and place for everything."

She was conscious of admiring glances in the restaurant and psyched herself up with wine, but not too much. She was planning a big night for Mark. She hadn't been pleased with her last escort, and he didn't throw money around like Mark.

When they left for her place she was in the mood and infected Mark. She tantalised him taking her clothes off and gave him a quick view before jumping into bed.

Mark was beside her in a second, and the touch of her erect nipples sent spasms through his veins. He teased with them until Carol gasped. Then she guided Mark's hands and, as her excitement raced and he responded, she pulled him hard against her.

It was a moment of suspended agony. Then Mark slid into her, and the agony was a rushing storm.

Carol whispered dreamily, "Great experience."

Mark nodded. He could hardly believe his luck. Twice running he'd hit the high spots.

Some days later Vince introduced Mark to Maurice Robens at his flagship club, and Mark's life took a different turn.

Maurice Robens was one of the modern day criminals and ran his empire from a comfortable London office in his glitzy West End club, *The Phoenix*.

He had his own agenda for Mark. He knew his big clientele were all wealthy, many well-known. Trap them and bleed them was Maurice's thought. Blackmail paid high.

He ensured Mark had a good time and fixed him up with a beautiful coloured girl, Rachel Threadgold, and he warned her to put in a good performance.

Rachel had no difficulty with this. She liked Mark and made him third time lucky in bed. Mark was ecstatic. Life was sweet.

The next day he examined the card Maurice had placed in his top pocket.

It was plain but gold-edged. It simply read, 'Private. Direct to Maurice Robens,' with a number to telephone.

Mark tapped it on his fingers, thinking about Rachel. You never know, he thought, and slipped the card into his wallet.

Maurice's objective with Mark was to persuade him to offer all his clients at 'Tall Trees' free membership to his clubs across London, especially *The Phoenix*. But what Mark didn't know was that Maurice had already taken steps to force him if persuasion failed.

When Mark had spent his night with Rachel at the club it had all been screened on camera.

Maurice was quite sure Mark would want to keep their amazing sexual antics private. But he was keeping this in reserve. He preferred co-operation.

Maurice also owned several big houses standing in their own grounds around London. But they were not what they seemed. They were brothels, each specialising in a particular type of debauchery.

Gay and lesbian sex, transvestism, sadism, even dominance.

Entry was strictly supervised, after careful surveillance. The joke around Maurice's inside circle was 'If you had to ask the price forget it.'

Considering that everything went on camera, the unsuspecting clients had to be very wealthy to keep up with his subsequent demands.

But that was only if their interest cooled. So long as the money tumbled in, Maurice was satisfied. Mark wanted more of this highlife, and he toyed with the idea of taking Barbara or Carol to the club. But he realised they would open their mouths. Not what he wanted.

He had quickly got the taste for the free and easy cosmopolitan atmosphere, and his appetites were racing.

Then there was Rachel; maybe others like her. His blood tingled at the thought.

He pulled out Maurice's card and rang him.

His voice came back immediately, smooth and assured; he couldn't have been more affable.

"You're welcome any time, Mark. I can introduce you to some very interesting people at *The Phoenix*."

"*The Phoenix*?" Mark repeated thoughtfully. "Interesting name."

"Oh! I've other clubs across London, but I like to regard *The Phoenix* as my star attraction," Maurice said easily. "I'll take you round any time you fancy."

"I'll keep it in mind," Mark said. "I might pop up Saturday evening." He hesitated briefly, "Rachel be around?"

"Of course. She mentioned she'd be glad to see you again," Maurice lied.

Carol was needled that Mark was not taking her out on Saturday. She'd had plans for a gay evening. But Mark told her on the phone he had to go up to London on business. She wondered if he was standing her up, and her thoughts immediately flew to Barbara, but, of course, she was looking in the wrong direction.

As soon as Mark entered *The Phoenix* on Saturday the receptionist asked him to wait a second, then Maurice came striding out and took his arm. "Few people I'd like you to meet," he said.

He threaded his way through tables and the dance floor to the bar, where he touched a tall man on the shoulder. He was slightly greying, but very assured.

"This is Mark, who I was telling you about," Maurice said.

"Mark this is Richard Hall, TV exec.," he said.

"Oh! The owner of "Tall Trees'," Richard said. "I've been hearing about your celeb retreat. I must try it some time."

Mark didn't correct him about the sole ownership; let him think that if he wanted. "Everyone is welcome," he said with a smile, "But it costs."

The lady standing by his side said, "Yeah! I've heard they charge you fifty pounds for a look at the menu."

"And fifty if you don't," Mark said. He was still smiling, "Money buys everything." He raised his brows. "You are?"

"Debra Morrison. I thought you might know me," she said, pouting a little. "I'm a TV presenter."

She was a smart blonde, on the tall side, and Mark thought he wouldn't forget her.

"I'm sure I OUGHT to know you," he said easily. "But I'm not hot on TV."

"I guess I can forgive you," she said.

The next moment Vince Adams tapped Mark on the shoulder. He had a big mean-looking man by his side.

"This is my associate, Dave Armstrong," he said.

Dave looked at Mark and nodded, but he didn't smile.

Unfriendly looking bastard, Mark thought. If he only knew it, Dave Armstrong was aptly named. He was Vince Adam's enforcer, or hatchet man, and he organised all his dirty work. In fact, he arranged the death of Mark's father.

"Seems to be a gathering tonight," Mark said.

"We've come to see the delicious Steff," Vince said.

"Steff?"

"Star of the cabaret. Wait till you see her. She'll knock your eyes out," he said.

He laughed and looked at his watch. "She'll be on in ten minutes. Don't miss it."

Curious, Mark took a table with the others, facing the stage, and ordered drinks.

The cabaret was high West End standard, and the dancers were not only gorgeous and scantily clad, they were well drilled too.

Then the star was announced, Steff Destry. Mark sat up as the spotlight picked her out, and a hum went round the audience.

A mass of blonde hair fell round her shoulders and her eyes were an amazing dark blue. She had tremendous presence and curved her vivid lips into a kiss as she sang. It was seduction of the first order, and her husky voice was a caressing whisper.

As she moved round the stage the dancers reappeared and gradually disrobed her. They took her last garment and left her with tinsels and beads with her red tips poking through, and nearly bare across her thighs, where a single rouged line disappeared between her legs.

At the final crash of music she stood statuesque, her legs parted, and briefly held the pose. Then the troupe wrapped her in a cloak and the curtain came down. The applause was rapturous.

"See what I mean?" Vince said.

Mark looked at Maurice. "Any chance of meeting her?"

He crooked a finger to a girl and whispered in her ear. Five minutes later she came back and leaned over him. Her voice was low.

He said to Mark, "You're on! Eleven o'clock. Go to Steff's dressing room."

Mark was delighted. "Thanks a million, Maurice. I owe you one."

Maurice smiled. Things were going his way.

At eleven on the dot Mark tapped on Steff's dressing room door but there was no answer. He pushed the door and went in.

She was just coming out of the shower.

Beads of water clung to her, and she looked like a young Diana emerging from the sea. She stepped into a pair of mules and her long legs looked even longer.

She took her time reaching for a gown, and Mark had a full frontal view. She really was gorgeous, and the smoothness above her milky thighs sent his blood pressure soaring.

The gown she had slipped on hid very little, and Mark had a job keeping his hands off her.

"So you are Mr Mark 'Tall Trees'," she said. Her voice still had that trace of huskiness.

She was impressed. Could hardly be thirty, she thought. And that huge business and all that wealth. He must have something.

She liked the glint in his eye and his ready smile, but thought she detected a trace of steel behind it all. Not surprising. He might turn out to be an interesting man.

Steff was thirty but wasn't going to admit it. She had come through a hard school trying to find her way, and suffered several knock backs. She was tougher than she seemed and could always put on an act when it was required.

After their survey of each other she said with a smile, "I think we might know each other again."

Mark liked her humour. "I think they once wrote a song about you," he replied."Unforgettable!"

Steff's eyes glinted. "You're quite a charmer, aren't you?"

Then she moved close, opened her gown, and pressed herself against him.

Mark's heart hammered, and his hands went round her naked flesh to fix in the mounds of her bottom, but as he reached further she drew away and closed her gown.

"Now you know how I feel," she said softly. "But you don't know how I think. Can we work on that?"

Mark was disappointed, and yet he wasn't. There was more to Steff Destry than he'd calculated. "Just let me cool down," he said. "Then we can start something going."

Steff was beginning to warm to Mark. Had she at last found that someone special? And wealthy, on top?

But she was not foolish enough to judge at first sight.

She led Mark to the dressing room sofa and sat beside him.

"You know, Mark," she said. "There's a possibility you might do more than just fancy me. Although I'm a theatrical I'm not a pushover." She looked at him rather solemnly. "I do not regard sex lightly."

Mark was disappointed but he was hooked. "We haven't even kissed," he said. "Surely we can improve on that?"

"Tomorrow," she said softly. "Come to the performance and my place afterwards, but don't think this means I'm going to fall on my back for you."

Mark's thoughts about Steff were beginning to turn in a different direction. He certainly had taken for granted she would be a gorgeous one-night stand, but he was having second thoughts.

What he didn't know was that, although Maurice was quite happy to use Steff for his own purposes, he regarded her as HIS woman, and expected her to be available whenever he wanted her.

The next night Mark was in the audience again and Maurice was happy to see his strategy working. He was waiting for the right moment to approach Mark and make his proposals, but he knew he'd have to be patient. Goodwill had to be built.

Mark saw the cabaret through and again got a kick out of Steff's performance. She seemed even better tonight, he thought. His desire was racing and his imagination running riot. Only the thoughts of their meeting kept him composed.

He went to her dressing room a little earlier and found her still in the shower. He had hoped for this piece of luck.

She heard the door shut and shouted, "Who's there?"

"Who are you expecting?" Mark laughed.

Steff didn't tell him it could have been Maurice.

"Just a sec, darling," she called, and appeared with her gown held close to her body.

Mark thought she was teasing him but she said coolly, "Just go into the other room while I dress, will you, Mark?"

He was taken aback. She was certainly full of surprises, and he realised he was taking too much for granted... Which is exactly what Steff had planned. She intended to make Mark forget all about a one-night stand.

She took her time and when she reappeared she surprised Mark again. She was wearing a classical white suit, beautifully cut, severe and smart, but not what he had expected.

This time Mark wisely kept his mouth shut. "Beautiful suit," he said.

Steff smiled and wondered what he'd really been expecting. She said saucily, "Offstage I'm a normal person." Putting Mark in his place once more.

But Mark didn't mind the surprises. She was making herself more attractive to him by the minute, and he was building a big hunger.

Like most of his previous female passengers, Steff commented on his red Lotus when they climbed in.

"More like a racing car," she said.

"I like fast cars."

"Not only cars," she said dryly.

Her flat was luxurious and well appointed.

This time Mark was not surprised. He was beginning to accept he would have to revise his whole opinion about Steff.

She got drinks then slid beside him on the cushions of a giant settee. She was still wearing her classical suit.

Mark wondered if she would change, and she read his mind.

"I'm sure you wouldn't want me to take this suit off, would you, darling? You did say how beautiful it was."

She'd scotched him again, but Mark was happy. For the second time she'd called him darling.

"I know you're a little minx, Steff Destry," he said. "But since you call me darling I'll forgive you. Is there any charge for putting my arm round you?"

"Yes," she said. "You have to dance with me."

"Dance?" Mark repeated blankly. "Where?"

She pointed, "On this lovely cream carpet in our bare feet. You'll enjoy it."

They rose, and as Mark pulled her close he immediately got the faint scent of hyacinths.

He had to say it... "Hyacinths!"

She smiled. "The welcome of spring."

The words hung in his mind while she switched on the video and kicked off her shoes.

He instantly followed. Then they were together.

The music was slow and they swayed as if locked.

"We shall soon be in each other's pockets," Mark whispered. His desire was killing him.

"I've a better idea," she whispered, and slipped out of her jacket. As Mark had suspected, she had no bra and her breasts stood out like sentinels.

Then she cast off her skirt and stood in G string and stocking tops.

"Now you," she said.

Mark needed no bidding and stripped to his shorts.

"H-mm!" she said, standing back. "Not bad."

They came together again, and this time Steff made love to him as they moved. She outrageously thrust her breasts into him and made sure her long legs caressed his, with her smooth front darting in and out.

Suddenly she felt his urgent demand and immediately put her mouth to his and slipped her tongue inside, but she wouldn't yield.

Instead, she tightened her grip, and Mark felt her hard breasts with the nipples biting into him like needles. A huge hot wave built up inside him and as Steff gloried in it and held him tight, he streamed against her. She was wet with desire and strained to find relief, but she wouldn't allow Mark between her legs.

When he got his breath back he said, "Does that count as masturbation or intercourse."

"Perhaps passion," she whispered. "Now we must have a shower, mustn't we?"

Mark's eyes lit up. "Together?"

"It would seem a good idea," And she took his hand and lead him to the shower room, where she slipped from her G-string.

Mark had stepped back into his shorts and stood hesitantly, until Steff reached across and yanked them off. "Now we're even," she said.

She stood with her hands to her breasts. "You are all over me," she said. "I'm going to massage it in. Then you're part of me."

"Allow me," Mark said quickly, and before she could protest his hands were on her in gentle circular movements.

When she could stand it no longer she pulled him tight and the prick of her enlarged nipples brought him up.

"No Mark!" she whispered, and he had to relent.

She started the shower and as the warm water cascaded she handed him the soap. "You know what to do with that, don't you?"

Mark could hardly believe his luck and soaped across her whole body lovingly, lingering round her bottom and between her legs.

"You know how to please a girl, don't you, darling," she said.

Then she did the same for him.

Mark had to stop her. "You know what will happen if you go on."

"Oh! What a crime."

She laughed out loud and Mark had to join her.

They went to bed, and as she curled up close to him Mark again got the scent of hyacinths. Those words of hers, 'the welcome of spring', again sprang to his mind, and before he drifted off to sleep he thought he'd forever associate Steff with hyacinths.

He felt he'd rarely enjoyed himself so much and knew he was going to have to do some serious thinking about Steff.

Back at Tall Trees Mark's phone was ringing. He had a premonition it was Vince Adams, and he was right.

He was in a foul temper. His directors were on his back. He'd promised them a deal in six months, and time was running out.

"Time to deliver, Mark," he spat out. "Or do I have to do another murder?"

Mark wasn't sure if he was serious but decided not to test his words.

"Look, Vince," he protested, "You know I've done all I can. I want the money as much as you. But I can't shift my mother.

Now that Sister Janet is supporting her she's found new backbone."

"I'm afraid the deal is fucked," he said.

For a moment there was silence at Vince's end. "I'll have to think about this." He said, "I'll be in touch." His phone went down with a bang.

Mark then endured a further unhappy phone conversation with Carol.

"Where've you been Mark? I ring your office and they say you're probably in London." She raised her voice, "Probably? And in London all the time? What do you take me for?"

Mark tried to soothe her and thought of a good lie. "Someone has to deal with my father's estate, the solicitors, accountants, Tax Inspectors. You couldn't expect my mother to do it, could you? These people are all in London, and I'm afraid I'm nowhere near finished yet."

Carol was stopped dead. Mark's explanation was good. "Well, when am I going to see you again?" She wasn't very happy.

"I hope next week, darling," he said.

She blew a kiss down the line. "Try to make it sooner."

Mark wondered if Barbara might ring but she didn't. Thank God for that, he thought.

The next day he attended a board meeting and got the shock of his life. He thought his mother looked unusually buoyant and he could hardly believe what she was saying.

"I've been talking to David," she said. "And he has advised me that our massive grounds could be turned into a luxury motel for celebs, and if I was interested he would take the matter further."

She looked at the others. "Why shouldn't we do something like this ourselves? It's our land... I had in mind," she said, "twenty or thirty luxury villas standing in their own grounds with their own pools and servants. Ideal for the rich and famous from London who are always asking for privacy."

She waited for Mark or Janet to say something but they were both temporarily stunned at her change of heart.

"The trouble is, of course, raising the capital," she said. "I am sure that with our holdings and land we could raise the money ourselves but I don't want to commit us too heavily. I'd like a partner."

She stared at them both. "For starters, ten million on each side. What do you think?"

To say Mark and Janet were flabbergasted would be the understatement of the year. But Mark's spirits were miraculously lifted. He could now offer Vince something.

He opened his mouth to speak but his mother held up her hand; she'd got the bit between her teeth. She said she was confident David's Group would be willing and that would make it nice and easy.

"Hold on!" Mark said. "Let's not rush in too fast. I know people in London who would be interested, and they'd bid against each other, which would give us a better deal." He looked at them both. "We want the best deal, don't we?"

For once Janet sided with Mark. "We do," she said firmly. "Mum, let Mark test the market."

She couldn't go against that, and so it was decided.

Mark rang Vince.

"Something for you at last," he said. "There's been an unexpected turn," and he explained the position. "Would you be interested in taking the contract? Big bucks!"

Vince was more polite this time, but he still grumbled, "Not what we were after."

"You know the old saying," Mark prompted him. "Half a loaf is..."

"I know, I know," Vince cut in. "But my outfit usually want full control. Still, I'll put it to them."

He was obviously uncertain. "Are there any other bidders?"

"Not at the moment but I suspect David Summers will bid, and obviously there'll be others once the news gets out."

Mark pressed his point. "I'm offering you first-in advantage, Vince; something for all our trouble. You say yes and you get the go-ahead. The others are dead."

Mark knew he couldn't guarantee this but his instincts told him that although there would be rich pickings Vince's outfit would reject his offer.... Company policy was Company policy, especially with the big nationals.

He knew he was taking a risk but he thought it was worth it. He wanted Vince off his back. He could be a dangerous customer.

Vince realised he was being offered a big advantage but he didn't think his directors would bite. Still, at least he was offering them something.

"OK, Mark," he said, "I'll get back to you."

"Don't leave it too long, Vince."

"You'll know this week," he growled.

He put it to his directors, and they suggested instead a sole purchase of the land only, leaving 'Tall Trees' as a separate company and plenty of seclusion.

But what mightily relieved Vince was that he was off the hook. His bosses recognised he'd delivered something.

He got back to Mark but, as he had expected, Mark received his proposal with derision. "You must be joking, Vince. Break up the golden egg! No way."

But Vince no longer cared. His reputation was safe. Move on to the next assignment... And as he anticipated, when he reported Mark's refusal to his directors they withdrew their interest.

But Vince couldn't keep his mouth shut about his near disaster. The following night at *The Phoenix* he told Maurice all about it.

Maurice didn't give a jot for Vince's misfortunes but he was delighted to hear of the development Mark was proposing. The more celebs on tap the better as far as he was concerned.

All he had to do was keep Mark sweet and wait for the right moment. Patience was not only a virtue, Maurice thought cynically; it could also be a useful tool.

The news went round, and Mark began to get a reputation as a business tycoon.

So far as Steff was concerned, it enhanced her view of him but she was not altogether surprised. Thinking unemotionally, it did remind her what a lot she stood to gain from Mark, but she was already putting in maximum effort because she was genuinely attracted to him... Still a reminder was not unwelcome, she thought.

Nearer home, Carol picked up the news and it jolted her. She had rather forgotten what a powerhouse Mark could be.

She wondered if perhaps she'd been taking him too much for granted, and her thoughts flew to Barbara.

She believed mistakenly that Mark had been waltzing her around town on his trips to London, and she decided a change of strategy was necessary to discourage her.

She came up with a little plan to create the belief that she and Mark were serious and Barbara would be wasting her time.

She also realised she must couple the plan with a sensational night on their next date... That was the easy part, she thought.

Barbara was now going to be around a long time. David's Group had agreed the deal, and she was appointed liaison officer between the two companies. She and David already occupied a suite at 'Tall Trees' but he would be moving out... Very convenient, Barbara thought, and her thoughts turned to Mark with redoubled interest.

But Mark only had thoughts for Steff, and to Carol's annoyance and Barbara's disappointment, he kept shooting off to London, where the eager Steff was joyously entertaining him.

Nonetheless, he did have to set aside a night to see Carol. She reminded him of his promise to see her during the week, and although Mark remembered he'd told her he'd TRY, he knew he'd neglected her and he didn't want a bust up... After all, before Steff came on the scene she was his number one; and now there was Barbara also, he thought ruefully.

Carol's plan for Barbara was suggested to her when she discovered Barbara had a suite at 'Tall Trees' and that invariably she dined late at night in the restaurant with David, then retired to the lounge bar.

She just hoped she'd choose a night when Barbara was not out gallivanting. If so, she'd have to try again, she told herself firmly.

Mark picked Carol up for the date and, with the engine revving, said, "Where to? Riverside?"

"No," she said coolly, "I've a surprise for you... 'Tall Trees'."

Mark took his foot off the accelerator. "What?"

"You know what a lovely restaurant they have... And," she said carelessly, "I've booked a suite so we don't have to bother about the time. A little luxury won't hurt, will it, darling? You can afford it."

Mark had to smile. Carol was unexpectedly adventurous tonight, and he shot a look at her. She was certainly dolled up.

Perhaps the night would have unexpected dividends.

"Well, the staff certainly know us," he grinned. "Perhaps they'll give us special service."

Carol put her hand on Mark's thigh. "You can count on it! And," she said sweetly, "YOU can count on me."

She crossed her fingers and hoped for a lucky night. Then she was jerked back in her seat as Mark put his foot down, and the Lotus roared away.

In the restaurant they were treated like royalty, as Carol had expected, and the food as always at 'Tall Trees' was superb. But Carol was edgy. Where the hell was Barbara?

She nearly gave the game away when she was staring round.

"What are you looking for?" Mark asked.

Fortunately Carol's nimble brain came to the rescue. "I was looking for the wine waiter," she said. "Do you think they have that delicious wine we have at *The Riverside*?"

Mark beckoned to a waiter, and in a matter of minutes he was uncorking the bottle for them.

Carol lifted her glass. "To 'Tall Trees' and us."

Mark sipped his wine. "Especially us."

He was beginning to enjoy himself. Carol was very buoyant tonight.

Then Carol's luck held. David and Barbara appeared, and they spotted each other at the same time. Barbara was smart in a business suit but not sexy, Carol was glad to notice.

"Would you like company?" David asked politely. "Or would you prefer to see our backs?"

Then Mark got another shock. "Pleasant surprise, please do join us."

This from Carol.

He was beginning to wonder what else she had up her sleeve.

Carol took the lead and said conversationally, "Been hearing about the big development. Should be quite something."

"It will be," David said. "Just the sort of private luxury the big stars look for. Near London and in the right place."

"It will be big money then?"

"The only reason for doing it," David replied.

"Will you be remaining?"

"No. Just Barbara. She's volunteered to run the villas."

Carol knew this already but she wanted to swing the conversation round.

"Oh," she said, looking at Barbara, "Won't you be lonely?"

Barbara got her message at once... Hands off!

Well that's up to Mark, she thought.

Carol drove on relentlessly, "It's not very often we come here. We usually go to my place but we thought we'd like a change and booked a suite."

Carol had put down her marker, and Barbara could be in no doubt. Now she felt quite gay.

She said to Barbara, "I suppose moving around a lot in your job you don't get much chance for social life?"

Barbara knew what she meant, but she wasn't going to let Carol have it all her own way.

"Oh! You have to take what you can get," she replied. And added mischievously, "Sometimes it can be quite exciting."

Mark was becoming impatient. "Well we've finished our meal. You're about to start. We'll leave you in peace." And he hurried Carol off to the lounge.

"What was all the lecturing about?" he asked. "You gave Barbara the impression we were a couple."

"Surely not," Carol said. "Still, I suppose it's not far from the truth is it?" she added with a little boldness.

"That's a further step forward, and you know it," Mark said, crossly.

Carol was momentarily put out of her stride, and she put her arms round him. "Darling, don't let's fight over trifles. I've a nice surprise for you later on."

"Oh?"

"I promise you'll like it."

She pulled him to his feet and linked her arm through his. "Come on. Let's go and have a dance," and she steered him through to the ballroom.

Once on the floor she sidled up close the way he liked.

She kept teasing him with little nudges, her thigh between his, her breasts touching and flicking, occasionally a quick brush across his lips.

She also kept the drinks coming... To keep him receptive.

When they at last retired to their suite she knew he was ready, and she was ready too for the last bit of her plan. A night to remember! And see if Barbara could match that.

"What do most men wonder about when they think of their girlfriends?" Carol teased him.

Mark wasn't sure how to reply. He could think of lots of answers. Many uncomplimentary, many downright saucy.

"You tell me," he said diplomatically.

"What does she look like without her clothes?"

Mark was astounded but agreed. "Right on the button," he said.

"Prepare yourself for the first surprise," she said.

Without another word, she strolled to the full length mirror and stood in front facing Mark.

There was the sound of a zip and her silk dress slid to the floor, leaving her in bra and G string.

Mark was goggle-eyed. Not often did he have such an opportunity.

Carol's best feature was her long legs, and she heightened the effect with high heels, which highlighted her narrow waist; and she gave Mark a slow spin.

Next she slipped off her bra, and Mark was pleasantly surprised. He'd always thought Carol had little up top, but naked, her breasts were well shaped mounds with strong red nipples.

She looked at him sensuously. "Now for your next surprise," and she slipped off her G-string.

Mark gulped.

She had removed all her hair and was entirely smooth. She obligingly parted her legs to emphasise her shadowy line, and Mark swallowed hard but couldn't take his eyes away. He also got the rear view picture in the mirror and the split between her tight rounded cheeks was nearly as erotic.

Carol slowly turned in a circle, taking care to space her legs. Then she put her hands on her hips.

"What do you think, darling?"

Mark was heavily aroused. "What do I think? I'm nearly having an orgasm. I don't know if that's the right word for a man."

"It'll do," Carol murmured.

She advanced towards him slowly, running her hands over her body, even her breasts. Her lips were a sensuous invitation.

Mark threw off his clothes and they jumped on the bed.

He immediately clamped his hands round her tight bottom, and she threw her arms round him and ground her breasts into him.

Mark had never known Carol so abandoned, and she sank her teeth into him mercilessly, and when they kissed it was almost a battle.

They were like two animals writhing together on the bed and Mark forced his hand between her legs. Then he pinched her breasts savagely and the pain was agonising to Carol but the sensation glorious, and to counter the pain she drove her fingernails into Mark. She felt him flinch but didn't stop.

Suddenly he reached his limit and lunged into her, which brought a huge O-h-h! from Carol, and she clung on for dear life as Mark ripped into her. She was on cloud nine, and only Mark's exhaustion halted the exquisite fantasy.

They looked into each other's eyes, breathless.

Mark was bruised and bloodied...He knew he'd never think of Carol in the same light any more, but he recognised the pure delight he'd enjoyed and wondered if perhaps there was something to be said for sadism.

"How you feeling, tiger?" he said.

"Battered but happy."

"I think I ought to call you that in future."

Carol was pleased Mark said 'in future'. "I think you could say we hit the high spots," she said.

"And how!"

"And shall we now attend to our cuts and bruises?" she suggested.

"In the shower," Mark said. He couldn't get enough of Carol now, and he picked her up and carried her through.

As the water warmed them Mark pulled her tight.

This time she didn't fight but opened her lips and Mark had a different Carol. She let him do what he wanted and eagerly co-operated as he kissed her all over. She knew Mark was fascinated by her smooth front and she opened her legs as well.

Mark put her on the floor and got the folds of her skin between his lips which gave Carol an almighty thrill and nearly another orgasm.

She didn't want him to stop but suddenly he came up to her mouth, and she felt him inside her.

The continuation was terrific and as he stroked into her she felt almost drunk with the sensation. It was as though her nerves were playing music, and suddenly she found herself surging out of control until all at once she was drained.

Mark was also exhausted. He had burst out almost as he entered her in yet another superb thrill.

"I reckon that cures our wounds," she murmured.

But Mark wasn't finished yet.

He picked Carol up and carried her to the bedroom, where he put her on the bed, then climbed beside her.

"We still haven't mended our cuts and bruises," he reminded her. "But let's have a few quiet moments first."

He was insatiable, and as he lay beside her he again ran his hands all over her, lingering particularly between her legs.

Carol realised he was fascinated by her smooth front and silently congratulated herself on a good move... I certainly know what turns him on, she thought.

She let him play with her for some time then said, "Time for real bed, darling. We don't have to dress. You can still love me as much as you like." She chose the word 'love' very deliberately and hoped it would strike a chord in Mark's mind.

In fact it did. Mark was changing his view of Carol very quickly, and when they were lying together he still couldn't keep his hands off her.

In the morning over breakfast his lip was showing a little damage, but Carol had covered up with lipstick.

She smiled at his lip and said, "I reckon my surprise worked out. What do you say, darling?"

"Surprise me again whenever you like, sweetheart," he said.

Carol had never heard him use that word before and she was well satisfied. Follow that, Barbara, she thought.

Mark couldn't help comparing Carol with Steff. Carol won hands down in the bed stakes.

What an incredible night she'd provided. The best he could remember. She had certainly been hot company and seemed to have lost that touch of ice.

Still, there was something about Steff. She was a beautiful mystery, still to be explored, and Mark recalled their exciting moments.

He wasn't going to give up. But his enthusiasm had taken a knock. Carol had certainly done a good job.

Maurice decided the time was now ripe to make his move with Mark and he called Steff into his office. He explained to her what he wanted from Mark, although he didn't mention the consequences that might befall some of his clients.

"It doesn't seem much to me," Steff said. "Why don't you ask him outright? You don't need me."

"The reason is," Maurice said patiently, "luxury establishments like 'Tall Trees' don't recommend entertainments in case their clients aren't satisfied. They reap big profits themselves and don't want to rock the boat... Although it's a simple thing to us to recommend someone, it could bring problems to them."

"Oh!... Well, what do you want from me?"

"I want you to arrange a meal with Mark in the restaurant, you can use that sheltered alcove I use, give him some drink and make sure he's happy. Then, when I come along and ask if everything is OK, you suggest I join you."

"I'll take it from there," he said, "Between the two of us we might pull it off."

He reflected for a moment. "If he is willing you can reinforce what I say and suggest you would look forward to meeting some of his celebs."

His face stiffened a little. "If he isn't willing you must work on him. Use your charms, Steff."

Mark, as usual, turned up at the club well before Steff's cabaret, and she had no problem suggesting a private meal after her act. "Make a pleasant change," she said.

Mark sat through the cabaret, and Steff gave an ultra performance in exposing her charms. All the men were agog, but she was doing it just for Mark, and in his front seat he caught her little sidelong pouts and gestures, and understood. He felt ten feet tall.

He swiftly went to her dressing room afterwards, and she was expecting him but pretended to be surprised. "You're on the ball tonight, Mark. I've not yet showered."

"Want any help?"

"Just be patient, Mark. You never know what you might get."

She fixed her amazing dark blue eyes on him and he felt himself weakening. Then with a swish of her gown she was gone and the shower room door slammed. Mark got the message and patiently waited.

She came out of the shower, threw off her gown, and, standing naked, she waltzed across the room and picked out her clothes. But first of all she slipped into her underwear. It was striptease in reverse, and Mark began to get hot.

"Call that underwear?" he scoffed. "Those wisps would go in my pocket."

"They are not for warmth, darling," Steff said, and put a quick kiss on his lips, but as he tried to respond she drew away.

She quickly dressed after the underwear display, and in half an hour they were sitting in Maurice's private alcove in the restaurant.

Steff followed instructions and kept the drink coming, although she was careful herself and sipped where Mark swallowed.

Then Maurice turned up. "Evening, Mark," he said. "Everything OK?"

"Fine, fine. Especially the company," he replied.

Mark was feeling well disposed towards Maurice. It wasn't only the drink. He knew he had the night ahead with Steff, and the anticipation warmed him. The outcome was a pleasant surprise for Maurice.

"Why don't you join us?" Mark invited.

Maurice pretended surprise. "You sure?"

"A pleasure! You've been very generous to me," Mark said.

Better and better, Maurice thought. He could have rubbed his hands, and craftily expanded his advantage.

"Glad you and Steff have hit it off so well."

"You know," he went on, "Steff has been attracting quite a few celebs to *The Phoenix*. In the last couple of weeks we've had several here."

He didn't mention they were minor celebs, not headliners. But Mark could believe him. *The Phoenix* was now a leading West End club.

Steff held her breath. She knew what was coming next.

Maurice said conversationally. "I'm sure YOUR clients would enjoy a night at *The Phoenix*, Mark. What do you say to scattering a few brochures round your place?"

Mark immediately clammed up and frowned slightly, "Oh I don't know."

Then Steff stepped in boldly. "Tell you what, Mark. Suppose I come down with a bundle of brochures; you can show me around."

Mark was still not sold but had to admit, "Yes I'd like that."

Steff pressed her advantage. "Perhaps we can also find something else to do."

Mark grinned. He was hooked now.

"How can I resist you, Steff?"

Maurice got up, well satisfied, and gave Steff a sly look of approval.

"Must go," he said, "Make sure you drink too much," and he went off smiling.

Steff had a good look at Mark. She sensed some of his bubbling enthusiasm had evaporated and wondered if her competition had been scoring. She was certain other women wouldn't leave him alone.

Handsome and wealthy, he had that arrogant air of power they all loved.

Well worth a fight, she thought, and she knew how to fight, clean or dirty.

"I think we should go on to my place," she said. "You seem a little jaded. You've either been working too hard, or people have been working YOU too hard."

Her acuteness surprised Mark. "Both," he said. "You got a remedy?"

"Wait and see," she replied. "Is the red chariot waiting?"

Mark had to laugh. "Ready to explode," he said. "Like me."

The hint was enough, and they were soon on their way to Steff's, where she hurried him inside.

Mark wanted another drink but Steff had other plans. "You've already had too much," she said. "It's coffee for you and black." She sat him on the settee and shot off to the kitchen.

She soon returned and handed him a cup but not before she had slipped in a little tablet.

As he sipped she slid off to change, and came back naked under a thin silk gown. Then she stretched out beside him.

Slowly she ran her hands over his body, easing, caressing, teasing, and Mark became like an upright poker.

Slowly she slipped lower and ringed her lips round him. Cannons began to go off in his head. It was exquisite agony, and he felt extraordinarily light-headed as though he was in some other world of feeling.

Suddenly Steff's lips were foraging between his and she slid him between her thighs. Somehow they seemed to be just one person imprisoned in furious movement, and Mark could only gasp until his body finally gave up.

He felt as though he'd been through a hurricane and his brain was reeling.

"My!" Steff whispered, "You did get heated, darling, really gorgeous."

She was lying through her teeth. She'd manipulated Mark from start to finish and had felt little. But she was elated, Mark wouldn't forget.

"I can't believe I was so wild," he said weakly. "I've never felt anything quite like it."

"It looks as though Doctor Steff had the right treatment, doesn't it?" she whispered. "I'm so glad it worked."

She was over the moon. She knew those tablets sent some people wilder than wild, and was thankful she'd stopped at one... More by luck than judgement, she acknowledged..

She sat back and soothed Mark. She felt she'd won a battle and when she visited Mark at 'Tall Trees' with the brochures she intended to remind him; and, you never know, she thought, be prepared, pack another tablet. Although perhaps not, suspicions could be aroused... She was in two minds..

Mark agreed a date with her, and the following week Steff turned up at 'Tall Trees' driving a silver Mercedes. Hired for the occasion.

Mark lifted his brows. "A Merc, eh?"

"I like to travel in style."

Mark liked that, and Steff scored another point.

He took her arm and steered her through to reception, a spacious and comfortable room with big armchairs and a bar. The client only had to lift a finger and the drinks were brought.

At 'Tall Trees' the clients only had to breathe for themselves, Steff thought, but she was impressed. The air of luxury was overpowering.

She went to the desk where leaflets and brochures describing the county, horse shows, and so forth were displayed, and scattered in a liberal supply of her own brochures. They were very tasteful. Maurice had seen to that. But also inviting!

The Phoenix. Leading club in London's West End. Mix with the latest celebrities. Enjoy our famous restaurant with world class chef and wines... Dancing. Gambling. Cabaret.

Then very discreetly at the bottom: -

Private rooms for special occasions.

Mark hadn't vetted the brochures and was unaware of a little lie Maurice had added:

As a token of past association with 'Tall Trees' we

offer all clients free membership.

Mark had carefully chosen a day for Steff's visit when he knew Carol would be at her office all day but he hadn't taken Barbara into account, and her eyes opened wide when she glimpsed Steff on Mark's arm strolling through the grounds.

She made up her mind to tackle him on the subject. Very politely of course.

Mark was hoping for some more sensational lovemaking with Steff and in anticipation was in an extremely light hearted frame of mind. He thoroughly enjoyed the compliments she passed on the opulence she met everywhere and introduced her to many wide-eyed clients as a London cabaret star.

Steff's eyes gleamed when she saw the sumptuous suites and she hoped Mark would reserve one for them, but she decided drugs were out this time. She was going to play it cool. Tempt him, give him a little, but make him understand he could not have the big prize just when he fancied.

They dined in the restaurant in the evening, and Steff was staggered at the huge choice of food, simple and exotic. And talk about service. There was almost a person on hand to blow your nose. She could see why only wealthy people came to 'Tall Trees'.

She kept Mark well plied with drink but was careful herself, and when he told her he'd reserved a suite she reckoned her plans were falling into place nicely.

When they finally retired the first thing she did was get him another drink and was pleased to see that at last it was having some effect as he noticeably slowed down.

She joined him on a long divan scattered with velvet cushions and as she sank down, Mark drew her close, but she didn't take the initiative, instead she allowed Mark to slip his hand inside her top.

"Knew you wouldn't let me down," he murmured. "No bra!"

His words were a little disconnected, and Steff knew she'd have no trouble controlling him.

She loosened his clothes. She'd tease him until he gave up, but it proved to be more difficult than she anticipated.

Mark tried to undo her top so Steff slipped it off. Immediately he cupped her breasts together and drew both nipples into his mouth almost together, and at the same moment he hardened.

A suppressed Oh-h-h! came from Steff, and she slipped off her skirt to reveal her bare skin.

Mark was loth to leave her breasts but his hand hovered until he found the right place between her legs and he massaged her fiercely.

Steff's desire suddenly exploded, and she flung off his hand and sat astride so he speared into her. She seemed to have the devil in her and she moved up and down wildly until Mark let out a yell.

Then his liquid hit her and she went berserk.

The thrill was indescribable, and she felt she was going to burst. Then suddenly she was shaking in wave after wave until a huge spasm drained her utterly. She couldn't remember stopping. She just fell upon Mark exhausted.

Unintentionally she had given him another unforgettable experience, and even in his half-drunk state Mark still marvelled.

'How does she do it?' he wondered.

Steff spread herself over Mark so they were touching all over. It was as if she was still drinking in the experience and unable to let go. And Mark seemed to share her mood and let his hands wander over her gently without motive, which pleased Steff immensely.

It seemed some time before they were finally spent, and Steff at last rolled off him reluctantly.

She rose to shower but this time it was on her own. Mark was nodding off.

As the water warmed her she thought how ironic it was. She had started out to control and tease Mark and ended up with the most fantastic orgasm she could remember...

Almost as if she'd taken a tablet herself...What a thought!

She had to admit her plans had gone wrong but she had a big consolation: Mark would not forget the terrific sex.

The next day Barbara sought out Mark.

"Who was that beauty you were showing round yesterday?" she asked.

He gave her a straight look. "Oh! She was just a messenger with some brochures from London."

But Barbara wasn't fooled. She'd seen how Steff was done up like a film star, and she'd seen her silver Mercedes.

Later she skipped over to reception and picked up a brochure. As she read her brain began to tick and she knew she was going to pay *The Phoenix* a visit before long. She intended to find out what Mark was hiding.

She enjoyed their sex together and was not inclined to let him go without a fight, particularly as she was going to spend a lot of time at 'Tall Trees' in the future.

In a few months the development plan would be under way and in the meantime she was going nowhere.

The following week she rounded up a boyfriend from her circle, Tim Howard. He was never very serious and always game for a little adventure.

She waved the brochure in his face. "I want an escort, and you're it," she said.

His blue eyes smiled. "Think you can trust me?"

"I'll chance it."

So two nights later they were in London and went across to the West End, where they quickly found *The Phoenix*.

Barbara was impressed at first sight. Imposing entrance. Big swing doors commanded by a uniformed commissionaire.

She wondered for a second if he'd let them in but his eyes just flashed at them and he opened the doors with a "Good evening, madam."

Barbara hadn't been called "Madam" for as long as she could remember and she nearly had a fit of the giggles, but she kept her face straight, gave him a smile and walked into the foyer.

The first thing that caught her eye was a huge framed picture of Steff, and the caption, 'London's Leading Cabaret Star.'

Her interest quickened as she stared at the picture.

Tim said, over her shoulder, "Some looker."

"You'll see a lot more of her in the cabaret," Barbara said.

And she was right of course. Steff went through her usual performance and when she ended with her nude display Barbara could see why Mark was smitten.

Tim was goggle-eyed. "Not much of that in my neck of the woods," he said.

"Just as well," Barbara said thoughtfully. "You'd get killed in the rush."

As she said this it occurred to her she was right, and she cheered up a bit. She felt sure Steff would not stick only with Mark when she had the pick of London's wealthiest watching her night after night.

She couldn't imagine Steff going home on her own.

She purposely stayed late to see if Steff reappeared and if anyone was waiting for her. And she got her reward.

Suddenly she was in front of her.

Steff was looking round and stood for a moment. Then she slipped round the tables and went straight to a man, who kissed her and took her into a private alcove.

Barbara asked a hostess who he was.

"Oh that's Maurice Robens. He owns the club, and thinks he owns Steff as well," she said.

"You mean they've a relationship?" Barbara asked.

"Relationship?" The hostess snapped her fingers scornfully. "He just snaps his fingers when he wants her and Steff goes running."

Barbara was warmed. And she had one important thing over Steff. She was always available.

Tim broke into her thoughts. "Time to go if you want any sleep tonight."

Barbara pressed his hand. "Lead on, darling. Whisk me back to reality."

Tim put his foot down on the drive back and he didn't delay her when they arrived. Just a brief goodnight kiss, and "Thanks a bundle" from Barbara.

He never asked any favours and Barbara didn't expect it. It had never occurred to her to wonder why.

In fact, Tim glorified Barbara but didn't think he had a chance with her so he kept his mouth shut. He feared a rebuff would spoil their open friendship.

The next morning Barbara chased around until she found Mark.

She said artfully, "Saw someone you know last night."

Mark pricked his ears up. "Oh?"

"Your messenger that came down the other day," she said.

Mark saw at once she'd caught him out but he kept cool.

"Lucky you." he said.

"Yes," Barbara said, "Star of the West End. Some messenger, I must say." She went on, "You're in good company. Half the men in the West End were after her. One in particular." And she waited for Mark's reaction.

He didn't move a muscle.

"Maurice, the owner of the club," she said. "Apparently she's his property."

The news shook Mark but he wasn't going to admit it.

"I suppose she has to be friendly to people in the club," he said casually

"This was one man and he took her off," Barbara said significantly.

Mark shrugged. "No skin off my nose." He kept his face calm.

Barbara wanted to accuse him of chasing Steff but common sense prevailed.

She said brightly, "These theatricals are anyone's, aren't they?"

She linked her arm through his, "Let's go and have some coffee."

Mark couldn't refuse; he was still trying to come to terms with Barbara's news. He had begun to entertain some long-term views for Steff and knew he'd have to tackle her.

One thing was certain, he wasn't going to mess with Maurice and the strong arm boys he employed.

Barbara saw she'd rattled him, but pretended not to notice.

She decided to press her advantage. "She'll be in a different bed every night," she scoffed. "Look at the temptations."

Mark's face was frozen, and Barbara knew she'd done enough. Best not to overdo it.

"Oh well! That's the West End life, I suppose," she said. She didn't mention Steff again.

But Mark had her in his mind all the time and not even a good display of Barbara's charms could cheer him up. This was a further warning to Barbara, and she knew she couldn't take Steff lightly.

Barbara had hardly disappeared before Mark's mobile was in his hands and he was speaking to Steff. "I want to talk to you," he said.

"You can talk to me next time we meet," she said with surprise.

Mark was insistent. "I want to see you tonight."

Steff had expected to be with Maurice but she relented.

"OK, darling, tonight it is," she said.

Mark came into the club late and just caught the last part of Steff's act but he didn't follow her into the dressing room afterwards, and she was a little alarmed.

He was waiting when she came out and hurried her off. "Your place," he said.

For once Steff didn't react when she was jolted back on the cushions of the Lotus as Mark put his foot down, and as Mark kept quiet she did the same. It was an uncomfortable journey.

"OK," she said, when they reached her place and were sitting together, "Spit it out, Mark."

He gave her a long look. "How serious do you take our relationship, Steff? You're a free agent and can please yourself, but I want to know where I stand."

She couldn't think of a single thing going wrong between them and was puzzled. "I should have thought," she said softly, "That our last meeting at 'Tall Trees' would have told you."

Mark didn't speak for a moment. "It did," he said. "But, unfortunately, since then a little bird has whispered to me that your number one is Maurice."

Steff quaked a little and forced a smile.

"Why, Mark, how silly. Somebody's got it wrong. Maurice is my employer and obviously buys my time and services. We may have the occasional kiss but that's club life." She challenged him with a lie. "You must know I could never sleep with him."

"Then is it OK if I mention it to him?"

Steff had to say yes and hoped she got to Maurice first, but Mark forestalled her, picked up the phone and dialled Maurice.

"Yes?" he said.

"Mark here. I know it's late but I want to ask you a question to avoid embarrassment."

"Shoot!"

"Is Steff your woman? Because if so I'll back off."

"Christ, no!" Maurice said coarsely, "I might tap her arse but then I'm her employer. Perks of the job."

"You with her now?" he asked.

"No, I'm speaking from 'Tall Trees'," Mark lied. "See you," and he put the phone down.

Steff could tell Maurice had backed her up and felt confident again. "You've just told a lie, Mark," she said.

"A white one," he said. "I didn't want to compromise you."

"Well, are you satisfied now?"

"Yes, darling," he said, and took her in his arms, but a nagging doubt remained. Barbara had been convincing.

When Steff saw Maurice the next day she said, "I was breathing heavy last night. Good job you gave the right answer."

"Piece of fucking cake," he said. "He gave himself away." He grinned, "Was he with you?"

"He was indeed."

Maurice laughed heartily, "He's not so fucking dumb then."

But Steff kept her true intentions to herself. It would be a huge mistake to have Maurice as an enemy.

Then the Hon. Derek Llewellyn-Wilson came to 'Tall Trees'.

He was a few years older than Mark and even richer. His father, Sir Reginald Llewellyn-Wilson, was Chairman of a multi-national electronics group, and one of the wealthiest men in the country.

His son Derek had long been a thorn in his side. Twice divorced, always looking for a thrill, he had been forced to get him out of trouble time and time again.

Derek was good looking and had a very racy manner, which got him friends instantly, and when Mark met him he reckoned they could have a few good evenings together.

He met him in reception, where Derek was fingering a Phoenix club brochure, and Mark liked his friendly style and carefree approach.

"Know anything about this club," he asked. "I could do with a good night out."

"One of London's best," Mark said. "Wine, women and song twice over. Plus some lovely escorts."

"Fascinating."

Derek hesitated. "You wouldn't fancy introducing me? I haven't brought a woman with me." He gave an easy smile. "Makes a change."

"You're on," Mark said, "If you can stand my driving."

"Fast and easy is how I like it. What's your car?"

"Red Lotus."

Derek clapped his hands. "Great! I've been meaning to get one. You must let me have a go at the wheel."

"I think that can be arranged."

They smiled at each other, and Mark thought he'd found a kindred spirit.

He rang Maurice and explained who he was bringing to the club, and Maurice was all smiles. Just the sort of dividends he'd hoped Mark would provide.

"Leave it to me. He'll be well looked after," he said. And he carefully chose Melanie to be Derek's escort. She was not only beautiful, she was absolutely loyal to Maurice. Not only because he rewarded her so well, but because he slept with her.

Mark let Derek take the wheel when they drove up to town that evening and was rather alarmed by his driving. Mark liked a fast pace himself, but Derek seemed to think everyone should get out of his way and raced in and out of the traffic like a madman.

Mark glanced at him. His eyes were alight and he was enjoying himself. Mark had to admit he was expert at the wheel, but some of the risks he took made his blood run cold. He was thankful when they arrived in one piece.

Maurice met them in the foyer and introduced Melanie to Derek. She gave him a dazzling smile, and her beauty did the rest.

Derek took her arm possessively and waltzed her off.

Maurice looked at Mark. " Arrogant bastard, isn't he?"

Mark grinned. "Ever met a rich man who isn't? But he's good fun. Just a bit wild."

"Just how I like 'em," Maurice said.

Melanie kept Derek well entertained, and eventually they watched the cabaret and Steff had Derek on the edge of his seat.

"She's a honey," he said. "What legs and where they lead."

"You haven't seen mine yet, darling," Melanie reminded him. "And you can handle those."

Derek took her hand. "I'm liking you more each minute, darling."

Melanie took him to a private room and put on a good performance, and when she was naked and Derek saw her body he threw off his clothes and took her in his arms.

He was so rough Melanie began to get alarmed. She knew there'd be bruises inside her thighs tomorrow and round her bottom. And when he seized her breasts and put his mouth to her she feared the worst.

She was right and he bit her. Then he transferred to her lips and was equally careless if he hurt or pleased her.

It seemed to Melanie as though he was a man being driven. He showed not a scrap of concern for her, and she was relieved when he savagely thrust into her.

She had a sudden idea when he withdrew. "I see you like things rough, darling," she whispered. "Would you like to see some really rough stuff and take part?"

Derek thought for a second. "The real thing? Sadism?"

"The real thing. Some of my friends have had wonderful experiences," she lied.

Melanie could see he was wrestling with the idea and she persuaded him with all her might. She would be on to a big bonus if she could get him to one of Maurice's special houses outside London.

Unfortunately, Derek seemed suspicious. "Is this place connected to the club?"

"Heavens, no! Maurice would have nothing to do with anything like that," she cooed. "This is between ourselves. Strictly for the few."

Derek couldn't resist. "Give me the address. I'll think about it."

Melanie picked up a little pad and scribbled on it.

"Don't leave it too long. There's a waiting list," she said.

Derek's face suddenly cleared. He'd decided.

He leaned towards Melanie and surprisingly gave her a gentle kiss. "Thank you, darling," he said. "I know I'm a rough bastard. Keep the change." And he handed her £500.

Melanie wasn't all that surprised. She'd met these rich young men before who thought money bought them anything on the planet. In the grip of passion, arrogant and savage, no concern for anyone but themselves. In everyday life quite different, perhaps quiet and charming.

She was going to have a look at the camera pictures with interest. Derek had seriously hurt her. But Maurice would be pleased. Especially if Derek went to the sadist house... If she'd read him right, she'd be surprised if he didn't.

It was very late when Derek went back to 'Tall Trees'. This time Mark was controlling the Lotus.

"Had a good time, Derek?" he asked.

"Terrific," he replied. "YOU?"

Mark laughed. "The same."

Derek went quiet, then suddenly flung at Mark, "That Melanie, the girl I was with, she was an adventurous bitch. Said she could fix me up to go to a sadist party. Even take part if I wanted." He said, lying, "I've often wondered what that sort of thing is like. Thought it would be a shame to pass up the chance." He hesitated. "I wouldn't have the guts to go on my own. I suppose you wouldn't fancy coming with me?"

Mark was startled. His knowledge of that game was secondary and very distant. "Why would you want company?" he asked.

Derek said, lying again, "I'd feel a fucking idiot on my own. You could say you'd come to watch."

His real reason was he wanted someone to watch his back. He didn't want to be fitted up.

"OK then," Mark said reluctantly. He hoped Derek would change his mind or have forgotten all about it by the morning.

He was disappointed. The next day Derek sought out Mark and said he was looking forward to the adventure. "You won't let me down, will you?" he pleaded.

Mark felt compelled to give in, and the very next night they were in his red Lotus outside London, looking for a house named 'The Beeches'. They found it at last, isolated and standing in its own grounds. It just looked an ordinary house, but what went on inside was another matter.

The girls recruited to perform in the debauchery were prostitutes drawn from the streets of Manchester or Liverpool. Never London. That was too close. They always kept their mouths shut afterwards. Not only from fear. They were heavily rewarded.

The recruiting was very clever so that it couldn't be traced, and done through a series of agents, only the last one knowing the venue. The house itself was rented for a period by an unknown name, cash in advance. Nothing could be linked to Maurice.

Mark drove up the drive and parked. Derek rang the bell.

A stern faced female answered the door.

"Yes?" she asked.

"I've come for a special party," Derek said. "This is my friend, Mark. He likes to watch."

"Name?" she said.

"Derek Llewellyn-Wilson."

"Who recommended you?"

"Melanie at *The Phoenix* club in the West End."

The woman pretended not to know the club. She had been well rehearsed. She pursed her lips. "Don't know it."

"The owner is Maurice Robens."

"Don't know him either." Her voice was loaded with suspicion.

"Just a minute," she said and shut the door.

She came back in a few minutes, and her face had relented a little. "It's all right," she said. "We know Melanie. Come in," and she stood aside.

"Christ! They're careful aren't they?" Mark whispered to Derek.

"Just as well," he replied, shielding his mouth with his hand.

They were ushered into a small bar that Mark could see was temporary, and they ordered drinks and sat down.

Then a mature young woman appeared and sat down with them. She was not a beauty but she had a certain animal magnetism that disturbed Mark. She said her name was Norma.

"Which of you gentlemen intends to participate?"

Her educated voice surprised Derek, but he answered quickly. "I am the one. My friend has come to watch."

"Really?" She made it sound depraved, and Mark could have squirmed.

"Follow me," she said and went through the next door. There was a fair sized one-way window facing them, and she indicated it and said, "Take your pick."

Derek peered through and saw a room where several girls were sitting in scanty dress. "Could you ask them to move?" he said.

The woman picked up a microphone and said a few words and the girls started a small parade round the room.

Derek pointed to one. "Her!"

The woman said into the microphone. "Kathleen, get yourself ready."

She turned to Derek and said quite evilly. "Do you want her tied up or do you want a fight?"

He said quickly. "Think I'd like a fight."

"You can do what you like," she said. "You'll find plenty of weapons at your disposal." She gave a grim smile. "We prefer you don't kill her."

She led them to another room that contained a long couch and a few chairs, plus a big cabinet full of various instruments of torture. The room seemed to be padded; Mark thought. And there were spotlights all round, with a one-way window along one wall.

As a final thought Norma said to Derek, "Do you want it silent or with music?"

Mark could hardly believe what he was hearing, but Derek said boldly, "Put on some crashing music, loud and repeated."

She spoke into her mike, and in a few minutes music echoed round the room. To Mark it appeared to be part of an opera but he couldn't name it.

Norma fixed her gaze on Mark. "Do you want to be present or watch through the window?" She pointed.

Mark felt dirty and wished he'd never come. "Outside," he said abruptly and followed her into the next room, where she stationed him in front of the window.

Kathleen came into the room. All in black. Brief bra and G string, high black heels, and long dark hair. Mark thought she had a dreamy look in her eyes, and he was right. She had been drugged with a little tablet in her drink before she appeared. He found out afterwards that this was supposed to subdue the pain.

She stared at Derek insolently. "You want a fight, pretty boy?"

Derek was in his shirt and he rolled up his sleeves.

She said impudently. "Why don't you take it off? Frightened of a little scratch?"

He cast off his shirt, and his eyes lit up. He was going to enjoy this.

Mark, watching, was transfixed. His idea of sadism was that someone got tied up and the other person wielded a cane. He hadn't expected to see a fight.

Norma was still by his side and saw his face.

"Doesn't it suit you?"

Mark didn't know how to take her. "I thought people got tied up and beaten."

"They usually do, but clients can choose."

She said with a slight sneer, "They get their money's worth whatever they pick."

Mark looked back through the window.

Kathleen stood hands on hips, taunting Derek, and she ran her tongue round her vivid lips. "I'm waiting."

Derek advanced towards her then got a huge surprise. As he got near, she suddenly launched herself at him and caught him fiercely round the face with the flat of her hand.

For a moment he stood dead still. The blow had hurt, but he was more shocked, and instinctively put his hand to his face.

Kathleen derided him. "Did that hurt, pretty boy?"

The repeated words pretty boy, infuriated Derek, and his temper rose.

He seized her shoulder and ripped off her bra, then her G string.

His eyes ran from her firm, thrusting breasts to the shaven space between her legs, then he swung her slender body round to glimpse her tight, rounded buttocks. He reckoned she couldn't be more than nineteen, and her firm contours stoked his appetite sky high.

She suddenly broke away and, before Derek could defend himself, she kicked her high heeled shoe into his groin, and he had to grit his teeth.

A few inches nearer would have doubled him up.

She went to kick him again but this time Derek was ready.

He seized her leg and upended her flat on her back. Then he opened her legs and pressed his knee into her, again and again. His excitement was burning, and her struggles goaded him further.

She screamed and without warning bent her knees so that Derek fell forward, and before he could recover she twisted away.

He got up and forced her to the floor where he cruelly twisted her nipples and again drove his knee into her. She screamed once more and hit him in the face.

He pushed his face into hers so she couldn't strike him and reached between her legs. Then, without a stab of conscience, he brutally twisted and turned the folds of her skin. He was absolutely inflamed and wouldn't let go.

The pain must have been awful and Kathleen shrieked and writhed. Then she did the only thing possible to save herself.

She ferociously sank her teeth into Derek's neck and held on till his hand came up. Then she spun away.

His neck was bleeding, and he stood up and glared at Kathleen's heaving body, but his appetite was undiminished and, with a quick stride he picked her up and mercilessly threw her across the floor. She careered into a chair and suddenly was still.

Derek stood over her and saw blood on her head. She didn't move.

Suddenly he was frightened and yelled out, "She's hit her head. Bring help."

Almost immediately the room seemed full of people and he saw Norma standing over Kathleen.

Then a man appeared with a bag and Derek saw he was a doctor.

Norma gave way, and after what seemed an eternity Derek saw the doctor was giving mouth to mouth resuscitation. Then he pumped Kathleen's chest vigorously but she didn't seem to stir. He stood up at last with a grim face and said, "This young woman is dead."

Derek was nearly paralysed with fear, his stomach a mass of pain. He'd killed a girl.

What could he do?

He dimly heard Mark's voice. "I've spoken to Norma. She said clear out and keep your mouth shut. They'll handle everything."

Derek nearly rushed out of the building. He couldn't get out quickly enough, and Mark was hot on his heels.

On the drive back he said, "What a fucking mess. Pretty grim stuff that, Derek. I didn't have you pegged for that sort of thing."

Derek forced a laugh. "Oh I'm not a pervert. Just looking for new experiences. Unfortunately, I lost my temper." He drew in his breath, "Don't worry," he said. "I've learned my lesson. There'll be no repeat of that."

He sounded plausible, and Mark decided to give him the benefit of the doubt, but at the back of his mind there was a nasty suspicion.

Maurice had done an in-depth check on the Hon. Derek and found that in the past he had similarly beaten a girl unconscious, and only his father's millions had saved him from an official investigation.

He was consumed with delight. Couldn't be better.

The blackmail didn't start until the Hon. Derek had left 'Tall Trees' and been back at his flat for two weeks.

He rang Mark. "I've had a bloody blackmail demand," he said. "Quarter of a mill. Fucking bastards!"

"Go to the police," Mark said.

"You out of your mind? I've killed a girl. My old man would crucify me."

"But what about next time? Blackmailers always come back," Mark said. "They're the original bloodsuckers."

"I know," Derek admitted. "I'll have to think about it. But I'll have to meet THIS demand."

"Why? Once they've gone public they can't come again."

"You fucking idiot!" Derek said. "I'll be up shit creek. My old man's reputation ruined! Me kicked out."

But Mark had a cooler head than Derek. "Play for time," he said. "They won't want to let a big pay-off slip."

He thought for a second. "Have they sent you the pictures?"

"You mean the tape?"

"What else?"

"No they haven't. They don't need to, do they?"

Mark said somewhat wearily, "Ask for it. It's a perfectly reasonable request which they can't ignore. They might be bluffing. There might not be any pictures. How do you know?"

Derek was silent. Then he said, "Yeah! You're right. Mark." He suddenly got a little more confident. "If they don't send them I'll tell them to fuck themselves."

"That's more like it," Mark agreed.

"But what can I do in the meantime?" Derek asked.

"Pray."

"I'll get back to you," he said.

Mark turned things over in his head. The blackmailers had got Derek by the balls. That was obvious. But he wanted to appear helpful to Derek. He didn't want to lose a wealthy client. They tended to talk to others.

He wondered who was behind the blackmail and straight away thought of Maurice, but he had to reluctantly disregard that theory. There was no way in which he could be connected.

Derek came through five days later. "Got the tape," he said gloomily. "Christ! It's worth than I feared."

"Any instructions for payment?"

"Oh yes, and very neat. A banker's draft through computer to an unnamed account offshore. Just a number."

"From where, of course," Mark said, "It can be transferred all over the place."

"I guess."

"You've no choice, Derek," Mark said. "Go to your father and tell him you did the whole thing for a dare, never dreaming it would be publicised. Unfortunately, there was an accident that could not have been foreseen." He said stalwartly, "I'll back you up. But if possible I would keep the pictures away from your father."

"You're fucking right about that," Derek said, "But gee! Thanks for your support, Mark. I won't forget."

Mark was satisfied. At least HE wasn't going to be a loser.

Derek plucked up his courage and went to see his father, but he was in for a huge shock.

First, Sir Reginald warned him very aggressively this was the last time he would dig him out, and stabbed him in the chest to emphasise his anger.

Second, he announced he wasn't going to lie down to the blackmailers.

He hadn't become chairman of one of the biggest public companies in Britain without knowing how to fight, and his ruthlessness was well known.

He barked at Derek. "You sit tight and keep your mouth shut. I'm handling this now. Any contact you tell me at once."

Then he shot a stream of instructions at him.

Derek was relieved his father didn't ask to see the tape, and thought he'd overlooked it. But his father knew his son and didn't want to be further disgusted.

When the blackmailers came through again Derek spoke to them in a manner approaching his normal arrogance; he no longer felt the same threat. He said nonchalantly, "If you want any money you'll have to contact my father. He's the money bags."

He gave them a private telephone number to contact him at night after eight o'clock. Before they could agree or disagree, he hung up, just as his father had instructed him.

Their next step was to ring the number, and they received a cool reception.

Sir Reginald Llewellyn-Wilson was a different cup of tea to his son.

He spoke in an icy cold tone to the speaker. "I am prepared to pay but not before I am satisfied there's no alternative, and I shall consult my solicitors."

The blackmailer started to speak but Sir Reginald cut him off.

"You want to get paid, you play it my way. I will instruct my bank to make a draft for the money but put a stop on it until I'm satisfied. You are welcome to check."

"But that could take weeks. Fuck you! We're in the box seat."

"Take it or leave it. Once the story's out you get fuck all." Sir Reginald jammed the phone down. He knew they would wait. There was no other way they could get the money.

His next step was to enrol private detectives in the area, and one of them was Alec Donovan. He was given the whole story and was on the job straight away.

He called on Mark first, and, considering his mission for his mother still ongoing, he studied Mark curiously. Could he be a murder prospect?

Yes, he thought, tough, intelligent and ambitious, but too much money too young. Plus a great deal to gain from his father's death. He was certainly in the frame.

But that was not his assignment at the moment, and he left Mark armed with the information he had asked for, the location of 'Beech Trees'.

He soon found the house and, as expected, found that that the tenants were no longer there. Their short term lease had expired, and there was no record of an address. The transaction had been cash in advance.

He obtained a key from the agents and went through the place. Then he got lucky. He found at the back of a drawer a handful of cards; the girls had not been as careful as the tenants. Alec knew at a glance they were the cards call girls used and he flipped through them.

One of them bore the name Kathleen, with a telephone number. He also knew the telephone prefix meant Liverpool.

He burned up the motorway the same day and arrived in Liverpool in the evening. Then he rang the number in case the new occupant could help him. Call girls were pretty clannish.

The girl who answered said her name was Kathleen, but Alec took that with a pinch of salt and arranged to meet her.

She welcomed him but was very cool when she found he only wanted information. "I keep my mouth shut," she declared. "You live longer."

Alec flourished some money, then a lot more. After all, Sir Reg was paying.

She suddenly found her tongue. She remembered the whole situation at *The Beeches* and identified the Hon. Derek as a fucking mean bastard. Alec got it all on tape.

He didn't tell her how she'd been used and was supposed to be dead. No need to frighten her. He might want her to repeat her story.

Alec reported his findings to Sir Reg, who immediately altered his strategy. The next time the blackmailers rang he went on the attack.

"Now you listen to me," he declared. "I have discovered the girl you said was killed is in fact alive and still operating in Liverpool, and she is prepared to talk."

He paused for breath and said threateningly, "This is final! I will release the money to you on one understanding. This is the one and only payment."

He wouldn't let the blackmailers cut in and raised his voice. "Don't think you're safe. I've an army of detectives on the job, and if you make any further attempts to extract money I shall have my solicitors take you to court for fraud and demanding money with menaces."

Once again he shouted them down. "If you take the money it confirms your agreement."

He wound up with the grim warning that all their telephone conversations had been recorded.

Finally, he slammed the phone down, and the blackmailers hadn't said a word... "That fucks you," he muttered.

When it was reported to Maurice he smiled. "Tough old sod! Still, quarter mill's not bad. There'll be others." He didn't want to invite trouble and he felt sure Sir Reginald would be a bulldog. He also thought how important it was to keep Mark sweet. These rich bastards were such easy pickings.

But Maurice would have been very uneasy indeed if he had known something else Sir Reg had done.

In his important position he had access to all the top men and he had dropped a hint to the London police chiefs that it might be worth their while to keep an eye on the West End's leading club, *The Phoenix*.

His acute mind had tried to find a source for son Derek's activities, and *The Phoenix* was the only prospect he came up with. Purely a guess, of course, but a very shrewd one, and the police took his words seriously.

And that is how DI Lew Green and his partner Sgt Sally Golding came to be in *The Phoenix* apparently as clients, and of course in plain clothes.

Their instructions were simply to survey the place and get an impression if underground activities might be taking place, and report anyone they recognised or had been through their records.

In other words, as Sally said, "A fishing expedition." She was thoroughly enjoying her experience at *The Phoenix*. Not very often she or Lew rubbed shoulders with the rich and famous in the country. And all on expenses.

They both regarded the assignment as a big perk and would have reported back no suspicions except for one unexpected event, and Lew was not sure whether he should report it or not, but Sally persuaded him.

Lew recognised the Hon. Derek from the pictures Sir Reg had passed on, and took the trouble to find out he was talking to Maurice and Mark.

Sally said matter-of-factly, "Not for us to decide who or what's important. Let the big heads in the office make the decision." So they informed them.

Their chief was pleased with their observation. It gave him the opportunity to mix with the upper level, and when he made his report he dressed it up a bit.

"Maurice Robens," he said, "has been suspected of different things in the past but always come up clean. We've had him under suspicion on more than one occasion."

"And what about Mark Addison?" he was asked. "Another very rich young man. Director of the 'Tall Trees' celeb palace."

The chief tried to think. There was something. He cudgelled his mind. Then it came to him. "There was something strange not long back," he said. "His father was killed in a motor accident, but his widow protested violently about the reported facts and point blank refused to believe the evidence. The family supported her, and she was very scathing about our enquiry. Said the accident was totally unbelievable."

"Get me all the files," he was told crisply, and the chief departed, feeling he'd made an impression.

He decided purely on his own initiative to keep the surveillance on *The Phoenix*. It seemed important enough to interest his superiors. You never know something might turn up. Nothing to lose if it didn't.

He instructed Lew and Sally to keep the survey on but pay particular attention to Maurice Robens, the Hon. Derek, and Mark Addison. Plus any interesting friends, of course.

Lew was inclined to think there was something going on that they hadn't been told about and he pressed Sally to take the assignment seriously. So far as she was concerned, it was a jaunt in the park, and all expenses paid, and she dolled herself up and even spent money on a new outfit.

It wasn't long before Lew noticed Mark's attentions to Steff, and also her apparent attachment to Maurice.

But it was Sally who spotted that, although Mark was quite open in his feelings to Steff, Maurice hid his from Mark. "I wonder," she said shrewdly, "If Maurice is using Steff to get something out of Mark?"

Lew didn't take her seriously, "What?" he laughed. "The colour of his next new car?"

Sally was stung and said hotly, "You just remember that the people we are watching have a connection to 'Tall Trees'. Even Steff has been down there."

"How did you know that?"

"I opened my mouth and asked a few people. It's no secret."

Lew went quiet. Perhaps Sally was more on the ball than he was, and he wondered if it might be a good idea to get down to 'Tall Trees' and have a scout round. Still, he could hardly expect the chief to sanction a stay there. It would cost a fortune.

Sally seemed to be reading his mind. "Might be worth having a look at 'Tall Trees'," she suggested. "Not to stay, of course. Some pretext, say checking the security?"

Lew had to admit she had a good notion.

"I'll speak to the chief," he said.

The chief was dubious. He didn't want a lot of wealthy people kicking up a big fuss. They had a nasty habit of complaining direct to senior officers.

Lew persisted, "We could make it sound we were doing them a favour checking their security." He said artfully, "They might consider that good service from the police."

The chief was persuaded. "But," he threatened, "I'd better not get any complaints."

Lew rang Mark and offered a security check at 'Tall Trees'. He explained that the police were concerned about mounting robberies, and his wealthy clients could be targets.

"But we've good security," Mark protested. "TV scanners, the lot."

Lew used his brains. "When were they last checked?"

This stumped Mark. "Well," he said thoughtfully, "I'm not sure."

Lew pressed on. "We'll do it for you free," he said. "And give you police approval or advice." He said carelessly, "Any time to suit you. But, of course, the sooner the better."

In two days time he and Sally were at 'Tall Trees' and met Mark, who introduced them to Barbara who was in his office.

She volunteered to take them round 'Tall Trees' and Mark was relieved to be rid of the chore.

But for Lew and Sally it was a lucky break.

As they left Mark's office Lew let Barbara get in front and whispered to Sally. "You chat her up. I'll do the checking."

She stuck her thumb up, and they were in business.

Sally was getting used to seeing how the rich lived, but 'Tall Trees' took her breath away. She said to Barbara. "I don't suppose you wipe their noses, do you?"

Barbara laughed. "These are seriously wealthy people. Every one a millionaire. The rest of us are just their servants."

Sally reckoned that wasn't far from the truth.

Then she started her campaign. She said conversationally, "Do you know Mark well?"

Barbara grinned and said quite unselfconsciously, "Does sleeping together count?"

Sally was stunned but covered it up. She said with a giggle. "Is it the rule round here?"

"Oh Mark's always being chased," Barbara said. "He's another regular girlfriend near here, name of Carol, but," she said, "He's got a stunner in London. A cabaret star and, believe me, she's like a film star. Talk about sexy." She drew in her breath.

Sally knew she was referring to Steff but kept her mouth shut.

"So you are not really serious?"

"I bloody am! I reckon she'll have strings of men lining up. I don't think Mark will get all his own way with her."

Sally changed tack. "Does Mark mix with the guests a lot?"

"One or two. But the one he's with most often surprises me."

She sniffed disdainfully.

"The Hon. Derek Llewellyn-Wilson." She put scorn in her voice when she said 'the Hon'. "A right rich rat," she said.

Sally pressed her luck. "You don't like him?"

"He's horrible. All pretence. Always smiling, but look at his eyes. Cold and mean." She gave a little shiver. "He always WANTS something, never gives. I wouldn't like to be in bed with him."

Sally was drinking this in and hoped most of it would record in the small mike she had concealed in her bag. Lew was in for a surprise.

But Barbara saved the best bit for last. "They go up to that *Phoenix* club in the West End," she said. "I reckon Mark meets his cronies up there. I'll bet there's some shady business conducted there."

"What, Mark?" Sally pretended to be surprised.

"Jesus! He's like all rich men, particularly the young ones. Think their money buys them anything."

Sally had to be careful now. "I can't imagine Mark doing something shady."

Barbara gave an empty laugh. "Where you been living this century? It's people like us who have to behave. The wealthy just pay."

"What do you mean?"

But Barbara suddenly dried up as though she realised she had said too much and regretted it.

She shrugged her shoulders. "You never know, do you?"

Sally realised her change of mood and got off the subject.

"What's with all this heavy plant and machinery going into the grounds?" she asked.

Barbara launched into the new development enthusiastically.

"There's going to be twenty or thirty luxury detached villas in their own grounds with pool and all services. Ideal for the London celebs trying to find privacy."

She laughed, "They'll be charged £500 to breathe, and," she said, "Guess who the liaison officer is for the development." She pointed a finger at herself. "Little me."

Sally said curiously, "Why would they want a liaison officer?"

"You any idea how much this is going to cost?"

"Millions, I reckon."

"And millions. My father's Company and Mark are 50/50 partners. That's why they want a liaison officer."

Sally wondered if she dare ask, then took the plunge. She tried to speak carelessly, "What's your father's company?"

But Barbara was completely unselfconscious.

"Oh! It's not HIS company. It's the International Hotel group. He's a freelance but does all their land valuations."

"I suppose there was competition for the contract?" Sally asked.

"Not much. I believe Mark said the other bidder wanted full control which was never a runner; but negotiations went on for some time."

Barbara said thoughtfully, "Mark used to speak to somebody called Vince Adams." She added with scorn, "Another *Phoenix* member."

Sally could hardly believe her luck. All this free information. She hoped Barbara wasn't telling fairy tales.

"Mark let you know his name?" she asked incredulously. "That was careless, wasn't it?"

"When you're with someone and his mobile rings, he answers it. I've got good hearing," she said defensively.

"But it was no secret to me. I knew what was going on from the start."

No more could be said as the tour and inspection came to an end. Lew raised his eyebrows to Sally and she gave a little tweak of her thumb.

He reported to Mark. "First class security; you should be complimented. You can put up a notice," he said. "Security approved by the police."

Mark was pleased but had no intention of putting up a notice; he didn't want his clients thinking about security.

Exactly as Lew reasoned, but it enabled him to leave Mark on very good terms. Should please the chief, he thought sourly.

He could hardly wait to get outside and question Sally but he waited until they were in their car. "Well?" he asked.

Sally gave him a look of triumph. "Pin your ears back."

She touched a switch, and the conversation came over sweet and clear from her recorder.

Lew was dumbfounded, and he said at last, "I could kiss you, Sally." Then he said doubtfully, "You don't think she was having you on? Trying to impress."

"Why should she? It was just girl to girl." She tapped her recorder. "She didn't know about this."

"True!" Lew smiled. Then he said thoughtfully, "I think we've just extended our stay at *The Phoenix*."

He tapped Sally on the shoulder playfully, "I'd like to see the chief's face when he hears this."

Sally broke into a smile. "Me too!"

She was also hoping for some praise from the chief. After all, SHE had extracted the information from Barbara.

The chief WAS pleased. "So you're instincts were right, Lew." But he also recognised Sally's work. "Smart work, Sally," he said.

He wrinkled his brow. "Play it over again will you? There's something stirring in my mind."

Sally played it again and when the name of Vince Adams came up he shouted. "Stop!"

"Well well," he said. "Vince Adams. He works for one of those big building outfits who try to bulldoze everybody out of the way, I think," he said grimly, "He's their strong arm man. He's never been charged but we don't like him."

Sally said innocently, "There's a big building development going on at 'Tall Trees'. Running into millions."

"Who got the contract?" the chief asked.

"It's a partnership. 'Tall Trees' and International Hotels."

"Oh they're absolutely straight. I won't say they're not ruthless but they keep strictly within the law."

The chief tapped his fingers on the desk, then snapped, "I still don't like Vince Adams in the picture. He's trouble."

"You'd both better stay at *The Phoenix*," he said, "Let's see who else comes along."

At Tall Trees Barbara seized the opportunity to get Mark's attention the next day. She loved a little mischief.

"Talk about questioning," she said to him. "That Sergeant Sally practically put me through a cross examination yesterday."

Mark was instantly alert but tried to conceal his interest. "Oh?" he said casually, "What about?"

"You mostly."

"ME?" Mark tried to laugh it off, but alarm bells began ringing in his head. He wondered if Derek's father had started something going and decided it would be a good idea to cool things with Derek. It never entered his head that it could be connected with his father's death.

Then he got a stroke of luck.

At *The Phoenix* Derek introduced him to Lady Olivia Lithgow, a tall elegant beauty with a very superior manner. She was sexy without trying, and Mark liked the look in her eyes.

To cultivate her, he spoke on the subject which seemed to be her major interest, horses, and, in particular, race horses.

The rather languid man escorting her, name of Geoffrey, didn't seem to mind Mark cutting in, in fact Olivia almost ignored him. Mark found out later that Olivia did the choosing as far as escorts were concerned, they didn't choose her.

She was used to bossing people. She ran a big stables her father had set up and wouldn't stand any nonsense.

She had that air of assurance men have, and Mark sensed a challenge.

Beauty and brains... What a combination, he thought.

"You like to do some gambling?" he invited.

"Oh I like gambling, but not on the tables of *The Phoenix*."

Mark raised his brows.

"Horses," she said. "And sometimes men."

Mark was beginning to get more and more interested in Lady Olivia.

"I suppose that could be arranged," he suggested.

She looked at him coolly. "Perhaps." Then calmly moved off with Geoffrey. She expected Mark to pursue her but he didn't and she gave him a second thought, which was unusual for her.

Mark didn't follow because he noticed Steff approaching and it wasn't long before all thoughts of other women disappeared from his mind.

Back at 'Tall Trees' the next day Lady Olivia came back into his thoughts, and for once it wasn't only sex he was considering. He wanted to impress her. He wasn't used to women who walked away from him. He considered she was a rather superior lady and wondered if adventures in bed would be superior too.

He asked Derek casually if he knew much about her.

"She's a haughty bitch," he declared. "Wants to boss everybody. She's always out with different men. No-one seems to get close to her."

"You don't like her?"

Derek sniffed.

"I'd probably do better if I was a horse."

Mark wondered if Derek had tried it on and been rebuffed. If so, he thought, one up to her.

"Yes, she did have horses on her mind," he admitted.

"You want to see the massive stables she's got," Derek said. "Not too far from here, just a bit further out in the countryside. Must cost a fucking fortune to run."

Mark didn't want to seem too interested; Derek had a big mouth, but there was one more question he had to ask, but carefully.

"She often at *The Phoenix*?"

"When the fancy takes her." A grin spread across Derek's face. "You interested?"

Mark was annoyed with himself. Just what he didn't want. Derek spouting off his mouth.

"You joking?" he said. "I just wondered if she'd walk away from me next time." He added for good measure, "Not a problem I usually have to face."

Then Derek gave Mark what he'd been fishing for.

"Sandown races in two weeks," he said. "If her horses do well it's a cert she'll be up at The West End celebrating."

Mark pretended not to be interested. "Fuck her and her horses," he said.

Derek smiled. "My feelings exactly."

Mark's next step went in the opposite direction. He enquired about dates and times for the races. Then he contacted a few people and got himself invited to Sandown by Jim Ferguson, a race horse owner and 'Tall Trees' client. In the private enclosure of course.

He could hardly wait for the date, and on the opening day met Jim Ferguson inside Sandown where they shook hands.

"Surprise," he said. "I didn't have you pegged as a race goer."

"I've recently become interested," Mark said smoothly. "I've even thought about buying."

"Really," he said. "You ought to have a look at Olivia Lithgow's stables. Not far from here."

Better and better, Mark thought.

Then he saw Olivia from a distance. She was on the turf talking to people surrounding a horse, including the jockey.

She gave the horse a pat and moved towards the private enclosure. She was wearing tapered black slacks and once again looked absolutely elegant.

Mark turned away and waited for Jim Ferguson to introduce him.

He heard him say, "Hallo Olivia. Someone I'd like you to meet." Then Jim tapped his shoulder and he swung round.

"This is Mark Addison," he said to Olivia. "He might be interested in buying so I mentioned your stables."

She looked at Mark coolly "Oh yes, *The Phoenix*, brief encounter."

Mark smiled, "Very brief."

She remained cool but relented a little. "You serious about buying?"

"I'm toying with the idea."

Olivia looked suspicious, and Mark guessed she'd sussed his motive.

Jim saved the day. "Why don't you go down to Olivia's stables, Mark? " he said. "They're not far away from you."

Olivia didn't like to be pushed into anything. Particularly regarding men. She was always faintly hostile when meeting a new man in case he thought he could dominate her.

Jim's urging swung the balance in Mark's favour.

"We can talk about it," she said shortly.

Then the racing started and she began to get excited.

Mark studied her as she followed the race through her binoculars. She was quite unguarded, and the tense set of her face changed to lively anticipation then almost the joyous thrill of a schoolgirl as her horse swept first past the post.

She turned to Mark looking radiant.

"What did you think of that?"

I must have her, Mark thought. "Wonderful Miss Cool," he said.

He'd hit the right moment with her, and she relented.

"You can take me to *The Phoenix* tonight," she said. "We'll celebrate."

Mark didn't tell her that he usually liked to do the asking. He felt it was almost a royal command... Still he'd got what he wanted.

She got third in another race and was delighted. Mark knew he would never have a more favourable time to proposition the ice maiden, but as they briefly parted before meeting again at *The Phoenix*, he was startled to feel a slight squeeze from her hand. He wondered if she was giving a message but wisely decided it was unintentional.

In the evening he was delighted to find that Olivia came to *The Phoenix* solo. He had wondered if she'd bring Jim Ferguson.

Earlier he had rung Maurice and Steff to tell them he would be escorting Lady Olivia. He explained she was the winning owner at Sandown races and it was a celebration... He didn't want Steff turning up with a frozen face.

As a result he got more of the red carpet treatment than usual, and Olivia was impressed. "Do they think you are Royalty?" she asked.

Mark turned the compliment gracefully, "It's you they want to impress, darling."

She raised her brows. "Darling?"

Mark smiled, "I apologise. Freudian slip."

Olivia liked that. He'd given a message but left her the option.

She'd had a few drinks and was pleasantly mellow, and she began to contemplate him more seriously.

He had an easy manner but a quiet air of arrogance, and she sensed he could be hard. She wondered about his self-control and if she would have an opportunity to test it.

Steff appeared after the cabaret finished and gave Olivia a quick look. "Hope you enjoyed the show," she said.

"Scintillating, Steff," Mark said smoothly. "You never disappoint."

She smiled and moved off. But Olivia's eyes were fixed on Mark, and he knew she wanted an explanation.

"I sometimes invite her for a drink after the show," he said. "Not on her own of course."

Olivia wondered if that was true, but she did notice Steff made a bee-line towards Maurice.

She was not really concerned and dismissed Steff from her mind. She had that upper class arrogance that working girls occupied a lower sphere, and she included Steff in that category.

Olivia did not consider running a stables was working; that was all apart of the superior life.

Although she would not have declared that view, it was part of her normal thinking.

She turned her attention back to Mark, her eyebrows slightly questioning.

He was turning over in his mind his next approach to Olivia. He knew for sure there was no question of spending the night with her but he wondered how far he could go towards that goal.

Then she made it easy for him. "The most silent we've been tonight," she said. "Something on your mind?"

Mark said boldly, "I was thinking about taking you home."

She smiled as though she was amused. "Of course. I didn't expect to walk."

They rose to leave, and again the staff put on the deferential treatment to Mark. Maurice liked to protect his investments and knew Mark would appreciate the build-up. They were almost bowed out to the door, and there was Mark's red Lotus waiting for them.

The treatment was not lost on Olivia. She knew only money brought such attention. But she wondered if it was Mark's money, or perhaps his family's.

As always, the red Lotus impressed, and Olivia was rather a racy lady. "Put your foot down Mark," she said. "Let's see what you can do."

Fortunately he had not drunk a lot as he had hoped he might be able to show off the Lotus, but he knew if they were stopped he would be in for a fine.

His luck held, and although he drove fast, he was a good driver and saved the speed for the open roads. Mark always maintained his motto was 'Safety fast', the old MG slogan, and he kept to it.

Again he chalked up a point. Olivia knew Mark would have been seriously tempted to show off, and his self control impressed her.

He found her place easily and was himself impressed with the size of the grounds and the establishment, and also the big villa dominating the countryside.

He pulled up with a roar and, although she invited him in for coffee, he refused politely. He knew she meant coffee only.

"Wait till we know each other more," he suggested easily. Then he thundered off.

Olivia stood at the door, reflecting. She was certainly surprised Mark had not accepted her invitation. She had been wondering if it might be a hard job to fend him off. "Interesting," she muttered.

The next day The Hon. Derek got a surprise telephone call from Lady Olivia. "Can you tell me anything about Mark

Addison? He's talking about buying a horse," she lied smoothly. "Is he well-heeled?"

"You joking?" Derek said. "He could buy and sell you twice over. He owns 'Tall Trees', that celeb retreat in the stockbroker belt."

"Oh thanks, Derek," she said coolly, and put the phone down. Her brain was beginning to synchronise with her sexual appetite.

She picked up the telephone and dialled Mark.

"Olivia here," she said. "I wondered if for a thank you for last night you might like to come to lunch and see round my stables?"

Mark was astounded. He regarded her as superior to his other women but still thought of her as the ice maiden, and had been idly contemplating a long term strategy.

His interest shot up. "What time?"

"When you like."

"Watch out for the red Lotus in the morning," he said gaily.

Olivia put the phone down slowly. She decided she would need to act quickly but carefully to start any sort of relationship with Mark. It was obvious he would be pursued by other women, and she needed to emphasise a distinction between her and the others. Show him she had a brain as well as sex to offer. Also play 'The Lady' card if necessary.

But not jump into bed too easily. He must be used to that, she thought.

Mark roared up about eleven and Olivia, who had been waiting on tenterhooks, put on a casual air. She was carelessly dressed in jodhpurs and boots, her working clothes.

She knew they suited her but she had also taken a little extra care this morning with her make-up, and made sure the top she wore showed a good outline but suggested more. Her final move was to comb her hair to the side so that it seemed careless but in fact was a perfect frame for her face.

She pretended to be surprised. "Oh you've come. I'm afraid I'm in my working clothes."

"They'll do for me."

Mark's immediate thought was exactly what Olivia wanted him to think.

Christ! This is something different.

She took his arm and led him across to the stable complex. She had already done a job on her staff as Maurice had the other night at *The Phoenix*, and they didn't let her down.

They usually called her Olivia, today it was Madam.

Olivia had also arranged a special act with one of her more intelligent stable girls and she acted perfectly.

After Mark had sampled the busy atmosphere she sang out, "Madam, Lord Waterton wants to know if you can see him tomorrow."

Olivia again pretended surprise. "What's it about?"

"He wants to discuss some new horses."

"Oh, all right. Tell him OK."

And she waved the girl away as though the matter was quite casual.

She said to Mark apologetically, "Some people can't seem to make up their own minds."

And to cap her virtuoso performance she took Mark to the back of the complex and pointed to the Surrey fields falling away. "Our exercise yard," she said.

The strange thing was that Mark, who was quite used to setting up other people, did not tumble that this time he was the victim. He was completely off guard and swallowed everything.

But it was fair to say his judgement was clouded. Olivia was at her best. Doing what she did perfectly. Showing off all her good points accidentally on purpose.

Mark was completely smitten and made the big mistake of thinking different was superior. Things couldn't have worked better for Olivia.

In her villa afterwards she entertained Mark royally. A feast of a meal, and coffee afterwards, followed by drinks by her pool, where of course she carefully displayed herself in a smart one piece, artfully cut around the front and breast regions. It really was not for swimming in, and she didn't take that chance.

Mark noticed that she seemed to have an army of girls running round at her disposal. He was not to know most of them usually did duty at the stables, and he soaked up the impression that she lived a very high life.

He was wondering what would happen in the evening but was not entertaining thoughts of getting Olivia into bed. He had already put her in a different category to his other women and was prepared to be patient.

Olivia deliberately delayed leaving the pool till quite late, and when they retired inside she left him with drinks and food while she changed.

She returned in a backless creation which seemed to fit her like a second skin, and it split open as she moved to emphasise her long legs. Made longer with high court shoes.

She arranged herself on a long couch and patted the space beside her.

"Come on, Mark," she said. "You don't need to be afraid of me."

He didn't need asking twice and he certainly wasn't afraid of her, but he WAS afraid of making the wrong move.

She had a huge television screen rigged up and asked Mark to select a video.

He looked through her library programme and was astonished to find soft porn quite prominent.

Olivia picked up his surprise.

"Shock you?" she asked. "It's human behaviour. It's only wrong in the wrong place."

Mark appreciated her intelligent approach. "Not shocked," he said. "Surprised."

"So?"

Mark selected a soft porn, and Olivia set it going. Then she put a drink at his elbow and sat closer.

Mark's hands were soon wandering and he felt her knee but she just lay back dreamily with her head against a cushion.

He slid his hand along to the split in her gown and brought his hand up till he found the bare expanse at the top of her legs.

Then her hand came down on his.

"Now you know I'm willing," she said. "But don't think I'm a one-night stand, Mark."

She gave his hand a little pressure. "Before we become serious we must become serious with each other."

"What on earth does that mean?" Mark almost shouted. "No-one can guarantee a permanent relationship."

"Of course not. This is the twenty first century, lust is everywhere," she said. "But I want more. Otherwise I might as well masturbate."

Her bold remark didn't shock Mark.

"We could have a whirlwind romance," he suggested.

"It might not work out."

"Then it's as well to know, isn't it?"

Mark had to admit Olivia's superior airs made HIM feel superior and stirred his sexual instincts like a bubbling cauldron. His desire was mounting by the minute.

She gave him a studied look. "Suppose we give ourselves a couple of weeks to explore each other."

Mark opened his mouth to object but she put her hand across it. "Then we shall know if the adventure is worth taking, won't we," she said.

She had every intention of driving him wild to get what she wanted.

Mark couldn't fight his desires. "You've got it, darling."

The next two weeks were the happiest of Mark's life.

Olivia made it into a honeymoon period and all they did was pursue pleasure. Even a couple of times flying across to Paris for a night out.

They excited each other to the full and kissed and fondled but Olivia would never give in fully.

At the end of the period they were back in her villa, lounging on her long couch, but this time she was leaning into Mark, and his hand was cupped idly around her breast.

"So what do you think, lover?" she whispered.

Mark had no caution now. "Thinking's over," he said, and reached across for her.

But with a big effort Olivia pulled away. She had another agenda. "Right, darling," she said. "Now before we go over the top let's be practical for one second."

She looked him full in the face.

"You have a business. I have a business. And as a regular partner I should expect you to take some of the financial burden off my father.... That's only fair, isn't it?"

Mark was taken aback, and for a moment his sexual urges froze, while his business brain jumped into action.

"What do you mean exactly?"

"Well, his money's running down. Income from stables is very erratic and they need steady funding."

"So if I don't come in, what happens?" Mark asked.

"My father will go on as usual."

Still struggling with the surprise Olivia had set him, Mark thought about the situation.

Olivia kept her fingers crossed while he was silent. This was the dangerous bit.

She coaxed him. "Come on, darling. If we were married there would be no question would there?"

Mark could understand her concern for her father but he was shocked by this totally unexpected proposal. On the other hand, he badly wanted Olivia.

His quick brain provided him with a compromise. Any finance he provided would finish immediately if THEY finished. Were it weeks, months, years.

"Tell you what," he said. "I'll put in 50 per cent of your monthly operating costs."

Olivia was disappointed, she had hoped for a capital investment. But still, half a loaf was better than nothing, and she could easily inflate her running costs.

"That would be fine darling," she said. "I wouldn't have expected more." The lie slipped out easily.

But Mark was equal to Olivia. He was a hard nut in business. "I'll get my accountant to contact you," he said.

Olivia tried to hide her disappointment. "Of course," she said. "I'll speak to mine." And she intended to give him some very specific instructions. The Battle of the Accountants, she thought.

In a way, Mark's tough approach drew him nearer to her. She admired strength and cleverness.

He was now in a fever of impatience waiting for the big moment with Olivia, and she was determined to make it memorable for him. She expected to enjoy herself, but it was more important HE did. She had to make sure he wanted more, and more important, wanted to come back.

Entering the bedroom, Olivia snapped on subdued lighting then appeared in a silk see-through gown, still wearing very high heels. Her legs looked longer than ever, and in the shadowy light as she swung about the room her nipples seemed huge.

She flashed the cleft in her tight bottom, and in her final swing she exposed her bare front and for a moment parted her legs. Mark was shedding his clothes and drew in his breath. Her line was shadowed but distinct, and his imagination ran riot.

She moved to the bed. "See anything you fancy, darling?"

Then without warning she threw off her gown and hurled herself on him, bearing them both to the bed.

Olivia was on top and ground herself into Mark and weaved and spun about with the whole contours of her body. She attacked his lips and rolled them round her teeth, then her tongue.

Suddenly she pulled away, but before Mark could be surprised, she was on him again, but facing the other way, and there was that distinct line between her legs, just in front of his mouth.

He had to go into it and as his lips closed around her she gave a violent jerk. Her folds of skin were magically wet and alive and Mark couldn't let go. The sexual force was frightening.

Her own lips moved across him like quicksilver, and suddenly she had him in her mouth. She seemed to be dragging out his lifeblood, and just when it seemed unbearable Mark started jerking like a madman and thought he'd never stop.

But Olivia still hadn't finished. Like a cat stretching, she swung round and got back on top of Mark. But this time she dragged his lips into her mouth, and forced her breasts into him. Almost by instinct Mark dug his fingers into her bottom and tried to pull her tighter, and if he'd had the energy he'd have started all over again.

Olivia whispered in his ear, "We can try something else next time, darling."

"That was pure lust," Mark murmured.

"The purer the better," she whispered. "Lust is not only for the ignorant."

Not for the first time, Mark thought Olivia might be too clever for her own good but she had him in her spell. He knew he couldn't wait for next time! Whatever next?

She had done her work well.

They didn't make an announcement of their affair and just moved in together quietly as they didn't want to disrupt existing relationships.

They decided they would share their houses, but from the beginning most of the time was spent at Olivia's villa. She had to be near her horses.

Mark didn't mind as he was still very near 'Tall Trees' and their days were spent much as they used to be .

But he did get interested in horses, although not the hard work of stabling, and Olivia made up he mind to take him to the next meeting at Sandown Park.

During this period both Carol and Barbara wondered what was occupying Mark, and he infuriated them by saying airily, "I'm considering some new developments not far away."

"What about the development taking place here?" Barbara demanded.

"Oh!" Mark said. "That's in your capable hands."

As for Steff, she guessed Lady Olivia was getting her claws in, but she was philosophical. It might not work.

Carol, however, didn't intend to take Mark's cavalier attitude lying down. She had her own plans for him, and decided to find out what he was up to. She suspected another woman and, if so, she wanted to know the competition.

Carol had a good opinion of herself, particularly in the bedroom, and was spoiling for a fight.

She rang Mark during the day at his office. She had a plan.

"What is the big secret, Mark?" she asked. "Why are you disappearing all the time?" She drew in her breath, "I shall begin to think you've dropped me if this goes on."

"I've told you," Mark said, "I'm tied up trying to get a new development off the ground. It's secret because it might not come off. If it does you'll know."

But Carol wouldn't be put off. "Look, darling," she said, "You can't tell me you can't spare me even one night away from work. Come off it!"

Mark saw he'd have to give in. He wasn't ready to dump Carol.

"Just a minute," he said, and pretended to go through his diary. "I'm free next Friday evening."

"Splendid," Carol said. "And I'm choosing where we go."

"Sure. Why not?"

"We're going to *The Phoenix* in the West End," she said firmly.

"Hold on," Mark said. "There's many better places nearer."

"I want to see where you've spent so much time."

"Not a lot," he lied.

Carol persisted.

"So you say. Now I want a look."

"OK, darling, if you insist." Mark tried to hide his annoyance.

Carol put the phone down with the gleam of battle in her eyes. She was going to keep her eyes wide open at The Phoenix.

Mark rang Maurice to tell him he was bringing a friend and to tell Steff not to get excited, she was a business commitment.

Maurice laughed to himself, "I bet."

He told Steff, and she got the message, but she was not going to miss the opportunity to view the competition. She didn't believe Mark's business commitment any more than Maurice.

On the drive up to London Carol was careful to let her dress ride up. She knew Mark's fondness for legs, right to the top.

And true to form, his eyes kept wandering.

"You still like them?" she asked saucily, and hitched her dress higher.

"Don't tempt me," he growled. But he was already wondering if she'd left off her G-string. She did that sometimes.

Carol read his mind exactly and smiled. "You'll have to find out, won't you?"...The evening had begun well, she thought.

So did Mark. He was all anticipation. Who was Olivia?

When they got to *The Phoenix* he was rudely reminded.

She turned up once again on the arm of languid Geoffrey.

Mark wondered what was going to happen but Olivia was the soul of discretion. She simply said, "Good evening, Mark," nodded to Carol and moved off as though he was a casual acquaintance.

But Carol was more sceptical.

"Who's she?" she asked.

"She's a racehorse owner. Has a big stables."

"What's her name?"

"Lady Olivia Lithgow."

Carol's brows shot up... The Lady was elegant and composed, definitely Mark's type.

Mark saw the suspicion in her eyes.

"I've only met her a few times." He said defensively. "She had that man with her then."

But Carol had already made up her mind about Olivia. She was definitely the enemy, or, at the very least, one of them.

Mark was not himself worried about her escort Geoffrey. He felt sure there could be no competition there. But he had yet to learn about Olivia.

Steff kept her distance but had a good look at sexy Carol.

"Business commitment, my arse!" she muttered.

She was not surprised. Young rich men, especially the good looking ones, were always fair game, and she was ready to step back into the picture any time. She had never thought Mark would be an easy capture.

Carol was beginning to realise how right her suspicions were. She'd certainly come to the right place. Anything could happen here. The place was alive with gorgeous women.

"I can see what attracts you here," she said to Mark. "Perhaps I should come more often." She displayed her legs to the top of her thighs. "I would fit in, don't you think?"

Mark had a job to drag his eyes away, and Carol said. "It might be your lucky night."

The next part of her plan was to get him full of drink so he couldn't drive back. Carol had a further suspicion about *The Phoenix* and she was going to test it.

They danced in close embrace, watched the cabaret, and were at last ready to depart well after midnight.

"You're not driving that bloody racing car after all that drink," Carol declared.

She looked round, then tried to sound innocent. "I'm sure these clubs have private rooms available; after all, this must happen fairly often. Rich people never know when to stop."

Mark was about to protest but before he could prevent her Carol said to one of the hostess girls, "Would you get me the manager, please?"

Maurice appeared instantly. He had been watching them.

Mark knew he couldn't drive back, but he didn't want Carol to think he knew about the private rooms. He said to Maurice, "Is it possible we could hire a room for the night?

He said apologetically, "I'm a bit over the top."

Carol didn't see his left eye flicker but Maurice did, and smiled to himself. A bonus coming up, he reflected. More adventurous pictures for his camera.

"Anything to oblige you, Sir," he said, and signalled to one of the girls, who took them through to a bedroom.

Carol was triumphant but not happy. She now knew what a liar Mark was! Business meetings! She nearly snorted.

But she reckoned the game was nowhere near over yet. She knew Mark was a rich playboy and he wouldn't change. It was all too easy for the wealthy. Anything they fancied they bought.

But she didn't care. She reckoned if she could finally get him into a serious relationship she'd be on easy street, and she could do the same as he did.

She had one big advantage over her competitors. She knew what Mark really liked. And she was going to see he got it tonight. In full measure.

She slowly undressed until she stood naked in her high heels. Then she caressed herself and became erect. She knew this set him going.

Mark bundled her into bed and fondled her swollen tips. It was exquisite agony for Carol, she felt really horny. But she pulled herself back. It was Mark who had to get the works tonight.

She eased him down to the top of her thighs and opened her legs. With her hands in his hair she guided him and he soon had her in his mouth. Then he touched her sensitive spot and for a moment Carol fizzed.

Mark felt her jerk, and his tongue nearly drove Carol mad, but with a big effort she encouraged him, and when Mark felt her wet he thrust hard into her, and at the same time his mouth came up over hers. He seemed to have a thing about mouth to mouth in the final moments.

This time Carol did not have to hold back and with a rush she let herself go. Perfect... They spasmed together.

She was more than satisfied. Mark had got the sensational sex he craved, and so had she.

She murmured to Mark. "What can better that?"

He grinned dreamily."The same again."

When Maurice watched the playback the next day he was thoroughly amused. "You naughty boy, Mark," he breathed. "Brilliant performance, and what a girl! You certainly know how to pick 'em."

He added the tape to his library. A real gem that one, he thought.

The next day Carol reflected on Lady Olivia. She reckoned Olivia was the new development Mark kept talking about. But realised there was nothing more she could do about it. On the other hand, she did not think Mark would stay faithful to Olivia, or her to him. It all depended, she considered, on what they were expecting from each other.

Mark had wealth. What did she have?

Carol reckoned she wouldn't beat her in bed but it occurred to her Olivia might not be in the same wealthy category as Mark, and she wondered if the Lady label and the big stables might be a front for shortage of funds. In that case Mark would find her out, she reasoned. If there was one thing Mark was, he was smart.

On the other hand, she might be well heeled, educated and witty. Carol took for granted she would be good in bed, but she consoled herself with the gloomy thought Mark's tiresome habits might get up her nose. His enthusiasms one day weren't necessarily the same next day. And she certainly couldn't see Mark taking to the horsy crowd. Well, if so, it wouldn't last. Of that she was sure.

Carol didn't realise it, but her analysis of Olivia had just explained why she had outlasted many other girlfriends. She understood what made Mark tick, and she didn't expect too much. She decided she would keep patient and wait for the Lady to overplay her hand. Meanwhile she had scored heavily at The Phoenix and Mark had been seriously impressed.

Unfortunately his thoughts were still directed at Lady Olivia. She was not only different, she was infuriatingly independent. And he anticipated some great battles to come with more glorious sex to follow.

He ran into Barbara the next day. "How are things coming?" he asked.

"On schedule, but it's a slow process."

She gave him a quick look. "Not seen much of you lately."

"You know how it is. Things change."

"What's the mystery about your new development?"

Mark stalled. "The mystery is, I can't make up my mind whether to put money into something different."

"I have a good listening ear," she suggested.

"Wish it was that easy."

Barbara said pointedly. "One or two people have been asking about you."

"Oh?"

Your sister Janet twice. Apparently she wants you to be here when someone important arrives."

"How important?"

"Don't know. But he's connected to the Government."

This jolted Mark. "Thanks, Barbara," he said, "I'll speak to her." He turned to leave and almost as an afterthought said, "We must get together again when I've some free time."

Barbara watched him stride away. The polite brush-off, she thought. Still there were other men, and she could bide her time.

Mark went to see Janet and apologised for his absences. "Been looking into something else we might be able to bring into our facilities," he said.

"What?" she asked.

Janet was a director, and Mark couldn't fob her off. He explained he had been toying with the idea of offering riding facilities to guests but he couldn't give names because a deal might not come off. He was only at the talking and looking stage.

To his surprise Janet took him seriously and was enthusiastic. "Great idea, Mark," she said, "I like it. Keep me posted."

Mark hastily jumped off the subject. "Barbara told me you wanted me to welcome some new arrival."

"Oh yes." She picked up a piece of paper from her desk.

"The first member of the government we've ever had. The right Hon. Arnold Bentley MP. Plus his wife Laura, who is a wealthy American heiress."

"What's his position in the Government?"

"Private Secretary to the Minister of Works."

"Hmm… OK," Mark said. "When are they due?"

"Three days time."

"Right, leave it with me, Janet."

He got up to go but she said, " Don't forget to keep me in the picture about the riding, Mark. I like it."

Mark nodded his head and left. A strange world, he thought. An excuse, a mere throw away notion gets Janet's serious attention. Normally he'd have a job to get anything at all past her.

Nonetheless it was a heaven sent opportunity to justify his contacts with Olivia, and it could even result in serious business.

He couldn't wait to see Olivia's face when he told her.

But that had to wait.

He was curious about the arrival of the Government Minister, and wondered if he would be pompous and expect all sorts of considerations; there was a limit to everything. There was also his wife to consider. But his visit would certainly add to the prestige of 'Tall Trees' and Mark fully intended to get out the red carpet without making it too obvious.

Quite by accident, he was in reception when they arrived and got a good view of their long dark car, with the chauffeur fussing around.

He immediately sent someone out to unload their baggage and stepped forward to welcome them.

He was not surprised to find the lady done up as though she'd just stepped out of a beauty parlour, high blonde of course, and she immediately showed her self-importance, looking round for attention. What we expect from American heiresses, Mark thought cynically.

His big surprise was the Minister, Arnold Bentley. A tall imposing figure, well spoken, and he could see why the American heiress had fallen for him. But he kept almost silent and simply nodded and smiled a little as his wife ordered people around. His gaze wandered about and Mark wondered where his mind was. Somehow it seemed a curious relationship, and Mark was intrigued.

"Any special services you require, Minister?" he asked.

"Very kind of you," he replied. "This is just a private visit."

He nodded to his wife. "Laura will let you know."

Mark next bumped into him in reception. He was on his own and going through the literature scattered about.

He had in his hand the Phoenix brochure.

"Curious about this club," he said to Mark. "Does the hotel recommend it?"

Mark was cautious. "We never accept a brochure that does not fulfil the highest standards."

Arnold gave a friendly smile, "That does not answer my question."

"Peoples requirements differ," Mark said. "I can tell you *The Phoenix* is one of the leading clubs in London's West End."

"They also provide a hostess service."

Arnold smiled. "I shouldn't require a hostess. Still I might go up one night."

Mark noticed he said 'I' not 'we', but knew he couldn't cross examine a Government Minister. Nonetheless his curiosity was aroused. Finally he went as close as he dared.

"Your wife not care for clubs?"

Arnold gave Mark a searching look. "She has her own itinerary... I like a break from the public eye."

Mark was now sure Arnold intended to visit *The Phoenix* and got on the phone to Maurice.

"Got some interesting news. We have a Government Minister staying with us, and I'm practically certain he intends paying you a visit. He questioned me about the brochure but seemed worried about being recognised."

Maurice was delighted. "We will be the soul of discretion."

But he had every intention of circulating the information. Good for business.

"Who is the Minister?" he asked.

Mark told him, and Maurice said he'd seen him in news interviews. "Bit of a public schoolboy," he said. "Would it be this week?"

"Almost certainly, I would think," Mark said.

Maurice left the phone thinking once again what a good move it had been getting Mark aboard. He would certainly have some plans for the Hon. gentleman if he turned up.

He arrived the next night with another man, who Maurice judged to be deferential to him. Perhaps a member of his staff, he thought.

He was nearly right. The man was not on his staff, but he was a House of Commons man.

Arnold was merely calling in a favour. He did not want to arrive alone.

But there was one person who was stupefied when she saw him.

Steff. She had passed thirty now, although she didn't admit it, but she still remembered Arnold from over ten years ago.

As a young girl struggling to start her career she had met him with a party of young men, and he had treated her viciously, she recalled, afterwards, as though he hated her. And in fact, that was the truth.

Arnold didn't like women and, as a younger man without responsibilities, he had been less guarded.

But Steff had neither forgotten nor forgiven him.

She was confident he wouldn't recognise her now. She had changed considerably and also assumed a fresh name.

As her thoughts went back to the past she felt violently angry again and was determined Arnold was going to pay.

She knew Maurice would easily blackmail him if he took the wrong steps, but that wasn't enough for Steff. She wanted to expose him.

Arnold was quite unaware of the tumult he had roused in Steff's mind, and pretended a false charm as Maurice introduced her as his cabaret star.

"A pleasure," he said. "I can hardly wait to see your performance."

Good, reasoned Steff; he had forgotten their previous encounter.

But she remembered afresh his light blue eyes, cold, and concealing his lack of compassion.

You wait, she thought. They say everything comes around, well I'm coming around to you, you bastard.

She decided for the moment to keep quiet. Maurice would keep her informed.

But her desire for revenge was burning.

She brought back the years in her mind... The calculating, callous man, and the defenceless girl. She had only escaped serious injury by luck.

One of his friends in the party had banged on her door and, before Arnold could stop her, she had screamed "Come in," then dashed past him as he entered, her clothes in her arms, battered, bruised and bloody. Next time she was resolute the boot would be on the other foot.

It all came rushing back to her in floods.

She thought she was about nineteen then and she was on the game to make ends meet.

It had started in a sleazy Soho bar. She, and a few of the other girls, got picked up by a bunch of rich young boys who took them to some rooms above the premises.

Because they'd paid they thought they could do as they liked, but Steff got the cream of the crop. Arnold, cold and merciless. She almost shivered again as she pictured him in her mind.

She snapped back to reality. Arnold had moved, but Maurice was looking at her strangely.

"You seen a ghost? You've been standing like a statue."

"Thought I'd seen him before," she said. Part of the truth.

There was also two other pairs of eyes glued to Arnold.

Det. Inspector Lew Green and Sgt. Sally Golding, both still on station at *The Phoenix*. Lew said, "I know that man, he's in the Government."

"So what?" Sally said. "He's entitled to a private life."

Lew stroked his chin and said thoughtfully. "I don't know." Then he made up his mind. "It goes in my report," he said. "Let the higher ups make a decision."

Sally shrugged her shoulders. She wasn't very interested.

But her attitude changed when later on Mark arrived and sat at Arnold's table.

She whispered to Lew. "That 'Tall Trees' connection again."

"Keep your eyes and ears open," he said.

After the cabaret Mark sloped off in one direction and Arnold another, where he got into a quick conversation with another man whom neither Lew nor Sally had seen before. Then they both disappeared through the bar, and Lew and Sally lost them.

Lew was annoyed,. "Fuck it! we were too bloody slow."

"What about Mark?"

"You know where he'll be."

"Steff?"

"What do YOU think?"

Meanwhile Arnold was installed in one of Maurice's private rooms with his male partner and proceeded to enjoy himself.

This time he was not vicious. This was Arnold's thing, and his partner knew how to rouse and satisfy him. It was a pity for Arnold he didn't realise the wonderful film he was making for Maurice.

There was no holding back. No squeamish pretence as he and his partner writhed together, and the final ferocious entry had Arnold on his back with his legs nearly round his partner's neck.

What a film for Maurice, and when he saw it he exulted.

Mark waited for the right opportunity to tell Olivia about the proposal to introduce horses to 'Tall Trees' clients.

She came in from the stables, took a shower, had a drink, and sat down.

Mark looked at her with a smile. "What would you think, darling, if I introduced my clients, my very wealthy clients, to your stables for discreet riding expeditions? Maybe even to learn."

Olivia's brows shot up. The scent of money was very welcome.

"What do I have to do, darling, to earn it?"

"Shall we try to find out after dinner?" Mark was eager for another exciting night.

They were soon in the bedroom after dinner and shed their clothes and slid into bed.

Mark held out his arms for Olivia, and she immediately crashed into him, stroking against him vigorously, her lips hard.

It was almost as if SHE was doing the kissing, not him, Mark felt.

But her forceful energy and darting tongue inflamed him, and he dug his fingers hard into her writhing bottom. He was already feeling the tips of her breasts like hard nails and tried to slide his hand between her legs, but she closed her thighs.

For a moment he was confused. Then Olivia changed position and straddled him. Almost in the same movement she laid flat on her back and slid towards Mark's mouth.

The sight of her shadowed line and the moist touch of her skin ignited him. His mouth went hard into her, and as Olivia thrust into his lips he lost control and streamed against her back.

There was a moment's silence, then she whispered, "Have I earned the deal, darling?"

Mark had been madly excited but felt oddly frustrated, and he was beginning to wonder if Olivia wasn't too masterful.

"Perhaps next time I'll do more of the work," he mumbled.

It was a dash of cold water and Olivia realised she would have to be more careful in the future.

She decided it would benefit her to take Mark to the next race meeting at Sandown Park. She always showed up well at the races, and she could introduce him to a few influential friends. He always enjoyed that.

When the time came it was sunny, and Sandown Park was crowded. Olivia was soon enjoying herself with people fawning around her, and Mark thought, a little sourly, 'Like a bloody queen.'

Suddenly she caught sight of Richard Haddon of the Haddon banking family. She had a note due to him next month for £100,000, and she had no hope of paying.

She tried to avoid him, but too late.

Richard very pleasantly reminded her the debt was due, and she tried to be casual. "Oh yes, so it is."

This cast a shadow over her day and she knew she would have to appeal to Mark, the only person who could rescue her.

When they returned home he said, "You suddenly got moody, Olivia. Not like you at the races."

It was her opportunity. She told Mark about the note, and he was furious that she hadn't told him.

"You can't expect to pick up a hundred grand off the streets," he shouted. "You haven't been fair with me, Olivia."

He wanted to use a stronger word, dishonest came to mind, but he curbed his temper.

He thought for a moment while she tried to appear contrite.

"Not the sort of thing I would want to mention, is it?" she said.

"There's one man I know who might help you," Mark said. "Maurice Robens, owner of *The Phoenix*."

Olivia pricked her ears up. She knew nothing about Maurice except he owned *The Phoenix* and always seemed very affable.

"What chances?" she asked.

"He has the money. Depends if he wants to trust you," Mark said.

Olivia took a trip to *The Phoenix* with Mark, and he left her to talk to Maurice.

Maurice took her to a private room and got her a drink.

"I understand you want to talk to me, Lady Olivia," he said.

"You can drop the 'lady'," she said. " 'Olivia' will do."

Being humble was not Olivia's style, and her lips went a little tight, but she had no option.

"The fact is," she said, "I've got a money problem, £100,000. Temporary, but it's there. Mark suggested you might be able to help me."

Maurice was not surprised. He could not imagine a lady of her class deigning to speak to him for any other reason, and he decided to enjoy his moment of power.

"You think I'm a moneylender?"

Olivia was embarrassed. "No no. Of course not. I didn't mean in that sense."

Maurice waited. He was enjoying turning the screw and he was not going to make it easy for Olivia. She had to ask straight out if she wanted his money.

Finally, she said, "Mark wondered if you had the finance available you would be willing, as a friend, to come to an agreement."

Maurice said quickly, "You mean he would guarantee you?"

Olivia was again embarrassed. "Not exactly. But I'm sure he would speak for me." She nearly said, we're living together, but just stopped herself.

Then Maurice startled her.

He said quietly, "I could let you have the money, pay back when you fancy. This year, next year, now, never. And no interest"... He lifted his arm... "But!"

Olivia tried to hide her eagerness. She would agree to anything to save the stables.

"What is the 'but', Maurice?"

"I would want you to act as a front for me, not only at your stables, also at the race courses round Britain."

Olivia was mystified. "What on earth are you talking about?"

"Laundering money," Maurice said laconically. "I'm sure you will know which bookmakers to use."

He added persuasively, "And you can have a cut."

Olivia's mind was working frantically. She couldn't let her lifeline go.

"I suppose this is criminal?"

Maurice laughed and said crudely, "I'm not paying a hundred grand for nothing."... He nearly said 'fuck all'.

Almost without thinking, Olivia said, "It's a deal."

She left Maurice feeling relieved. But she should have been worried. Maurice wouldn't hesitate to put the pressure on a bit of class. Mark flicked his brows up when she rejoined him.

"Thanks, Mark," she said. "We've done a deal."

Arnold returned from *The Phoenix* feeling quite happy and he continued to be until one week later he got a phone call.

'His night out with his partner at *The Phoenix* had been fully caught on camera. Would he like a copy of the film? It would only cost him a quarter of a mill.'

Arnold was stunned and his legs went weak. But he tried to bluff.

"I'll call the police," he yelled. "They know how to treat blackmailers."

"So do the public press," came the answer. "We'll be in touch in a few days."

So Arnold sweated for two days until another call came.

He was astonished at their seeming crass arrogance. But, in fact, it was clever. The blackmailers weren't asking for cash but a cheque, made out to Soho productions, to be posted to a PO Box number. It was payment for an important video they were selling.

They warned if he did not pay they would offer it to the public press, and gave him seven days.

Arnold had to tell Laura at this stage. She was the moneybags. At least, her family were.

He was not as embarrassed as he might have been. Laura had known about his sexual activities for years. She had simply insisted there was no publicity. She lived her life. He lived his.

She said in a matter-of-fact way, "It's no use paying blackmail. That won't stop it."

She said firmly, "There's only one way. My father in the States knows some very nasty people." She picked up the phone and made a transatlantic call.

Before the week was out, two tough-looking Americans appeared on the scene. Frank and Rob. They were grim faced and didn't smile much.

They got Arnold's full story, then they took charge.

"You do nothing," Frank told him. "Wait till they call. Then tell them you are not sending a cheque that can be traced. It's cash or nothing. £100s and £50s."

"Suppose they won't agree?"

"They'll agree. They want the money. Ignore their bluff."

"We'll be here to back you up," Rob added.

The seven days passed, and the blackmailers rang again. This time Rob and Frank had briefed Arnold on what to say, and were listening in.

"If your cheque does not reach us within three days we go to the Press," the voice said.

Rob nodded to Arnold. "I'm not sending a cheque that can be traced back to me," he said firmly. "I'll give you cash, in £100s and £50s. You name the pickup."

There was silence at the other end, then a voice said, "OK but no tricks. We still have the video."

There was another delay, then their instructions started. "Go to Waterloo station on Monday at ten in the morning and place the case of money in Left Luggage. At eleven a young woman will appear and ask for a case for which she has lost the ticket. You step forward and give it to her. You found it outside.

"Don't think of following her. She has a waiting taxi and we shall be watching."

The phone went dead.

"I don't like it," Rob said. "It was agreed too quickly. It's a set up."

"We get down to Waterloo tomorrow and check the place out," Frank said.

And they were there first thing in the morning.

They examined the place thoroughly but could find no alternative exit. The people and luggage came and left in one single entrance.

Rob sat on a bench, thinking. "There's something we're missing here," he said.

Frank suddenly cracked his fingers. "Remember the Brooklyn fuck up?"

Rob cracked back. "Sure thing! Yeah! maybe you're right."

They tracked back to Left Luggage department and asked one of the men behind the counter if there was another entrance. They reckoned there had to be.

He shook his head. "Only the one."

Then Frank and Rob got a piece of luck. One of the other men standing near piped up, "Don't forget the fire exit for the staff at the back Eric."

Rob and Frank exchanged glances and nodded their thanks.

"That was all a lot of malarkey about the girl and the ticket," Rob said. "They fuck off quick while we wait for the girl."

"Won't they get a pleasant surprise," Frank said.

Monday came, and they were stationed in a concealed position long before ten, then as the time approached for the pick-up they saw a man arrive in a car, look round and make for the Left Luggage fire exit. He fiddled for a moment at the doors then disappeared inside.

Five minutes later, he came out carrying the case and made off in his car.

The blackmailers worked out of a Soho address and used portable cameras.

Although they worked for Maurice, any connection would have been denied. They knew if anything went wrong Maurice would look after them, and if they crossed him they could start making their wills.

The man with the case stopped his car outside the Soho office with Rob and Frank behind him, and they trailed him up some stairs, where he disappeared through a door.

They waited a few seconds then slammed the door open and went in with their guns pointed, and they were big guns.

There were three people in the room. One standing who had just entered with the case, and two others clustered round the case on a big table.

The Americans roughly shoved the standing man aside and levelled their guns.

The men in the room all froze.

Rob playfully tapped one of them on the side of his head, but drew blood. "You tired of living?" he snarled. "We don't give a sod for your videos but we hate blackmailers."

"Who you working for?" he yelled.

"We don't work for anyone." His reply was a sullen mutter.

Rob hit him harder round the head, and he staggered and blood ran down his face.

"Give me the right answer and you might live," Rob threatened.

One of the others growled, "We have a contract with a few clubs." He pointed behind him. "There's our equipment."

Rob looked over his shoulder and saw the portable equipment and the cameras. It sounded plausible.

"It's your lucky day," he said. "I believe you. But if we come back you go out feet first. We're not coming all the way back from the States for fuck all."

To emphasise his point, he smacked the other man round the head too, but harder. It was an awful crack, and as his face spurted blood he nearly fell over.

He looked at the third man who had brought the case in. He was standing back petrified.

Rob thrust his gun in his face. "You'll get it too if we come back."

Then they were gone with an almighty slam of the door.

"Jesus!" one said. "Fucking Yanks. Bloody animals."

The man who brought the case snapped it open. "Still we've got the money. Those bastards only wanted blood."

Then his jaw dropped as rolls of newspaper fell from the case.

Frank and Rob reported back to Laura and told her she could forget the blackmail.

Laura gave them both a big bonus. "Sometimes there's only one way, isn't there?" she said.

When Maurice was told he was displeased but reacted typically. "Some you win some you lose." That's why he was so dangerous and why he kept so safe. He always knew when to quit.

But Arnold's troubles weren't over. Steff was still thirsting for revenge, and when Maurice told her Arnold had escaped a blackmail threat she decided to take some action herself... He wasn't going to get away scot-free she told herself. Fuck that!

Not knowing sufficient about the blackmail, she wrongly concluded he'd been saved because he was in the Government, and this further example of pulling strings angered her.

When Mark came up in the evening and went to her flat he noticed her preoccupation.

"What's on your mind, lover?" he asked.

Steff was bursting to tell someone else and get their point of view, but she didn't want to give away too much about her early days. "I heard that man Arnold Bentley, the MP, got away with a blackmail threat," she said.

Mark said quickly, "Who told you that?"

"It's all round the club."

It was news to Mark, and he didn't like it. He recalled the Hon. Derek and his blackmail episode.

Both had been to *The Phoenix*. Yet he still didn't link it with Maurice.

"So why are you so blue?" he asked.

Steff told him part of the story, omitting she'd been on the game.

"He ought to pay, didn't he?" she said.

"Yes, he should," Mark said. "But it would be impossible for the police to bring a case now."

"I wasn't thinking of the police," she said. "Suppose his wife knew?"

"That would be cruel."

"Or more cruel to leave her in ignorance," Steff replied firmly.

Mark wondered what kind of reception Steff might receive from Laura. She was pretty hardboiled. She might regret telling her.

"Don't forget," he said, "She might want to protect her husband and tell you to fuck off."

"She's a fairly tough customer, a Yank," he added.

But Steff's mind was made up. "I'll chance it," she said, and picked up the telephone.

Mark felt a sudden alarm. "What now? In front of me?"

He didn't want any part of it. "Look at the time," he said feebly. "She's probably asleep."

"Then I'll fucking wake her up." Steff was crude, deliberately. She was annoyed Mark wouldn't back her up.

Laura answered the phone on the second ring. She was relaxing in bed with a magazine and a drink.

"Yes?" she said.

Steff started off very politely. "I hope I'm not disturbing you but I would like to make an appointment to come and see you. I am Steff Destry, cabaret star at *The Phoenix* club in the West End."

Mark was listening at her side and breathed a sigh of relief. At least there wasn't going to be a confrontation.

But Laura's reply rattled him. "Course you're disturbing me. It's well past fucking midnight."

Steff kept cool. "I have something to tell you about your husband. Not an affair. Nothing so simple. And I'm not seeking anything."

Laura would have hung up, but Steff's words 'nothing so simple' got her attention. "Spit it out," she said.

"Not on an open line," Steff said. "How about tomorrow afternoon?"

Laura said tersely, "After two," and slammed the phone down.

The next day Steff turned up in the silver Mercedes just before two and went to reception. The girl at the desk saw her approaching and immediately called Mark. She remembered Steff with Mark from her previous visit.

Steff reached the desk and asked for Laura. The girl said apologetically, "I've just called Mr Addison," and at that moment Mark appeared.

He waved away the girl's apology. "It's all right," he said. "I was expecting this lady."

He escorted her to Laura's penthouse suite and said to her, "Watch what you say. She might be recording you."

"I should care," Steff said defiantly. Then she gave a ring at Laura's door, and as it opened Mark drifted away with a brief "See me before you go back."

Laura matched Steff for makeup and style and planted herself vigorously on a long settee. Steff sat facing her.

"Perhaps you'd better spit it out," Laura said.

Steff explained herself and said she intended to give her story to the papers. "I can produce the other girls who were present that night," she finished.

Laura heard her out and didn't interrupt once.

"So why are you only coming forward now?" she asked.

Steff pursed her lips insolently, "Because I saw Arnold again and because he has just escaped a blackmail threat, obviously because he's a Government boy. Why should he get away with everything? It's only fair to tell you first," she declared.

"And watch me squirm?" suggested Laura.

They looked at each other then both laughed.

"Arnold is a rat," Laura said. "I've known about him for years. He lives his life. I live mine. But no publicity, that's the deal... This alters things."

"Why have you never divorced him?"

Laura gave a thin smile. "My Mom and Dad in the states are king-sized Catholics and opposed to divorce. They control the money."

She smoothed her hair. "I'm going back to the States next month and I believe they might relent if I humble myself and tell them Arnold's a homo. They hate that even more."

Steff stared at her, "So you're going to ditch him?"

"Leave it with me and watch the papers in a few months," Laura said. She leaned back against the cushions. "Now I think we can have a drink."

Mark had been waiting nearby on tenterhooks and could hardly curb his impatience as the time slipped by. He must have glanced at his watch twenty times.

Steff came out at last and looked like the cat that got the cream. She was positively beaming.

"Well?" Mark raised his brows.

"We had an interesting talk."

This infuriated him, as Steff intended. She was still sore Mark hadn't backed her up.

"I think Laura's going to put the knife in," she said. "But we'll have to wait and see."

"Is that all?"

"We had a few drinks."

Mark realised she was teasing him.

"OK," he growled, "I tried to put you off. I thought you'd be getting trouble. You blaming me for that?"

Steff relented. "Laura knows Arnold is a rat and is probably going to divorce him now."

"Probably?"

"Have to wait and see. Honest, that's it."

"You were together a long time," Mark said suspiciously.

"We both put the dagger into Arnold and consoled ourselves with a few drinks."

That was all Mark could get out of Steff. But he insisted on driving her back to London because of the drinks she'd swigged down.

He actually had a dual purpose. He would be quite happy to spend the night with her and he wanted a word with Maurice.

As he got behind the wheel of the Mercedes, Steff said saucily, "Now you've got the chance to drive a proper car."

Mark didn't reply. He was still worried Arnold could bring trouble and hoped Maurice would be able to reassure him.

Steff dozed off when they started the journey, which suited Mark. He couldn't get his thoughts off Arnold.

Maurice met them as they entered *The Phoenix* but in answer to Mark's inquiry he was a clam. "Know nothing about the affair," he said.

"Well it's all round the club," Mark said.

Maurice shrugged. "People gossip."

Mark heaved a sigh of relief. Looked like he was rid of Arnold.

But he was mistaken.

To his amazement the following week two plain clothes policemen from Special Branch called on him. They had been alerted by Lew Green's report to his superiors.

One of them said smoothly, "We are investigating the possibility that the Hon. Arnold Bentley may have been the subject of blackmail, obviously a matter of serious concern in a member of the government."

"Yes?" Mark said cautiously. He wanted to say as little as possible.

"We understand he vacated your hotel last week?"

"That's right."

"Could we view the suite he used?"

Mark didn't like this. "My guests pay for privacy," he snapped. "Surely that isn't necessary."

The second man said, "We can always obtain a warrant, but I would have thought," he said suggestively, "That you would have been pleased to co-operate."

Mark pursed his lips and said stiffly, "All right, but you'll have to wait until the present occupants are out. I'm not having my guests upset."

"How long will that take?" The question was a little more hostile this time.

"I'll let you know," Mark said coldly. "Leave your telephone number."

A card was handed over, and Mark went to the reception desk, handed it over, and gave instructions to the girl on duty.

He then expected the men to leave, but they still stood their ground.

"Is there something else?" he demanded.

"We should like a few words with you personally, Sir."

Mark's face set in a scowl but he took them to his office, and they sat facing each other.

He glared at them.

They could see they were unwelcome, which they were used to, but they were hesitant to bully Mark. He would have influential friends, they had no doubt.

The first man spoke up again. "I realise we are unwelcome Sir, but we have a job to do and we regret any inconvenience."

Mark felt slightly less aggravated. "So what are your questions?"

"Did you introduce the Hon. gentleman to *The Phoenix* club?"

This was an uncomfortable question for Mark because of course, he had introduced him. But he didn't want to be dragged into their calculations.

"He picked up one of our brochures from reception," he said.

"But we understand you accompanied him there."

"I am a member and it was only polite."

The other man said courteously, "It would help if you could tell us the man you introduced him to, and who he met afterwards."

Mark could see a long round of questions ahead and decided he wasn't going to play.

"I simply introduced him to reception and left him," he declared. "I've no idea what he did with his time."

Both officers stared at him suspiciously, thinking the same thing; he doesn't want to finger his friends.

Their next strategy was a little gentle bullying.

"It was reported to us that you and Arnold were seen talking with the owner, Maurice Robens." This wasn't strictly true, it was more of a guess, but they wanted to put pressure on Mark.

They hit the spot.

Mark said defensively, "Same thing. I just introduced Arnold to the owner as a new member."

"Do all new members get introduced to the owner?"

Mark was getting hostile himself now. "How do I know? I introduced him because he was a member of the Government."

He clammed up and wouldn't say anything more, and the plain clothes men left dissatisfied.

The first man said, "Brush off. He doesn't want to talk."

"Bloody obvious!"

"Well we can always come back."

The first man started the car and they drove off.

Mark cursed Arnold under his breath and hoped he'd seen the last of these men. He intended to be absent when they returned to examine Arnold's former suite.

He toyed with the idea of confiding in Steff. She always seemed tuned in to activities at *The Phoenix*, and in the end he did tell her.

He was very concerned that 'Tall Trees' might be dragged into the picture, and hoped she could give him some reassurance. He spoke to her on the phone the same evening, and to a large extent she did reassure him.

She repeated what she'd told him before. "Arnold got away with it. The blackmail fell down." But she also added importantly, in answer to further prompting from Mark, "The police haven't been involved."

Mark at once concluded the Special Branch officers had been brought in as Government routine. The suggestion that a minister might be blackmailed would alert them immediately.

He felt huge relief. 'Tall Trees' was in the clear.

Steff later told Maurice that the plain clothes had interviewed Mark and he thought, 'knew I was right to pull out.' He was smug.

Olivia was tickled pink with the new deal Maurice had engineered with her. She didn't see how she could be found out.

It was quite neat. Maurice would commission her to buy horses for him and pour money into the stables. And when the horses were sold he would receive the proceeds.

The only thing missing was she would never buy any horses, and if ever she was challenged she could produce any horse she fancied from her own stock.

In addition, there would be large cash sums on occasions, which would be dispensed on the race courses. The winnings going to Maurice, less a cut for Olivia.

She began to feel more settled, and when Mark questioned her about the deal with Maurice, she said casually, "He put me on the right road."

She decided that only two people should know. She and Maurice. And for once Olivia exercised absolute discretion.

Mark didn't want to pursue the subject. He felt he was putting enough money into Olivia's establishment, so the whole thing was put to bed.

Olivia continued to drag him round different race courses, and he began to enjoy the meetings, even getting acquainted with some of Olivia's circle. He also had a few bets occasionally.

In addition, he went riding with Olivia out of her stables. Something else she did naturally and gracefully, although Mark thought she was a bit callous sometimes. "You have to show who's boss with a horse," she said.

Their sex wasn't quite as satisfying to Mark now.

Now that Olivia felt financially safe she showed her true colours. Her desire was to dominate, and, although their sex was always exciting, Mark was fighting her half the time. At first it was a joy, then he became frustrated.

Finally he said to her, "I've got to spend more time at home, Olivia. The new development at 'Tall Trees' now needs hands on. Too many problems are occurring and we've millions invested."

"Fine, darling," she said, "Business comes first."

But she didn't really care now. She had her own circle and she knew she could always call on Mark. Olivia was a very resilient lady.

One morning, Steff received a package in the post. When she opened it she found an American newspaper inside, and it contained an article of news, heavily underlined:

'Laura Bentley divorces. Husband resigns from Government.'

Steff muttered "Thanks, Laura," and there was a huge smile on her face for the rest of the day.

When Mark came up and saw the paper he said to Steff, "Thank God that's buried."

They both felt pleased for different reasons and when they later had sex it seemed to have an extra edge. Mark particularly felt a rush of joy when Steff yielded to him. He couldn't help the comparison. Not like that animal, Olivia.

Steff sensed a change in Mark. "You fallen out with Olivia?"

Mark was astonished. "Why do you say that?"

"Grow up," she said. "Do you think people don't talk?"

But Mark wasn't giving anything away. "We all have our ups and downs," he said.

Steff's enthusiasm was rekindled. The game wasn't over yet, and she was right, she was still in it.

Mark also wondered if Carol and Barbara could forgive his inattention.

The new development in 'Tall Trees' grounds was now quite advanced and taking shape, and when Mark visited the site, his arm was promptly taken, and he looked into the smiling face of Barbara, fresh and friendly.

She said mockingly, "So you didn't get lost?"

Mark gave her arm a gentle squeeze. "You know I've been tied up in that stable prospect with Olivia."

"You don't mean tied up with Olivia?"

Mark had to laugh. "She is desirable."

"Well I won't say I've been saving myself for you, but I am available," and Barbara showed her white teeth in a big smile.

She'd hardly finished her sentence when there was a call from nearby, and Mark turned and saw Carol advancing towards him. 'Oh lord!' he thought.

He prepared himself for a blast but she said apologetically, "Sorry I couldn't contact you before I had to go away. It was very sudden and you were hard to find. Hasn't the time flown."

What a gigantic piece of luck, Mark thought.

"Where have you been?" he asked.

"France. The Firm needed a sudden replacement and as you know, I speak French."

Mark didn't know but pretended he did. "Oh yes."

He chanced his luck. "You could have left me a message, Carol."

"I did," she said.. "I posted it to your office."

Mark didn't know if she was telling the truth or not, but it didn't matter, he was off the hook.

"Well I didn't get it," he said. "Still, some things get lost in office traffic, don't they?"

Carol wasn't arguing, said hallo to Barbara and joined them.

She was looking for a chance to make a date with Mark but he gave her no opportunity so she decided to force her luck.

"How about celebrating my return?" she asked.

"Why not?" he said.

She promptly said, "Saturday. *The Riverside*." Then with a big smile she swept off.

Barbara said, "You didn't fix a time, Mark."

"Carol knows," he said.

That's some understanding, Barbara thought.

"You've jumped Friday," she said. "Must be my lucky day. You free?"

Mark laughed. "No dates for months, now two together."

Barbara said, "Well we won't talk about the new development."

"I think I can agree to that. Where?"

Barbara thought she'd put one over Carol.

"How about I come to your place and cook you a meal?"

"You're kidding."

"You wait and see. I'll bring all the stuff."

Barbara intended to be a very sexy cook. She had the same serious intentions of enjoyment that Mark had and she intended to knock his eyes out.

Mark continued his inspection of the site, and Barbara guided him to the first nearly completed villa, and immediately it was business again.

He was extremely impressed. It was an oasis of luxury. High walled garden. Private drive in with big iron gates. Green lawns with super swimming pool and patio.

The rooms were the last word in design and space, with oceans of glass overlooking the pool and gardens, and aluminium shutters at the touch of a finger. All the bedrooms were en suite and contained a huge sunken bath in marble.

Mark wondered what else would be installed.

He tried to imagine the place completed, decorated, furnished, finished, and he promised himself a look when it was ready for occupation.

Barbara tugged his arm. "You like?"

"How couldn't you like? This beats Hollywood."

Mark's brain was ticking over. Perhaps they could charge even more than they'd planned.

"What about services?" he said, "Our guests won't want to lift a finger."

"Each villa will have its own cook and servant."

Barbara pointed across the grounds. "In addition, see that long low building beneath the trees? When completed that will house a permanent staff available night and day for those that might want a banquet or party or something special.

"The kitchen will be a chef's dream with a dining room that wouldn't disgrace Royalty."

She gave a little smile. "The guests will only have to breathe for themselves."

Mark's business instincts were charging up. This really was going to be something extra special and he'd see the news got round *The Phoenix*. Maybe also think about some discreet advertising.

Friday came, and Barbara prepared for her night out.

She sensed Mark had cooled with Olivia and wanted to make a hit with him. She knew she shared a sense of fun with him and he was always exciting, ready to do or go anywhere.

She smiled. Exciting in bed too.

Well worth an effort.

She first of all raided M & S food section. Then prepared and cut the food in advance. She wasn't intending to sweat in the kitchen. She had in mind teasing as well as cooking.

She drove up to Mark's place about six and staggered in with armfuls of bags. Then she went back to her car and returned with a small suitcase.

She scattered the bags around the kitchen then said to Mark, "I'll just strip for action," and went into his bedroom with the suitcase.

His stunned gaze followed her but she shut the bedroom door.

She took off her clothes and selected a thin bra from her suitcase. She'd bought it especially for the occasion and when she put it on her nipples stood out like little towers.

Good, she thought, glancing in the mirror, Mark likes nipples.

She didn't go for a G-string. She thought that might be a bit too much, she chose instead a pair of brief shorts. She knew she had a good tight bottom.

Then she tied an apron round her neck that would flap about as she walked, she intended to be rather careless.

She slipped on white heels, and finally plonked a tall chef's hat on her head.

She looked in the mirror and smiled. "You'll do."

She flung open the door and strode past a startled Mark.

He started to smile at her cheeky face under the chef's hat, then he took in the whole picture.

"Jesus, Barbara!" he said. "You can cook for me every day if my blood pressure will stand it."

"Nothing wrong with a little excitement," she said demurely. "You just keep simmering."

It was the only time in Mark's life that he remained in the kitchen whilst a meal was prepared. He couldn't take his eyes off Barbara and he thought simmering was hardly the right word.

She pretended to bustle about and gave Mark flashes of her assets, but finally she stood up and said, "Ready in five minutes. I'll just change." She swept out of the kitchen.

She came back in a slinky gown, shimmering from head to foot. The transformation was amazing.

Mark was bowled over. "Reckon you're my kind of girl," he said.

His words stuck in Barbara's mind and warmed her for the rest of the evening.

She said saucily, "I have another asset. Try my food."

Mark poured the wine and looked at her over the edge of his glass.

"It'll be like you," he said. "Delicious."

Barbara wasn't sure how to react; chat lines weren't taken too seriously these days.

"Well you can sample both, can't you," she said.

She knew perfectly well the food was going to be first class. Whilst at college, she had taken a chef's course, but such things she kept to herself.

Mark was a steak man, and she had prepared what she called steak a la grande.

It nearly melted in Mark's mouth, and he thought you can't top that, but she had two more courses of Mark's favourites equally appetising, and finished with another big favourite, Stilton cheese and biscuits.

Mark drained his glass and looked at Barbara. "You're an eye opener," he said. "Anything else up your sleeve?"

She had, and when they retired to a long settee up came another Mark favourite, black coffee and cognac.

He was amazed. "How come you know all my favourites?"

Barbara tapped her nose. "I've got a mouth and ears, haven't I?" She wouldn't go beyond that.

They lay together for some time with few words between them, just enjoying the contact and video music, until finally Mark said, "How about bed, or do you fancy going home?"

Pretending to be serious, Barbara said, "I suppose I'd better go. Do you think I can drive or should I call a taxi?"

Mark played the game. "Oh I'll drive you," he said, and got to his feet.

Then they linked arms and walked into the bedroom.

Mark repeated his earlier words, "Yeah! I reckon you're my kind of girl," and Barbara thought, mission accomplished. Then she was in his arms and they were kissing.

She slipped off her gown and for a moment stood in front of him nude, then she kicked off her heels and slid into bed.

Mark was beside her in a flash.

He cuddled her, and she responded and teased him, but HE was in charge. This is more like it, he thought. First Steff, now Barbara. Back in the real world.

Olivia and their battles to dominate seemed a dark dream now.

He soon had his mouth round Barbara's nipples. He'd been aching to do it ever since she flashed them in the kitchen, and as his teeth touched her she flinched but didn't draw away.

Mark took his time to enjoy Barbara's body. She was so eager, so vibrant, and when his hand wandered to the top of her thighs she obligingly guided him to explore the folds between her legs.

He shrank from putting his mouth there. She seemed so fresh and vivid it seemed more natural to kiss, and when his lips met hers he realised they were on the same wave length.

She was warm and exciting without being forceful, and he was delighted when her teeth gently nibbled at him, and when she opened her lips wide it seemed a huge caress.

Suddenly she went tense and drew Mark inside, and she replied to every thrust he made.

They clung together during the non-stop fury, and when it was all over they still remained tight. Almost as one, he thought.

For a moment Mark's mind was unclear. He didn't know what to think. Somehow the experience seemed different. But he felt full of new life, and as Barbara hugged him as though she'd never let go, he knew she felt the same.

He said at last. "Worth coming up, Barbara?"

She said a little breathless. "I think you can call me darling now."

Mark wished he hadn't made the date with Carol now. He thought it might be anticlimax after this night with Barbara... 'How can you follow that?' he thought.

Still he couldn't put it off. He was fond of Carol and couldn't let her down.

He needn't have worried. Carol was no fool, and reckoned Barbara might have got him into bed. She certainly seemed up for it when they parted, she thought.

She decided on a change. A low key evening. See what developed.

When Mark picked her up she was elegant, not sexy, and he immediately noticed.

"Very smart," he said. "Like the pearls. Didn't know you had any."

"There's a lot more you don't know," she replied.

Mark sent the red Lotus thundering off and thought he might be in for an interesting evening... Carol had already scored.

At *The Riverside* Mark received his usual royal service, and Carol was witty and charming, perfect company.

She read his mood just right, and when they left *The Riverside* Mark was relaxed and chatty.

He went into Carol's place wondering if it was to be coffee only, and as she went to change he stretched out on her settee.

She returned in a kimono that flapped about loosely and just covered her nudity. Next she started a video of the latest film release and sprawled against Mark, encouraging him to touch and fondle her.

Before long his fingers began gliding through the hairs at the top of her legs until he was between her legs. Carol eased her position so he could explore and began to react herself.

She slipped off her kimono and teased Mark with her swollen nipples, and suddenly he was no longer indolent. His mouth went round her nipples, and he began to roll them fiercely.

Then Carol opened her legs.

He kicked off his trousers and Carol tugged off his shirt.

Almost in one movement she eased him up and worked their lips together. Then with a delicious thrill she steered him inside her.

He was like a violent spear but she was more than ready, and forced her fingers round his bottom and pulled him in as far as she could.

An agony of pleasure hit them both, and when the sudden relief came it was like an explosion.

"Nothing like it," Mark breathed.

Carol was ecstatic. "You've said it."

Much better than she'd anticipated.

Mark's mind now focussed on the Villas and he cudgelled his brains to think of suitable advertising. Nothing vulgar like competing with masses of other hotels in the media columns. Something on its own. Something discreet.

Then he thought of TV, and the names of Richard Hall TV Executive, and Debra Morrison TV Presenter, came into his mind. He'd met them at *The Phoenix*. Time to get in touch with Maurice again, he thought, and try to get them on board. A small TV film would be absolutely ideal. He thought he could coat the pill as far as Debra was concerned with the promise of a free stay in one of the Villas. She could then work on Richard Hall.

He rang Maurice and explained what he wanted.

Maurice was only too happy to act as go-between. He was glad of any opportunity to put Mark in his debt.

The following week Mark and Barbara shared a table at *The Phoenix* with Richard Hall and Debra Morrison.

She was a tall blonde, smart, but rather dictatorial. Richard was affable but cautious.

Barbara had thoughtfully prepared with a photograph of the first Villa, and Mark let her do most of the talking.

She was enthusiastic and convinced her guests the Villas would become internationally famous.

"Why don't you come down for a look round?" she suggested.

Debra immediately agreed, and Richard said, "Give me a full report, Deb."

When she came down Barbara put out the red carpet and Debra couldn't help but be impressed. She recommended just what Mark wanted, a fifteen-minute documentary to come out in a few months when they could offer more completed Villas.

Richard agreed to Deb's recommendation instantly, and Mark could hardly wait for the film to be shown.

When it came out and was shown on TV he had to admit Richard and Debra between them had done a superlative job.

The film was headed *Millionaires Roost*.

And their finishing line was a quote Mark had remembered. He couldn't recall where it came from.

'All they ask you to do is breathe for yourself'.

Vince Adam's bosses saw the TV advert, and their interest was fired again. They told Vince if he could bring off a deal he could name his own price.

He contacted Mark on the phone and used as a lever the knowledge of his father's murder.

"Yes, but YOU are implicated," Mark protested.

Vince laughed, "The police would find nothing on me. I'm afraid the trail would lead direct to you, Mark. You can't do much business in prison, can you?"

Mark felt trapped.

Everyone wanted the Villas now; they were perfect for London celebrities and were becoming internationally famous.

Mark knew they could charge the earth and still have a waiting list of millionaires. And he also knew his mother and Janet would never agree to sell.

"You know very well, Vince," he said, "I cannot do the impossible. Even if I agreed to sell my mother and Janet certainly wouldn't. So there's not much point in putting me in prison is there?"

But crafty Vince had guessed this would be Mark's defence.

He said brutally, "That's your problem. You'll have to find a way." He didn't care how Mark tricked or harassed his family.

"I'll give you two months," he said, and hung up.

But for once Vince made a mistake. He misjudged Mark as a rich boy who would flounder under pressure and ask his family to bail him out.

Mark thought about the matter hard. His own skin depended on it, and he found the decision easier the second time. Vince Adams would have to be removed.

A certain grim amusement flicked across his mind. It would be poetic justice. One murder for another. Vince for his father.

He was certain there would be no number two to step in. This would be a one-man campaign with the bosses shutting their ears.

He arranged a private meeting with Maurice, convinced Maurice would know a man who would know a man who would do the job. But he realised he would have to be careful.

Maurice received him in his office. "What's on your mind, Mark?"

Mark swallowed. He was taking a big risk, and he started cautiously. "I've often heard it said that awkward people can be removed," he said. He looked at Maurice for reaction but he didn't move a muscle.

"Yes?" Maurice encouraged.

"I wondered if you could put me in touch with someone." He added defensively, "Such a cosmopolitan crowd pass through your doors. They can't all be good guys."

Maurice said casually, "Obviously all sorts of people come here. Some I know are unscrupulous, but that's not a problem, that's life."

Mark knew he had to take the risk and plunged, "Well, Maurice," he said quietly, "Is it yes or no? It's important to me."

Maurice would do the job with his own men, but he was not telling Mark.

"I certainly know of someone," he said. "Who is it you want removed?"

Mark suddenly became anxious. "Do YOU need to know?"

"Jesus, Mark!" Maurice said, "Do you think I can approach someone without saying who is to be hit?"

Mark screwed up his courage. "Vince Adams," he said. "He wants the new villas and he's threatening me."

Maurice was rocked. Still Vince Adams wasn't valuable to him, Mark was.

"How soon?" he asked.

"Within two months."

"Oh, easy! Time for a nice comfortable accident," Maurice said. "But it'll cost."

"What's money for?"

Maurice stroked his chin then said very deliberately, "Can I take it then, Mark, this is a definite instruction to do the job? There's no backing out afterwards."

"It's a definite instruction," Mark confirmed. "Go ahead." He hesitated, "You're a good friend, Maurice. Thanks."

After he'd left Maurice ran through the conversation, which he'd recorded, and put the tape in his safe.

"Yes, and you're a good friend to me, Mark," he muttered. "And you're getting in deeper and deeper."

Mark hoped that was the last he'd hear of Vince Adams but he was disappointed. At the end of the month he was on the line again, threatening him. "Don't forget you've only a month before the balloon goes up."

"Don't worry," Mark replied.. "I shall be taking some action." He nearly rang Maurice to check if he'd done anything but second thoughts stopped him. If Maurice hadn't done anything he wasn't going to, or couldn't. He tried to calm himself. He'd have to live on his nerves a little longer. The rest of the month dragged by for Mark and he was dogged by thoughts of disgrace and humiliation. Both Barbara and Carol wondered what was eating him. Steff didn't even see him, but she was always philosophical.

The end of the month came without word from Maurice, and Mark was beginning to despair. Was Vince going to bring his whole world crashing down? Mark knew he would tell him, if only to gloat, and he was dreading his call.

Then he nearly jumped out of his skin. The phone was buzzing. "Yes?" he said. He was fearful Vince would answer, but to his relief it was Maurice.

But Maurice didn't dispel his anxiety.

"You heard from Vince?" he asked.

"No! And I don't want to." Mark was tight with anxiety. "You got any news for me?"

"Could you come up tonight and have a talk? Steff will be here." Maurice sounded unbelievably casual, and Mark's mood got blacker.

"I'll be there," he said. But he couldn't think about Steff. Vince Adams menaced his mind like a black cloud.

When he arrived at *The Phoenix* Maurice quickly took him into his office.

"I've some bad news for you," he said.

Mark's nerves jumped, "Go on."

"I'm sorry to tell you," Maurice said, "Our friend Vince Adams has met with an accident. A hit-and-run driver. Unfortunately, he didn't recover."

Overwhelming relief surged through Mark, and he could have jumped for joy. "What a shame!" he said.

"Isn't it." Maurice agreed. "Such a pleasant fellow."

Mark smiled, "Yes, I'll miss him." But he couldn't help adding, "Worth every penny, Maurice."

Just what Maurice wanted. A further admission of guilt on tape. He passed over a piece of paper. "You can make a bankers draft here, Mark."

Mark signed the draft and suddenly felt buoyant, the world was bright again. His thoughts turned to Steff and there she was, coming through the door.

"Hallo stranger," she said. "I thought you'd forgotten me."

"Let's make up for it tonight," Mark said. "You can dance for me in the cabaret. Then we'll have our own private dance in your bedroom."

Steff could see Mark was charged up and wondered what had happened, but he didn't enlighten her.

She gave several longer flashes of her charms in her performance and lingered in suggestive poses, and Mark was grateful. He loved her smooth front, and as she danced she exposed the space between her gorgeous legs.

Steff wasn't surprised at the ringing applause she received, but she'd done it for Mark. He was her audience tonight, and she wanted him fizzing.

He always thought the most fabulous part of Steff's body was her beautifully rounded thighs exhibiting her thin hair line, and he believed she knew it.

In her dressing room afterwards she gave him a smile. "Did you enjoy the show?"

"The show was perfect," Mark said. "The others were just lucky to be there."

He took her to the couch and slipped off her dressing gown. She didn't resist, indeed she was up for it.

Mark laid her flat on her back and gazed again at the smooth expanse between her legs, and the thin line dividing it. She looked up and obligingly parted her thighs.

Mark's fascination for this area never waned. To get inside was not enough. He could never see enough, feel enough, and he wanted to roll and caress and kiss all the folds in her skin.

He knew it was sheer lust but he was not dismayed. Why shouldn't lust be shared and enjoyed?

He looked at Steff's face, and she was flushed and excited. She knew what he wanted.

"Do it, Mark," she said. "We can always fuck later."

He ran his hands along her thighs and slightly widened them, then drew her into his mouth.

Steff leaned back and sucked in her breath. It was easy at first to stay calm but as Mark got her excited strong urges took over and she began to thrust against him, almost artificial intercourse.

Suddenly she let out a cry. She felt as if she was ejaculating and couldn't stop until a final huge lunge stilled her. Then she was exhausted.

"What about you, Mark?" she whispered.

"You kidding? I couldn't hold back. I was so hard it hurt."

"So we don't need to couple up in future?"

"You joking? We don't want to kill ourselves." He grinned broadly, "We can do it for a holiday."

Steff laughed back at him and ran her hands through his hair.

"You're an outrageous bastard, Mark! But there's some truth in there somewhere."

She wondered what would happen when they went back to her flat. Can't see how you can top that, she thought.

But Mark's appetite had not lessened when they reached Steff's flat AND he persuaded her to walk about the bedroom nude.

"You can't imagine the things your wonderful body does to me," he said.

Steff was used to showing her body and didn't regard it as a big thing. But Mark did. He knew none of his other women would give him this privilege.

He pulled her close and ran his hands over her, lingering between her legs, but Steff expected that.

She was prepared to give him all he wanted, not only because of his fortune and her distant hopes, she really felt Mark innocently enjoyed her body, and it gave her a sense of power which she enjoyed.

She slipped off his clothes and kissed him slowly, and he put his hands round her bottom and worked her close.

She felt him respond and smothered him with her breasts. They were firm and hard and to Mark they felt huge and pricked him.

He rose against her and she straddled him then hung on tight as he stroked fiercely until a violent spasm stopped him. But he didn't withdraw immediately, and the passive contact somehow seemed extraordinarily sensual.

"You never have enough do you, Mark?" she whispered.

"That makes two of us. Nod your head if I'm wrong," he smiled

"You're welcome," she said. "The night's not over."

True to her words, when they went to bed she caressed and fondled Mark and he thoroughly enjoyed the feel of her body all over again, and Steff made sure he didn't forget his favourite spot. She still had sexual energy to burn, and on this night Mark matched her.

They had a final pulsating burst together and Steff really let herself go and surprised Mark.

"Where do you get all your energy?" he asked.

She smiled, "The same place as you."

Mark was surprised he'd not heard from Olivia. He had put up notices in 'Tall Trees' reception advertising her stables and wondered what the response had been. She had been very keen on the idea when he suggested it.

He decided to pay her a visit, unannounced, surprise her.

He did surprise her. She was ranting at one of her stable girls in very unladylike terms. "When I tell you to do something you fucking well do it." She glared at the girl. "Or piss off and find another job."

She spun round in a temper, and her brows lifted in surprise when she saw Mark, but she didn't attempt to excuse her coarse behaviour.

"My!" Mark said. "So this is the lady in action."

She sniffed. "Fucking staff. Not worth a light, some of 'em."

She became businesslike, "What can I do for you, Mark?"

He was surprised at Olivia's curt attitude. Still he had neglected her for some time. "I was wondering what the response had been from 'Tall Trees'," he said. "I've advertised the stables in very favourable terms."

She was casual. "Oh I believe we've had one or two."

Mark was nettled. He'd taken a lot of trouble to help her. He said sarcastically, "I suppose you wouldn't object if a worldwide celebrity wanted a ride?"

Her attitude changed. Prestige was different.

"Who is it?" she asked eagerly.

Mark said coldly, "No-one now. But there could be tomorrow, next week, who knows?" He finished abruptly, "If you're still interested."

Olivia tried to soothe Mark. An international celebrity photographed at her stables would be great advertising and enhance her social standing. Not to be missed. "Of course I'm interested, darling," she said. "But you can see I'm up to my neck in it." She spread her arms out wide.

But Mark wasn't fooled. He had detected the change in her manner straight away. He was curious. Had her money troubles suddenly gone away? He said cautiously, "You still stretched for funds or did Maurice come across?"

Olivia wanted to get away from this dangerous ground straight away. "He did suggest someone," she lied, "But I was able to manage through a family friend." She added to make it sound believable, "Thank goodness for banking friends."

Mark didn't buy her story, and he went away with a big question mark in his mind. One thing he was certain about. He wasn't going to exert himself promoting her stables any more. Fuck her!

The more he thought about it the more certain Mark was that Olivia had done a deal with Maurice. So why didn't she say?

Mark didn't like being pushed aside and he was deadly curious why Olivia would want to keep her deal secret. For all he knew, she might have involved HIM without his knowledge.

He could imagine Olivia's haughty drawl to Maurice. "Oh Mark would always step in if necessary." Not beyond the bounds of possibility.

He determined to find out who was behind her and decided to employ a private eye. His immediate thought was Alec Donovan, the man who'd interviewed him over the Hon. Derek business.

To say Alec Donovan was surprised at Mark's inquiry would be the understatement of the year. Here was his quarry seeking to employ him. He gave a cautious "Come and see me" to Mark and prepared to receive him.

Mark drew up in his red Lotus with a roar, and, looking out of his window, Alec thought, typical.

They sat facing each other and Alec asked how he could help.

Mark said prudently, "I take it anything I tell you is strictly confidential?"

"Of course," Alec replied, "Unless I have a police directive."

"What does that mean?"

"If I am questioned by the police I would have to answer their questions in the same way that you would."

Mark deliberated on this. Still the police weren't involved.

"This is a private matter," he said. "No question of police."

Alec nodded. "Go on." He was prepared to listen unless it affected his inquiry for Mark's mother.

Mark cleared his throat. "You've probably heard of Lady Olivia Lithgow and her stables?"

Again Alec nodded.

"We have a business relationship," Mark said. "And I think she is keeping something from me."

"Can you be specific?"

"She has suddenly come into funds that she won't account for, and I want to know why. I'm not talking about small change."

Alec stared at Mark. "How far do you want me to go?"

"All the way until you get the answer. At her stables, on the race courses, wherever you like. The cost doesn't matter."

"Any suspicions?"

Mark said unhesitatingly, "For a kick-off, Maurice Robens, owner of *The Phoenix club* in the West End. I know for sure Olivia approached him when she had money problems."

Alec knew a bit about Maurice. "Well that's a start," he said.

Mark left Alec, feeling more reassured, but his mood would have changed if he could have looked into Alec's mind.

In addition to his new assignment he intended to study Mark close-up. His main inquiry was still his father's death, and so far as Alec was concerned Mark had a big question mark over his head.

Alec drove up to Olivia's stables and, fortunately for him, she was away so he was able to walk round and talk to whoever he wanted. He soon found that in the past Olivia had kept a tight rein on spending but the money problems had miraculously disappeared. The stable staff said things were easier now and they could get all the things they wanted without any fuss.

So Mark had good cause for his suspicions. Alec's first finding.

He continued on his tour and very conveniently found tacked behind one of the stable doors a list of the race meetings Olivia intended to visit.

"Thanks," he muttered and took it down and put it in his pocket.

He asked one of the stable girls if the stables were full and she said yes they always were. In fact, they had a long waiting list.

"What about any new horses bought in?" Alec asked.

The girl looked at him a little suspiciously, "You selling?"

Alec laughed. "Not me. But if you're full you've no room for any new ones, have you?"

"Not my problem," she said curtly.

Alec thought for a moment. He was missing something. Then it struck him... Winnings! Racehorses were supposed to win races.

He said to a passing stable lad. "You won any races?"

"One or two," came the reply, "But not the big ones. That's where the money is."

Alec now began to see some daylight. Olivia was not earning enough from her horses. And when you tacked on her high living style the problems mounted.

He decided his next call had to be *The Phoenix*, and he timed his visit for a morning, when Maurice and the night staff were nowhere to be seen.

He posed as a Council Inspector for Hygiene and had an official looking card to back him up, which nobody ever challenged when it was flashed.

He went first to the kitchens and made a pretence survey.

"Do you ever see Maurice Robens?" he asked one of the white-aproned staff.

"What the owner? Lord no! The chef Jermaine is our boss."

Alec walked round the dance floor and came to the restaurant where a few people were tidying up

He said to one of the ladies, "Where's Mr Robens' office?"

She took him outside and pointed down a passage. "At the end, but you won't find him in." Then she turned and walked away.

Alec couldn't believe his luck, but he'd yet to test it.

He walked boldly to the door and knocked. There was no answer, and he turned the knob. The door wasn't locked, and he pushed it open.

He quickly swooped to the big desk dominating the room and glanced at a few papers. Then his eye took in a square piece of paper tucked into a corner of the blotter, where people jotted reminders.

It contained one small sentence circled. O 13.30.

Alec's fertile brain immediately jumped to Olivia 1.30. But where? Today? Tomorrow?

Then he heard footsteps coming down the passage and he swiftly got to the door and swung round. A rough voice said, "What you doin' here?"

Alec flourished a piece of paper. "I want a signature for the inspection." He flashed his card quickly. "I'm from the Council."

The man, a tough looking character, seemed undecided.

"Where's the manager?" Alec asked. "I've got to have a signature."

This seemed to prompt the man, and he shouted down the passage, "Alf! Fetch Arnold, will you?"

In a few minutes another man appeared. He was wearing a suit and was obviously office staff. He said self-importantly, "I'm the day manager. What do you want?"

Alec held out an official looking certificate, entirely bogus. "Will you please sign that I've inspected your premises?"

But Arnold was no fool. "We've never had to do that before," he said.

"You will in future," Alec said. "New regulations."

He helpfully held out his pen and Arnold signed. Alec left the premises with some relief.

He sat in his car and considered the note. It was a reminder. Likely to be today. But where?

Then he had an inspiration and pulled Olivia's list of race meetings from his pocket. Sure enough, there was one today, at Kempton Park. Just outside London near the Thames.

Alec glanced at his watch. Plenty of time to make it.

He was there with time in hand and kept his eyes open for Olivia in the Members' Enclosure. Alec had a card to get in. He had cards for everything.

She appeared about 12.30 with a small group round her, and they drifted off to the bar. Alec kept her in sight although he could not mistake her rather haughty drawl which kept rising above the other voices. She doesn't hate herself, he decided.

From about 1.15 she kept glancing at her watch, and Alec knew he had guessed right. But he didn't know what to expect.

Just before 1.30 she drifted out of the bar and, of all places, went to the car park. Alec followed at a distance.

She had a quick glance round then made for a car.

Alec moved quickly and was just in time to see a man hand her a suitcase.

She had another look round then walked off towards the public enclosure, the opposite direction.

Alec was close enough to see her disappear into a tent on the grass and watched at least half a dozen people go in and come out.

Olivia was the last to exit and made her way back to the private enclosure without the suitcase.

Alec quickly focussed his attention on the people who had come out of the tent and soon picked up two of them placing bets. Then he spotted two more doing the same.

He was jubilant. He'd sussed it: Olivia was laundering money for Maurice. That suitcase contained cash.

Suddenly he had second thoughts. An occasional cash windfall wasn't enough to keep up Olivia's big complex and her high living. There had to be more from somewhere.

He sat in his car and puzzled but couldn't work it out. All he was certain of was that racehorses were at the centre of the jigsaw.

He made a report to Mark and said quite bluntly what he suspected but that he was only scratching the tip of the mystery.

"There has to be a lot more money coming from somewhere," he said, "And it's definitely connected to racehorses."

Mark was amazed what Alec had found out so quickly and commended him.

"Do you want me to stay on the job?" Alec asked. "It seems to me the key is in these stables."

Mark didn't want to give up half way and agreed.

Then he got a piece of luck from Steff.

They were lying in bed, just chatting, and she said innocently, "Maurice has bought another horse. I wonder what it's called."

Bells rang in Mark's brain... Racehorses! Just as Alec said.

He said carefully, "Did you say ANOTHER horse?"

"That's right. He did have three but he sold one."

"Since when has Maurice been interested in the gee gees?"

"Since he met the charming Lady Olivia." Steff didn't hide her sarcasm.

Mark was thunderstruck. The plot was opening out.

"So how many does he have now?"

"Three."

"You ever seen them?"

"Course not. They're in the Lady's stables."

The next day Mark contacted Alec on his mobile. "Got some interesting news for you. Maurice has bought three horses and they are in Olivia's stables."

"Impossible," he said. "They were full when I first visited and had a long waiting list, and it hasn't changed."

"Could you check it out?"

"You bet."

Alec tripped back to Olivia's and sought out a friendly stable girl he'd chatted up.

"Remember telling me the stables were full?" he asked.

"Sure. They still are."

"I was told today that you've had three new horses in the past few months. One was sold, then another came in its place last week."

"You're living in dreamland?" she said scornfully. "I know every horse in this stable. There's been no change."

"Have you any other storage spots for horses?"

"Certainly not," she said indignantly. "What are you suggesting?"

Alec had got what he wanted. Now he had to stop the girl talking.

He made a show of pulling papers from his pocket and going through them. "Oh! I'm terribly sorry," he said. "It's stables at Newmarket."

"There you are," she said. "I think I know my own stables."

Alec was perked up. He'd found the scam. But how was it worked out? It would have to be watertight. Nothing else would do for Maurice.

He confirmed the news to Mark and said, "Now I'm stumped. Do you want me to pack up?"

Mark had great faith in Alec. "Stay on the job," he said. "This isn't over yet."

Alec thought what a determined character Mark was and had to smile to himself. He was doing very well out of the 'Tall Trees' family. First Helen, now son Mark.

But Mark would have been seriously worried if he knew how far advanced Alec's inquiry was into his father's death.

After unofficially perusing police records, Alec had succeeded in tracking down the articulated vehicle that killed Mark's father and where it started its journey.

He had also discovered that it had not been delivering anything, and he asked himself why had it been setting out so late without a load? His suspicious nose was twitching. His next step would be to trace the driver.

Mark decided to confront Maurice with Steff's comments and challenge him to produce some paperwork for his horses.

He met him in the evening over a drink. "Steff tells me," he said, "You've been buying horses from Lady Olivia. I told her she must have got things wrong but she insisted. Said the paperwork would prove it."

Mark paused, "It's not true, is it?"

Maurice silently cursed. Fucking big mouth Steff!

His mind raced. If he didn't produce some paperwork Mark would go on blabbing to everyone. Show him once and it was over, no mystery. Nothing more to talk about.

"Steff's got it right," he said. "Come into the office."

He went to a cabinet and pulled out paperwork, together with an invoice for £250,000 for a horse named Rainbow Boy.

"That's the latest," he said. "It's no big deal. An investment really. The charming lady persuaded me."

Mark was elated and memorised the horse and the date on the invoice. He had something on Maurice now.

He shrugged his shoulders, "Oh well that's the end of that. Sorry to trouble you, Maurice."

Maurice didn't want hassle with Mark and was relieved when he walked away, satisfied.

Mark's thoughts about Olivia, however, were different. He realised he had a hold over her as well. But he knew he'd have to be careful if he wanted to exercise it. She would certainly tell Maurice, and that was a different cup of tea.

He turned things over in his mind. He was reluctant to abandon an advantage, and decided he could frighten Olivia without making Maurice suspicious if he pretended to inquire about Rainbow Boy. What more natural than to have a look at a friend's horse?

She wouldn't come the haughty madam then, he thought. The idea appealed to him. It could be useful to have Olivia willing to oblige.

He went up to her stables the next day and didn't see Alec but he knew he'd be lurking about somewhere.

Then Olivia came marching up to him in her imperious way. "Why, Mark," she gushed. "What brings you up here?"

Mark silently savoured the bombshell he was going to throw at her.

"I've come to have a look at Rainbow Boy," he said.

He might have imagined it but he thought she lost some of her colour, and her imperious manner fell away instantly.

"Rainbow Boy?" she gulped.

"Yes. Maurice told me he'd bought him. Where is he?"

Olivia was a tough nut and regained her control. "He's out exercising," she said. "Be a few hours. Let me know another time, and I'll keep him back for you."

Very cool, Mark thought.

"Oh it doesn't matter that much," he said. "Just curiosity." He went on jovially, "Just wondered what Maurice got for his money."

Olivia insisted Mark go up to the house for some refreshment, but Mark knew she wanted to find out how much he knew.

Sure enough, her first words. "How did you know?"

"Just an accident. Steff, you know the cabaret star, told me Maurice had bought a horse, and I didn't believe her. She insisted and said the paperwork would prove it, so I asked Maurice, and he showed me the invoice."

Mark tried to sound casual. "Not that I care. Maurice can do what he likes with his money."

Olivia was worried. Mark might open his mouth.

"You can see Rainbow Boy when you like," she said. "Just give me a bell."

She could bring out any old horse. No-one would know.

"Oh I shan't bother now," Mark said. "It was just an impulse."

He felt he'd said enough to keep Olivia ready, willing and able.

No threat, but the fact that he knew and appeared to accept the position innocently would certainly make her careful to keep him sweet.

Mark guessed it would be a matter of minutes after he left before she was on the phone to Maurice, and he wasn't far wrong.

Maurice picked up the phone. "Yes, Olivia?"

His face darkened as she told him about Mark's visit.

"It was fucking awkward, Maurice," she said.

"You're sure he suspects nothing?"

"No way. He was just curious. I told him to give me a ring if he wants to see the horse." She laughed, "I can trot out any old horse."

"OK," he said. "But if he starts getting curious you tell me."

"He won't," Olivia said confidently. "I think he's already lost interest." She badly wanted to say "Why the fuck did you tell Steff?" but she didn't dare, and the conversation finished.

Mark's next thought was to put Alec in the picture, and pay him off. He'd found out what he wanted to know.

He called him into his office and thanked him and paid him.

Alec sat facing Mark. "What are you going to do now?" he asked.

A grim smile crept across Mark's face and he pointed to his head. "I shall keep it all up here," he said. "Until I need it."

Alec stared at Mark. His eyes looked cold and he thought, 'wouldn't like to be his enemy'; once more his thoughts jumped to his father's death. Yes, he thought, Mark could murder.

He took his leave with his thoughts re-focussing on the mother's inquiry, and he wondered if he would be confronting Mark again in the future.

Out of sheer devilment and to try out his new found power, Mark decided to test Olivia.

He rang her up. "Hi," he said. "I've got a couple of guests who'd like to see Rainbow Boy. They've tons of money and, if they like the look of him, I think they'll plunge heavily when he runs."

It was a good job Mark couldn't see Olivia's face. She was furious and pursed her lips angrily, but she was cool when she spoke. "Of course, Mark. When do you want to come?"

"Would tomorrow be OK?"

"Sure. Around two o'clock?"

"Fine." Mark was grinning as he put the phone down. He would easily find two people to look at a racehorse. Betting was a regular thing with the rich.

He turned up at Olivia's with a sporty middle-aged couple and she greeted them warmly.

"I've got the horse ready," she said. "We'll walk him round for you and show him at a gallop if you wish."

She brought out a handsome looking grey with a shaggy mane and a stable boy by his side.

She said jokingly, "I believe they called him Rainbow Boy because he has none of the rainbow's colours."

It was her bad luck that the man Mark had invited was a genuine racegoer, and he ran his hands over the horse lovingly.

"Looks good," he said. "I'd fancy a few hundred on him. Where's he running next?"

Olivia was prepared now and said coolly, "Probably Newmarket but of course it depends on the going and if he's ready."

"Has he won any races?"

This was a nasty one for Olivia. If she plucked one out of the air this man might know better. She had to play safe.

"We've had problems," she said, "And not run him seriously yet."

"Pity," the man said. "Nice looker."

Olivia thought her problems were over but Mark got back into the picture. He was loving Olivia's embarrassment.

"Has he a good pedigree?" he asked. "He cost enough."

Olivia could see Mark's guest anticipating her reply, but she kept calm.

"Good enough," she said. "I'll root out the papers for you next time."

The man waved her away. "Oh that's all right. I'm satisfied with what I see."

He turned, "Could I have a look at some of your other horses?"

Olivia was only too happy to oblige, and a stable girl took over.

She breathed easier. Problem over.

She stared at Mark, and, although he was loving Olivia's embarrassment, he managed to look innocent.

"He seems too know a bit about horses, doesn't he?" he said.

"Seems so."

"Reckon you'll have any luck with Rainbow Boy? I might put on a bit myself."

"You never know," she said.

Mark saw his guests returning and went to meet them.

He gave Olivia a wave. "Thanks, darling, very interesting... See you!"

He'd had his fun and found Olivia was vulnerable. He was pleased.

Olivia was enjoying her freedom from money worries and began to get greedy. She wondered if there was any way to raise even more finance. She had plans to extend her stables, and her ambitions were now flooding in other directions. For a start she'd love to make her jumping area into a real professional arena with seated accommodation.

She tackled Maurice the following week at *The Phoenix*.

"Can we have a private chat?" she asked.

He sat her down in his office and looked at her. "So, Olivia?"

Now that the time had come she was embarrassed. She'd never liked asking for anything, she was used to taking, and this was the second time with Maurice.

Maurice prompted her, "Yes, Olivia?"

She still couldn't bring herself to ask straight out and said cautiously, "I've been so pleased with our arrangement I wondered if there was any way it could be increased."

Maurice had a big laugh to himself. The aristocratic lady was getting greedy. But he wouldn't look a gift horse in the mouth.

"Possibly," he said. "There are ways and means. Your valuable connections make you very useful to some people."

"What does that mean?"

Maurice gave a small laugh. "There are a number of establishments that provide special services for those willing to pay."

Olivia interrupted. "You mean sex?"

"What else?"

Olivia thought for a moment. She was perplexed. "What could I do?"

"Simply introduce people. Nothing more. These places aren't advertised."

"That doesn't sound like big money to me."

"The big money is what they have to pay in blackmail," Maurice said. He paused, "On a 50/50 split."

"That's criminal."

"Of course it is. That's why the money's big." He shrugged, "I can give you addresses. If you're serious contact them and mention my name."

"You own these places?"

"Don't be ridiculous. I make my money legitimately at *The Phoenix* and my other clubs. But from time to time my girls get asked for these places."

Olivia was torn. But greed won.

"And no-one else would know?"

"How could they? You are merely giving someone an address you know about. Nothing more."

Maurice tried to be casual. "Best I can suggest to you, I'm afraid, if you want to make big money." He gave her a stare. "I'll leave it up to you."

Olivia rose. "Thanks, Maurice. I'll think about it." But they both knew she was going to do it.

And once she'd started she found it easy. The blackmail didn't bother her, being found out did. But she felt safe.

The development of the villas was in full swing, and half a dozen were now completed. Well on schedule.

They were instantly occupied, and all the others to be built were reserved in advance. The Villas were a huge success story. Enquiries were still coming in from all over the world.

As Mark said. "Didn't know there were so many millionaires in the world."

Barbara was preening herself. She had played an important part in the development and she told Mark David was coming over soon to inspect progress.

Mark was pleased but also concerned. When David had agreed the contract he had insisted on an option to continue the partnership after development, which at the time appeared reasonable, and cemented the deal. But the runaway success of the Villas had made Mark regret it. He could see no end to the money that could be squeezed from the willing millionaires and he wanted full control.

He suspected David might be an immovable obstacle.

His thoughts immediately went to Barbara. If she started shooting off her mouth with high praise about the Villas and the millionaires rush to become occupants, he would have no hope. He wondered if he could persuade her to be loyal to him instead.

He decided a night out might help his cause. The question was, did he try to persuade Barbara things were not as rosy as she might think. Or was it honesty first and tell her straight out he wanted David's option. After all, it was no skin off her nose.

Mark gave the first option only a moments' thought. Barbara was far too bright to be taken in. It had to be honesty, but he wasn't confident she would support him.

At least it would be fun trying, he thought gloomily.

He tackled her the next day.

"I want to talk to you," he said.

She smiled. "Shoot!"

"No no, this is not business, it's ABOUT business. How about coming for a meal?"

"And after?"

"You took the words right out of my mouth."

She had a roguish smile. "Would tonight suit you?"

"Perfect."

Barbara thought no more about Mark's words. She just reckoned they had a date and was ready to enjoy herself. She always felt she could abandon herself with Mark.

He took her to *The Riverside*, and she was flattered at the attention she received. Was the wine just right? Did Madam like her coffee black or white? Would she like a cognac with it? Or cointreau? Which cheese would Madam prefer? There was someone at her elbow the whole time.

The meal was perfection, and Barbara said, "Anyone would think I was the queen."

"You are tonight," Mark said.

She looked flushed and excited, and Mark thought once again how appealing she was.

He omitted to tell her he'd bribed the Riverside to give her special attention.

She looked at him over the top of her glass. "I think I'll have just one more then I'm ready for action," she said saucily.

"Action?"

"Pleasure without speaking," she said.

Mark had to laugh. "You'll be the death of me."

"So long as it's after and not before," she said.

Mark had to laugh again, and his hopes rose. Barbara was certainly in a carefree mood.

When they got into the Lotus to drive back she lifted her dress to the top of her legs.

"If you like them," she said, "I'll show you a bit more."

She was wearing hold-up stockings, and Mark glimpsed her bare thighs and not much else.

"We'd better get home first," he said. "Or I'll be arrested for carrying a nude passenger."

When he pulled up he asked, "Why do we nearly always come to your place?"

"So I don't have to walk home."

She wouldn't add to that and put her fingers to his lips.

"I have to have some secrets," she said.

She changed into a loose gown that kept swinging open, but she kept her high heels. She knew how attractive her tight bottom was in high heels.

She lay against Mark on a long couch with her legs on full display, and he cupped her breasts and played with her nipples.

They seemed slightly swollen, and Barbara soon threw off her gown... Mark was already nearly naked.

He felt the tension across her taut stomach as his hands wandered and when he came to the top of her legs she immediately opened them.

She seemed in such a willing mood, he said quickly, "You ever been kissed down there?"

"No," she breathed. "I've often wondered but thought it was asking too much."

"I'm offering."

She promptly stood up and gave him a full view between her parted legs, then straddled him and slid towards his mouth.

Mark rolled her in his lips, and she gasped and began to finger her own breasts. It was delight.

Then all at once she felt violent surges. It was almost agony and she nearly shrieked. Then suddenly, like a cloudburst, she was throbbing in wonderful relief and felt she was gushing out floods.

Mark said softly. "Lust at its best."

"Whatever it is you can do it again," she said.

She hesitated, "Do you want me to do it to you?"

"Do you really imagine," Mark said, "That I held back? Not a chance."

He pulled her on top, and as she lay against him he still felt a thrill as her pointed tips jabbed into him and his hands wandered between the rounds of her bottom.

She helpfully spread herself and it was almost like cool sex. Neither of them wanted an end.

"Seems like we're sex maniacs," Barbara observed.

"That'll do for me," Mark said. "It's enough when you can't do it any more."

Barbara had a memory flash. "You wanted to talk to me, Mark."

Her reminder struck Mark with full force. The sex could look like a bribe.

"Oh, it can wait," he said. He tried to sound casual.

"Go on. Don't keep me in suspense."

Mark crossed his fingers. "It was just that when David comes over I want to persuade him to give up his option when the Villas are completed, and I wondered if you'd back me up."

Barbara was surprised. "What option?"

"Under the contract either party on completion can withdraw or continue in partnership."

"I didn't realise that, but I'm sorry, darling, I couldn't be disloyal to David."

There it was. A big No!

Mark tried to hide his disappointment but he admired Barbara's stand.

It was two more weeks before David appeared, and he brought a big surprise.

He confided in Barbara that his group wanted to buy out Mark and take full control of the villas.

He went on to say that his directors wanted full control or nothing. They had their own very definite ideas on the way the

Villas should be run, and for a start the name 'Tall Trees' would be ditched.

Barbara smiled to herself. She could imagine Mark swallowing that.

She went to see him with some thoughts whizzing round her brain.

"I bring you some interesting news," she said. "David's bosses want to buy you out, and I'm sure they'll offer big money. But if you stand firm they'll go away. They want full control or nothing."

Mark was overjoyed. "You sure?"

"I'm sure."

Mark was suddenly suspicious. "You said you could not be disloyal to David. Remember?"

"I remember, and I'm not. He's turned up under orders. Full control or nothing. I couldn't influence him if I wanted to."

She gave Mark a stare. "The rest is up to you. I'm sure they'll offer you a fabulous sum of money. You must decide." She gave him a smile and walked away.

The next day David appeared in Mark's office and offered him a million for his option.

Mark laughed, "These villas are goldmines, David. No deal. But there's enough for us both. Stay with us." He said this with his tongue in his cheek.

David came back the following week with an offer to double the figure, and in addition, pay Mark an overriding commission when figures reached a certain level, quite a complicated contract.

But Mark wasn't interested and as he knew David would pull out if he sat tight he said, "I'm quite happy to share with you. As I said before, there's enough money for us both, but I definitely won't withdraw. That's my last word."

David consulted Barbara. "Any way we can persuade Mark? There's big money in it."

She gave him a sunny smile. "You're wasting your time, David."

"You sure?"

"I'm sure."

David made one last try. He said to Mark. "You know, a couple of million cash down opens a lot of doors, and my Group are prepared to offer all sorts of other inducements."

"I don't need the cash, David."

That was the weakness in David's armoury, and he knew it.

"All right!" he said finally, "Name your own terms."

Mark smiled, "Five billion. Every year."

David gave up and shook Mark's hand.

"OK and good luck," he said. "If ever you do think of selling give me first shout, will you?"

Mark was exuberant. He'd got full control and without a pay out. What a scoop. He knew that would impress his mother and sister Janet, and it did.

"How did you manage that?" Janet asked

Mark tapped his nose. "I did my homework." He grinned as he thought of Barbara.

Then he had a bright idea. He would need someone to run the villas full time. Who could be better than Barbara? She knew the place from A to Z. He'd been very impressed with the loyalty she'd shown to David, and he knew he'd be able to trust her completely.

He waited a few days and thought things over and couldn't think of one objection.

He wasn't influenced by their relationship. Mark was cold-blooded about business and had no difficulty in viewing her quite impersonally. But once he'd decided, he had to smile. He'd have her charms as well.

But there was one final hurdle. Barbara herself. She might want to go back to her life with David. Marauding round the globe. Mark decided to find out. He caught up with her as she was striding along and fell into the rhythm of her steps.

She turned and smiled at him. "I thought I was being stalked."

"You are."

She lifted her eyebrows.

"Do tell."

"I want to talk to you again."

She said with a chuckle. "Like last time?"

"That can be arranged. But this is more serious."

She raised her brows higher. "I'm listening."

Mark took her arm. "Not here. Come to my office when you're free."

"I'm coming now," she said.

They sat facing each other, and Barbara gave him such an elfin look he nearly smiled.

"I want to make you a proposition," he said. "How would you like to run the villas in sole command as a permanent job?"

Barbara was startled then excited. She loved it at 'Tall Trees' and the life near London, and also working with Mark, and she knew she'd never get a better boss. Better wasn't quite the word, she thought.

But she had to consider David. He may have plans for her.

"Will you give me a few days?"

"Of course. I didn't expect an instant decision." Mark wasn't quite honest.

Barbara tackled David straight away. "Mark's offered me the job of running the Villas as a permanent job," she said. "I'm very tempted but I owe you. Have you any plans for me?"

David knew he had a lost cause on his hands and he was generous.

Barbara had served him well and he would be sorry to lose her, but he'd always realised this could happen.

"The job is made for you," he said. "Take it and be happy." He gave her a look of affection. "I'll just have to find another daughter."

He gave her a hug and kissed her on the cheek. "Good luck to you."

Barbara felt a bit emotional. "It's been great fun working for you David," she said, and she nearly shed a few tears.

She didn't see Mark until the next day.

"Well?" he asked.

"The answer is yes."

"Brilliant! Now we can have that other talk." Mark was all smiles.

Olivia was very happy at the money beginning to generate through her introductions, and, although she still saw Mark from time to time, they were no longer a pair, and Mark was quite happy with the arrangement.

Then she ran into some serious trouble. One irate man, not married, refused to pay blackmail, and told Olivia he would name her to the police.

She knew she couldn't run to Maurice so she chose Mark.

Mark picked up the phone and heard the familiar voice again.

"I wonder if you can help me, Mark. I've got myself into a spot of bother."

She explained that she'd introduced a man to a house that catered for special sex and he was being blackmailed and threatened to name her to the police. She allowed Mark to think it was a purely one-off situation and she was just unlucky.

Mark didn't feel any obligation towards Olivia now, but he could offer help quite easily, and she would owe him a favour... Mark always thought about the long chance.

"Leave it with me," he said. "I'll get a private detective on the job. He'll be round to see you in the morning. His name is Alec Donovan. He's a very smart operator."

He put the phone down and immediately rang Alec.

Olivia was impressed with Alec, although she felt uncomfortable about some of his questions, and she had the feeling he wasn't fooled when she told him her introduction was a one-off.

He was unmoved by her story. He was used to the sleazy antics of rich people, and just stuck to his job.

He came away from Olivia with what he wanted, the irate man's address.

He interviewed him the same day. "They can go and fuck themselves," the man said. "I'm going to the police."

Alec pointed out that if he did it was probable HE would be prosecuted for immoral activities in a house of ill-repute.

"That is the legal term," he said apologetically.

The man stared. That hadn't occurred to him... "So what can I do?"

"When the blackmailers ring again you tell them you're not going to pay, and if they publish the video you'll sue whoever publishes it. I assure you," he said solemnly, "That is the last you will hear of it."

The man pulled his lip and was silent for a moment. "What about Olivia?" he said. "She gave me the address."

"Don't waste your time," Alec said. "She and her friends know several addresses where you can get kinky sex. She just thought she was doing you a favour."

The man was satisfied, and Olivia was home free.

Maurice, prudent as usual, did exactly what Alec predicted when his crew reported the man's threat to him. "Forget him," he said. "Move on to the next one."

But he began to wonder if Olivia might become a dangerous leak. He knew perfectly well if the police came in she would finger him without hesitation. Olivia didn't know it but she was on thin ice.

Alec told Mark he'd settled the matter, and Olivia was safe.

He added, "If I were you I'd have a word with that lady. I think she's mixing in dangerous company, way out of her depth."

"What do you mean?"

"Suspicions," Alec said. "But strong ones. You take my tip if you care about the lady."

Mark decided to frighten Olivia while she was vulnerable, and see what he could shake out and he went up to see her.

He could see the strain on her face, and he went straight on the attack.

"You bloody fool, Olivia," he said. "I know what you've been up to. Do you realise you're risking a long prison sentence?"

She lost a little colour but tried to defend herself. "I've only given introductions," she said.

"In a court of law that is conspiracy to demand money with menaces. In other words," Mark said brutally, "touting for blackmailers."

He went silent while she digested this news, and he could see she was shaken. The seconds ticked by but Mark still kept his mouth shut; he wanted the whole story.

Olivia said at last, "Maurice's girls gave me the addresses, apparently they often get asked." She said weakly, "I didn't realise I could be in such trouble, but I need the money."

"You can't spend it in prison."

She got a little tight-lipped at the lecture she was receiving, although she was still frightened. "I should think this man was a one-off," she said.

Mark said, "For fuck's sake, Olivia, get real. They're all one offs. The next man might go straight to the police. How do you know?"

Mark had said 'The NEXT man,' and Olivia picked up his words eagerly. "Do you mean I'm off the hook?"

"Yes!" he said, "But there can't be a second time, Olivia."

She felt an immense relief, but couldn't shake off her financial anxiety.

"Unfortunately, Mark, I'm trapped," she said. "Like I said, I need the money. I've already committed myself to expansion and given the orders. I'm really scared" She spoke the truth. "Do you think you could help me out? If you backed me I'd give you a proper legal agreement."

Mark could easily put money in. His board had liked the idea of the stable facility, particularly being linked to a titled Lady. It fitted in with the luxury style of living they promoted.

But Mark wanted an advantage for himself.

Suddenly he had a bright idea. Tie her down strictly on a commercial mortgage, and, if she defaulted, as he was sure she would, take over the stables as a 'Tall Trees' facility.

Then Olivia would work for him. Mark loved the idea.

"Tell you what, Olivia," he said. "I'll get my solicitor to arrange a proper mortgage for you." He added, so it was on the record, "But don't forget, you can't play fast and loose with a mortgage."

Olivia was so relieved she didn't even consider the implications. "Come up to the house," she said, "We'll seal the bargain."

Of course that meant staying the night, and this time Olivia had to consider Mark rather than press her own desires.

Nobody could teach Olivia much about the antics of sex, and she brought out all her tricks. She even took Mark in her mouth, which was a first for them. The sensation left him breathless, and he could hardly stop shaking. The fact that Olivia achieved small satisfaction didn't seem to matter to either of them, and in the morning they parted on friendly terms.

On his way back Mark's thoughts drifted towards Maurice, and he wondered just how much he might be involved in underworld activities. He resolved to be on his guard in future. Just in case.

There were now more than twenty Villas completed, and Barbara had christened herself Director of Villas.

She walked about with an air of importance that amused her. In anyone else it would have been pompous.

She also had a side advantage in that Mark was frequently by her side. He didn't interfere but was very anxious that nothing went wrong, and in these early days in particular, kept his eyes open all the time.

There was one couple in the villas Barbara rather liked. Matt and Beth Saunders from the good old USA. They had with them an eighteen-year-old son Marty who made eyes at her, but she took this lightly.

Little did she know he had serious intentions.

He was a headstrong young man used to getting his own way. He had never lifted a finger to do anything, and he spent his time ordering people around or cursing at them if they objected. When he got in trouble Daddy spent some of his millions to bail him out.

He was undeniably a handsome youth but Barbara didn't like the way his mouth turned sullen very easily and thought he could turn nasty at the drop of a hat. She thought it was a pity Matt and Beth had to be saddled with him.

One night she got a telephone call from Marty. "Could she come up? It was urgent."

"What!" Barbara said, "It's gone seven thirty. You're lucky I'm here."

Marty persisted. "It's mama," he mumbled. "She's really distressed."

Barbara couldn't ignore a distress signal. "I'll be over," she shouted, and slammed the phone down.

She hurtled over and rang his doorbell furiously. The door opened in a flash, and Marty stood there.

"This way," he cried, and Barbara scooted after him to the master bedroom.

She'd hardly put a foot inside when he suddenly turned and gave her an enormous swipe across the jaw. Her knees went, and she blacked out.

When she came round she was naked and spread-eagled face down on the bed with her hands and feet tied to the corners. She jerked her head round, and Marty said with an evil grin on his face, "Good! doll. I've been waiting for you to come back to life. We're going to have a picture show. I like a nice tight ass."

Barbara felt her bruised jaw as she moved her head. Then she glimpsed a tripod and camera set-up pointing at her and she had an awful feeling of fear.

The next few minutes, she thought, would live in her mind forever.

Marty took off his clothes then pushed his hand between her buttocks and smeared her with some kind of grease.

He went back to the camera and sighted it, then she felt his weight as he speared between the cheeks of her bottom.

Barbara screamed at the pain and wrenched at her bonds but the more she struggled the better Marty liked it, and he furiously stroked into her until, horror of horrors, she felt him shooting into her. At that moment she could have killed him. She felt her whole life was collapsing in filth. For a moment he lay on her panting, his full weight pressing her down, and he was a six footer. Then he wrenched himself off and gave her even more pain.

Barbara hoped her ordeal was over but it wasn't. Marty stood over her, smoothing and patting her bottom. Then he opened her cheeks wider for a better camera shot. Finally he gave her a quick smack across the bottom.

"Think that will do, doll," he said, and, to Barbara's amazement, tore off the restraints, and she was free. She couldn't believe it.

Hurting as she was, she jumped off the bed and scrambled into her clothes while Marty just watched.

She shot him a contemptuous stare then dashed to the door. She shook it but it wouldn't open.

Marty mockingly held up the key between his thumb and forefinger. "Hard luck, doll. Here! This should keep your mouth shut," And he flung a bundle of banknotes at her.

"Five thous!" he shouted. "Now you can piss off."

Barbara furiously threw the money back. "You think you can buy my silence? Not with a million, never mind a miserable five thousand. I'm off to the police."

Marty was still mocking. "And who do you think they'll believe? The poor little rich boy, eighteen years old, or the sophisticated lady who came to his villa to seduce him. You're on a loser, doll."

He threw her the key. "You'd better think again."

His words penetrated Barbara's mind, but she couldn't digest them. She could only think of escape and revenge.

"You vile bastard," she shouted, "You're not getting away with this," and she stamped out.

She stumbled into her suite and collapsed into a chair, where she began to sob. She thought she'd never stop, but as the pain stabbed into her again she finally pulled herself up.

She took a trip to the bathroom and gingerly examined herself and, as she suspected, found traces of blood. She cleaned herself up then stepped into a bath. She thought she could never feel clean again.

She sat down to think, and her mind began to clear.

It was then that she realised she would have a struggle to convince the police of her story. Marty's version, no doubt delivered with teen-age innocence, would be persuasive.

She picked up the phone and surprised Mark. It was about 11.30.

"Come over, Mark," she gasped. "I'm in serious trouble."

He was there in a flash.

One look, and he took her in his arms, and she started sobbing all over again. His face went like granite when he heard her story.

He immediately took her over to Matt and Beth's Villa, and they went inside.

"I'm afraid I've a very serious accusation to make against your son, Marty, and it may be impossible to keep the police out of it," Mark said.

Beth went a bit pale.

Matt said with a set face, "Spit it out."

Barbara took over and retold her story, and Matt's face went darker and darker.

"Unbelievable!" he said at last.

He shouted upstairs, "Marty. Come down here."

Marty took his time then strolled casually into the room.

He looked at Barbara and said insolently, "You've a cheek to come back. Didn't you get enough before?"

Mark could have hit him.

"You know why we are here," he said quietly. "In this country people get locked up when they rape a woman, particularly when it's obscene."

Marty sneered at Barbara. "What, is she trying to get money out of us? I call that blackmail."

He said defiantly, "I didn't ask her here. She came over here unannounced and seduced me. I'm not saying I didn't go a little wild but it was all her fault. Apparently, she wanted kinky sex."

"What about your phone call asking me to come over?" Barbara said coldly.

Marty scoffed. "Any more fiction?"

Everybody in the room knew Marty was lying, but it was also true Barbara's version couldn't be proved.

Then Mark had an inspiration and told a wonderful lie.

""I take it, Barbara," he said, "You took Marty's call on our Company line?"

He said to Matt, "We record our tele-conversations for one day in case any instructions are disputed."

Barbara took the hint. "Of course."

She said contemptuously to Marty. "That sews you up."

He said coolly, "Doesn't make any difference. She still seduced me."

Matt's father said crossly, his face like thunder, "Stop it, Marty, and get back upstairs."

When he'd gone Matt said apologetically, "Can't say how sorry I am. How much?"

Mark spoke. "I don't want your money," he said. "I want to protect my staff. Your son is a danger to them, and it's a matter for the police."

Beth reached across and took Mark's arm, "Don't take him away from us," she pleaded, "He's our only son."

Mark was silent then said stiffly, "I'll leave it up to Barbara."

But Barbara could only see Beth's tear-filled stricken face and knew she couldn't go ahead.

She came to a quick decision. "Two conditions," she said. "One. Here and now Marty comes down and admits the offence and apologises to me. Two. I'm afraid you'll have to leave. I couldn't bear to have Marty near me any more."

Matt said, "The second is easy."

He shouted up the stairs again, "Marty!"

He came down, sullen. "Yes?"

His father said to him grimly, "You're a lucky boy, Marty. Barbara has agreed not to inform the police if you admit the offence and apologise to her... Then we leave."

He prompted him loudly as he stood silent and rebellious. "Do you prefer prison?"

So Marty had to admit the offence, and Barbara made him admit everything so that his mother and father were in no doubt.

"Now the apology," she said. "And on your knees."

She had swiftly scribbled the words she wanted him to say and thrust the paper under his nose.

He said all the words, which included 'and I acted like the worst kind of animal,' and was about to stand up when Barbara clouted him round the face with all her might, and he nearly fell over.

"Well at least I've got some satisfaction," she said as he glowered at her. "Now YOU can piss off."

She stalked out of the room.

That same night Marty was on the phone to his pals in New York.

"Wait till I get back, fellas," he said. "I've got some great pictures of a lovely tight ass with me sticking it right up her till I came. Best I've done."

"Reckon I'll take the prize," he added, and he hung up, basking in their admiration.

In three days the Saunders had gone.

Christmas was approaching, and 'Tall Trees' usually held a Ball to mark the occasion. It was always a very special event and it was guests and friends only. The event was organised by sister Janet and it was obligatory for Directors to be present. But this year Mark wanted to give it a miss and was looking for a good excuse.

He'd been invited by Steff to what she called a very special party in London. "Make your hair stand on end," she said.

It was to be held at *'The Kink's Palace'*, and Mark knew perfectly well what to expect if he went, but he craved excitement and his curiosity to witness different sex was compelling. There were no reservations as to dress or behaviour, and entrance was by invitation only. Privacy was ensured.

Both Carol and Barbara expected to be invited as Mark's partner to the 'Tall Trees' Ball. More so Carol as she had been Mark's partner before. But Mark kept them maddeningly frustrated as he tried to think of an excuse not to go.

Then he got lucky. He received an invitation from the Hoteliers Association to represent 'Tall Trees' at their festive occasion in London on the same night. He immediately refused but showed their invitation to 'Tall Trees' to explain his absence from their Ball.

The night before the party Steff warned him there were no morals at *The Kink's Palace*. "There's no such thing as husband and wife or partners," she said. "It's a jungle, and you fight for what you want."

"That's what attracts me," Mark said. And he was speaking the truth.

On the night he parked his Lotus outside Steff's and they took a taxi to *The Kink's Palace*.

Steff looked superb in a silver sheath that shamelessly failed to cover her breasts and exposed her legs to the top with every step she took. Mark did not have to guess she was nude underneath, he knew.

Just inside the entrance, a sort of mini foyer, a tall black girl greeted them. Except for high heels, she was entirely nude. And she placed a card in their hands. She said with a big smile that showed her white teeth.

"There is only one rule here. Nothing is barred."

Mark dragged his eyes from her huge dark nipples and glanced at the card. It included a sort of diagram and showed the layout of private rooms, stage and dance floor, bar and restaurant, plunge bath, steam room. And a big message ran across the top.

IF YOU CAN'T GET IT HERE IT'S YOUR OWN FAULT.

He said to Steff. "There must be a lot of money behind this place."

"There is," she replied. "If you want to become a member it will cost you £10,000."

Mark whistled.

"And there's a waiting list," Steff said.

She pointed, "There's the owner standing over there."

Mark looked across, expecting to see a much older person but he found himself looking at a woman in his own age bracket.

She was tall, slim, and smart and very sexy in an understated way.

Mark was intrigued. "She must have made a lot of money quickly to set this place up," he said.

"Nobody knows much about her, but I believe she comes from a very wealthy family," Steff said.

"What's her name?"

"Aimee la Salle."

While Mark was digesting this information Aimee caught his eye, and Mark had the feeling she was amused. She was better covered than most of the guests, yet her suggestion of sex was overpowering.

He made up his mind to meet her, and while he was thinking, someone took Steff's arm and wheeled her away.

For a moment Mark was annoyed then he saw Steff grinning at him over her shoulder. "Told you so," she mouthed.

Then somebody touched Mark's arm, and he looked into the face of a lithe young woman whose eyes were burning with desire. A mass of unruly dark hair flopped around her face and added to her aura of abandonment.

"You are mine," she said.

She wore what appeared to be a handkerchief across her thighs which displayed her wonderful legs, and she didn't conceal her breasts. Her bra encircled them and left the points free for public gaze.

"I hope you like what you see," she said. "That's only a sample." She put her arm through his and hauled him off to the dance floor, where slow music was encouraging close movements. The floor was dimly lit and surrounded by long low couches which some couples were already using.

In her high heels she was only a few inches shorter than Mark, and he found her lips in the exact kissing position. He also immediately found that her handkerchief skirt concealed nothing, there was only flesh underneath.

Then he glimpsed Steff moving round. She was with another woman, and they were about to kiss.

It suddenly hit him that in this bohemian world everyone was equal.

Nobody had an edge, there was no superiority of position. The power was sex.

He drew a deep breath. He was going for it.
"What do I call you?" he whispered.
"Sam. And you?"
"Mark."

She opened his shirt. "I like to flick my nipples across," she said.

She said it in a matter-of-fact way, and Mark began to think he was holding dynamite.

"Be my guest," he said.

She was gay and frolicsome. She pushed into him, thrust her leg between his thighs, and flicked him with her lips, but Mark knew she was only teasing.

Then he saw two entirely nude women dancing and fondling each other.

Sam followed his gaze. "That excite you, Mark?"

"I'm only a man." he mumbled.

She laughed. "You like two women together?"

"Yes," he said. "But I like one to myself."

"Good," she said, "I'll give you a show."

Mark could hardly wait. He reckoned he'd struck lucky with Sam.

She whipped off her handkerchief skirt. "Put your hands there," she said. "I'm sure you like a tight bottom."

Mark did indeed, and he cupped the mounds of her flesh.

"A bit more," she coaxed.

Mark slipped his fingers between her cheeks and pressed and as he did she slipped her leg between his and stroked against his thigh.

Her bare flesh made him hard, and instantly Sam unzipped him and Mark felt a thousand times more stiff as she took hold. She massaged him up and down, slow, quick, slow, quick. Then so violently he nearly jumped and spurted torrents all over her.

She laughed and said softly, "A good start."

She led him to the plunge bath where she whipped off her bra and plunged in.

"Come on!" she coaxed, and Mark shed his clothes and followed.

They pretended to wash each other, then she backed into him and brought his arms round so that she was in his embrace.

Immediately, she guided him all over her body and when she felt him harden she edged him between her cheeks.

"Just a little masturbation," she said. "My turn now." And to Mark's amazement, she proceeded to do exactly that, and fingered herself until the final surging movement.

Mark found another thrill between her cheeks, and as she finally jerked so did he. This was becoming unbelievable, he thought, and he wondered about his stamina.

They clambered out and Mark stared at Sam unashamedly.

She pirouetted. "You like it?"

Mark certainly did, and his fascination for the space between women's thighs was magnified.

Sam didn't even have a hairline. She was completely smooth all over, and Mark glimpsed the shadow of her true line.

"I'll show you more later," she laughed. "Let's eat."

Mark slipped on his clothes and Sam put her bra and handkerchief skirt back, and they drifted off to the restaurant.

Not that it mattered. No respect had to be shown. People were lounging at the tables in all sorts of undress, some entirely nude.

And, of course, the waitresses were in G-strings or nude, and the men, gay and normal, in practically nothing, or cross dressed.

The food was good, and Mark found himself hungry but he was equally matched by Sam. The champagne tasted like nectar. Or was it their mood? Mark wondered.

Then he glimpsed Aimee la Salle at a table with a woman by her side.

She still had that suggestion of sex lurking, but she was quiet.

"Who's that woman with la Salle?" he asked Sam.

"Oh that's her secretary, she's always with her," she replied. "Fay Harrison."

"Blue-eyed blonde, pretty girl," Mark said.

Then, to his surprise, a waitress put a card in his hand.

It was gold-edged and read: Aimee la Salle, with a telephone number; nothing else.

Mark turned the card over. There was a small scribble. 'Try to see me before you leave.'

Mark looked across to her table but she was talking and didn't look up.

"What's on the card?" Sam asked.

Mark showed her.

"You're honoured," she said. "Aimee doesn't mix."

"Must be my fatal charm," Mark suggested.

He knew he would see her. She had intrigued him from the start, and he sensed a great deal more than sex in Aimee la Salle.

Sam swigged down her champagne. "Another bottle?"

"Sure it won't slow you down?"

Sam laughed, "Can a duck swim?"

So they opened another bottle. And finished it.

"What now?" Mark asked.

"You like cabaret?"

"Sure."

"Well this is a cabaret of sex, if you know what I mean."

"I think I can guess."

So they watched.

The first act was a line of gay men performing as dancing girls, and they looked the real thing.

Next was a solo strip act, and the man appeared exactly like a woman. His breasts would have been the envy of many; and his legs were long and slim.

As his last garment fell, he stood in a G-string and still looked suspiciously like a woman. He let it fall, then parted his legs.

"Fooled you, eh?" he laughed. "Now you know."

"Can't think how he does that," Mark said.

"Oh there are ways," Sam said. "Some a bit painful."

Then the lesbians came on and opened their legs to each other in all sorts of unusual positions, and the climax was four of them playing about with a dildo. And did they get excited!

"I think I've seen enough," Mark said.

"Good," Sam said. "Nothing like the real thing."

She took him to a private room, luxurious and en suite.

"La Salle doesn't miss a trick, does she?" Mark said.

Sam said sensibly, "Rich money, rich returns."

She stripped naked and jumped on the king-size bed and Mark slipped beside her, but Sam said, "No. I promised you a show," and she spun round and spread her legs within inches of his gaze.

"Go on," she said. "Have a good look and feel free."

Mark couldn't resist. Her entirely smooth area got him going, and he stared as if hypnotised. Then he put his fingers on her and smoothed and turned over the delicate skin between her legs until she was almost inside out.

Sam put her hands on his head, "Now you can love me with your mouth," she said, and moved him into position..

Mark was wildly excited, but he was anxious not to do harm, and he was gentle as he took her in his mouth.

It brought an immediate rebuff from Sam.

"Come on, Mark!" she said. "Get rough. I want to feel something."

That was enough for him. He spread her legs wider and revolved her in his lips savagely. Then he felt the soft skin inside with his tongue and, as he moved upwards to her most sensitive spot, she gave a convulsive jerk.

Suddenly she surged, and Mark felt her moist against his lips. Unthinkingly, he reached for her nipples and squeezed. She let out an enormous shout but Mark held on until her hands restrained him.

"Did I do good?" he asked.

"You did good," she repeated. "It will do as a starter."

"Do I get a break first?"

"Yes," she said, "Champagne, a dance, then a glorious finish."

"Where do you get all your energy?"

Sam puckered her lips, and suddenly there was a faraway look in her eyes. It seemed very strange.

"I had a radical mother," she said. "She taught me that sex was to be enjoyed and there were no barriers. Adventure and excitement was the key to her attitude, and she reckoned there were no rights or wrongs. If it felt good it was right... I reckon that's me as well."

"Amen to that," Mark said.

They drank the champagne then danced quietly and returned to their room.

"I'm remembering what your mama told you," Mark said as they fell on the bed, naked. "If it feels good it's right."

Sam spread herself out, and once again Mark was unable to resist her smooth front area. He had his hand there immediately, and as Sam moved he pinched her in the right place, and for a moment she went taut.

"You're learning," she whispered.

Then her arms came over and she dragged him on top. "I want you to kiss me all over," she said. "The grand finale."

She stretched her arms wide. "You know where to start. My nipples already know."

And sure enough, she was enlarging.

Mark marvelled as his lips went round her. How did she keep it up?

She was soon swollen, and twisted and turned as he teased her, but she wanted more and pushed his head to her navel.

Mark was unaware this was an erotic area and he was surprised as she drew him against her skin and in particular wanted his tongue to drive inside the cavity.

At he same time she brought his hands up to her breasts again.

He couldn't help feeling she seemed to have sex in every particle, and when she finally whispered, "You know where to go next" he was excited as if it was a first time.

His mind told him Sam was definitely something different, and then he was between her legs and she was pulling his hair.

He didn't know if it was EXcitement or INcitement, but he couldn't stop.

She lurched and almost kicked as he found the spot. Then she screamed "Now Mark... Now!" and dragged his mouth up to hers.

He was grateful he'd been able to wait, and with immense relief he gushed out torrents as she heaved against him like a wild animal.

Only exhaustion stopped them, and at last Sam whispered dreamily, "I'm all lit up, darling."

It was the first time she had called Mark "darling", and for some obscure reason he felt ten feet tall.

They cuddled, then he said. "It's two thirty, and I've got to see la Salle."

"Why bother?"

Mark's mind was still agile. "She probably wants to know about 'Tall Trees'. You know, my hotel."

"Oh! OK."

Mark didn't know how near he was to the truth but when he tapped and walked into her office he found out.

He wondered idly how long she'd been waiting.

Her office was luxurious, like the rest of *Kink's Palace*, and she leaned back in a big leather chair and signalled him to another.

Mark was completely undecided about Aimee la Salle. She had an air of mystery and sophistication, and he picked up an unusual impression of hard/soft; that she could be hard like him or abandoned like Sam. He sensed sex powerfully. She also seemed aloof, almost haughty and he was puzzled.

"Have you seen enough?" She gave him a long stare.

Mark didn't think she was impressed...

"I apologise," he said. "Can't say I'm at my best at two thirty in the morning."

Aimee knew Mark had been assessing her but she had to admit that was a smooth reply.

"I'm surprised you're not on your knees," she said, "Don't you know Sam Steel is a nympho?"

Mark grinned. "I do now."

"I hope you've enjoyed yourself."

"Couldn't have been better."

"Good. I wondered if you might return the compliment. I've been thinking about a break and thought your villas were exactly right for me." She smiled, "Unless the TV's lying."

"Sorry. There's a huge waiting list," Mark said. "Tell you what, though. 'Tall Trees' is private, and the suites and facilities are equally luxurious."

He looked at her thoughtfully. "If you're interested be my guest for a day."

He fished a card out of his pocket and handed it to her. "You've only to ring. I'll rush up and drive you there and back."

"That seems exceptional service."

"Not if we become friends."

"That's a big jump, isn't it?"

"I shall know if you ring me."

Mark rose, and gave her a good stare... What was it that was particular about her?

Her eyes met his, unmoving, and he still didn't know.

She tapped the card between her fingers. "So you are Mark, I am Aimee, au revoir."

Au revoir, until we meet again. Mark turned the words over in his mind as he left. He couldn't get Aimee out of his mind. He didn't have another thought for Sam.

On his way home he wondered how Steff had ended up. He couldn't conceive her night had been as tempestuous as his; stormy Sam was one on her own. But he was sure she would tell him.

The next day at 'Tall Trees' Barbara asked if he'd enjoyed his night out, and for a moment Mark was stunned. How could she know where he'd been? Then he remembered where he was supposed to have been.

"You know, the usual thing," he said. "Fairly formal, nothing outrageous." God! If she only knew, he thought.

"How did it go here?" he asked.

She mocked him. "You know, the usual thing."

Mark had an uneasy feeling she'd found him out but he kept cool.

"Did you miss me?"

"I did, and I think you ought to make it up to me."

Mark breathed a little easier, she didn't know.

"Choose a date," he said. "I'll try and put things right."

Barbara was pacified, "Next Saturday," she said. "Tell *The Riverside* to be on their best behaviour."

Mark grinned. He'd certainly see to that.

He wondered if Carol would be the next to speak up, and she was.

Two days later she rang. "Since you did me out of the 'Tall Trees' Ball," she said, "You can make it up to me."

Almost Barbara's words, Mark thought. So now he had a date for the following Saturday as well.

Then Barbara and Carol vanished from his mind.

Aimee la Salle came on the line. She went straight to the point.

"I should like to have a look at 'Tall Trees'. If you are still willing could you pick me up at ten tomorrow morning?"

Mark was a little amused. It was more like an order than a request, and he decided to soften her up.

"You'll have to hang on to your hat," he said. "I drive a Lotus."

Surprisingly she said, "A red one, I hope."

"I'll do my best to oblige," Mark said.

"Excellent," she said. There was a click. She'd hung up.

Mark was puzzled at her abrupt manner.

"I'm going to unravel you, Aimee la Salle," he muttered.

The next morning he turned up at *Kinks Palace* only a few minutes after ten and she came out immediately reception buzzed her.

"Not bad," she said, glancing at her watch.

But Mark had eyes only for her. She was wearing a figure-hugging dress of dark velvet that emphasised her slim lines, and high heels that made her long legs even longer.

"Your chariot awaits," he said.

They marched up to the car and she said, "Red it is. You ARE obliging Mark."

She settled herself in the front seat with her long legs on full display and made no attempt to cover them.

Mark made no comment. He wasn't sure he was on her wavelength.

But he was sure the display was for his benefit, and he intended to give her his own display with the Lotus... See HER reaction.

He slipped in the gear and roared off.

Aimee leaned back in her seat, and Mark could have sworn there was a slight smile creeping across her face. This provoked him even more.

Once on the dual carriageway, he let the car rip and shot past everybody, edging dangerously close at times.

Aimee seemed unmoved, even to be enjoying herself, but at length she said, "Who are you trying to kill, Mark? You or me?"

He was annoyed but bit back a hasty reply.

He had been correctly reproved, but he wasn't going to lie down.

"Sorry if I frightened you," he said. "I thought you'd enjoy some real speed."

"With safety, yes," she said.

"The spark comes with the danger."

"In the right place, yes."

Mark was not used to people correcting him, and she'd just done it twice. But he had to stop speeding or look foolish, so he slowed.

"That suit you?" He tried to hide his ruffled feelings.

"No," she said. "But it will keep us alive."

Mark realised she was letting him down lightly, and suddenly he laughed. He knew he was in the wrong.

"You must forgive me," he said. "I got the bug."

"Bug?"

"Speed!" Mark said.

She was enigmatic. "Ah! Yes."

Mark drove in to 'Tall Trees' sedately, and Aimee was immediately impressed with the privacy and space, and more so when she saw the individual suites and realised the facilities available.

She picked up a brochure from reception and said, "I see you have horses available. My real outdoor love. Could I see them?"

"Of course," Mark said. "But I'll show you the villas first. Your original choice."

He introduced her to Barbara, and she toured round with them.

She could see immediately that Aimee was more than an ordinary enquiry, and thought she had the slightly superior air of the career woman: smart, severe, and aloof.

Not Mark's type at all, Barbara thought, and she was intrigued.

She kept her ears open, but learned nothing except Aimee obviously had some familiarity with Mark.

But where? How? She was puzzled.

She tried her luck, "You live in London?"

Aimee was amused. She was aware of Barbara's scrutiny. "I have a business there," she said, "I live over the shop."

Mark gulped. What a description for the luxury *Palace*.

He dragged Barbara off the subject. "When would be the earliest vacancy?"

"Not this year, I'm afraid," she said. "But, of course, if a cancellation came along we could ring the lady."

An obvious suggestion for Aimee's telephone number but she fielded the question expertly. She said to Mark. "You could let me know."

"Of course."

When they left her Barbara watched them out of sight. She felt vaguely disturbed by Aimee. She didn't fit into Mark's world so what was beneath that cold veneer?

She knew she'd remember her.

Mark drove up to Olivia's stables, and she came out as he blared his horn.

"Hallo, stranger," she said. Then she saw Aimee and raised her eyebrows.

Mark allowed Olivia to think she was a 'Tall Trees' guest. "This is Aimee," he said, "She wanted to see your stables."

"And have a ride, if possible," Aimee said.

Olivia said mischievously, "Your dress would jump up round your navel."

"I throw myself on your mercy," Aimee said. "A pair of slacks and a top?"

"Fine," Olivia said. "Have a look round. Then come up to the house."

She signalled to one of the stable girls to show them round, and Aimee was delighted when she saw there was a jumping course.

"I must have a go at that," she said.

She sauntered into Olivia's house, and Olivia watched through a partly closed door as she slipped off her clothes and changed into slacks and a top. Her lithe body excited her.

They rejoined Mark at the jumping course.

Olivia wasn't keen on Aimee jumping, and Aimee said to her boldly, "You let me pick my horse and I'll out-jump you, Olivia."

Olivia was proud of her prowess on a horse, and her vanity was pricked. "In your dreams," she replied.

She watched with interest as Aimee selected a horse. She had to admit she was a good judge, or else she was lucky. We'll soon find out, she thought grimly.

Olivia jumped first. A perfect round. Not a fence disturbed. "Follow that," she said to Aimee.

Aimee also cleared each fence, no problem, and Olivia was nettled. She wanted to come out top on her own ground.

She signalled to the girls to put the fences up. "We'll have another round," she said.

She waited, then jumped again and came back triumphant, another clear round.

She was cock-a-hoop now and smiled at Aimee "Your turn."

Aimee startled her. A clear round for her too. She said to Olivia, "Put the fences up, we'll have a jump off."

But Olivia declined, "Not fair on the horses," she said. She gave Aimee a good look. "You're a surprise packet. What do you do?"

Aimee gave her a good look then said calmly, "I sell sex."

Olivia's brows shot up, and Aimee said, "You heard of *The Kink's Palace*?"

Olivia shook her head.

"Perhaps it's just as well," Aimee smiled. "We have no rules, no limits."

Olivia's appetites were roused. "Give me the address."

"I think it would be too rich for your blood."

"You think so?" Olivia felt challenged. "Give me your card."

Immediately Aimee changed, she put her card in Olivia's hand and she glanced at it.

But she had one final question for Aimee. "How come you can jump horses?"

Aimee laughed. "I haven't been in business all my life. In my teens I did the jumping circuit."

"Well, at least that makes me feel a bit better," Olivia said.

There was a tap on Aimee's door, and to her surprise Mark entered her office.

He smiled, "Did you think you could get rid of me?"

"My best surprise today."

She got to her feet. "Let's go to my own quarters," and she took him to her penthouse at the back.

Mark said approvingly, "How the rich live."

"You should talk," Aimee said.

She gazed at him. "Let me guess. You want to arrange a party."

"Yes. But with only one person."

"You are making a big assumption, Mark."

"No risk, no gain," he said calmly.

Aimee was undecided about Mark. He was a powerful man, and likeable, and therefore good to have on her side... But what would he expect from her? She decided to play safe.

She got him a drink and sat beside him. "Well?"

"I'll be honest," Mark said. "I was impressed with your one-woman domination and I was hopeful we might get together."

"And see what drops out?"

"Something like that."

"You might not get what you want."

"Life is full of ups and downs," Mark said, "Do you want to give it a go?"

"Why not? But I warn you, I have to be very convinced before I think of sex. You can forget any ideas of a one-night stand."

"I didn't expect to get that lucky," Mark confessed, but he was a little surprised at Aimee's frank comment.

"Well, that's a good start," Aimee said, and leaned over and kissed him. Her lips were cool and she moved them over his until she had full contact, and Mark found it pleasingly sensuous.

"I'll take that as goodwill," he said, and made no attempt to respond. Aimee was a power, and he knew he'd have to battle to get what he wanted.

For her part, Aimee was satisfied Mark wasn't going to be bull at a gate. She intended to have him under the microscope before she committed herself.

They separated on those terms, with Mark expecting more than Aimee.

A few days later Aimee got another surprise. Olivia telephoned and asked if she could come up.

Aimee warned her what to expect but it didn't daunt Olivia. "I've been around, darling," she said.

But when she arrived at *Kink's Palace* she had to admit she was astonished. She hadn't expected such large scale opulence.

"I see why it's called a Palace," she said.

"You spend money you receive money," Aimee said.

Olivia and Aimee hit it off, and Olivia soon revealed her desire.

Aimee wondered if she would be dominant in bed. That she could fancy.

They stoked each other up, and when they reached the touching stage they went into the bedroom.

Olivia admired Aimee's lithe lines and firm breasts and clamped on them savagely. Aimee was hurt but couldn't draw back. There was a rush in her blood, and she opened her legs.

Olivia's hand came down and smacked into her cruelly, and she pushed her way in until she found the right spot.

Then she pounced with ferocity and guided Aimee.

Aimee nearly screamed, then she was lost. Her body heaved and she seemed to be pouring out torrents, but for once she was exhausted and satisfied.

She said to Olivia expressively, "You?"

"The same as you," she smiled, "But you didn't notice." She planted a kiss on Aimee. "You have a wonderful firm body, and legs that are a dream, they go on forever." She wagged a finger at her in mock protest. "You're not going to escape me now. If I have to I'll come up here on a horse and drag you out."

"What about Mark?" Aimee said sweetly.

"We're not that close."

"I meant me," Aimee said.

"Oh!" Olivia was startled. "Well he's a powerful man. Are you into him?"

"I haven't made my mind up," Aimee said. "He wants me."

"And you?"

"When I've decided my feelings will follow."

"That's a strange reply," Olivia said.

"Not for me."

Aimee wouldn't say any more but Olivia wasn't going to leave things there.

She was intense about Aimee and didn't want Mark interfering.

She reflected as she drove home. She might have to drop a few hints to him. Never mind how untrue. All's fair in love and war.

It was Saturday, and Mark had his date with Barbara at *The Riverside.*

He never tired of female company, he loved the challenge and the excitement, and Barbara always got him going quickly. She had a vivacious quality of innocence that always seemed fresh, and he wondered why he didn't see her more often.

But then what about Carol? Or Olivia? And what about Steff?

And could he add Aimee to the list?

He suddenly started thinking about them.

Carol was smart, sophisticated, not to be taken lightly, good in bed.

Olivia was a hard nut. Quite selfish really. Fierce in bed but often disappointing. Wanted her own way generally.

Steff was tops for glamour. Full of surprises and seemed to anticipate all his desires, especially in bed.

Aimee was the puzzle. Mark hadn't yet worked her out. She had an aura of powerful sex, and, although she was not so willing to yield, he sensed if the floodgates opened it would be unforgettable.

He was also aware of a mental equality in her that would have to be overcome... Or was cooperation possible? That might be exciting.

He asked himself a question.

Who would he choose long term?

Surprisingly, he concluded Carol, and he also surprised himself. Apart from the bed stakes, she could stand up for herself but she could also be charming. She was also adept at smoothing sharp corners.

Of course he'd known her longer. Perhaps took her for granted?

He was sure of one thing. He wasn't ready to settle down.

He laughed to himself and turned the question round. Would any of them fancy HIM long term.

With a start, he realised he hadn't been out with Barbara since the rape from that confounded Saunders boy, and he suddenly wondered if she would be different. He could hardly imagine a worse ordeal for a woman.

He was prepared to be surprised when they met and Barbara did surprise him.

"I've changed my mind," she said. "Not *The Riverside*, somewhere else."

Mark agreed without argument. He knew several more good places.

"Let's try *The Bluebell* on the Brighton Road," he suggested.

She touched his hand. "Great."

Mark wondered why she changed her mind. She must know he would keep his mouth shut, so people at *The Riverside* couldn't possibly know about her ordeal. Then he suddenly thought of the Saunders boy. That little bastard might have opened his mouth, even boasted.

The Bluebell was more merry than *The Riverside*, and, although the food and service was very good, Mark missed the attention he always got at *The Riverside*.

He studiously avoided talking about the rape, and Barbara never referred to it, but Mark got the impression she seemed uneasy, and he resolved to speak to her about it as soon as the opportunity came. He felt a responsibility apart from his concern, but he knew she would have to open the door.

Barbara accepted automatically that he would go back to her place afterwards, and when they were in her lounge drinking coffee she suddenly brought up the subject without warning.

Mark thought she must have been burning to unburden herself.

"I suppose you're wondering why I haven't mentioned the rape," she said.

"Not at all. You wouldn't want to talk about it."

"That's just it. I DO, although in a way I don't."

Mark looked at her. "I'm a good listener."

Barbara drew a small breath, "I've become a little more wary of men," she said. "I don't mean I've gone off sex but I've had a fright."

She opened her handbag. "I'm carrying this with me now." She put a small spray in his hand. "Am I over the top?"

Mark kept his face straight. "Good thinking, Barbara."

"Listen," he said. "If you don't fancy sex tonight I shan't be offended. I do have some understanding."

"I fancy it more than ever," she said. "Come on." And she led the way into her bedroom where they quickly undressed.

Mark was very gentle, and Barbara said at last, "Come on, Mark, don't be frightened."

Then she suddenly started crying with great big sobs that shook her body and she clung on to Mark as though he was her lifeline. She couldn't stop and seemed to go forever, and when it was all over they were both wet with her tears.

Mark said, "You needed that, darling. Pressure has to burst."

Barbara's tearstained face hit him hard and he kissed her, then soothed her. "Now you just go to sleep," he said. And she did.

He realised that he had put someone else first, an unusual experience for him. Perhaps I'm maturing, he thought cynically.

In the morning Barbara said, "You know, Mark, you surprised me last night. You've hidden depths."

"I am human," he protested, but in fact he was a bit embarrassed. He secretly thought he had been effeminate.

But Barbara felt a lot better for relieving her feelings. Mark had brought her back to the real world. I think if I loved somebody he would have to be like that, she thought.

Mark looked for something different when he picked up Carol the following Saturday, and this time it WAS The Riverside. Be nice to get back to normal, he thought. But his surprises weren't over.

Carol was at her best, witty, charming, and looking a million dollars, and Mark was eagerly anticipating events to come later.

But at the end of the meal, over coffee, she said, "Mark, I want to talk to you seriously."

"Sure," he said, "When we get back to your place."

"It has to be now," she said.

Mark was not perturbed, Carol liked a joke. "I'm listening," he said.

She paused for a second, put her elbows on the table and clasped her hands together.

Mark was amused at the pantomime. "You've got my attention, darling."

Carol wrinkled her lips a little, anxious to make a smooth start.

"Mark, we've known each other a fair time now but we don't get together as much as I would like."

"Well, let's see each other more often."

"What's wrong with seeing each other all the time?"

"Marriage is for older people."

"What about partners?"

Mark was startled. He didn't want ties, but he didn't want to lose Carol either. "Tell you what," he said, "We'll make a regular arrangement every week, more if you like."

Carol slowly shook her head. "I'm heading for thirty, Mark, I want to be more settled. Why not move in with me? Or me with you?"

Mark shook his head almost by instinct. "Wouldn't work, darling. I have so many people to meet you'd wonder where I was."

"You sure you can't do better than that?"

Mark sensed this was an ultimatum but he couldn't give up his freedom.

He tried to be jovial. "Come on, Carol, what about all the good times we've shared? And plenty more to come."

She nibbled her lip. "I've had an offer to move in with someone, Mark, but I would have preferred it was you."

Mark was a little petulant. He didn't like losing Carol.

"The so-called brother you introduced me to way back?"

Carol wasn't going to give way. "That's right," she said. "That equals your pretty business appointment."

Mark had one last chance to keep Carol, but he couldn't take it.

"All right," he said breezily, "One last night together?"

"Certainly not," she said tartly. "You know the old saying; you can't have your cake and eat it." And she swept out, leaving him sitting at the table.

Mark was particularly sorry about Carol; he'd regarded her as a fixture. Perhaps that was part of the trouble, he thought; still, she should have known better.

He consoled himself with the challenge of Aimee and got up from the table, thinking things could only improve. In fact Mark wasn't the only one exercising his mind about Aimee. Olivia was busy too, but in the opposite direction. She was desperate to stop Mark pursuing her.

It occurred to her that if SHE could give him what he wanted the problem might be solved, and she would also have the opportunity to sow a little poison.

She decided her own feelings would have to come second as far as he was concerned. But there was the problem of getting him up to her place. Things had gone cool between them.

After some consideration she rang him. "Hallo stranger," she said. "There's something I'd like to talk to you about." She added craftily, "It concerns Aimee."

She had Mark's attention at once. "Oh? What about."

"We need a chat," she said. "Could you pop up and see me?"

"I'm free tonight," Mark said.

"Lovely," she replied. "See you later."

He has the hots for Aimee all right, Olivia concluded. He can't wait to get his leg over.

She had already decided on her strategy and waited for Mark with mixed feelings.

He arrived about seven, and Olivia made sure she looked particularly attractive. Slinky dress, nice display of leg.

Mark was impressed, and Olivia could see it.

"Thought we'd make an evening of it," she said, taking his arm. "They say absence makes the heart grow fonder."

They sat in the lounge with a drink, and Mark raised his eyebrows. "What's this about Aimee?"

"I've got a plan to get her back into horses. She's too good to be wasted. I'd like her to ride for me on the jumping circuit."

"Where do I come in?"

Olivia chanced her arm. "Well, you're close to her. If you backed me up it would help a lot."

"Who said I was close to her?"

"Well I certainly got that impression when you brought her up here."

Mark was silent for a moment. "I certainly know her, and I think she's an interesting woman. But you're a bit off the mark there, Olivia."

You fucking liar, she thought; well, try this one, Mark.

"I have heard it said she's not particularly interested in men." She shrugged her shoulders. "Of course, I can't say for sure."

Mark was staggered. "That can't be true."

"Why not?"

"Well, she's so attractive."

Olivia scoffed. "Lesbians don't have to be ugly."

Mark was horrified. "Come off it, Olivia. That's a horrible thing to say. Have you ever seen Aimee with a woman?"

"I haven't. I'm just telling you what her club members say."

"So you've been up to her place," Mark accused.

Olivia silently cursed. She'd slipped up there.

"I tried to get her to change her mind about the horses," she lied.

Mark went quiet, and Olivia could see she'd shaken him. Time to move on before he undid the poison she'd put in.

She said brightly, "Another reason I wanted you here is to put you straight on my lovemaking."

Mark raised his eyebrows.

"I believe you think I like to dominate. Well, it's true I've played that part, but I mistakenly thought that was your preference. It is with a lot of powerful men," she said astutely. "Tell me if I'm wrong."

"You are."

"Well, welcome to the new Olivia," she said.

But Mark wasn't so easily persuaded. "What made you think you were mistaken?"

Olivia threw out her hands. "You stayed away."

Mark couldn't argue with that, and Olivia pressed her cause. "I'm offering you a night to make it up," she said.

Mark weakened, then grinned.

"Best offer I've had today."

Olivia knew she had to put on a command performance, and when they went to bed, she suggested Mark should undress her, something she had never done before.

"I am yours from the start," she said.

Mark did like undressing a woman. He felt it was like his own striptease, and he slipped off Olivia's dress with mounting desire.

She had of course carefully chosen her underwear, and Mark was fascinated with her see-through bra silhouetting her tremendous nipples. They always looked slightly swollen and sexy and as her bra fell they seemed to leap out like little mountains. He couldn't resist fingering them before his hands fell to the wispy froth round her thighs.

He stood back and looked at her. High heels, hold-up stockings, and nothing else. She had long slim legs and obligingly parted them. Mark glimpsed her outline and wondered if she had trimmed her hair.

His temperature was rising by the second, and Olivia, eager to please, swung away and walked a few steps to show Mark her tight, rounded bottom. She also played with her nipples. To her surprise she was enjoying her unusual role. She felt a power over Mark.

He now had his clothes off and she came back and pushed her bottom into him, and put his hands to her nipples. "Just feel them now," she whispered.

Mark dragged her on to the bed and cupped her breasts so the swollen tips stood out, then worked them round his mouth.

Olivia gave a little start, and immediately he ran his hand down her taut stomach to the tight hairs at the top of her legs.

She eased his fingers between her thighs and when she felt him stiff she stretched her legs and pulled him tight into her.

Mark tried to be steady but a furious energy drove him and he thrust madly, each stroke inflaming him more until he thought he would burst. Then he did, and he seemed to be shooting into Olivia like a waterfall.

He came to a gasping stop and hugged her tight. His heart was beating like a trip hammer.

He said at last, "I suppose I was selfish. Sorry, Olivia."

"Darling," she lied. "It was wonderful."

And she hoped it was worth it.

She certainly impressed Mark. He thought he'd had one of his hottest nights, and the sight of naked Olivia in stocking tops and heels lingered in his mind.

Unfortunately for Olivia, his pursuit of Aimee was undiminished. The sex in her case was distant and still beckoning. First she had to be conquered.

Mark reckoned Olivia's suggestion she might be a lesbian was founded on her stand-off attitude and he dismissed it.

Two nights later he was at Aimee's door again.

She smiled. "You won't give up then?"

"I wanted to invite you to a meal."

"Where?"

Mark suddenly had an inspiration. *The Phoenix*. He had tons of respect there, and they could clear out before the late cabaret and Steff appeared.

If she spotted Aimee she could be a business prospect.

"*The Phoenix* in the West End," he said.

"Oh yes, I know it," she said.

She looked him up and down. "But I haven't decided yet."

"Better than doing your knitting."

She had to laugh. "All right, Mark, you're on. Get yourself a drink while I change."

She came back, rather surprisingly wearing a close fitting trouser suit with velvet lapels over a heavily embroidered cream top that went high up her neck.

Not what Mark had expected, and he was quite taken aback, although he had to admit she looked sensational.

Her high cheekbones gave her a Russian look and her height emphasised her long slim legs.

Mark had the feeling she'd deliberately dressed to intrigue him, and he was right, but her main reason was to emphasise that she made her own rules.

"Rather startling," he said. And he wondered if there might be any difficulty in getting into *The Phoenix*. Some of the top clubs were particular about dress.

"I like it," she said.

Mark wondered what would happen to a doorman who tried to bar Aimee la Salle but he held his peace.

Fortunately, they sailed into *The Phoenix* without any bother, and Aimee soon had people running around. She wanted this, she wanted that. And she chose, chose isn't the word; she DEMANDED a table facing the cabaret stage. People already occupying it were told, unfortunately, it had been reserved.

Mark was bothered by her attitude and was wondering when somebody would object. But nobody raised a finger.

He took her on the dance floor, and she moved expertly and teased him with the occasional touch. In her heels her eyes were nearly level with his, and he could have sworn as he looked into them she was mocking him.

He suddenly felt annoyed. She'd behaved like a bitch. Time to speak up.

"Why are you set on annoying everyone?" he said.

"Not everyone... You!"

"Perhaps you will explain."

"I wondered how much you would stand."

"Fuck you!" Mark said. "Behave or we leave."

"Reckon I'll have to behave," she said, and her eyes flashed with devilment.

Mark took her back to their table to order a meal. "No more tricks," he said.

But she wasn't finished. She wanted some sea food the chef didn't have and demanded to see the manager.

They waited, and at length Maurice turned up.

Mark's face was grim. Christ! Now there'll be a row, he thought.

But his evening of surprises continued.

Maurice smiled. "Hallo, Aimee," he said, "What brings you on to my territory?"

Aimee started laughing. "I've been putting my friend through the wringer."

"What, Mark?" he said.

The surprise on Aimee's face was almost comical, and she turned on Mark. "So you know Maurice. The joke's on me. You must have had a good laugh."

"If that's your name for embarrassment," he said. "I was unaware you knew Maurice."

"Huh!" she said. "I'm not so sure."

Maurice sat down with them. "This is an unholy trinity, isn't it?" he said.

"*The Palace, The Phoenix*, and 'Tall Trees'."

He was semi-serious. "You'd think between us we could drum up a lot of trade."

Mark's eyebrows shot up.

Aimee said, "I think Maurice means trade outside the law."

"Outside the law?"

"You know as well as I do rich people want kinky sex. It comes expensive."

"Yes," Mark said curtly, "Particularly with blackmail on top."

"The risk they take," Maurice said. "There are always people to screw others. Human nature."

"Blackmail's nasty," Mark said bluntly.

"Some pay up. Some face up. Why should we care?" Maurice said. "We aren't responsible for what others do." He told the lie with a straight, serious face.

Aimee knew otherwise and also knew she had to keep silent.

But she thought if Maurice was trying to drag Mark into his net he was making a big mistake.

In fact Maurice was only fishing for Mark's reaction. He suspected the same as Aimee that Mark wouldn't want to dirty his hands, and he wasn't surprised at his final comment.

"Blackmailers should be put against a wall," Mark said. "In fact, shooting's too good for them."

Aimee looked at Maurice, "Now you know," she said.

Mark was a bit surprised at her remark, but, before he could pursue it, Steff put in an appearance.

"Hallo, Aimee. What you doing here?"

Aimee indicated Mark. "He brought me."

Steff gave him a stare then looked at Aimee. "How's trade?" she joked.

"You know," Aimee said. "Up and down."

They both laughed, and Steff sat with them for a while, but when she got up to go Aimee said to her quietly, "Give me a bell soon, will you?"

"Will do," Steff said.

Mark took Aimee back to her penthouse, and they chatted over coffee but she didn't allow even a suggestion of sex to arise and ignored Mark's hints. He finally left for home frustrated, without even a kiss.

'What the fuck is she up to?' he thought.

He didn't realise that was exactly what she wanted him to think.

Steff couldn't wait to find out Aimee's interest in Mark, she was still interested herself and, as requested, she rang Aimee the next day.

"This is Steff. You wanted to speak to me."
"I want to know about Mark."
"Interested?"
"Curious," Aimee said.
"Oh yeah!"
"Come on, what do you know?"

Steff thought for a moment. "Well you know he's wealthy, and he's generous, but I think he's deeper than he seems. I think he could be tough."

"Could you fancy him long term?"

Steff was guarded, she didn't want to give too much away and tried to sound casual. "Well, who wouldn't? Where there's wealth there's competition."

Aimee sensed Steff was protecting her interests, and tried to sound offhand herself.

"Guess you're right, Steff. We met on business. I don't actually know him."

Steff's mind immediately told her... Liar!

"I wouldn't like to cross him," she said... And she thought, swallow that, Aimee!

Aimee was thoughtful after their conversation. She still couldn't make up her mind about Mark.

She was always keen to have wealthy friends, but she was very careful when it came to a relationship. She found it easier with a woman where there were fewer consequences, but there was no denying Mark would be a powerful friend. On the other hand, he could also be a powerful enemy.

Slow and easy, she decided. Sex could wait.

Mark's thoughts about his love life came to a jarring halt as out of the blue he got an enormous shock. In fact a full blown crisis.

His mother Helen announced she was going to retire with a very generous pension and that she was splitting her shares between Mark and sister Janet fifty – fifty, so they each had equal voting rights.

"There's likely to be a clash," Mark complained.

"That's exactly the point," she replied. "You'll have to work it out. No bulldozing one over the other."

This seriously disturbed all Mark's plans. He often didn't see eye to eye with Janet, and while she had religiously stuck to her own duties when her mother held the balance of power, he knew it would be a different proposition when they were on equal terms.

Janet could be very determined. Mark knew there were stormy waters ahead, and he tried to think of ways to protect himself.

Thank goodness, at least she would have no power to push a project through or dismantle one without his agreement.

But fifty - fifty worked each way. He couldn't compel her either.

There would certainly be a stand-off regarding Mark's pet project, the money-making villas.

Janet didn't approve and considered the villas were a business distinct from hotels and should be sold off to become a separate company, although she would have no objection to holding shares.

Mark thought her attitude was that of an imbecile. To lose control of this huge money-making machine and the prestige that went with it he regarded as criminal, and the very thought made him furious.

The villas were already better known than 'Tall Trees' itself, and this was something else Janet disliked.

As a counter Mark knew there was one project she WAS keen on developing: Olivia's stables and horses. She reckoned they were exactly the 'Tall Trees' style, particularly when hosted by a titled lady, and she would happily pour money in to further this ambition.

At the moment Mark couldn't see how this would help him, but he knew it could be a bargaining factor if it came to head-to-head conflict.

There was one other possibility that might help him, but it was even more distant.

Janet cherished the idea of marrying her long term fiancé Cliff and bringing him into the business. Mark had always opposed this strongly.

But the changed circumstances of equality between them completely altered his thinking. He could consider relaxing his opposition on condition that any shares allocated to Cliff came from Janet. This would, of course, give Mark superior voting power over her, although not over their combined vote.

But men were human and open to change. You never could tell what might happen. Persuasion or dirty tricks might work on Cliff.

Mark was full of doubts and possibilities and he wasn't a happy man.

As he anticipated, Janet called a meeting in her office and made it plain that her new powers would be exercised.

"No more of you shooting off and doing a deal and telling us when it's done," she said to Mark. "Mother's era is over."

Mark took the opportunity to sound her out about Olivia.

"I suppose," he said, "You'll be thinking about putting more money into Olivia's stables."

"It's a logical step isn't it?" she replied. "As one of our facilities it gives a top class impression." She repeated what was in their brochure, "Stables under the exclusive management of Lady Olivia Lithgow."

"Yeah! It sounds good," Mark said, "But there are other things we can think about now we have a free hand. What about our own helicopter pad? Make things a lot easier for the celebs, and in particular the villa clients."

Janet pursed her lips. "The helicopter pad is a good idea but I don't think we should slant our policy towards the villas. By definition they are not hotels and will be catering for a smaller number of clients."

"But producing a great deal more money per head."

"I can't argue with that, but the two don't mix."

She pointed out triumphantly, "You have to have a separate manager."

Mark opened his mouth to reply, but Janet rushed on, "The ideal arrangement would be for a separate company to run the villas. We could hold shares but be able to deny or confirm any publicity that might link us."

Mark wasn't surprised at Janet's words. Her attitude hadn't changed.

He decided to test her reaction regarding Cliff. He let the conversation drift then said casually. "I suppose you've dropped the idea of bringing Cliff into the business?"

He knew perfectly well this was Janet's strongest wish and that she would marry straight away if it could be arranged.

"I think we've been over that a few times already, haven't we?" she said tartly. "You know perfectly well Cliff would be willing."

Mark said as though he was chewing the matter over, "Just a thought. Things are different now. He could fill the hole Mother left, and we could rearrange our duties."

Janet was immediately suspicious. She knew Mark's repeated hostility and his oft-repeated words 'The business is for the Family.'

"So you've suddenly changed your mind?" she asked sarcastically.

"No, I haven't. But the landscape has changed. I was thinking we're going to be pretty tied down, just the two of us."

This was something Janet could understand. She knew how Mark loved a free hand floating off all over the place. But she was still suspicious.

"Are you being serious?"

"I could be. Of course you'd have to give him some of your shares. I'M not marrying him."

The light dawned in Janet's eyes. "So that's it," she said scornfully, "so you can outvote me."

Mark said semi-humorously, "Well yes, if you think Cliff would vote with me and against you."

Janet put her lips together and pondered as new hope sprang into her mind. "I'll certainly think about it," she said.

Strangely enough, she had the same thought as Mark but in the opposite direction. Cliff and Mark knew each other and had always got along well. It was possible Cliff might put some pressure on Mark to support HER. But Janet never rushed into a big decision. She would turn it over in her mind until she felt sure.

Mark was happy to end the meeting on that topic and was satisfied to let the idea stew in Janet's mind.

He wouldn't mention it again; he knew that sooner or later she would return to it.

Then she would have to seek his approval, and when that happened he was going to drive a hard bargain to make sure she kept off his territory. He had every intention of getting back more than he gave.

He was confident they would develop the helicopter pad but he wasn't sure yet what he wanted from Olivia. When he had decided he would dress up a good story for Janet that would further enhance his bargaining position.

While she was still in his mind, she telephoned him.

"Come up for the evening, Mark," she urged. "Last time was so good. And I'd like your advice about something."

I bet it's money, Mark thought. Olivia had never mastered the art of living within her means. Still, last time was good and he was at the moment in gloom. She'd rung at the right psychological moment.

"Fine, Olivia," he said, "See you later."

He arrived around seven. Olivia looked very glamorous and while they ate she kept him entertained with small talk about the aristocracy and her horses.

Then they retired to the lounge for coffee, and Mark thought, now for the serious business.

She moved close to him on the settee.

"Let's relax," she said. "The whole night is ahead."

Mark ran his hand under her dress to her stocking top. Then her hand came down on his. "Later, darling. Something I must ask you first."

Here it comes, Mark thought.

"It's about the mortgage on my property. I've received threatening letters from the company," she said in an aggrieved tone.

"The reason being?"

"Because I've missed a few payments."

"A few?"

"It doesn't matter," she said defiantly. "Surely they must know who I am and they'll get their money eventually."

"Eventually is not good enough on a mortgage," Mark said, "You have to keep to your agreement or forfeit the property. It's a lawful contract."

He patted her hand. "If you recall, I told you this at the beginning."

"So what can I do?"

"Did you reply to their letters?"

"No. I thought they'd wait until I got the money."

"Well, I'll tell you what to do. Write to them. Tell them you're sorry you've had a financial setback but you will start the monthly payments again, plus an amount off the arrears." He concluded, "I assure you they will listen."

"But I still don't have the money," wailed Olivia.

She started a little sob.

Mark's long-term plan with Olivia's mortgage was at last working out, and inwardly he was jubilant. At last, something was going his way.

His face went thoughtful. "Tell you what, Olivia," he volunteered. "Suppose 'Tall Trees' bought out your property from the Company? Then you would work for me, but only we would know. The sign at your entrance would still be the same. Lady Olivia Lithgow's stables. Just remember," he coaxed, "If you agree, 'Tall Trees' would have to foot all the expenses, including taxes. You'd be home free."

"But I wouldn't own my own stables." Olivia was genuinely near tears.

Mark said brutally, "If I don't step in you will have no stables and be pitched out of the property. I'm offering you a way to keep control and be free of expenses."

He added quickly before Olivia could reply, "I'm not saying my Board will agree to my proposal but I think I can swing it."

He stared at her. "Up to you, Olivia. Do you want me to try or are you going to wait for the chopper?"

Olivia's face was grim. She was in a corner but she had no option. At last she whispered, "All right, Mark, but I don't want my friends to know. I'll have to trust you."

"No worry," Mark said. "Now let's make love."

Olivia had received a big shock, and realised she needed Mark more than ever.

"Do you want a show first?" she whispered. "Like last time."

"You're reading my mind," Mark confessed, and followed her into the bedroom.

Despite her frame of mind, Olivia rallied and when she stood before Mark again in stocking tops and heels she was more daring, and swayed and spun with legs apart and even held her own breasts so the nipples looked like angry red peaks.

Mark's desire went skywards. He pulled off his clothes and took her where she stood, and she immediately felt him between her thighs, with his hands clawing at her buttocks. Then his mouth clamped her hard, and her arms went round his neck.

She had never known Mark so dominant, and his fierce movement rocked her to and fro until his final strokes, when a deluge hit her.

Olivia enjoyed the sensation without satisfaction, it was all too quick. But at least Mark was happy.

"Christ, Olivia!" he exclaimed. "I don't know what you're doing to me. I was finished before I started."

"My fatal charm," she suggested.

It wasn't until Mark had left in the morning that Olivia remembered she'd forgotten to ask him about Aimee.

Ah well! she thought philosophically. There's always another day. At the moment her mind was burdened with Mark keeping his mouth shut.

She hoped she could trust him.

Mark approached Janet and asked her what would be her reaction if he could buy Olivia's stables and control all future development.

She said suspiciously, "With her still in charge?"

"Of course," Mark said. "The lady is all important."

"Come off it, Mark. She won't sell."

"I can push a deal through if you want it."

"How come?"

Mark tapped his nose. "I'm not telling you all my secrets." He gave her a long look. "You owe me one, right?"

Janet said stiffly, "If it comes off, yes."

Mark set the wheels in motion, and the deal was agreed.

Then he saw Olivia. "I've got board approval," he said. "Say hallo to your new boss."

"You WILL keep mum?"

"My lips are sealed."

She gave him a kiss. "Hallo, boss," she said. "Welcome to Lady Olivia's stables."

With Olivia in his pockets Mark's thoughts went back to Aimee.

Her coolness nettled him; he reckoned they were made for each other. Similar in outlook and mentality, he reckoned sex between them would be a dream.

More annoyingly, he felt Aimee understood this. So why was she so obstructive?

He was impatient to contact her again but he needed a good excuse in case she thought he was chasing her. Then she would have all the cards, and Mark had no intention of being whipped around at her whim.

He wanted an approach of equals.

Then he remembered Steff took him to *Kink's Palace* where he first met Aimee, and it occurred to him he could use her again.

He turned up at *The Phoenix* in the evening, with the express purpose of tackling her, but immediately bumped into Maurice, who was always pleased to see Mark.

He said breezily, "Steff wants to see you." He lifted his brows in a smile. "If you've the time?"

Mark slid open the door of her dressing room silently. She was sitting at a mirror with her back to him, and he moved quickly and put his hands across her eyes. "Guess who."

She drew his hands down. "The King of Siam, or is it Mark?"

She spun round. "I suppose Maurice told you. I've another invitation to *Kink's Palace*, but I need a friend."

Mark could hardly believe his luck. Then his scheming mind suggested Aimee had engineered the invitation, expecting Steff to bring him again. Not an unpleasant thought.

"So you thought of me?"

"As a matter of fact, Aimee did."

"Oh?"

"Yes. She said, why don't you bring Mark again. I'm sure Sam Steel would be pleased."

Mark had no doubt it would be Aimee he would see if he went, not Sam Steel, but he decided not to seem too eager. Two can play the devious game.

"When is it?"

"Next Saturday."

"Rather short notice."

"Don't you want to come?"

"Well, I must confess I wouldn't want to miss Sam Steel if YOU don't object."

Steff smiled. "It's not a lovers' conference." She pulled her lip, "Just all the sex you can manage."

"You keen?" Mark asked.

"Of course. Free sex, no comebacks."

She said firmly, "A little adventure is good for you, Mark... You're coming."

So that was that, and Mark was happy his meeting with Aimee had been engineered so easily and when Saturday came, Steff entered *Kink's Palace* on Mark's arm.

They'd hardly been there a few minutes before Aimee appeared, looking dominant as usual. She still held that suggestion of powerful sex and Mark guessed she could have nothing on beneath the figure-hugging sheath just clinging to the top of her breasts.

She gave him a smiling invitation. "Sorry to disappoint you. Sam's not here tonight."

"But YOU are." Mark kept his face straight.

"I'm not part of the merchandise."

"It isn't possible to be that stupid," Mark said. "But are you available to talk business?"

A daring idea had just shot into his mind.

Her brows shot up. "Business?"

Aimee glanced at Steff. "You know about this?"

She shook her head.

"Nobody knows," Mark said. "Because it's only in my head at this moment."

"I'll give you half an hour," Aimee said, and strode off to her office, Mark following. She was prepared to be annoyed if this was a clumsy ruse from Mark to get his leg over.

She plonked in her chair and faced him.

"The floor is yours, Mark," she said imperiously.

For a moment he was quiet then he said, "You're vexed."

"Possibly."

Mark smiled. "You're on the wrong track. I want to talk about money, lots of it."

"Oh?"

"You are, of course, aware that I am surrounded by millionaires every day down at 'Tall Trees'. And with the addition of the villas, this is multiplied over and over."

"So?"

"Rich people like to indulge their fantasies. That's why *Kink's Palace* is a big success. I want a *Kink's Palace* near 'Tall Trees'. Under a more discreet name, of course, but the same thing."

Mark paused and gave her a hard stare. "I shall need tutoring, or a partner."

Aimee sat with her hand clasped against her jaw and her eyebrows high. "You are serious?"

"Deadly. There's millions to be picked up."

She rose from her chair and took Mark's hand. "Shake, partner" Then she half-pulled him from his chair, leaned tight, and kissed him.

Mark felt her lithe body hard against his and longed to wrap his arms round her naked flesh and press her firm buttocks, but he had to be content with the firm imprint of her lips. No tongue, no emotion, but none the less, sensual.

He tried to go further but Aimee drew back. "Pleasure comes later," she said.

She began to see why Mark was wealthy and was admiring him more by the minute.

"Have you a place in mind?" she asked.

"I have. Within ten miles. A quarter of an hour's drive. An old mansion standing in big grounds and deserted. We can convert it in months." His mouth curved in a smile. "It's surprising what money can do."

"I'll match you pound for pound."

"Brilliant. And how's this for a name? *Fantasy Palace*, a select new members club."

"Sounds good, Mark. But have you thought about the difficult part. Who's to run it?"

Mark gave a broad smile. "I have. But she doesn't know it yet."

"Spit it out."

"Steff."

"Jesus! Absolutely brilliant." Aimee reached for Mark's hand and pressed it against her breast. "Feel my beating heart. It's going mad."

"It would feel better against the skin," he said.

She loosened her top and Mark had his wish to touch her naked flesh.

He was not surprised there was no bra and he was impressed with the delightfully small droop to her firm shape.

The beating of her heart was far from his calculations, and he trapped her nipple between his fingers and closed them, but her hand came down on his. "Not in the contract, Mark," she said. "Yet."

She held his gaze. "When are you going to ask Steff?"

"Tonight."

Aimee pressed a buzzer on her desk, and a girl appeared. "Find Steff," she said. "And bring her here."

"But..." the girl protested.

"Tough!" Aimee said. "Someone will have to be disappointed."

It was at least ten minutes before a flushed looking Steff appeared. "This had better be good," she said.

Aimee said callously, "Male or female?"

Steff tossed her head. "Who I fuck is my concern."

Mark grinned, "Take a seat. You're going to get a shock."

Steff crossed her legs defiantly. She was simmering.

Then Mark explained the whole proposition.

"Just think, Steff," he finished, "More money, security, your own boss and a free penthouse thrown in."

"Plus," Aimee put in, "all the perks you can pick up. Millionaires can be very generous."

Steff's annoyance vanished. "I certainly go for the idea," she said.

"But what about Maurice?"

"Leave him to me," Mark said. "He'll have two or three months to find a new star... So are you in, Steff?"

"I will say yes for the moment but will you give me a few days to think about it? It's a big step."

Mark told a small lie. "Just what we expected," he said.

He and Steff left together, and Mark pointed out she would see a lot more of him if she took the new job. But he needn't have bothered. Steff had already taken that into account.

Her worry was Maurice. They were close, and he could be very nasty.

Maurice wasn't pleased when he was told, but, as it was Mark doing the asking, he pretended to be generous.

"You're the only one who could take Steff away from me," he said. Jokingly he added, "I won't kill you this time."

He said to Steff later, "London's only half an hour away. You can always reach me."

And she thought, yes, and you can reach me too. She knew too much about Maurice to get the wrong side of him and she was relieved that she could leave amicably.

So it was finally settled, and the trio of Aimee, Steff and Mark put their heads together to plan the new Palace.

After the initial solicitor's work and obtaining the building and arranging the conversion, Mark gave what time he could to the project, but the rest of the development was mostly left to Aimee, with constant help from Steff.

With his mother now retired, Mark had his hands full with 'Tall Trees' business, and fencing with Janet had become a regular routine. She seemed to delight in opposing him, and Mark reckoned she was making up for previous years when her parents ruled and she'd had to bite her tongue.

She was frequently chasing him on the subject of Olivia's stables. She was impatient for enlargement, and also to enlarge the 'Tall Trees' brochure, but, strangely enough, she never went near the stables. She didn't like horses personally, her concern was prestige, and Mark was relieved and able to satisfy her questions easily.

Janet didn't mention the subject dear to her heart, bringing Cliff into the business, and day after day Mark got more impatient, and wondered if she was deliberately frustrating him. But at last she broke her silence.

"I've been thinking about bringing Cliff in," she said.

"Taken you long enough!" Mark snapped. Janet had been getting on his nerves all day.

She was riled but persisted. "I certainly think it will give us some relief," she said, "but I'm not happy at giving up my shares."

"Then you'd better forget it!" Mark said brutally, and went to rise from his chair.

Janet stopped him. "I've another idea."

He paused and sat still.

"What's wrong with bringing him in without a shareholding?"

"Don't be ridiculous. How could he be a director without holding shares?" Mark was annoyed.

"He could be an employee with management status," she said.

"Wouldn't work," Mark growled. "He would still expect the privileges of a director, and the other staff would be resentful. And if he didn't have those privileges the other staff would wonder why. It's a recipe for trouble."

He got up from his seat. "Let's forget it."

But Janet again restrained him. "All right," she said, "We'll do it your way. But don't imagine," and she waved an accusing finger at him, "it will give you an advantage in voting. Cliff will never vote against me."

"It never occurred to me," Mark lied.

So Cliff came into the company and Mark made it his business to be very friendly and welcomed him warmly. He was well aware the goodwill might pay dividends later.

He also kept closer to Olivia, she was delighted that Mark in no way exercised his ownership rights, and they discussed the improvements in her complex amicably. She was not slow to show her gratitude.

As always, Mark had an ulterior motive, and when the *Fantasy Palace* was near to opening he suggested that some of her friends might care to know that a restricted membership club was opening locally that would satisfy all their fantasies... Both sexes, or no sex.

At the same time Aimee had suitable entries made in particular magazines, and sent down a few of her girls to assist Steff.

Steff also recruited some theatricals waiting for work, so that when the club was ready to open they got a kick-start.

Naturally 'Tall Trees' could not be associated with the enterprise but Mark made sure the news reached his clients by the simple expedient of telling his staff. He knew they wouldn't be able to keep the news to themselves.

Aimee had thoughtfully mentioned the new club to some of her regulars in London, and curiosity brought some of them down for the opening but she needn't have bothered. Members poured in, and Mark said cynically to Steff, "We should have called the place 'Millionaires Paradise'."

Mark, Aimee, and Steff were all smiling.

Steff settled in immediately and she felt like a queen parading before her subjects. But, like women before her, Mark was her first choice. She admired his power and the way he got things done; and he wasn't so bad in bed either. She hoped he was going to be a frequent visitor to her penthouse.

Olivia was no fool and she wondered why Mark should want her to spread the news about the *Fantasy Palace*. He was a devious bastard.

He'd given her a card, and she looked at it. It simply read *Fantasy Palace* with the number. But you couldn't call it plain. It was gold edged.

She dialled the number and a female voice said "Reception, can I help you?"

For a moment Olivia floundered. She hadn't known what to expect. Then her composure came back and she said in her accustomed drawl, "Can I speak to the owner?"

"You wish to become a member, madam?"

"Perhaps. Get me the owner!" Olivia snapped.

"Just a moment, madam."

Then a new voice came on the line, almost as haughty as Olivia's.

"Who am I speaking to?"

Olivia started to laugh. She recognised the voice. "Belt up, Steff," she said, "This is Olivia. LADY Olivia. Does Maurice know you're out?"

"That's past history, Olivia."

"So you've got yourself a new brothel. Trust Maurice to soak the rich."

"Not Maurice. Private backer."

"Who then? Come on, Steff. spit it out. I'll find out."

"You won't, and it's more than my job's worth."

"Don't piss me around, Steff. It IS Maurice isn't it?"

Steff raised her voice, "If I were you I wouldn't let Maurice hear you say that. I tell you loud and clear, Olivia, its fuck all to do with Maurice." Then she said sweetly, "Do you wish to become a member?"

"I'll turn up one day, don't you fear," Olivia said.

She didn't believe Steff. She thought *Fantasy Palace* was exactly Maurice's handwriting, bringing a bit of the dirty West End to the stockbroker area, and she determined to make sure.

The fact that Steff had moved from *The Phoenix* made it a certainty in her mind. Maurice would never let Steff go. And if he WAS operating so close to her she wanted to know. He could be dangerous, but there could also be perks.

It never occurred to her that Mark might be involved.

Her next step was to ring Aimee. She reasoned there had to be a tie up, another Palace was no accident. But she wasn't going to ask her straight out about Maurice. It seemed he wanted privacy so she'd carefully work her way round.

"Hallo, lover," she said. "Olivia here. Fancy another night?"

Aimee couldn't resist. Olivia was rough but madly exciting. Definitely her number one.

"You're on," she said.

Then Olivia had an idea. "You wouldn't fancy coming down here?" she asked. "I'll give you another jump-off."

That did the trick for Aimee. Her love for horses had been regenerated.

"Name the day, darling," she said.

"Tomorrow?"

"Can't do."

"The next day?"

"Perfect."

Olivia was pleased with herself. She'd take Aimee to *Fantasy Palace*. Somebody could easily let something slip.

Aimee turned up at the stables the following morning with a small suitcase.

Olivia had to ask. "What's in the case?"

"My battle gear."

Olivia laughed. "It won't help you. I'm having some real big jumps this time. But I'll let you choose from my best two horses."

Aimee rose to the challenge. "What are you prepared to gamble?"

Olivia thought for a moment. "The winner gets an option. The loser has to accept."

"That could be anything."

"Got the wind up?"

"OK," Aimee agreed. "But suicide's out."

They had a leisurely meal, then Aimee changed and came out for the fray in smart jodhpurs and boots with a red cap.

Olivia stared. "This isn't the Hickstead derby."

"It's my Hickstead. I'm going to show you how it's done."

"Just wait," Olivia said, and off she went and returned in her own jodhpurs and boots with a black cap.

"We start even," she said.

A stable girl brought two horses forward, and Olivia said to Aimee, "Your choice."

She selected her horse and mounted, and Olivia climbed on to the other one.

"Three rounds, smallest number of total faults wins," Olivia said. "You can go first."

"Oh no!" Aimee said. "We toss." She called to the stable girl.

"Toss a coin, will you?"

The girl fished out a coin and flicked it in the air.

Aimee called tails.

"Tails it is," the girl said.

Olivia reined her horse back but Aimee said, "No Olivia. You first. I get the choice."

Olivia set off and clattered the first fence, but it didn't fall, and she went clear.

Then Aimee went round and was also faultless.

Olivia had the fences raised for the second round. She had the first one down, four faults.

Aimee went clear to the last fence but tapped it, four faults.

Last round, and they were level. Olivia touched two fences but nothing fell, clear round.

Aimee had a clear round to the last fence but tapped it once more and over it went, four faults.

Victory to Olivia. She was all smiles.

Aimee didn't like being beaten but forced herself to be gracious. "Good jumping, Olivia," she said. But she couldn't stop herself from saying, "I'll beat you next time."

Olivia was generous; it was easy when she'd won. "I'll tell you something, Aimee," she said. "You did wonders. You picked the wrong horse. Mine is our number one jumper."

Aimee's wounded pride was slightly relieved, and she managed a smile. "You've won. What's your option?"

"Can you stay overnight?"

"I can if I make a phone call."

"Fine. You'll find out tonight."

Olivia touched her heels to her horse. "Let's go riding."

She intended to keep Aimee guessing, and surprise Steff, and as they rode through the countryside she kept her mouth buttoned despite Aimee's promptings.

But Aimee guessed they would be going to *Fantasy Palace* and later rang Steff on her mobile to warn her.

It was after nine when they arrived at the Palace, and Olivia said, "What do you think of that?"

"Looks like another *Kink's Palace*."

"Let's see inside."

They entered reception, and in a minute Steff appeared. She'd been waiting for them.

"So you couldn't stay away, Olivia," she said.

"I wanted to show Aimee."

Steff nearly grinned. "I'll show you round."

The tour quite overwhelmed Olivia and she agreed it rivalled *Kink's Palace*. She was particularly impressed with Steff's penthouse, where they finished up.

"Think you'll get used to the luxury?" she joked.

"I'll give it a go," Steff responded, and poured some drinks.

Then she gave Olivia a long look.

"What do you think, Olivia?" she asked. "Does it stir your juices?"

"I'd like to come every night."
"Seriously, would you like to be a member?" Aimee cut in.
"How much?"
"Ten thou for membership. For you... nothing."
"How can you say that?"
"Can't you guess?"
Olivia's eyes rounded. "Are you saying what I think you are?"
"You are looking at the owner."
"You bitch, Aimee, stringing me along."
She laughed. "You shouldn't beat me up with the horses."
"And where does Maurice come in?" Olivia was a little short.
"Nowhere."
"Listen Aimee, I'm no fool," Olivia snapped. "And I know Maurice. He wouldn't let Steff go unless he's involved."
Steff interrupted, "He WAS a problem but I agreed to stay with him until he got someone else in my place."
She gave a small laugh.
"Fortunately we solved the problem."
He's now got Holly Spring, a young coloured girl, who doesn't much like wearing clothes and with good reason. She's as good to look at as to listen, but the main thing is, she's taken a shine to Maurice and he isn't resisting."

She said sarcastically "I think he fancies her huge dark nipples."

Then she pointed to a big glass cabinet on the wall. "I also had to promise to advertise *The Phoenix*."
The placard inside the cabinet read:
'Whilst in the West End we recommend you
visit *The Phoenix* starring Holly Spring. If
you're thinking of sex you're thinking of her.'

A daring picture of Holly followed, featuring her enormous nipples.

Olivia said stubbornly, "Fair enough but I still don't believe you set this up entirely on your own, Aimee. Too big a risk. There's someone else's brain and money in this."

Aimee told a neat little lie to keep Olivia quiet. "You're on the ball, Olivia," she said. "I have a sleeping partner. One of my London guests, a banker, too respectable to have his name linked."

"But not too respectable to collect the profits."

"The way of the world, darling," Aimee said.

Then she took the lead.

She stood up abruptly and said, "Come on, Olivia. You've satisfied your curiosity. Let's leave Steff to attend to her clients," and without further ado she ushered her outside. Olivia barely had time to brush her lips over Steff's cheek in a quick goodbye.

When they were motoring back she said, "You were in a hurry to get out, Aimee. Why the big rush? I wanted to ask a few more questions."

"You should have said," Aimee replied. But of course that was exactly why she pushed her out. The last thing she wanted was Olivia grilling Steff.

She gave her a provocative smile."There's a lot of the night left, darling."

That was enough for Olivia. Another session with Aimee was just what she fancied, and quite unconsciously her foot went down harder on the accelerator.

Later, when they were in bed naked, Aimee's slim body and narrow hips excited Olivia all over again. She reckoned Aimee had the figure of a model, and when she teasingly parted her long legs Olivia got a big rush, and put her mouth straight between them.

Aimee closed her thighs on Olivia's head, and the insanely sensuous pleasure nearly drove her mad.

But of course, Olivia had to be violent, and she forced her hands under Aimee's buttocks and squeezed them so hard Aimee shouted.

That stopped Olivia, and she ran her hands up Aimee's body in strong pinching movements, until she reached her breasts. Then her mouth took over and came down hard whilst at the same time her hand went low and her violent fingers mercilessly turned Aimee inside out.

Aimee went wild with excitement and was ready to explode, and when Olivia's teeth went into her nipple the floods broke, and she felt she was pouring out Niagara. But she had a wild impetus and pulled and jerked Olivia until she had no more strength.

The relief was an exquisite agony.

She whispered to Olivia breathlessly, "Did you get off?"

"You kidding?" she said. "You nearly took the skin off me."

Aimee showed her sore nipple. "You nearly bit it off," she said.

They looked at each other and laughed. Then Olivia pulled Aimee against her roughly. "Now we can rest," she said. "Don't wake up too soon. I might be playing with your wonderful body."

"You like it?"

"You could be a model."

And on that pleasing note Aimee closed her eyes, whilst, true to her words, Olivia continued to stroke Aimee, but for once gently, until she at last closed her eyes as well.

Olivia was fired afresh with Aimee and she now had the excuse of the horses to link her closer.

In the morning she said, "I want to see you at the stables regularly, Aimee. You can choose your own horse, and it will be yours."

She added with a laugh. "You'd better choose well, because you'll be jumping against me and I don't like losing."

"Very tempting," Aimee said, "And I'll accept your offer and choose a horse, but I can't come regularly. Will as often as I can do?"

Olivia pouted a little. "I suppose I can't have everything."

She was pleased and she wasn't pleased. While she wanted Aimee closer her big fear was Mark could always turn up at the stables, and she desperately wanted to keep them apart.

She was still not sure about Aimee and Mark.

Before Aimee left, however, Olivia had a consolation. Aimee promised to come next week and choose a horse. She was really delighted with the idea, and her love for the sport was taking hold again.

Olivia saw her off with mixed feelings. Delight at her swift return next week, but troubled that Mark might appear at the wrong moment. He'd been seeing Olivia much more since the ownership change, and of course she'd been encouraging him.

Aimee reappeared the following week, as promised, and she was gay and enthusiastic. "Trot out those horses, Olivia," she demanded.

Olivia took her round the whole stables and was impressed with the way Aimee spoke about them and the way she touched and assessed them.

She already had a high opinion of Aimee's knowledge and she'd made a private bet with herself as to the horse she would choose, but she was wrong. And not only wrong... surprised.

Aimee chose a white horse that was a newcomer to her stables and was entirely untested.

"You sure?" she asked.

"Dead certain," Aimee replied. "That's my horse. And it's called, Myon."

"Myon?" echoed Olivia.

Aimee smiled. "MY own. Myon's near enough."

Her enthusiasm sparked Olivia. "Come on," she said, "Let's go for a ride. Christen your horse."

Aimee couldn't resist, and they set off through the countryside.

She trotted and cantered Myon, then set off at a gallop, leaving Olivia well behind.

When she caught Aimee up she said. "Well, you satisfied?"

"Absolutely."

"You've not seen him jump yet."

"You told me he could jump," Aimee protested.

"That's what we understood when we took the horse but we've not tested him. You may find you'll have to change your mind."

"He'll jump," Aimee said confidently. "Like an angel," She'd already fallen in love with the horse and patted his neck.

When they trotted back through the stable gates the first thing Olivia saw was Mark's red Lotus parked next to Aimee's big car, and her heart sank.

Aimee also noticed. "Why, Mark's here." she said. "You expecting him?"

"Not really," Olivia said. " 'Tall Trees' send their guests up here, and they've also put money in. He's liable to turn up any time."

Then Mark came striding towards them. He must have been watching from the house.

"Well well," he said. "My two favourite ladies."

He looked at Aimee. "So Olivia persuaded you. You look good on a horse, Aimee. White suits you."

Aimee knew he was being sarcastic. "And red suits you," she replied.

"Touché!" Mark said. "See you up at the house."

Olivia was livid. All her plans down the drain. And what might Mark let slip?

They stabled the horses and walked towards the house.

Aimee noticed Olivia had gone quiet. "You seem upset, Olivia," she said. "Is Mark bad news?"

"No, no," Olivia said hastily, "Shall we say, an inopportune moment."

She hoped he wouldn't stay now that he'd seen Aimee, but he showed no signs of moving when they reached the house and Olivia was forced to entertain him.

Maddeningly, he directed the conversation at Aimee, who repeated her big love of horses and her desire to take up riding again.

"Olivia's given me that white horse," she said. "I'm calling it Myon."

Straight away he said, "My own... Cute."

Olivia was annoyed he'd instantly spotted the link that she hadn't. She silently raged to herself. Fuck it! He's spoiling the evening.

Her big problem was that both Mark and Aimee would expect to stay the night with her, and after they'd eaten, Olivia became increasingly apprehensive as neither showed signs of moving.

It got to ten o'clock, and Mark said to Aimee, "You going back to London tonight?"

"Bit too late now," she said.

"Well, Olivia's plenty of bedrooms," Mark said.

Olivia held her breath.

Aimee said, "You only live round the corner, don't you, Mark?"

"That's right," he smiled. "But I'm tempted to stay. Olivia's got plenty of room for us both, eh?"

Olivia was alarmed. What was he implying?

But Aimee realised Mark didn't know about her and Olivia and kept her composure.

"Guess you're right, Mark," she said coolly.

He was thoughtful for a moment. "Still," he said, "Perhaps you two would be uncomfortable with me in the way."

With hardly a pause, he got to his feet, gave them both a kiss on the cheek and left, and in barely a few moments they heard the loud roar from his speeding Lotus.

"Thank Christ for that!" Olivia said. She pulled Aimee to her feet and led her to the bedroom. "Come on, get your clothes off."

Aimee lay back on the bed with her arms clasped behind her head.

"You do it," she said.

Olivia didn't need a second invitation and in a flash she had Aimee undressed, except for a wisp clinging round her waist.

She gently pulled it off and stared between Aimee's legs, which she obligingly parted.

She smoothed her with her hand and said, "Perfect."

She moved to kiss her there, but Aimee feared a quick climax, and pulled her up.

Then she wished she hadn't. Olivia's lips crushed down and she ground her breasts into Aimee until her nipples felt like little daggers.

Then, without warning, she spun away and turned Aimee over, and without pause wound her arms round her from behind and grasped her breasts brutally.

The pain was intense and Aimee flinched, but she couldn't move. The agony was part of a huge thrill rushing through her like a hot tide, and her whole body tightened.

As if on cue, Olivia reached between her legs with both hands and at the same time rocked into her. Aimee nearly went mad. Olivia was pulling her apart in front and driving into her from behind. It was almost like a man stroking.

She felt herself scream, then she was thrusting uncontrollably until at last she seemed to burst.

The relief was magical, and she could have enjoyed the feeling forever.

They came to a standstill, and Aimee was hoarse. "Christ Almighty!" she muttered.

There was a huge smile on Olivia's face. "Our best yet, darling."

Aimee fingered her nipples gently. "They're nearly in rags," she protested, "and sore as hell."

"The scars of love," Olivia whispered, and gathered her up again..

Jesus! Aimee thought, does she never stop? I'll have to cut this down. But she knew she couldn't. Olivia seemed to have new tricks up her sleeve all the time.

On his way home, Mark thought what an opportunity missed. And he meant Aimee, not Olivia.

The next day he got a phone call from Maurice, and he was unusually conversational. "You coming up this week, Mark?" he asked.

"Quite likely," Mark said. "I've not seen the new sensation."

"Oh, you mean Holly... Yeah! She'll knock your eyes out." He paused for a moment. "Do you think you could bring Olivia?"

Mark was surprised. "I dare say. Why?"

"Tell you when you come," he said mysteriously.

Mark pondered whether to go up and see Olivia or give her a ring. He thought she might be a bit uneasy about being summoned by Maurice. Because that's what it amounted to.

He decided to take the short trip so he could see her reaction, and drove over in the morning.

She raised her eyebrows. "Why so early? Couldn't you sleep?"

Mark reckoned she was having a dig at his abrupt departure last night, but he swallowed it. "Maurice wants to see you," he said.

He wasn't sure, but he thought Olivia lost a little colour. Certainly her lips went tight. "What does he want?"

"He didn't say. Perhaps you're the flavour of the month."

"What do you think he wants?" Olivia was showing a few nerves.

Mark decided to release the screw. "Don't worry," he said. "I think he wants something from you."

Olivia was relieved but not totally. "Did he say when?"

"Some time this week."

"Oh!" She mulled things over. "I take it he meant you as well."

"He did. You get another ride in the red Lotus."

"Tomorrow's OK for me."

"Tomorrow it is." Mark drove off.

He reflected on how nervous Olivia had become. The tough Olivia! Maurice seemed to have that effect on lots of people.

He greeted them affably at *The Phoenix* the next evening and said to Olivia, "You're looking gorgeous."

But Olivia wasn't going to be reassured until she knew what he wanted, and anxiety drove her.

"Well I'm here, Maurice. What's on your mind?"

He took them to his private alcove and ordered drinks.

"There might be something you can do for me, Olivia," he said.

"Shoot," she said.

Maurice made a little apex with his fingers on the tablecloth. Then he said, "Are you acquainted with Sir Robert Buckingham?"

Olivia was really surprised. "Bob Buckingham? Sure, but he's not one of my favourites. He's a bully. The way he behaves you'd think he came from the gutter. And he likes knocking women about."

Maurice was nodding his head in assent, as though he knew the man.

Then he said smoothly, "I understand he's a riding man. Do you think you could get him down to your stables? I've got a man who'd like to confront him but Buckingham won't let him get near... He's an absolute army of people protecting him."

"Well, he'd surely do the same thing again, wouldn't he?"

"The difference is they'd be face to face. Not so easy to ignore," Maurice said. "At the very least the man could get a camera shot of him."

Olivia was puzzled.

"What's this all about, Maurice?"

"It's a bit complicated," he said, "Robert Buckingham is mixed up with an arrogant crowd of aristocrats who always have to have their own way, and one of them battered a girl senseless when she wouldn't give him what he wanted at a boozy party. Buckingham is the chief suspect. The police interviewed them all but they backed each other up and the police couldn't take any action."

He waited a second while this sank in. "Her father wants words with him, and a photo shot to show his daughter. They intend to take further action."

"Why doesn't he try his address?"

"His estate is like Fort Knox," Maurice said. "You can't get in. But if you can get him to your stables they can have a man to man."

"He might be told to piss off."

"He can still get a camera shot."

"So you're asking me to finger one of my friends." Olivia was annoyed. "Fuck you, Maurice!"

Maurice corrected her, "You said he wasn't one of your favourites, Olivia. Surely you wouldn't support knocking up a young girl? Picture the scene," he suggested. "A leering bunch of drunks who've scattered money like confetti and think the girls should all line up for them. One objects, so she gets a battering."

Olivia sneered, "How is it you've suddenly become whiter than white, Maurice?"

He went a bit quiet. "The man in question is my brother," he said. "Nothing like me. He's an honest berk. But he's still my brother."

"Oh!" Olivia said. "But ratting on one of my own?" She shook her head.

"It might NOT be him," Maurice said. "Then you'd be doing him a favour. Come on, Olivia," he urged, "I'll owe you one. Some time I'll be able to do something for you, I'm sure."

Olivia knew this was an inescapable truth, and at last she said grudgingly, "All right, Maurice, I'll do it... I'll let you know."

"I won't forget, Olivia," he said. "Now you two go off and get a gander at the gorgeous Holly."

They waited for the cabaret, and Mark was seriously impressed.

Holly was like a young dark panther. Long dark ringlets of hair fell across her sensuous face, and she had superb breasts with huge black nipples. Her high heels made her long legs go on forever, and she kept flashing open her voluptuous thighs to give off an animal vitality.

Unlike Steff, she rolled and exposed her body with such abandon that nobody bothered about her singing.

She finished completely nude and did a full circle before she left the stage.

"I can see why Maurice likes her," Mark said.

"What man wouldn't?" Olivia said. "I'm sure there's a lot of stiff pricks in the audience." She pretended to reach across to test Mark, but he smilingly shook his head.

Olivia was quiet on the way back, and Mark guessed she was still unhappy about what she'd agreed with Maurice.

"You could be getting Buckingham off the hook," he said. "If he did it then, fuck him, no sympathy."

But Olivia was still gloomy and made no comment.

The next day she rang Buckingham. "Olivia here," she said.

"Long time no see," he said. "Got any good horses in your stables?"

Olivia couldn't believe her luck. Just the opening she wanted.

"That's why I've rung," she said. "I've just got a young jumper and I'd like your opinion." Buckingham was an expert on horses.

"Fine," he said. "Say when."

"Next Wednesday afternoon suit you?"

"You've got it."

Olivia was astonished it had been so easy and felt some relief her part in the big scheme was over. The rest was up to Maurice, and she got on the phone to him. When he answered she just said two words. "Wednesday afternoon." Then there was a click as she rang off.

Maurice grinned as he put the phone down. Olivia must have been scared witless to be so brief. She even forgot her pompous manner.

Wednesday came, and mid-afternoon Olivia saw a big silver Rolls Royce pull into the car park. Its number plate was JB 111.

Big head! Olivia thought. Not enough to have a Rolls Royce. He has to stick on his own number plate.

Buckingham jumped out of the car. He was a big man and, like many wealthy aristocrats, he was arrogant.

He could be charming, and women liked him, but if you crossed him that was a different matter.

"Hi!" he shouted to the advancing Olivia. "You've done a lot since I was last here."

"We DO progress, Bob," she said. She took his arm. "This way."

Then somebody shouted, "Hey!" and Buckingham turned.

A man was coming towards them.

"Can I speak to you?" he shouted.

"Fucking Press," Buckingham muttered. "Ring my secretary!" he bawled, and turned away.

The man shouted again. "I say!"

Buckingham turned once more and, as he did, the man snapped him on his camera.

"Bastards!" Buckingham muttered, and strode away from the man.

He said to Olivia suspiciously. "How did he know I'd be here?"

Olivia shrugged, "We often get the press here," she lied.

Buckingham thought no more about it and went with Olivia to the horse she'd picked out. He examined it closely, and watched its movements. "Have you jumped it?" he asked.

"Once," she lied. "Seemed nice and easy."

He patted the horse. "Think you've a good one here, Olivia. If ever you think of selling give me first shout."

"Sure thing, Bob," she said.

Then she took him to the house for a meal and drinks, after which he left.

Olivia fervently hoped that was the last of the matter.

Two weeks later Buckingham was badly beaten up by a gang of thugs after he left a London Club and was put in hospital for several days.

When he came out he started thinking. One of the thugs had muttered something about a little girl. What was it? Then he remembered. 'This is for the little girl.'

It all came back to him. He and his crew. Half drunk and one little girl who wouldn't play like the others. He'd tried to force her but she kicked him and he saw red and struck out. He acknowledged he'd had too much drink. In fact, the others had to pull him off.

Still, the bastards that put him in hospital weren't drunk, and Buckingham wanted someone to pay.

His mind started working overtime, and he considered the events leading up to his beating.

One person stood out like a shining star. Olivia! Lady fucking Olivia!

Yes it had to be her. That man with the camera wasn't there by accident. It was a set-up.

He'd thought at the time it was a little strange to suddenly hear from her. Especially as she was herself an expert judge of horses and had heaps of people nearer than him she could consult.

His jaw set... Well that's one lady I will teach a fucking lesson.

A week later he drove back to Olivia's in the evening and rang her door bell.

She came to the door looking very glamorous, and he wondered if she was expecting someone.

"I'm your fucking date for tonight," he snarled, and pushed her into the house.

Olivia retreated to the lounge and faced him.

"You fingered me, you lousy bitch," he shouted. "I'm going to give you a few slaps to remember. Then I'm going to tell all our friends that the charming Lady Olivia is a fucking sneak."

He advanced towards her and raised his arm, but Olivia quickly darted across the room to a table and whipped open a drawer. When she turned she had a gun in her hand.

Buckingham laughed. "You can't frighten me, Olivia. You wouldn't have the guts to press that trigger. In any case," he said. "The safety catch is on."

Olivia glanced at the gun, and Buckingham launched himself at her but he was the loser. She got off two shots, and his legs gave way and he fell, with a sort of moan.

For a moment she was frozen...Would he get up?

But he didn't, and she knelt and couldn't detect breathing. She panicked and her mind rushed round in circles. Murder... Police... Prison... Ridicule.

Then she got control of herself and picked up the phone.

Mark answered. "Yes, Olivia?"

"Get over here quick," she said. "And don't tell anyone. I've got a body on my hands."

Mark was always good in an emergency. He said crisply. "Do nothing. Touch nothing. I'm on my way." Then he scooted out to his car.

It wasn't long before Olivia heard the Lotus and rushed to the door.

Mark pushed in, and Olivia threw herself into his arms and started to shake. "It's that fucking Buckingham!" she gasped. "He tried to attack me and I shot him."

Mark hurried into the lounge and stooped over Buckingham. "Yes, he's dead all right," he said. "You sit down. I'll get some coffee going."

Olivia gratefully subsided on the settee until Mark came back with the coffee. He held up a whisky bottle. "Put a slug in?"

"A big one," she said. And as she sipped she felt mightily relieved Mark was there.

"We've got to think about this, Olivia," he said. "You've shot a man, and for all we know the police might call it murder."

He tried to marshal his thoughts. "We've got to do two things," he said. "Lead the police the way we want them to go, and avoid publicity."

"The first is for you. The second is for me. 'Tall Trees' has to be squeaky clean. Any scandal and the stables are stone dead."

He studied Olivia. "Are you up for questions?"

"Not at the moment."

Then she had a thought. "Mark," she said, "Maurice owes me one. Could there be a better man to handle this?"

Mark agreed and picked up the phone. "Maurice, this is Mark. I'm with Olivia. She said you owe her one."

"Yes?"

"You remember the man she fingered for you, Sir Robert Buckingham? He came back tonight to do her over and she shot him. We've a body on our hands."

There was a small silence, and Mark wondered what was coming. Then Maurice said firmly, "Leave it to me. Do nothing until I get down. I'm on my way."

The waiting seemed an age but in fact it wasn't long before Maurice pulled up in a big black Mercedes, and two men got out with him.

He swiftly summed up the situation and took charge. He behaved as though it was part of his normal business, and both Mark and Olivia were impressed with his coolness.

He put out his hand. "Give me the gun, Olivia."

He held out a little bag, and as she dropped the gun inside Olivia began to think for the first time she might get out of this mess.

Maurice put the bag in his pocket.

"Was this gun registered to you?"

"No," she said. "It was given to me many years ago as a precaution against intruders. My family worried there was no man in the house."

"Excellent," he said. "So far as the police are concerned you've never owned a gun. I suppose," he said, "The big Rolls is Buckingham's car?"

Olivia nodded.

He bent over Buckingham's body and fished out his car keys. Then he turned to his men.

"Get him in the car and drive down the nearest dual carriage-way for a couple of miles. Then swing over to the opposite side as though you're coming back, and park in the first lay-by."

He looked at them to make sure they understood then said, "Put the body in the driving seat. I'll follow to check things over. Then we all get back to London."

Mark was full of admiration for Maurice's astute thinking. The impression would be that Buckingham was shot before he got to his destination, not after. And if by any chance someone knew he was going to visit Olivia it would still ring true. As far as Olivia was concerned, he didn't turn up.

He touched Maurice on the shoulder. "Many thanks. Terrific thinking."

"It's not over yet," Maurice said.

He turned to Olivia. "When the news breaks you must phone the police and tell them Buckingham was on his way to see you. That will be the normal thing to do.

"If you keep mum and they find out, and they will, they'll wonder why you kept quiet and you'll be under suspicion. Just act normal. You know nothing."

He added a little warning. "But be prepared for the police. They sometimes act clever and try to trick people."

"What do you mean?" Olivia was alarmed.

Maurice ran his hands through his hair. "Well, for instance they might say we understand Buckingham visited you. A total lie, but testing you. Just stick to your simple story. He didn't arrive, finish. They can't know any different."

He gave Olivia a long stare. "Think you can handle that?"

"No sweat," she said.

Buckingham's body was taken out to his car but Maurice came back for a last look round. "There's nothing here of Buckingham's is there?"

"Nothing," Olivia said. "Dead sure."

Maurice showed his approval and touched her arm. "Fine," he said. Then he swept out, and the cars drove off.

Mark said. "Thank God for Maurice."

"Amen to that," Olivia said.

Maurice was very particular how the Rolls was parked in the lay-by, and he had the front wheels driven over the verge to give the impression of hasty driving.

At last he was satisfied and he and his crew drove back to London.

The news broke the very next day and in the afternoon Olivia telephoned the police.

"Lady Olivia Lithgow here," she said. "Sir Robert Buckingham was on his way to see me yesterday, and I wondered why he didn't arrive."

The police sergeant said respectfully, "I expect we shall want to speak to you, my Lady."

"Of course," Olivia said, "Call when you like."

The sergeant didn't point out that usually people went to them at the station. He was a bit in awe of Olivia's title, and when he passed the news to D.I. Lew Green that was the first thing he said.

"Why didn't you ask her to come in?"

The sergeant fidgeted, "Well, she seemed a bit haughty. I thought, bugger that. She IS a Lady."

Lew laughed. "It may surprise you to know, Sergeant, that aristocrats are not a different race. They even bleed like us."

The sergeant looked embarrassed but Lew had no sympathy for his craven attitude. "Get hold of Sally Golding for me," he said crisply.

She was his personal sergeant and came charging into his office with enthusiasm. "What's up?" she asked.

Lew told her, and the following day they called on Olivia and they sat down together.

Sally put her mike on the table. "OK, my Lady?"

She nodded and Lew kicked off. "I understand Sir Robert Buckingham was on his way to see you on the day he was murdered."

"That's right," she said. "He was going to give me an opinion on a horse. He was an expert."

"Did he say what time he would be arriving?"

"Just Wednesday afternoon."

Sally asked a question. "Didn't you get concerned when he didn't arrive?"

"Not concerned. I intended to ring him the next day if he didn't ring me, but you know what happened."

Lew took over again. "Were you close friends?"

"Not close but we've known each other a long time. We used to bump into each other at some race meetings, and compare notes. Occasionally we had a drink together."

Sally said quickly, "AFTER the races?"

Olivia was a little cool. "AT the races. They all have bars."

"Do you know if he had any problems, business, social?" Lew asked.

"Didn't know him well enough, but I wouldn't have thought so. He was very wealthy."

Lew thought he'd take one last shot. "Well somebody didn't like him. Do you know if he enjoyed the London round? Clubs etc?" He said craftily, "*The Phoenix* for instance."

Olivia laughed. "Bob certainly liked a woman on his arm, and I'm sure he went clubbing. But not with me."

Lew rose. "Thank you very much, Lady Olivia. We won't trouble you further." He and Sally left.

On the way back to the station she said. "Not much there." She wrinkled her brow, "Tell me," she said, "Why did you link Buckingham with *The Phoenix*?"

Lew gave a small grin. "Fishing! You never know. Don't forget the Lady socialises there."

"I do declare," Sally said, "You're more devious than I thought, Lew Green."

"Has to be done," he said. "Now we'll have to start digging through the computer records. See if we can find who didn't like him."

Sally got the job of checking the computer records, and she quickly came across a recent entry about Sir Robert Buckingham.

After leaving a London club he had been attacked by a gang and put in hospital.

She rushed the news across to Lew.

"We certainly can't disregard that. Violence incites violence," he said. "Apparently no police action was taken. Let's speak to the Met."

The Met Police were quite informative. The club Buckingham had left the night he was attacked was *The Phoenix*. And they weren't very complimentary about the owner, Maurice Robens. They suspected him of being the Mr Clean behind several unpleasant episodes which they'd been unable to solve.

Lew asked them if they had any ideas about Buckingham's attackers, and they said they could name one or two gangs who'd be up for it but Buckingham had kept his mouth shut, and they guessed he was being paid back for something.

Lew was quite thoughtful after receiving this information, and said to Sally. "It seems there's a lot more needs to be known about Sir Robert Buckingham."

He told her to go back to the computers and check the last year prior to Buckingham being attacked. She did, and she came up with gold.

There it was in black and white. Buckingham had been involved with others in an assault on a girl who had been beaten nearly senseless; but he was the chief suspect.

No action was taken because all the men supported each other and nothing could be proved.

Lew immediately said, "Check this out, father, husband, somebody would have been sore about this."

Sally came back two days later triumphant. "I've found the sore person," she announced. "The father. Living this side of London, near Wimbledon."

"What are we waiting for?"

Inside an hour they were knocking at a door, and a man opened it.

"Yes?"

They showed their warrant cards. "We should like to talk to you about the assault on your daughter," Lew said.

"That's all over." The man wasn't friendly.

"If you will let us in we'll put your mind at rest," Lew said mildly.

He ushered them into his lounge and they sat. "So?" he asked.

"We know all about what happened," Lew said. "And that no police action was taken."

The man remained tight-lipped.

"You must have been angry."

"I wasn't pleased."

Lew then told a lie. "We know from the gang that attacked Sir Robert Buckingham afterwards that you ordered it."

The man was about to protest but Lew went on smoothly, "That doesn't interest us. We are looking into the murder of Sir Robert." His voice got a bit threatening. "Beating a man up is one thing, murder quite another."

The man went a bit pale. "You think ' I ' murdered him?"

"You are the obvious suspect."

"What! After I've given him a bloody good hiding? Where's the sense in that? Besides I wouldn't know how to use a gun."

"I haven't said a gun was used."

"I do read the papers."

Lew had got the information he wanted and decided to bring things to a close. But he wanted to scare the man. He might spill something.

"Where were you on that Wednesday afternoon?" he asked.

"With several people at a meeting," the man said triumphantly. "You can check, The Wimbledon Bowling Club, Worple Road."

Lew and Sally left.

In the car Sally said, "You're not really going to check his alibi?"

Lew laughed, "Of course not. That was simply to put a bit of pressure on him. He might have dropped something. Besides, we might want to go back to him."

"So in fact our trail has led to an innocent man."

"It has for the moment. But I'm convinced Buckingham's attack on this girl is the source of his murder."

Lew reflected, "HIS violence, gang violence, finally murder. What do you say to payback?" He thought for a moment, "We're missing something here, my girl."

Sally said, "It would have been quite different, wouldn't it, if the car had been going towards London."

"Of course. It would mean Buckingham had been to Lady Olivia Lithgow first. But you can't alter the facts to fit a theory."

"So is it another one for the computer file?"

"Afraid so. But you never know what might turn up."

Olivia was still nervous about the Buckingham shooting and the police enquiries, and was relieved to have her thoughts distracted with a call from Aimee.

"Get the horses ready," she said. "See you Saturday."

Just the push Olivia needed. She couldn't get Buckingham out of her mind, and the anxiety hovered over her like a dark cloud.

Aimee arrived on Saturday full of enthusiasm, and she and her horse jumped like angels, completely outclassing Olivia.

She was all smiles, "You've got to be consistent, darling."

Olivia was nettled, but for once she had little to say.

To add to her annoyance, Mark turned up again, and she wondered if his real object was to contact Aimee.

"Looks like you've met your match, Olivia," he said gaily.

This was rubbing salt in the wound. "I had an off day," she said stiffly. "I'll get my own back next week."

"Oh! Is this a weekly arrangement?"

Olivia could have bitten her tongue out, but it was too late.

"Well, not always," she said defensively.

Aimee joined in and laughed, "Whenever possible, darling. I've got the bug again."

Mark didn't want to get in their way, but he took the opportunity he'd been waiting for.

"If you come next week pop in and see me afterwards, would you, Aimee? I'd like to talk some business."

Aimee knew perfectly well this meant a visit to *The Fantasy Palace* to see Steff but she was quite pleased. Business apart, Mark was still high in her estimation, and she hoped exploring him was going to be a pleasure.

"Expect me," she said.

He left soon afterwards, and when he was out of sight Olivia said to Aimee suspiciously. "What's this guff about business, Aimee?"

"Oh," she said coolly. "Mark gets people interested in *Kink's Palace* and he likes me to give them an introduction."

It was a thin lie but Olivia couldn't contradict it.

"Huh !" she breathed.

Her moodiness spoilt the evening, and when they eventually went to bed Aimee was not surprised that she was disappointing.

In the morning she asked, "What was wrong with you last night, darling?"

Olivia of course couldn't tell her.

"I had a bad day," she said. "Every fucking thing went wrong, and to cap it all, I lost a horse. You know how that hurts."

This was a total lie but got Aimee's sympathy at once.

"Oh I'm sorry. You should have told me, darling."

Before they parted she kissed Olivia and said, "Don't be frightened to confide in me darling. I have plenty of sympathy for friends."

At least something salvaged, Olivia thought sourly.

The following Saturday evening Aimee arrived at 'Tall Trees', and Mark came out to welcome her immediately he heard from reception. Then he took her to the restaurant for a meal.

As always, he was waited on hand and foot, and Aimee of course received the same consideration.

"I see you're king here, Mark," she said.

"What's money for?"

They agreed to visit Steff, and she was composed, as always, when she saw them. One of her many good qualities, Mark thought. She never panicked.

"How's tricks?" he asked.

She lifted her arms. "Can't stop the flow."

She said archly, "Want to make a booking?"

Mark smiled. "Any problems?"

"Not enough hours in the day."

Mark sampled the atmosphere. The place was jumping and he and Aimee could hardly keep the smiles off their faces. What a good choice Steff had been, he thought... And they were going to make another fortune.

They had drinks with her in the penthouse then left for Mark's place.

It was quite late when they arrived, and they had a quick coffee.

Lounging on the settee, Aimee said, "I know you're anxious to take me to bed, Mark, but I'm not ready for it yet. I'll show you my body but that's as far as I'll go."

She gave him a long look. "You decide."

"I don't think I could keep my hands off your naked body," he said.

She looked at him teasingly, eyebrows raised and hands on her hips. "Well?"

Mark knew he couldn't resist. "I'll screw myself down."

She got to her feet, smiled and unzipped her dress.

She was left with a wisp of lace round her thighs, high heels and stocking tops, no bra.

Her high breasts were almost pointed, and her long slim legs ran into narrow hips.

Mark couldn't wait for her to discard the wisp round her thighs, but she delayed and delayed, and he wondered if she would...

Then she did a swift turn and flashed the lace hovering between her legs.

Mark swallowed. "Aimee, how can you do this to me?"

"Easy," she said. "It's called control, and that's what I'm looking for in you."

Mark's desire was smothering him. "Get on with it, Aimee."

She stepped out of the lace, and Mark could hardly restrain himself.

She was entirely smooth with no hairline, and the naked skin between her legs set his pulses hammering.

Tantalisingly she posed, "One embrace?"

Immediately Mark had her in his arms and one hand slipped down her back and spread between her legs, while his mouth explored her open lips.

He became so hard it was almost agony but abruptly Aimee thrust him away, "You're getting too heated, Mark."

He was thunderstruck.

Having gone so far he'd thought she would relent, and he found it hard to draw back. With any other woman he wouldn't... But this was Aimee; it was on her terms or nothing.

He struggled with his emotions, and stared at her steadily. Finally he said, "You've a lot of nerve, Aimee."

She looked him straight in the face. "We've plenty of time, Mark. You've got to understand my mind goes with my body. I don't jump in and out of bed at the flick of a man's thumb."

Mark now had himself under control and he managed a half smile. "It seems you like to live dangerously, Aimee."

"I knew I could trust you, Mark," she said enigmatically.

She managed to be at Olivia's again the following Saturday, and, much to Olivia's approval, suggested another jump-off.

Olivia was dying to get her revenge. She took her role as horsewoman seriously, and it had rankled how Aimee had humbled her last week.

She challenged her. "You wouldn't care for a little wager?"

Aimee smiled, "How little?"

"A new dress?"

"That all?"

"Mine are designer dresses," Olivia said haughtily.

Aimee laughed, "You beat me, I'll buy you two."

Olivia picked out her best horse and Aimee mounted Myon.

"You first," she said to Olivia. "Mugs away."

Olivia was taken aback. "Mugs away?"

"Haven't you heard the phrase? The mug is the loser."

"Really!" Olivia was not best pleased. Mug she didn't like. And because of her annoyance she had the first fence down, which annoyed her further. But she pulled herself together and rode the rest of the course clear.

Aimee took off in great style and raced round for a convincing clear round. "That's how it's done, darling," she said.

Olivia was furious but she said, "Best of three. Don't count your chickens."

And she sent her horse round in a superb exhibition to register a clear second round.

Aimee took off again and, to her exasperation, she touched the first fence and it fell. So they were level again.

"Can't understand that fence falling," she said. "I hardly clipped it."

"Take it up with the fence," Olivia said.

She was elated. When she'd put the fence back after her first fault she'd balanced it thinly on the edge and not pushed it fully home. Following Aimee's fault, she did, ready for her third jump.

She went clear and said to Aimee, "You'd better be in form, darling. Two dresses hang on this."

Aimee again jumped clear and they were level again.

"Only one way to settle it," Olivia said. "Much higher fence. One jump settles it."

"Fair enough."

Olivia put the first fence up six inches, which was a massive margin.

"Think you can handle it, darling?" she asked.

"It's a huge increase."

"Same for us both," Olivia said. "Of course, if you're not confident I could lower it." She knew Aimee wouldn't be able to ignore the challenge. But she also knew something Aimee didn't.

Her horse had already jumped that height. She was doubtful if Myon could tackle a fence that high.

"There's no mugs now," she said. "Who's first?"

Aimee flipped a coin. "Call!"

"Heads."

Olivia was right and prepared for her jump.

To Aimee's amazement, she didn't retreat to get a good run at the fence but stood off quite near.

She approached from the side slowly and as she got near the horse launched into a huge spring.

She heard an ominous click but to her delight the fence didn't fall. The good old first fence she'd pushed fully home. She was over the moon.

Aimee was dumbfounded. "Christ! How ever did you get over without any speed?"

"Bit lucky, really," Olivia replied. "Thought I'd try it slow. Mine's not a fast horse."

She didn't own up to the fact that she'd experimented with the horse over and over to find its best technique.

Aimee was now extremely doubtful about her chances. She'd seen the enormous leap Olivia's horse had made and she was frightened her horse might pick up an injury.

"I give in," she said. "I don't think we can manage that."

Olivia was happy again. Her superiority had been demonstrated.

"It was a big jump," she admitted. "But don't forget my dresses."

"Just send me the bill," Aimee said. "You've earned them."

They stabled the horses and retired to the house, and Olivia was buoyant and hoping for a good night with Aimee. Her one fear was Mark. If he turned up anything could happen.

She was still undecided about Aimee and Mark as a pair but she didn't like it. She didn't like anything that might separate her and Aimee, and she knew Mark was a powerhouse and dangerous.

After they'd eaten it was obvious Mark was not going to appear and she was relieved, but she was anxious to get Aimee to voice her thoughts about Mark.

"Seen Mark recently?" she asked.

"Not since last week. Why?"

"I thought there was something going on between you two."

"I'm just interested. Haven't made up my mind."

Her cool reply infuriated Olivia, and she realised Mark was still a danger, but she had to hold her tongue. She couldn't dictate to Aimee.

She made sure the drinks kept coming, and with one or two caresses thrown in they were both halfway amorous when the time came for bed.

Aimee stripped off, and Olivia said, "I'd die to get a body like yours, darling. So slim and legs that never stop."

Aimee posed roguishly and parted her legs. "And what about this?"

"Don't tempt me. I'll ravish you now."

"I don't mind rough, darling, but don't kill me."

Olivia smiled. "I'll stop when you shriek."

She lay against her, and the touch of Aimee's naked body was like raw electricity shooting into her.

She pulled her so tight it hurt then her mouth closed on Aimee's. It was almost like swallowing her lips but Aimee loved it.

Suddenly she stopped and put her mouth on Aimee's enlarged nipples. First one, then the other... Ferociously... Olivia knew no other way.

Aimee felt the pain intensely, but it was also exciting, and when Olivia felt between her legs and pinched and pulled her she gloried in the agony because of the sheer intoxicating delight.

She didn't realise she was heaving and rolling like a wild animal, but that was what Olivia thrived on, and she locked her mouth on Aimee's to stifle her cries.

"Jesus, Olivia!" she whispered when it was all over, "You nearly torture me and I do practically nothing."

"You only had your fingers inside me nearly up to your wrist. When you go, darling, you go."

"Did I?"

"I made sure you did."

Aimee stared at her, then a smile broke across her face. "You are a fucking bitch, Olivia." she whispered.

"You love it."

And Aimee knew there was no answer to that.

"You can kiss my sore parts better," she said.

"And down there?" asked Aimee, pointing between her thighs.

"I guess that's too dangerous."

Then they lay together, and Aimee winced as Olivia fondled her sore body. But she knew she couldn't give her up.

Olivia was thinking the same, and her fears about Mark came rushing back.

The big barrier! Christ! Can't have him getting between us, she thought.

She said to Aimee impulsively, "You fond of Mark?"

Aimee sat up, astonished. "You mesmerised with Mark?

"He frightens me a bit. Like Maurice. I wouldn't want you to get hurt."

"Poor lie, darling. What's on your mind?"

"That's it."

Aimee was peeved. "If you don't level with me I'm not coming again."

"You don't mean that."

"I do. And if you won't tell me I'll ask Mark."

"Ask him what?"

"I'm not an idiot, Olivia. This has to be something recent, and I can make a good guess."

Olivia lost a little colour. Aimee seemed to be drawing entirely the wrong conclusion, and it could be dangerous if she opened her mouth.

"You've got it wrong, Aimee," she said. "I wish I hadn't spoken."

Aimee stared at her. "I think you're lying to me, Olivia, but I'll give you the benefit of the doubt... For now."

This was a sour finish to their evening and Aimee was still a bit cross in the morning, although she did kiss Olivia.

She said haughtily, "I didn't think I'd have to say this, but I'm disappointed in you, darling, I like to lie with someone I can trust."

Olivia deeply regretted her impulsive comment but she couldn't take it back.

She pleaded with Aimee, "Don't let a silly moment spoil things, darling. I promise there's nothing to hide."

Much against her inclinations, she added, "You ask Mark." Safety has to come first, she reasoned.

Aimee thought for a moment then she said, "I'll see." She waved and stepped into her car.

Olivia was in a panic and got on the phone to Mark straight away.

She explained what had happened and insisted she hadn't told Aimee anything. "Unfortunately," she said miserably, "I suspect she's piecing things together about Buckingham."

"You bloody fool, Olivia," Mark shouted. "Do you want to get us all locked up?" He paused for breath. "You'd better hope Maurice doesn't hear about it. He'll kill her."

"He wouldn't!" Olivia was shocked.

"Believe me, he would. Maurice is particular about not spending his days in prison. What about you?"

Olivia felt an absolute fool. But she was also frightened. She said in a small voice. "Can we do anything?"

Mark was still annoyed. "So it's WE now, is it?"

Then he cooled down. "Perhaps it's not gone too far. Aimee wouldn't dare open her mouth at present. She's not got enough." He halted for a moment, "I'll work on her."

"You think you can swing her?"

"I'll think of something. You can calm down."

Olivia put the phone down with great relief. She knew she could rely on Mark and immediately felt safer.

Mark was confident he could retrieve the situation but, for once, he underestimated the other party.

A few days later Aimee was on the phone to him.

"Think you could come up and see me, Mark. Something I'd like to discuss."

Mark wasn't altogether surprised. "Of course. When?"

"Tonight? Tomorrow? You choose."

"Tomorrow night will be fine," Mark said.

When he arrived the next evening she took him through to her penthouse and sat next to him. She was looking very glamorous, and Mark was wondering how she was going to approach the delicate subject.

Then he got a big shock.

"I've been thinking, Mark," she said. "Of the huge success of our Palaces. It's money for jam and millions of it."

She gave him a long stare. "I think we should open another but I'm heavily mortgaged, and you're the only one I can think of for the rest of the money. Naturally," she said with a smile, "I'll raise what I can."

She paused as Mark was grappling with the shock.

"How does the idea grab you?"

Mark was silent. Her sheer audacity had taken him by surprise. But as always he was a quick thinker. He knew she was saying. 'I know. Pay me off.'

The question was how much did she know? Always a gambler Mark took a chance.

"What makes you think I want to open another place?"

"The money."

"I've enough already."

"I haven't. Come on, Mark. You know another Palace can't fail."

Mark shook his head. "Maybe some other time, Aimee. Not interested at the moment."

Now the ball was in Aimee's court. But she knew how to play her hand.

"Well, that's a shame. I've already made tentative enquiries and know where there's a very good site."

She gave him another smile. "Well, I'll just keep it on hold in case you change your mind."

"I expect I shall be at Olivia's on Saturday for the horses," she said. "May see you."

This perked up Mark. "Is this a date?"

"Not firm... Maybe. I want you to tell me something first."

Here it comes, Mark thought, and this time he was right.

"Last week Olivia hinted at something you'd done which seemed to frighten her but she kept mum. Naturally, that incensed me."

She looked at Mark but he was calm.

"I've made a good guess that it had to be something recent and I immediately thought of Robert Buckingham, who was on his way to Olivia when he was shot. He had a name for manhandling women, and my guess is he tried it on with Olivia and you covered up."

Mark started a slow handclap, and Aimee thought he was applauding her reconstruction, but she was wrong.

"What an imagination!" he said.

He leaned towards her. "All right, Aimee, I'll give you the truth but if you ever let on to Olivia I'll rip your heart out. Is it too much to ask for your word?"

"Since you put it so prettily, you've got it."

"The truth is, I got Olivia into a commercial mortgage knowing she wouldn't be able to pay, and when she defaulted I took her property away. Olivia doesn't own the stables now. She works for me. I'm not surprised she feels I'm ruthless."

Aimee looked startled then started a slow handclap herself. "Good story, Mark, but I have an ace up my sleeve."

"One of the stable girls saw Buckingham's car parked at Olivia's on that day. It's a very distinctive Rolls with a personal plate."

She smiled at him, and he couldn't tell she was lying. "Answer that one."

"The police found Buckingham's car some distance away still headed towards her place," he replied. "You're a fucking liar, Aimee."

Annoyingly, Aimee still smiled. "Cars can be turned round, Mark."

"This is just fantasy. The police would laugh at you."

"Not if they knew Buckingham's car was at Olivia's on that day."

"I give you that," he said grudgingly. "If it was true."

"But you wouldn't want them thinking in that direction?"

"Of course not, and you fucking well know why! How would you like police and newspaper men crawling all over your business?"

"I concede that."

She thought for a moment. "Is it really true you own Olivia?"

"Gospel."

"Jesus!"

Mark thought he'd won the day after all.

Then Aimee said, "Well no strings. You think about another Palace, Mark. We couldn't go wrong, could we?"

She added tantalisingly, "I've even thought of a new name."

Mark couldn't resist. "Spit it out."

"Palace of Pleasure."

"Yeah! I like it. I'll give it some thought."

Aimee then gave him some food and a few caresses but she wouldn't let Mark get serious, and he drove back home very late with a big problem on his mind.

He realised afresh what an acute mind Aimee had. Her reconstruction had been breathtaking.

He drove up to Olivia's the following Saturday, still thinking about a new Palace.

In fact, he was warming to the idea. He knew it was a sure fire money mountain, and the bigger his Empire became the more he liked it. Success and money was power and prestige, and Mark enjoyed them to the full.

But his growing enthusiasm was clouded. Aimee might think he was giving in to her pressure. This was dangerous, and could open the door to further demands. Totally unacceptable.

He arrived as Aimee and Olivia were walking up from the stables.

Olivia looked pleased, and he guessed she'd won their contest.

"Who won?" he asked.

Aimee jerked her thumb towards Olivia. "The lucky lady."

"Lucky?"

"She's a sore loser," Olivia interrupted. "I've won the last two."

"Don't bet on a third," Aimee said.

Mark realised there was real rivalry between them and bit back a flippant comment.

"Nobody wins all the time," he said.

"Except me," Olivia said. She had to have the last word.

They walked up to the house and she said, "What brings you over again, Mark?" She put in the 'again' deliberately. She wanted to discourage his Saturday visits when Aimee came.

"I thought," he lied, "that I might have a quiet canter through the countryside with you, but I see I've arrived too late."

"Come and have a drink instead," Olivia said.

They moved into her lounge, and Aimee looked at Mark but said nothing. Mark realised she was waiting for him to say something, but he still couldn't make up his mind about another Palace.

Then he had an inspiration.

Discuss the idea, then call Aimee's bluff and turn her down. After a few months, change his mind, and everybody would be happy.

The only risk was Aimee opening her mouth, meanwhile, but Mark was ready for the gamble. He felt sure she'd keep mum with the prospect of changing his mind. Like him, money ruled.

"The second reason I've come is to have a chat with you both," he said.

He noted with satisfaction Aimee's immediate surprise. She had obviously been expecting privacy.

He said to Olivia, "Aimee has been thinking about opening another Palace and invited my advice. But I'm not sold. Do you reckon it would work?"

"Well, I'm not sure," she said, to Mark's delight. "It would have to be around London, and that would be three. After all it IS a restricted market isn't it?"

Aimee said firmly, "London's a big place with a lot of big wallets. I don't see how it could fail."

"What about the money?" Olivia asked. "You'd have to find a lot to match the other two Palaces. Is it worth it when the money's rolling in so well?"

Mark could have hugged Olivia.

Aimee's face was frozen, "Money rolls in better from three."

"Well, it needs more thought," Mark said. He was delighted Olivia had strengthened his strategy and now he was confident.

He broke away from the subject.

"Have you any plans for this evening?" he asked Aimee.

Stony faced, she said, "I shall be staying with Olivia."

Olivia was delighted.

Mark drove back self-satisfied, and when he arrived the phone was ringing.

It was Barbara.

"Mark I've got a little problem," she said. "Could I have a talk with you?"

She couldn't have chosen a better moment. She could fill the gap Aimee had left by staying with Olivia.

"I'll come over and see you," he said.

Barbara was delighted. She was always keen for a night with Mark, and it did no harm to please the boss, especially when he was generous. She, in fact, reckoned he was extravagant.

She gave him a warm kiss when he arrived.

"A good start," he said. "But let's get the business out of the way."

"I've one villa, two people wanting it," she said. "One is a business man who would want it more or less permanently, the other is a Hollywood actress who would want it short term, but I know how you like celebs in the place."

"How big is the actress?"

"Norma Golding."

"Oh! Well in the public eye. Go for the actress. Tell the business man he's next," Mark said.

Barbara greatly admired Mark's swift decisions. And, in fact, she would have chosen the business man so she was glad she'd consulted him.

Mark patted the settee. "Now come and sit here, Barbara. We mustn't waste a good opportunity, must we?"

Her warm lips on his was the answer.

Mark always marvelled at the warmth and freshness of Barbara, and she didn't disappoint him.

She persuaded him to stay the night, and when he cuddled up against her nude body he felt it was a perfect end to a good day.

In the morning, Barbara said, "I always enjoy myself with you, Mark. I wish it was more often."

Still flushed with pleasure, Mark took the hint. "You ever been to *The Phoenix* in the West End?"

"I've heard about it."

"I'm going soon and I'm short of an escort. Want to come?"

Her face lit up, and she rushed across and kissed him. "That would be great. Is it long dresses?"

"Anything smart and daring."

"Leave it to me, darling."

Her enthusiasm touched Mark, and he was glad he'd asked her.

Nearly two weeks had gone by. He suddenly remembered Aimee, and rang her.

"Mark here," he said.

"Yes?"

"I've decided against a new Palace," he said. "It's not right for me at the present time."

Aimee pretended great surprise in a long drawn out "Wha--a--a----t? You can't mean that, Mark."

"It's no go, Aimee, I'm afraid. It's thanks but no thanks."

"You might regret it."

"I might. Then I'll have to bounce back."

Mark waited but Aimee had nothing more to say. "See you soon, darling," he said and hung up.

Aimee gripped the phone in a fury. She had not been prepared for the brush off and muttered through tight lips, "You're a fucking cool customer, Mark."

But for Barbara, it was *Phoenix* night, and Mark tapped on her door, which opened immediately.

She was in very high black heels and a shimmering white creation that appeared to be skin-tight against her youthful breasts. A black slash outlined her waist. And her big brown eyes stared out under long black lashes. The black and white effect with her close cropped dark hair was terrific.

She spun round and asked saucily, "Will I do?"

"You're a star," Mark said.

When they arrived at *The Phoenix* he saw how the eyes followed Barbara and he was proud to have her on his arm.

Then Maurice arrived on the scene. His gaze swept over Barbara from head to toe, and he took his time. He seemed to stare at her, and Mark tried to fathom his thoughts. He would have been surprised.

Maurice knew about Mark and Aimee and they were both here with separate escorts.

Wait till they see each other, he thought. Fireworks. Bang! Bang!

Quite oblivious, Mark enjoyed a splendid evening dancing and drinking with Barbara, and she made sure he realised there was nothing beneath her dress.

They stayed to watch the late-night cabaret, and the sexy Holly appeared.

"Jesus!" Barbara said, "She's sex on fire. What nipples."

Mark was amused. "So you noticed?"

But he wasn't amused a moment later when a hand lightly touched his shoulder, and he looked into the face of Aimee.

She wasn't exactly smiling, and whispered in his ear, "How many more have you got in your stable, Mark?"

His mood changed in a flash. He was likely to lose both ways. Barbara wouldn't be over the moon, and Aimee certainly wasn't.

Aimee had her secretary, Fay, with her. She was smart, but Mark thought she was a strange escort.

He had to admit he hadn't fathomed Aimee. She was like him, she made her own rules.

Barbara joined his arm. She was staring at them, eyebrows raised, and Mark was forced to make the introduction.

"This is Aimee, a business partner," he said. "And Fay, her secretary."

"Barbara runs the famous villas," he said to Aimee.

There were nods all round but nobody moved to kiss or shake hands.

Aimee said pointedly, "Are YOU a business partner Barbara?"

She replied sweetly, "Absolutely! Full time."

Then she conspicuously turned away to watch the cabaret.

Aimee had no choice but to move off with Fay, but she was riled at her cool dismissal.

Barbara had snubbed her deliberately. She resented Aimee's possessive manner. She whispered to Mark. "Does she think she's the bloody Queen?"

He said smoothly, "You're right. She does give herself airs." He added truthfully, "I've never really understood her."

Barbara pressed his hand. "I hope you wouldn't say that about me."

Mark was truthful again. "That would be impossible."

He laughed, "Let's get back to Holly's nipples."

"She's showing a bit more than that now," Barbara giggled. "You comfortable with that?"

Barbara grinned. "She's super. I could fancy her myself."

With which comment Mark heartily agreed.

Aimee, at her table with Fay, was miffed.

"Mark's a real stud, isn't he?" she said.

"What do you care?"

Aimee was of course well aware that Mark had other liaisons. But she was annoyed to find the competition so stiff.

Barbara's vivid personality had impressed her straight away, not to mention her strong sexual magnetism.

"Her fucking dress was skin-tight," she muttered.

Fay laughed. "Am I hearing this? You jealous over a man?"

"Not jealous, irritated." She said tartly, "I have plans for Mark."

Fay touched her hand. "Don't forget I'm always here, darling."

Aimee smiled faintly. She took Fay's loyalty for granted.

Nonetheless she had told her the truth. She wasn't jealous, but she did dislike the thought of Barbara's warm young body in Mark's bed. She felt Barbara was chipping away at her power base, and she wondered if she might have to do some more work on Mark.

Barbara saw Holly's act through to the end.

"How would you like Holly's nipples on me, Mark?" she joked.

He had to laugh.

"I could put ice on mine," she suggested.

"What about the black?"

"We'll see what we can manage tonight," she said mischievously. "Perhaps you could put the black on."

Mark grinned, "Give me more jobs like this."

Now he couldn't wait to get back home.

"Get your coat, darling," he said. "Let's see what the Lotus can do."

Barbara grabbed his arm. "Take it easy, Mark. You don't want my nipples falling off, do you?"

He doubled up, and suddenly realised he had more fun with Barbara than anyone else and wished he could see her more often.

But there was Aimee standing in the way; his obsession.

She could be a real bitch, but she was a match for him and a challenge, and now that he had seen her nude body his desire was almost out of control.

Abruptly he turned his mind off her. There was a joyous night ahead with Barbara.

They roared off in the Lotus and reached Mark's place in record time. The first thing Barbara did was to strip off her clothes and put on a dressing gown. Mark did likewise.

Then she marched into the kitchen and came back carrying a tray of ice cubes, which she put into Mark's hands.

She opened her dressing gown and said, "You know what to do."

Mark had taken on her gay mood and said with a smile, "They won't bite, will they?"

Barbara squeezed her breasts so the tips stood out straight.

"Try them."

Mark put on the ice, and she drew in her breath.

"Pretend it's Holly," she urged. "Flick them about a bit."

Then she brought his head down, and Mark went from one to the other. She seemed huge now, and he was almost mesmerised at the sensual touch from her yielding skin.

He was reluctant to move but Barbara obligingly parted her legs and he progressed downwards, but in a slower tempo. They seemed to have a silent understanding not to hurry and took their time right up to the final breathless moments, when a wild emotion swept them like a tidal wave. Even then Mark couldn't let Barbara go and he locked his fingers into her bottom and pulled her tight.

'Can it get better than this?' he wondered.

Barbara seemed to be reading his thoughts. "This one was special, Mark."

She ran her fingers through his hair. "You know," she went on, "Ever since you came to my rescue over that rape business I've felt I've known you better. Perhaps we don't always understand our motivations."

Mark was surprised. "Why, Barbara, you're quite the philosopher."

"Did you think I was just a pretty face?"

Then she burst out laughing, and Mark joined her.

Aimee's phone rang. "It's Mark."

"Yes, Mark?"

"I've been having second thoughts about another Palace. Do you think we could get together?"

Aimee woke up as if a burst of electricity had hit her... Were things going to go right again?

But she pretended not to be overwhelmed. She wasn't going to give Mark all the advantages.

She told a total lie and said coolly, "I thought that one was dead. What changed your mind?"

"You did."

"I did? I haven't mentioned the subject since our discussion."

"I wasn't ready then. Other things were crowding my mind." Mark halted. "Well! Is it yes or no? I seem to remember you saying you had a site picked out."

"Quite right. But of course I don't know if it's still available." Another lie. Aimee knew perfectly well the site was still available, but she wanted to mislead Mark. "If you're sure," she said, "I'll check it out."

Mark knew Aimee's devious mind worked like his and he was not surprised at her reaction. He was certain she had everything under control and ready to go.

"So is that a yes?" he said.

"It is, partner. You'd better get up here as soon as you can."

"Tomorrow?"

"Excellent."

Aimee put the phone down, her eyes bright. She was going to get her way after all.

The next day Mark arrived at her penthouse door early in the afternoon.

"You're early," she said.

"We've a site to inspect. I take it you've checked?"

"Naturally."

"Let me guess," Mark said. "It will have to be the other side of London. Say going towards Bucks?"

"Spot on. We think alike, Mark. The perfect partnership."

"Come on," he said, "Get in the Lotus."

Aimee swiftly changed into slacks, got in beside Mark and they roared off.

Mark hurried, and in half an hour he pulled up outside a big old house in deserted grounds. It was screened and it was isolated, but not far from a dual carriageway.

"Ideal," Mark said. "Let's get hold of the agent."

"I'm seeing him tomorrow."

Mark grinned. "Aimee, you're a fucking bitch. You're so much like me I'm almost frightened."

"That's why we're so good together."

"When are you going to share your body with me?"

"You'll know when I know."

After that little exchange Mark drove back to Aimee's penthouse, and they sat drinking coffee.

"We'll employ the same people," he said. "And I want a rush job again. The sooner we're in business, the sooner the money flows. The design can be the same, unless you have other thoughts."

"I'll see... Is the name agreed?"

"*The Palace of Pleasure?*"

Aimee nodded.

Mark grinned. "Sounds just right to me."

"One thing!" he said. "Same old problem. Who's going to run it?"

"We'll have to think about it." Aimee said. "Plenty of time."

"It's no good leaving it to the last minute," Mark said sharply. "We might be forced into a decision. We start now."

Aimee was reminded what a dynamo Mark was. But she knew he was right. The wrong person would blight the business.

She gave him a mock salute. "Action tomorrow," she said.

"I might talk to Steff," Mark said. "She knows all the talent. Could come up with something."

Aimee nodded, "Good idea."

"Now then," Mark said. "We've had an interesting day. What about the night?"

Aimee had no intention of giving Mark what he wanted, although she was quite happy to tease him, but she knew she'd have to be careful.

She said carelessly, "Stay if you want, Mark, but I'm not in the mood for careless rapture."

"What about CAREFUL rapture?"

"Never mind the words, Mark. It's no to bed."

Mark wasn't surprised. It was tease, tease, tease with Aimee. Then he surprised himself with a sudden rush of blood.

He seized Aimee roughly in his arms and slid his hands under her clothes to touch her naked breast.

Her reaction was immediate. She threw off his hand, and Mark felt a stinging slap round the face.

"Once more, Mark!" she said fiercely. "And it's finish. It's together or nothing."

Mark was cross. He'd hoped for a different response.

"I'm only a man, Aimee," he protested.

She said stiffly, "Goodnight Mark. I shall expect to see the other Mark next time."

Mark stared at her then said, "Fuck you, Aimee!" and stalked from the room.

Aimee smiled at his retreating back. She still had the upper hand.

She busied herself the next few weeks with the new project and in particular tried to find another Steff for the new Palace. But she found it hard going.

Then a friend recommended Cathrin Metz. She was the right age and for nearly ten years had been a very superior call girl.

Aimee had her up at her penthouse.

She was a dynamic brunette with big eyes and vivid lips. She really did shriek sex but it was nicely controlled in her manner, and she spoke intelligently.

"Why do you want this job?" Aimee asked.

"I've had enough freelancing. But sex is my game and so is money."

Aimee was impressed and asked her to meet Mark.

He came up to Aimee's to meet her, and Aimee wanted to sit in on the interview, but Mark insisted he see her alone.

"I didn't sit in on your interview," he pointed out.

He didn't want Cathrin to have an ally, and he knew Aimee was already sold.

"What makes you think you could run the *Palace*?" he asked Cathrin.

"I know sex. I love sex. I'm experienced in sex." She smiled. "Plus I have some brains. I'm not uneducated."

Mark was impressed with her assurance but he had a big doubt. She'll work for herself, he thought. Not us.

Aimee asked Cathrin to wait in reception and asked Mark, "Well?"

"No," he said.

"What! She's brilliant for the job."

"Yes she is, but I think she'd work for herself, not us."

"You're crazy."

"I've not built my business by being crazy," Mark said.

His words pulled Aimee up short. She couldn't deny his comment. But she wouldn't retreat from her position.

"So we have a stand-off," she said. "What do we do?"

"Third party decides," Mark said.

"Who?"

"The obvious choice, Steff."

"Let's get her over here," Aimee said.

"What NOW?"

"Now! I don't want you speaking to her beforehand."

Mark had to smile to himself. You'd have a job to put one over Aimee, and in fact she'd read his mind with pinpoint accuracy.

Aimee picked up the phone, and Mark heard her say "Yes now, darling, please hurry."

Steff was with them in less than an hour, and they explained what they wanted. So, Cathrin had her third interview, then they let her go home.

"Well, Steff, what's the verdict?" Aimee asked

"I was very impressed. She's very capable, sexy, ideal for the job."

Aimee looked at Mark triumphantly until Steff spoke again. "But I wouldn't employ her. I don't think she really wants to work for someone else. Just a change. I wouldn't back her long-term."

Mark looked at Aimee. "That's no twice."

"Fuck it," she fumed. "We've got to start all over again."

Steff interrupted. "I might be able to help. My chief assistant Leanne would be absolutely ideal. I would be sorry to lose her but I wouldn't stand in her way."

"I'll come over and see her," Mark said. "Thanks, Steff."

Aimee said tartly, "You won't forget I want a say, Mark."

He smiled at her cheerfully, "Noted, darling."

Mark liked Leanne on sight.

She was tall and slim and she gave off an air of glamorous devilment.

She had startling auburn hair that fell loosely about her shoulders in ringlets you were tempted to touch. And Mark liked the little smile that appeared to be lurking at the corners of her curved lips and echoed in her clear green eyes.

Nonetheless that didn't count at the interview.

Mark was tough and detached in business, and he didn't flinch from grilling Leanne.

He soon found out her history.

She had been an escort girl for some years but the experience hadn't hardened her, it had matured her, and it was Mark's impression that her mind was as open as her clear green eyes.

"What do you feel about sex?" he asked.

"It's good," she said, "But better when it's exciting."

"Think you can handle the awkward sods?" Mark asked.

"A smile goes a long way," she said.

Mark felt she was right for the job, and he liked her, but he had one concern.

"I just wonder if she's tough enough," he said to Aimee. "We can't have someone who's bulldozed all over the place. You know what arrogant bastards we get."

"Let me have a go at her," Aimee said.

Like Mark, she was immediately struck with Leanne's vivid colouring, and her quiet style impressed her. She also thought she could be very sexy and thought she'd test her.

She put her hand on Leanne's knee, but as she was about to open her mouth, Leanne calmly detached it and said coolly, "I only swing one way and it's not that way."

Aimee wasn't put off. In fact, she rather admired Leanne's boldness and thought it was a good example of toughness.

"You don't mind who you offend then?" she asked.

"Yes, I do. But I'm not going to offend myself."

"What about the exotic crowd?" Aimee asked.

"People can fuck who they like, how they like, and that applies to me also." Leanne was very assured.

Aimee was leaning very much in Leanne's favour, when she recalled Mark's concern about her.

She said candidly, "I just wonder how tough you are, Leanne. Could you be a bitch and make an unpopular decision? Or stop a row?"

" 'Fuck off' means the same whether it's shouted or spoken," she said coolly. "You will have to judge me for yourself. But I can give you some help... Ask Steff."

"Why Steff?"

"She's seen me in action. Cooling hot tempers."

Aimee picked up the phone, so Steff had no warning.

"Aimee here. Leanne told me she's handled some hot situations in your place. Give!"

Steff had been half expecting the call. She knew Aimee would test anything Leanne said immediately. No time for a tip-off.

"You don't want to be fooled by her quiet manner," she said. "I can remember one occasion in particular. It could have been very nasty. A regular turned up and found his preferred girl, Leonie, with another man, and threatened him."

"And?" Aimee prompted.

Leanne stepped between them and said to the aggressive man. "Bob! I want to talk to you," and she led him off.

"You're an intelligent man, Bob," she said. "If you want Leonie again you'd better not embarrass her."

"Come and have a drink," she coaxed, "While you look at the rest of the talent."

"And?" Aimee said.

"He apologised, and Leanne found him another girl."

"I thought that was beautiful," Steff finished. "Good enough?"

"How is it you can remember the conversation so clearly?"

"Well, I admit it may not be word for word," Steff said, "But near enough. It was in her early days and I was watching to see how she'd cope."

"Good enough," Aimee said, and rang off.

"Well you've got some support, Leanne," she said. "You can expect to hear from us."

In the evening she telephoned Mark. "I think we've found our new boss."

Mark was in absolute agreement when he heard what Aimee had to say but decided to wait a few days before he told Leanne their decision. He didn't want her to think there was no competition for the top job.

He finally told her after four days had elapsed.

He went into the *Palace* and beckoned to her. "You're the new boss," he said. "We expect to open in less than two months."

He stroked his chin for a moment.

"Tell Steff I want a couple of her girls to go with you when the opening is launched."

"She intended to anyway," Leanne said sweetly.

Mark raised his eyebrows.

"She was that certain you'd get the job?"

"SHE was. I wasn't."

She looked at him. "Do I get a penthouse like Steff?"

"You do."

"Lovely," she murmured. "I think I'll take to wearing a tiara. Queen of the Palace."

Mark had to laugh, but he injected a note of caution.

"Take care it doesn't slip," he said. "You're taking on a tough job." But he had confidence in Leanne and was relieved the hunt was over.

His thoughts went back to Aimee and he surveyed his position.

He decided it was ridiculous the way she was holding him off, and he made up his mind to play her at her own game. Let things cool. He didn't know what was in her mind but he did know what was in his, and it wasn't one-way traffic.

The lovely Leanne would be an excellent distraction and he would have every justification for keeping an eye on her. New job, new enterprise.

He went up to *The Phoenix* to spread the news about the new *Palace,* and Maurice immediately realised the quick and enormous profits to be made from these Palaces. Far outstripping his own out-of-town establishments.

They weren't in the same league.

"If you think of opening up any more and you want a partner," he said. "Count me in. Money no problem."

Maurice had been very deliberate before he made his offer. He knew better than anybody that sex sells and he regarded Mark as an ideal partner. Plenty of money, respected, secure, and, although Mark didn't know it, under his control.

Maurice still held videos of Mark's sex antics at *The Phoenix*. His reserve of power, he called it.

"I'm serious," he said. "I like to back winners."

Mark's mind ticked over furiously.

Further Palaces could open up a bonanza of riches. And with Maurice as a partner, he would have available protection and also a strong arm crew.

He realised that sooner or later others were going to be attracted into this easy money market. Maurice could then be very important. Nobody would tangle with him.

"I'll bear it in mind," he said.

But he wasn't ready to commit himself to Maurice without a great deal more thought. He had one big doubt about a partnership with him: his inclination to blackmail, and he feared he might not be able to resist the temptations in a new *Palace*. He would undoubtedly think it was the ideal place.

Unfortunately, Mark knew that any suggestion of blackmail would kill the Palaces stone dead. It was such a closed exclusive clientele the word would go round immediately. Even one victim would be too much. There would be one worry: who's next?

Mark was moody for the rest of the evening, thinking about new riches but mostly he was engaged with the pitfalls in the way.

Even the delicious Holly failed to stir him, and when he drove home his mind was unsettled, but he knew he couldn't disregard the opportunity from Maurice. His greed was too strong.

He could open up a chain, an Empire awash with millions. The thoughts jumped about in his brain like a charge of electricity, and he knew he would have no rest until he reached a decision.

He had one small consolation. For a change Maurice wanted something from him and he would plug his advantage as much as he could.

It was opening time for the new Palace, *The Palace of Pleasure*. Mark was keen to see how Leanne performed at the beginning of her reign, and he was hoping she would make a big impact.

She was like a dog with two tails. Her enthusiasm was tremendously heartening to Mark, and it seemed to encourage the others. Particularly, he thought, the girls who had come across from Steff's Palace.

Steff herself was there in full support and glittered like a jewel as she moved around with an eye on everybody, but she was generously unobtrusive, and Mark thought Leanne stole the show. Her tawny locks seemed to bob up everywhere.

He was well pleased with the opening night and reckoned Leanne was going to be another big winner.

To mark the opening, she provided free champagne for everyone, and this little touch put everyone in a good mood and provided the frame for a riotous evening.

Mark asked her who had authorised the free champagne and she smiled at him. "You did."

The surprise shot his brows skyward.

"I took the decision for you," she said. "I thought you could afford it." She added with an impudent smile, "I'm willing to pay if I've sinned."

Mark found her smile infectious, and Leanne gained another bonus point.

"Small sins are forgivable," he said.

To his surprise, late at night Maurice looked in, and, although he didn't stay long, Mark realised he was reminding him of his serious intentions. It was very unusual for Maurice to desert *The Phoenix*.

"Some place!" Maurice said to him. "Free for all but smooth. I like it. Particularly that flame-haired beauty running things. She's a wow!"

He gave Mark a long stare. "We must talk again, Mark."

Actually Mark didn't need the reminder. The subject of further Palaces kept nagging him like a sore finger. Making money was his big obsession. Even before sex.

He put his hand on Maurice's shoulder and said non-committally, "I hear what you say, Maurice. I won't forget."

In the morning he retired to Leanne's penthouse at her invitation.

"Well?" she challenged, over coffee. "What did you think?"

"In the words of somebody important, you were a wow."

Leanne tossed her head.

Mark was to learn this was a characteristic of hers.

"How important?"

"Very rich, AND powerful. He owns *The Phoenix* in the West End."

"Oh! You mean Maurice Robens. I've heard of him." She said thoughtfully, "What would bring HIM here?"

Mark wasn't giving secrets away. "He's a friend of mine," he said. "Just showing support."

"So what about the whole show, Mr Addison?"

Mark laughed out loud. "Leanne, you're a boss now. Call me Mark."

She quickly adjusted, "So Mark, what did you think?"

"I think *The Palace of Pleasure* is in safe hands. First class opening."

He rose and kissed her on the cheek.

"I shall be around for a while in case you run into any problems," he said. "But feel free to call me any time." He handed her his private card and left.

Leanne tapped it with her fingers. She was still somewhat overwhelmed with her meteoric rise, and also with Mark.

She knew all about powerhouse rich men used to getting their own way, and she knew from bitter experience that they tended to buy what they wanted and treat women like merchandise.

Nonetheless, she had to admit she liked Mark, and her instincts told her he was more than interested, but she didn't intend to be another one-night stand.

As a matter of fact, Mark intended to go very carefully with Leanne.

Although she attracted him, he sensed an independence in her similar to Aimee, and he decided he wouldn't push, but watch and wait.

At the moment his prime objective was the same as Leanne's: the success of the new *Palace*, and he intended to give her his full support. Business and money always came first with Mark.

He let a few days go by before he turned up unexpectedly about ten o'clock in the evening.

He went in unannounced, and Leanne didn't know he was there until she spied him talking to a very exotic looking brunette who was obviously disappointed that he had declined her invitation.

Mark laughingly waved her off but didn't say who he was, and this impressed Leanne.

She stood off and watched him circulate, and it was clear he was getting close up views from everybody.

It occurred to her he would be a very hard man to fool.

It was at least half an hour before he went in search of her, and she took him to her office where they sat facing each other.

"Well, you've got a lot of satisfied customers," he said.

"They're entitled," Leanne said. "It costs them an arm and a leg."

"I'm not about to cry," Mark said. "Any problems?"

"I'm not sure."

"Not sure?" he said sharply.

"It's Yvonne," she said. "One of two girls we recruited locally."

"Yes, I know Yvonne," Mark said. She was an attractive intelligent looking blonde. "What's she done?"

"It's not what she's done. It's what she's not done."

Mark was all ears. "Explain."

"She's hardly had a man in her embrace but she does an awful lot of talking. I'm afraid I've got a nasty suspicion."

Mark said grimly, "Is it the same as mine? That she's wired up and eager to make the news with a story?"

"Spot on."

Mark stood up. "Get hold of her and bring her here immediately. No buts!"

Leanne left and came back with a surprised-looking Yvonne a few minutes later.

"Lock the door," Mark said to Leanne. Then he said pleasantly to Yvonne.

"Yvonne, we know what you're up to. Are you going to come clean?"

She bridled, "What do you mean?"

Mark then stunned Leanne and Yvonne at the same moment.

He walked up to Yvonne, and although she backed away, tore away part of her dress. Then he put his fingers round her waist and pulled up a wire.

"You can't do this!" she shouted and tried to struggle, but Mark was too strong and ripped it from her body.

"Can't do what?" he said quite pleasantly. "I didn't see anything. Did you, Leanne?"

She shook her head, and Mark turned back to Yvonne.

In a voice full of menace he said, "Now get the fuck out of here and don't you ever come back."

He threw open the door and pushed her out.

"Problem sorted," he said to Leanne. "Well spotted."

"Phew!" Leanne said. "Man of action," and in that moment she really admired Mark.

"Suppose you'd been wrong?" she said.

"I back my judgement," he said.

And in that quick episode Leanne saw the ruthless streak in Mark that had made him rich. She wasn't sure whether she was more frightened or impressed, but she knew she wouldn't like him as an enemy.

Strangely she felt drawn closer to him.

"Come back to the penthouse," she said. "Coffee on the house."

Mark followed her and in a short while sat next to her while she filled his cup.

"Not bad," he said.

He had a further sip. "How are you finding things?"

"I was thinking I was doing a good job until you just shook me up," Leanne said honestly. "I couldn't have done what you did."

"The buck stops with the owner," Mark said. "You did what you should have done. Kept vigilant and told me. I ask no more."

Leanne was warming to Mark but kept her feelings tight.

He made no amorous move of any kind and, after further conversation, rose and left, leaving Leanne a little disconsolate.

She had wondered if he might make a pass and had to admit she was disappointed.

The next day she rang Steff and told her what had happened.

"His ruthlessness frightened me," she explained. "And yet he was right."

"That's part of Mark's charm," Steff said. "His ruthlessness."

Leanne thought about that and had to agree.

She had an afterthought... So long as they were on the same side.

Mark didn't appear again until the following week, and Leanne felt some frustration. She thought she had sensed an interest in him and wondered if she was mistaken.

Again Mark stuck solely to business and, illogically, it needled Leanne. While she dismissed quick sex, his lack of interest was like a shower of cold water.

Mark's tactics were paying off. He didn't want Leanne to think he was chasing her, and she didn't. In fact, she didn't think he was interested.

The next time she saw him he again walked in unannounced, and once more Leanne saw him before he saw her.

She began to realise he was unpredictable but she didn't dislike this quality.

She gave him a wave when he turned towards her, and he came over. "Everything OK?" she asked.

"Fine," he replied. "I suppose you didn't hear any more from the charming Yvonne?"

"She rang me and threatened to report to the police."

"And what did you say?"

A smile lurked round Leanne's face. "Do you want me to be honest?"

Mark nodded.

"I told her to fuck off."

Mark smiled delightedly and touched her on the arm. "That's my girl."

"You're teaching me to be decisive, Mark."

"That's the nicest thing you've said to me, Leanne."

She gave him a warm smile. "I can still learn."

And in that moment they both recognised an intimacy.

Leanne squeezed his arm. "I'm sure you'd like some coffee, Mark?"

He grinned. "Thought reader."

They retired to the penthouse, and when they'd had their coffee Mark put his hand on Leanne's.

"Perhaps we're friends now."

"Perhaps more," she whispered. An obvious invitation.

But Mark was still backing his instincts. He believed Leanne would not be impressed with a big rush.

He knew what a lot of women thought about rich men. They got what they wanted and moved on. He had even heard it called 'rich man's syndrome'.

"More comes later," he said. "But there's nothing wrong with a little kiss," and he leaned towards her.

Leanne was unprepared and her lips were slightly parted so the kiss was more erotic than Mark had intended. Leanne's lips moved slightly, and it was like a small caress.

Mark withdrew first, and she felt discouraged. She was also a little bewildered. He didn't strike her as a patient man.

Although, if she was to be honest, she preferred gradual to grab.

The weeks went by, and coffee in Leanne's penthouse became a regular habit. But Mark still played his cat-and-mouse game with the occasional kiss, and Leanne was getting exasperated.

At the end of the sixth week she said to him plaintively, "Don't you fancy me, Mark?"

"Of course I do," he said. "But I want YOU to fancy me."

Leanne rose from the settee, pulled Mark to his feet, and folded her whole body into him.

Then she kissed him hard and made sure he felt her breasts. She lifted her head. "Is that enough fancy?"

"Loud and clear," Mark said. "Make up your bed for two."

Leanne was elated and felt like racing into her bedroom. Although she was particular in her private relationships, she had been a call girl and knew all the tricks, and when they retired to her bedroom she was ready willing and able.

She undressed to her underwear. Cute lacy french knickers and a lacy bra that failed to conceal her large nipples.

Unlike his other women, she kicked off her shoes and still looked exciting. In fact, Mark thought she looked better without heels, and so did she. Tall, slim and exciting, he thought.

As she slid off her bra she said, "I hope you like large nipples, because that's what you're going to get."

"You've been reading my mind."

Then with a flourish she stepped from her knickers.

Mark couldn't tell if she was clipped. There was a small reddish cover at the top of her thighs but sufficient space to follow the curve between her legs.

"Guess you're a true redhead," he laughed. "My favourite colour."

Then he was alongside her on the bed.

She opened her lips and drew him in, flicked her tongue in little darts, and with constant movement let him feel her teeth.

Then she put his hands on her huge nipples. "Wait for it," she said. "They'll get even bigger."

Mark was getting roused by the second. "Do they embarrass you?"

She gave a joyous smile. "Not in bed."

Then she twitched, and Mark let his hand glide down to her reddish crop which he explored until he found the right spot in her warm centre.

She gave a gasp. Then a whisper.

"You can do whatever you like, Mark."

Immediately his mouth was between her thighs and he enveloped her, and when he felt her ready he hastily withdrew and drove straight into her.

She drew her knees back and Mark thrust so far into her he thought he was going to reach her heart. Then it was all music and he thought he'd never stop, but at last it was a shuddering standstill.

"My God! Mark," she whispered, "You been saving that up?"

""Perhaps I've been waiting for you."

"Even if it's a lie," she said, "I like it," and she gave him a little squeeze.

Mark did not make the mistake of thinking he now had rights over her, and in the following weeks he gave Leanne room, which pleasantly surprised her, although she did wonder if, having submitted, he was no longer interested.

But crafty Mark had something else in mind as well. He wanted Leanne to realise that, although their relationship had changed, business still ruled. Sex was second. Unfortunately, he nearly went too far.

She didn't invite him for coffee on his next visit and was noticeably cool.

"Have I done something?" Mark asked. "No coffee?"

"I thought you'd gone cool on me."

"You're surely joking?"

"Well I've hardly seen you for weeks. Did that lovely night we spent together mean nothing to you?" Leanne was emotional, and Mark could see he'd made a mistake.

He could have cursed.

"Accept my apology, darling," he said. "Unfortunately there will always be times like this. Problems and problems. I've been run off my feet."

The magic word that swung Leanne back was 'darling.' A word Mark had never used to her before.

For a moment she was like a statue, then she said softly, "Come and have a coffee, darling number two. I'm sorry I misjudged you. I suppose I expected too much."

"You can always ring me on my private number," Mark said. "Whenever you like."

They kissed and made up but stopped short of full sex. "When we've more time," Mark said. "It's too good to be hasty."

Afterwards he congratulated himself. He'd stopped false expectations from Leanne but left the door open. And he badly wanted that door left open. Very wide!

Aimee was perturbed that she hadn't seen or heard from Mark for some weeks, and she rang Steff.

"You seen Mark recently?"

"Not a lot," she replied. "He's been spending his time bedding-in Leanne."

"Oh! has he?"

She was even more displeased with the word Steff used. 'Bedding'.

Knowing Leanne, she realised that bedding might be nothing but the truth, and she knew Mark wouldn't forgo an opportunity. Aimee's lips tightened. She was not disposed to let Mark slip away. Never mind the sex, his weight and power could open many doors, and she anticipated further golden partnerships. She thought up a little plan then rang Leanne.

"I have been warned," she said, "That it would be a good idea to employ security men at the Palace. Will you see to it?"

"I'll speak to Mark," she replied.

"Good idea."

This was exactly what Aimee had expected. Now Mark would have to contact her and she would have the chance to compete with Leanne. And was she going to take it!

She was not surprised when he rang her. It was later on the same day, and she thought viciously "So he can't keep away from the lovely Leanne."

"Yes, Mark?" she said.

He was quite hostile. "What's all this crap about security men?"

"The police have been circulating the information."

"We've not heard anything."

"I suppose," she said easily, "It depends on your district. I'm all for safety."

Mark was silent for a moment. "I'll be up to see you." he said. "Tomorrow OK?"

Aimee pretended nonchalance. "If it suits you, Mark."

He was at Aimee's door the next evening.

She had dressed carefully for the occasion. A tight-fitting trouser suit that emphasised her slim lines and a top that was not revealing but dipped suspiciously when she leaned.

She wanted to appear businesslike and sexy, all in one, and she did a good job.

Mark gave her a second glance as she stood back to let him enter.

"Like the suit, Aimee."

"My business uniform," she said casually.

She got drinks and they sat together

"Now then, Aimee," Mark said. "What's all this fucking nonsense about security men?"

"Fucking sense. Not nonsense!" she said promptly. "I'm advised the Insurance Company will not look favourably at a claim in the absence of proper security safeguards."

Mark gave her a look of derision. "You can't be serious, Aimee."

"Where my pocket is concerned, deadly!"

"But Jesus, Aimee, we're an exclusive membership club! Not open to the public."

"What about guests that any member can sign in?"

"That's small beer, Aimee." Mark said ominously, "Either forget this stupid scare, Aimee, or give me the letter you received, or a name. I'm not taking this lying down... Fucking needless expense is just what I need!" he snorted.

Aimee saw she was defeated. But she was not surprised and didn't care.

Mark was there... Her real objective.

"All right," she said, in a resigned tone, "I'll bow to your superior knowledge."

But she couldn't resist a barb, "You'd better be right."

Mark grunted. "Just trust me, Aimee."

She stared at him, pretending to weigh up the subject, then said brightly, "OK, your responsibility," and dismissed the matter. Now she could tackle Mark. Her real purpose.

"I've seen little of you for some weeks, Mark," she said. "You gone cool on me?"

He pursed his lips. "I'd like to get hot on you, very hot, but you don't let me pass first base."

Aimee made a little mountain with her fingers, looked over the top and said softly, "Tonight might be different. I think you could say we're past the casual stage."

Mark brightened immediately. Aimee never failed to rouse him. Her slightly hollowed cheeks and the way she held her head always made her appear haughty, but tonight she seemed to have her guard down, and there was a glint in her dark eyes.

His longstanding desire began to simmer, then it took hold. "I can't wait," he said.

Aimee knew she had to deliver something special. Leanne was a big problem to overcome.

"Let's drink to that, darling," she said "And it has to be champagne. Special occasion."

She left the room and came back with a bottle and two glasses.

But she omitted to say Mark had something extra in his glass. A little help wouldn't go amiss, Aimee thought cynically.

Mark drank swiftly, then another, and they didn't retire to the bedroom until the bottle was nearly done. He felt really hot with desire.

Aimee then decided to tease him. Something extra. Prolong the show.

"Shall I jump into bed, or would you like a show?" Her face was a question mark.

With a lot of champagne on board Mark felt bold. "How about both?"

"Well, don't forget I'm not a professional," she mocked, "But perhaps I can interest you."

She threw off her jacket, her top, and her see-through bra. Then she immediately covered herself with her hands.

"That's not fair," Mark protested.

She smiled and uncovered her small tight mounds. Her nipples were pointed and vivid red, and Mark wondered if she'd put something on them.

"How many women can match that?" she asked, fingering them. "I could go without a bra."

Mark had to agree. They were like small defiant mountains, with hardly a droop, and he badly wanted to feel them in his hands.

Aimee moved again and stood entirely nude except for a tiny G-string. Her long slim legs and narrow hips were a model's dream, but Mark's gaze was fixed to the top of her thighs.

Her last wisp started to fall, and showed the smooth hairless curve between her legs, but as it fell she spun and flashed her tight rounded cheeks.

It flashed into Mark's mind that 'tight bottom' was a phrase that exactly suited Aimee. What a body, he thought.

"Tonight, Mark," Aimee whispered. "You're the boss. Whatever you want, just take."

"When you go overboard, darling, you do it in style," Mark muttered, "And I'm going to take you at your word."

He had another good look at her figure, now still. "I'd like you to lay on the bed, face down," he said, "So I can play with your body."

She immediately complied and obligingly parted her legs.

Mark was bemused at the amorous feast before him and advanced towards the bed slowly. He was so roused he could almost drive into Aimee from behind as she lay there, but he held his control and caressed her. He let his fingers glide round her bottom, then into the space between, and, as he touched the warm nude skin between her legs, he could hardly hold back.

He was hoarse with excitement. "Can I come at you now? I'm nearly gone."

She raised herself. "Do it, darling. Do it."

Mark was hard like a sword, and with the close feel of her buttocks exciting him, he stroked into her wildly.

His hands, almost unconsciously, wandered underneath to seize her breasts and he pinched them mercilessly. He hardly knew he was doing it but his impulses were out of control, and when sheer exhaustion at last brought him to a standstill he still lay on Aimee, inert.

She was more than satisfied. Mark had been sensationally excited. Mission accomplished. She was not concerned about her own feelings... Follow that, Leanne, she thought maliciously.

A little shamefaced, Mark said, "Sorry, Aimee. Shouldn't think you had much fun. I felt really wild tonight."

"You were rough, but I enjoyed it, darling," she lied. "I don't like a man to hold back. If you want to make amends," she cooed, "You can kiss my sore nipples better." And she displayed them.

They certainly looked angry, and Mark needed no urging to take them in his lips. If he'd had the energy he would have started all over again.

Aimee had won her battle.

Mark had felt as if a raging fire was sweeping through his veins, and Aimee was seriously back in his thoughts as someone special.

He now returned to his earlier thinking about opening new Palaces.

He knew Maurice was eager to back him, and he knew money galore would be the outcome, but he still had that big doubt about Maurice. Blackmail! Would he be able to restrain himself? Or want to? And suppose he gave a promise and broke it? Mark knew he couldn't battle with Maurice.

He was very tempted. Although rich, the pursuit of money was his holy grail and drugged his mind entirely. He would never have enough...

Money was power.

He decided to open things up and rang Maurice, "Remember our conversation about opening up new Palaces?"

Maurice's mind, like Mark's, was ever alert to make money, and ticked into gear immediately. "You having serious thoughts?"

"I am. Can we meet?"

"Come up this week. Perhaps you can stuff Holly afterwards," he said crudely.

"Doesn't she get a say?"

Maurice grinned. "She gets a say, then she says yes." He rang off.

Mark walked into *The Phoenix* two nights later, and Maurice promptly took him to his office, where they sat facing each other.

"So what you got in mind, Mark?" he said.

"To open up a chain, but only one at a time, because each one requires personal attention. Apart from the actual site, what is paramount is getting the right personnel."

"So?"

"I would want the next one on the Essex side of London. When we've encircled enough we branch out round the other big cities."

"Sounds good," Maurice said approvingly.

"But I'll be frank, Maurice." Mark said earnestly. "I know such establishments would seem to welcome blackmail, and it's easy with clubs, but blackmail in the Palaces would kill them stone dead and it has to be excluded.

"The members are closed groups of people who know each other and know they are committing misconduct, but feel safe. They would run a mile at even the scent of publicity."

He stared hard at Maurice and said, "If we cannot agree on this there's no point in going further. But, bear in mind the gold will flow by just playing it straight. No hassle."

He said persuasively. "Just think about the figures. Ten thous for membership. A minimum of 300, there will undoubtedly be more. That's three mill without the takings from drinks, drugs and so forth. And this is at each Palace we open. You can do sums can't you, Maurice?"

He put his hands together and stared at him. "On this basis, you in or out?"

Maurice was taken aback. "Seems like tossing away golden opportunities."

"The first time, maybe. Possibly the second also. Then you might as well close down. And our money's down the drain."

"Don't you think, Maurice," Mark went on convincingly, "That I would be all in favour if blackmail paid off? Am I a business man or not?"

Maurice realised Mark knew what he was talking about, but he took his time before he finally growled, "OK. You've got my vote. I'm in."

They struck a fifty-fifty partnership, with Maurice agreeing Mark superintended everything. "But don't forget," Maurice said ominously. "I still want a say. My money's as good as yours."

They shook hands on the deal, and had a couple of drinks. Then Maurice said. "Go and watch Holly. I've got a room reserved for you later." He added coarsely. "Work up an appetite."

Mark wandered out to watch the cabaret and waited till Holly appeared. She still seemed just as sensuous, and her enormous black nipples certainly did work up his appetite.

She was one big sex bomb and as she wriggled her way round the stage and unashamedly showed herself Mark reckoned he was in for a hectic night. In fact, hot would have been a better word.

When they got together Holly was insatiable and nearly wore him out. Once, twice, and she still wasn't satisfied.

"Jesus, Holly!" he said. "Where does all your fucking energy come from?"

She smiled sweetly and said, "Between my legs."

Mark gave her a good present of money, and she took it without a qualm. "Easy money," she said. "The way I like it."

Mark now had the next Palace on his mind and started his enquiries in Essex with the people he'd used before. "You know what I want," he said. "Ring me when you've got something."

It wasn't long before a place in Essex was offered to Mark, and so that he had a second opinion he decided to take Steff with him. He couldn't involve Aimee. If she knew she'd been cut out there would be ructions and he didn't fancy Maurice and Aimee striking sparks off each other with him in the middle. He hoped it would be a long while before she found out. Time to prepare a good lie.

Steff of course was surprised when she was invited and the first thing she said to Mark was, "What about Aimee?"

Mark put his finger to his lips. "She's not involved in this contract. Don't rock the boat."

Steff shrugged off her surprise. "No skin off my nose." She was chuffed Mark had chosen her to go with him. It made her feel important. Even more, to be trusted with a secret.

The next day she had a ride in the Lotus to Essex, and Mark's judgement in selecting her was fully vindicated.

She surprised him with her acute observations. One in particular that would never have entered his head.

They were discussing the layout, and she said, "It would be a good idea to have the chief's office on the upper floor overlooking the car park."

Mark was amazed. "Whatever for?"

"You can see who's coming and going."

"So?"

"Suppose you see somebody who's barred? Or somebody you might particularly wish to welcome? Even suppose it might be the cops or one of those confounded council bodies?"

She gave him a good stare. "You could get down to reception to welcome someone, or warn security to kick their arse out of the place. If it was the cops or suchlike you'd be glad of all the time you could find. The old boy scout motto," she said, "Be prepared."

Mark gave her an appreciative look and touched her lightly on the shoulder. "Nothing like experience, Steff. Glad you came."

She was pleased with the compliment. "Worth a good lunch?"

Mark took the hint and, before they motored back, he gave her a slap-up meal in the best restaurant he could find.

Neither of them had the same strong impulse for sex with each other these days. Mark was getting plenty, and he strongly suspected Steff was too. She would have a huge pick from her clients and she was enormously attractive.

Nonetheless she invited him in to her penthouse when they got back, and when she floated about, carelessly revealing her charms, Mark's pulse rate jumped. But for once his willpower ruled and Steff was safe.

He fancied she was teasing him, and the little smile lurking round her mouth gave the game away.

He got hold of her shoulders and swung open her gown. "Is it still on offer?"

She grinned. "If you like but I'd sooner have a cuddle and a drink." She added, still smiling, "Like a mature old lady."

"Some old lady," Mark said.

He took her to the settee and kissed her, but he couldn't resist testing her, and when he felt her tips enlarge he said, "So you're still horny."

She laughed. "They come up on their own now."

Mark couldn't stop laughing, and humour took them over. For once sex was relegated.

He said seriously, "Are you really happy in your job?"

Steff's eyes shone and she took his hand. "Enormously," she said. "The best thing that ever happened to me."

"Good," Mark said. "I might want to use you again, Steff. You opened my eyes today."

He gave her a warm embrace and light kiss and they parted on very happy terms.

Mark decided the place in Essex was suitable and informed Maurice but he simply grunted and said, "It's in your hands, Mark." So he went ahead and prepared to launch the next Palace.

He knew this one would take less time because the building would convert very easily. His most urgent job was to find another Steff to run the place.

He began to think about the women in his circle. For this sensitive position Mark preferred to choose someone he knew, if possible. An outsider might be disloyal. A risk that could cause enormous trouble.

He didn't fancy any more wired-up women rolling round the place.

Barbara came into his mind. Charming, intelligent, motivated, but he doubted she would take to the scene. She was sophisticated but not that loose in her standards. Besides, she was already doing a good job and he'd have an awful task to replace her. He reluctantly ruled her out.

What about Olivia? She would take to the scene like a duck to water and love ordering people about, and also Mark had a hold over her. His ownership of her stables was still a big secret.

The big snag was her heart was in her stables, and she wouldn't give them up. Divided loyalty was no good.

He shelved the problem, and it was left unsolved. But a few days later he got an unexpected slice of luck.

Carol telephoned him to say her relationship had broken down, and she wanted him to know she was available again.

His thoughts immediately brought her into the reckoning, and he wondered if an approach would be worthwhile.

Her credentials were first class. She was intelligent, sophisticated and strong in business. Her loyalty would be unquestioned, and he knew adventurous sex wouldn't bother her, quite the contrary.

The big snag was she'd have to give up a good well-paid job which made her independent, and for which she'd studied, but Mark thought he might be able to tempt her with money and the boss position; in his mind she was an immediate favourite and he decided to sleep on it.

In the morning he was still uncertain. He wasn't sure if Carol would be willing to make the psychological change of dealing with people rather than the figures that came across her desk and didn't answer back.

But he knew he wanted her and decided to make the first move.

He telephoned. "Hallo again, darling, Couldn't resist your invitation. How about the Riverside? Say Wednesday?" He kept quiet about his real purpose.

"Delighted," she said. "Pick me up? Red Lotus?"

"My pleasure." He hoped it would be, but knew he had a tough task.

Carol looked very glamorous when he picked her up and still stirred him. She welcomed him with a warm kiss and made sure he had a good leg show in the car.

Mark was encouraged, "So you still fancy me?"

"Just about," she said cautiously. She didn't intend to let Mark have things all his own way.

"So what broke you up?"

"He wasn't as serious as I was."

Mark digested this and wasn't pleased. Then he realised that if Carol took the job she would probably think she had even greater access to him. A plus mark in his favour after all.

At the Riverside, Mark got his usual royal welcome and service. Carol had missed this with her other partner, and it added spice to the splendid meal they enjoyed.

Towards the end he said, "I've suddenly had an idea, Carol." He looked at her enquiringly. "You completely happy in your job?"

Her surprise was obvious. "Of course I am. I've had to work bloody hard to get where I am."

Mark persisted. "But you're not a boss."

She laughed. "I'm with a big outfit. There might be a chance when I'm ninety."

"How would you like it to be now?"

Carol's head jerked up. "You serious?"

Mark nodded.

"Go on."

"I don't know if you've heard of *Fantasy Palace*."

She interrupted him. "I once went there as a guest. Phew! Half of them were naked and nobody turned a hair."

"Did it offend you?"

"Not at all. I just wanted to have a look."

"And what did you think?"

"All right for those that wanted it, and absolute luxury. Waited on, hand and foot."

Time for the plunge, Mark thought. "Guess who owns it," he said.

Carol said coolly, "You do."

It was Mark's biggest surprise for some time, and his voice went a bit weak. "How did you know?"

"I didn't. Your questions gave you away."

Mark had forgotten how quick Carol was, and it reminded him what a capture she would be.

"I'm opening a new one," he said. "Exactly along the same lines. I want a boss. Top money, far more than you could ever earn, a penthouse, security, and absolute authority."

The offer staggered Carol, and she was impressed, but she was also uncertain. "I've no experience, Mark," she said. "I might fall flat on my face."

"You'd have two months to understudy Steff, the boss at Fantasy Palace."

"We might not get on."

Mark was getting a little cross as she put obstacles in the way, but he realised she was right.

"We can soon find out, can't we?"

"All right," she said. "Lets find out. If I like her I'll think seriously about joining you."

She gave him a smile. "Now then. Your place or mine?"

"Yours. After we've been to see Steff."

"What now?" Her eyes opened wide.

"Let's see how serious you are."

Mark pulled out his mobile. "Steff, I'm bringing somebody over about the Essex job. I might have another Leanne for you. OK?"

Steff got the message. "Fine," she said.

Within the hour Mark drove up to *Fantasy Palace* and parked.

Steff was waiting for them and gave Carol a searching look. She was good on faces. "Haven't I seen you before?" she asked.

"I was here once on a short visit."

Steff's face cleared and she gave Carol a warm clasp and kissed her on the cheek. "Knew I'd seen you."

She said generously, "The glamorous ones make an impression."

She made an immediate friend. Carol had already sized up Steff and glimpsed the intelligence behind her beauty.

"You're not so bad yourself," she said.

"I'll wait in your penthouse, Steff," Mark said, and turned away.

He was pleased they seemed to gel. Good start.

Steff took Carol on a long tour and explained a few things she didn't appreciate. For instance, although there was an unwritten rule that advances should not be refused by either sex, it was not obligatory. And in fact some couples went together. Some split up, some didn't.

Carol began to realise that managing people was full of pitfalls. "What happens?" she asked, "If someone goes too far?"

"Be precise."

"Suppose a man tries to force anal sex but the woman objects."

"She presses a nearby bell and instantly a girl appears to intervene. She always has to support the person who objects, whichever sex. We do not support rape or force. Only mutual acts."

"What about the aggrieved person who is stopped?"

Steff smiled. "The manager steps in and spreads charm."

"I can give you a few tips," she added. "One big plus thing," she said. "You'll find you make lots of important friends. All our clients without exception are wealthy. They have to be."

Carol was warming to the challenge but she had a final question.

"What sort of boss is Mark?"

"He leaves you alone but you can run to him if you're in trouble."

This was what Carol had anticipated, but she was glad to have it confirmed.

"OK, back to Mark," she said.

"Well?" he asked. "Anything settled?"

"In my mind, yes," Carol admitted. "But I'd like to sleep on it."

This satisfied Mark, and as they left the Palace he gave Steff a confident grin.

He put his foot down in the Lotus on the return journey. He guessed Carol would be lit up and was hoping for a good night.

They were in her bed soon after arriving and she didn't disappoint him.

She seemed to be on fire almost instantly, but she took her time, teasing him until he was at his limit. Then she stretched her legs wide and pulled him up tight so she felt every stroke.

Mark was breathless. "You still know how to do it, darling."

Carol grinned. "It takes two."

Mark now waited for her decision.

He was not surprised at her caution, he knew she was very level-headed and had a lot to consider, but he was confident she would not refuse him.

Nonetheless it was three days before she rang him, and the delay was making him edgy. He didn't fancy starting the search all over again.

"Carol here, Mark," she said, "I'd like to see you again about that new position."

Mark was surprised. "You've not decided then?"

"Half."

"I'll come over tonight," he said.

He added with grim humour, "Perhaps I can provide the other half."

Carol received him in what she called her working clothes, a well-cut suit and top. Still smart but without her usual glamour.

Mark joined her on the settee. "What's troubling you, darling?"

"I'll be quite straight with you, Mark," she said, "The job appeals to me immensely but I don't see I have any security. Suppose we fell out. I should be out on my arse, wouldn't I? And nothing to go back to."

Mark saw her reasoning. In her present occupation she had all sorts of safeguards, plus a gilt-edged pension, and if she broke away she threw it all to the winds. There was no walking back.

"Suppose I give you a written contract?"

"Then you've got your new boss."

"You've got it," he said. He was highly relieved the problem was solved and he gave her a quick kiss.

The timing was perfect. The new Palace would open in about eight weeks, just the period for Carol's training.

"I want you to get in touch with Steff," he said. "She'll probably want you to stay at her penthouse for the probationary period. Anyway, you can work it out."

Carol fetched a bottle of champagne and two glasses.

Mark was surprised, "That's not your drink."

"Celebration."

"So you were expecting to get your way?"

"Nothing like being prepared."

Mark immediately thought of Steff. She'd said the same thing.

"You and Steff should get on well," he said.

They clinked glasses, and he nodded, "To our partnership."

"Not forgetting the old," Carol corrected.

Mark left her place happy, and as soon as he stepped into his car he rang Steff on his mobile. "I've landed Carol," he said. "The new place opens in about eight weeks. I want you to get her ready."

"It won't be hard," she said. "She's got what it takes, and I like her."

Mark was pleased. "Thanks, darling, you're a jewel."

He was constantly at Steff's side during the following weeks, but she didn't need to tell him Carol was progressing. He could see it in her confident air.

"What are your thoughts?" he asked her.

"I'm eager for the fray," she said. "Steff's promised to help me at the start and she's also promised to send over some of her girls. They'll soon get things going."

The grand opening came, and Steff was generous enough to make the trip to Essex herself. Carol was grateful, as they had become good friends.

She gave her a kiss and thanked her. "I hope I can help YOU some time," she said. A sly smile slipped across her face. "How do you like the new name?"

Steff was quizzical, "Golden Palace! Not sure," she said. "How about you?"

"Love it," Carol said.

"That's all that matters," Steff said.

In a month Carol was in full control and her doubts had vanished.

Mark was gleeful and reported the success to Maurice.

"Never had any doubts," he grunted. "I only back winners."

Then a bombshell exploded in Mark's lap.

He received a message Janet wanted to see him.

He picked up the phone. "What do you want, Janet?"

"You'd better get over here pronto, Mark," she said.

"Couple of hours do?"

"NOW!" she snapped. "This won't wait."

Mark was intrigued. Forceful! Not like Janet. He sauntered over to her office and saw the accountant sitting by her side. Her face was as black as thunder.

He slid into a seat. "What's up?"

Janet looked at him with a grim face. "Up to now the finances have all been in your hands," she said. She tapped the pages in front of her, then said ominously, "I have a report here which does not account for huge sums disappearing from the company's account."

Mark was unprepared for this setback and said cautiously, "As you say, since Dad died the finances have been under my control, and I have used my judgement to improve the company's position, especially in the long run. You must be aware, Janet, we have spare capital, and it cannot be left idle."

"Then perhaps you will explain where the money has gone." Janet was stiff and unrelenting, and the accountant sat by her with a set face.

Mark had regained his composure and was annoyed with the accountant. "Edward why didn't you come to me? I'm in charge of finances."

He said defensively. "Janet asked to see the figures."

This was quite true. Janet had decided it was time she had a look at the company's finances, but her interest had only been casual until she examined the figures and asked questions.

"Same question to you, Janet," Mark said.

She said hostilely, "I'm coming to you now! I would like an explanation."

"I think," Mark said smoothly, "The best thing is for me to go over the figures with Edward, then we'll get back to you with all the information you want."

Janet's suspicions were red hot but grudgingly she had to accept this compromise. "All right!" she snapped. "We'll talk again in seven days." She added forcefully, "No longer."

"I'll start with Edward this afternoon," Mark said, and he got up and left. His mind was seething. Was all his enterprise to be wrecked by strait-laced Janet? Not if he knew it!

Edward was the key. Janet knew very little about the financial side and relied on him exclusively, both for information and guidance.

Mark reviewed Edward's career.

He had been Company Accountant for many years. Engaged by his father and respected by him. But he was eligible for retirement in about five years, and Mark thought he would probably want to extend this. He was well paid, had a company car, many perks, and a comfortable existence.

He had a lot to lose. He was only in his fifties.

A plan was already beginning to form in Mark's mind, and he went to Edward's office with his confidence restored.

Edward greeted him deferentially. "Where would you like to start, Mark?"

"Before we start, Edward," Mark said, "I just want to recap. How long is it you've been with us? Is it fifteen years?"

"That's right," he replied. He felt a little unease at this line of conversation. Exactly the psychological effect Mark had intended, and he deliberately paused for a period as though he was considering Edward's position.

One thing Mark was certain about. Edward was no fool. He had always held his own with Mark's father, who had been an expert on finances, and he would not have put up with anyone incompetent.

He said at last. "I'm going to take you into my confidence, Edward, and I shall expect you to honour it." He stared at him.

"Apart from the big outlay on Lady Olivia's stables, which were bought as a service to our clients, I have put money into entertainment establishments that my sister would condemn, but which are going to produce huge profits."

He refocused his eyes on Edward. "So the position is I have to dress up these establishments for the benefit of my sister or cost the company a lot of money." He gave a tight little grin. "Mind you, she will be happy enough to draw the profits."

Edward asked, "What are these establishments you wish to conceal?"

Mark had to tell him because he could have found out quite easily.

"Good Lord!" he said. "They're pretty blue, aren't they?"

"That's why they pay well."

Edward was silent, and Mark wondered what was going on in his mind.

At last he said, "If I agree to the deception I shall be in breach of my duties as Chief Accountant."

"But not to your employer," Mark said. "And I would naturally see you benefit from supporting me."

"Well," Edward said, "I did hope to continue after my retirement date."

"I hope you do," Mark said. "I am intending to improve your contract substantially, and we can talk about it over the next few weeks."

Edward was won over. "So what heading shall we use for this extraordinary expenditure? It's still difficult," he said.

"How about 'Associated Entertainments Ltd.' with a London address?"

"But that company doesn't exist."

"It will immediately I can get to a solicitor," Mark said. "Technically it will be a holding company with no practical effects."

He leaned towards Edward conversationally, "Then we can honestly say the money has been invested in Associated Entertainments Ltd, a London company building up its capital buildings programme with a promise of high profits."

"So can you produce some figures for me from these enterprises?" Edward asked. "We can then present them as outlets under the company name. A perfectly proper procedure."

"No problem," Mark said. "Each place keeps its own books under strict accounting standards."

He studied Edward. "So are we agreed?"

"We are."

His lips moved in what Mark supposed was a small smile. " 'Associated Entertainments' is an excellent choice of words. Covers a multitude of sins."

Mark rose and left his office, and when the door shut Edward switched off his recorder. "Just as well to be safe," he muttered.

Mark made a mental note to inform Aimee and Maurice about the 'Associated Entertainments' heading. But there was no problem there. He would simply say it was a tax dodge.

At the end of the week they all met again in Janet's office. She seemed a little less hostile this time. Perhaps she'd had second thoughts, Mark thought.

"Hope you've some good news for me," she said.

"I'll let Edward explain," Mark said. "He's the figure man. But I'll answer any questions."

Edward started off confidently. "I'm glad to report that Mark's investments are sound and, in addition, will be very profitable."

He named 'Associated Entertainments' Ltd and quoted the figures from Mark but skated over the names of their outlets.

"Who are these people?" Janet asked.

Mark cut in. "It's a limited company but their interests run from dance halls to clubs. The entertainment industry is a booming place for investment nowadays," he said.

Edward continued very cleverly. "As you can see," he said, passing over sheets of figures to Janet, "These initial returns are extremely good. Even better than Mark had anticipated, and those projected are even better."

Janet didn't see, but she did see the profits quoted, and as it was Edward doing the quoting she was completely won over.

"All right," she said. "I can see I jumped too quickly."

"But," she said, addressing Edward, "I want to be kept informed of outside investments in future. I don't want another embarrassment blowing up."

She eyed him deliberately, "Will you make sure of this, Edward?"

"Of course I will," he said.

Mark left Janet's office completely happy; he'd have no more trouble with her. Future investments would be lost under the heading of 'Associated Entertainments' and the continuing profits would keep her quiet and satisfied.

He was more concerned about Edward. He hoped he hadn't foiled one enemy to be presented with another. If Edward opened his mouth Janet would completely lose all faith in him.

He knew he'd have to give him a good deal when they talked but this was no problem. As usual with Mark, money was the key.

A few days later an irate Aimee rang Mark.

The balloon had gone up.

"So another Palace has opened," she complained, "And I'm shut out. What the fuck are you playing at, Mark? I thought we were partners."

"We are. We are," he soothed. "How can you doubt it?"

Then he said sharply, "Are you in your penthouse?"

"Yes. Why?"

"I don't want to be overheard. Now listen," he said. "My partner in this new Palace in Essex is Maurice. You can guess why, can't you?"

"You mean he's got something on you?"

"Well said, and, as you know Maurice, doesn't go for three-way splits. It hurts him enough to accept two."

"So can I take it the door is still open for us?"

"You can. You find your half of the money, and I'll find mine."

Her tone dropped in relief. "Great."

For a brief moment she was silent then she said abruptly, "Can you come up to see me?"

"Urgent?"

"For me, yes."

Mark was intrigued. This wasn't like Aimee.

"You can expect me within two days," he said.

He was there two nights later and sat with Aimee in her penthouse.

"So, spit it out," he said.

Her face went a little tight and she said, "I've had a blackmail demand."

Mark's surprise showed. "Go on."

"Obviously it's connected with my past," she said, "But the story would embarrass me now."

She hesitated, "It's not that I can't meet the demand, but it will continue, won't it?"

Mark looked at her. "Are you going to tell me the secret?"

"Certainly not. I want it kept in the past."

"I suppose you don't know who it is?"

"He thinks I don't know, but I do."

"Well, that makes things easier, doesn't it?"

"No, it doesn't," she said. "He's a journalist, not a prominent one, but he can get the story spread across all the papers."

"So you want him out of the way?"

"I want him stopped."

"You mean beaten up and warned off?"

"I suppose so," she admitted.

Mark still couldn't stifle his curiosity. "Come on, Aimee," he urged. "You can let me into the secret. I'm a big boy."

"Definitely not," she said. "You know what secrets are, Mark. You tell one person. He tells his best friend, etc. etc."

"So you won't trust me?"

"I don't want you to know, Mark. Sorry!"

He stared at her, annoyed. "All right!" he said, "I'll see what I can do. Give me his name."

"Roger Harrison. He's a reporter for one of the daily papers." She scribbled on the back of one of her own cards. "Here's his address."

Mark tapped it on his fingers. "You sure about this, Aimee? There's no backing out afterwards."

"I'm sure, and the sooner the better."

Mark rose. "Right! I'll get on with it."

Unusually, he left Aimee without even thinking of sex. He was consumed with curiosity and wondered what on earth she could be hiding. Under-age sex? An abortion? Something she'd done? The thoughts pounded in his brain.

His first act was to contact Maurice and he explained the position to him. "Aimee wants him roughed up," he said.

"That's no fucking good!" Maurice growled. "It might shut his mouth for a month but he'll be back."

"So?"

"Leave it to me," Maurice said, "But don't forget you owe me."

Mark knew what Maurice's solution would be but he couldn't object. At least it would keep Aimee safe, and he was sure she would be grateful.

"One thing." Mark said. "I don't want a motor accident."

In his mind it was too near to his father's accident, and he was mindful that the police had a nasty habit of matching events on their computers.

They particularly didn't like coincidences.

"Does he drink?" Maurice asked.

"He's a journalist."

"Easy meat," Maurice said callously.

Mark decided not to tell Aimee what Maurice intended, and hoped whatever happened looked accidental.

He simply told her the matter was being taken care of and she said, "Thanks a million, Mark. I'll show you my gratitude."

"Can't wait," he said.

Two weeks later Roger Harrison died after a late-night punch-up outside a London club. He breathed his last in hospital after an injury to his head. The police said it was impossible to say who started the fighting but, according to witnesses, the men were all drunk.

Mark rang Aimee with the news.

She was almost tearful. "Jesus, Mark! I didn't want him killed."

Mark said calmly, "It was a genuine accident. Apparently Roger struck his head when he fell. Nothing anybody could do about that."

He added, without sympathy, "But I shouldn't be too sorry for a blackmailer."

Aimee went silent, but her relief was immediate.

She said at last, "Suppose you're right."

Mark was now determined to unearth Aimee's secret. He calculated it had to be something important and could well affect his attitude towards her. He decided to tackle her long-time friend and secretary Fay. She might loosen up after enough drink, he reasoned.

He turned up at Kinks Palace when he knew Aimee was absent.

"Perhaps you can help me with one or two things, Fay," he said. He carefully enquired about business matters well within her province, which she was able to answer, but when he slipped in one or two personal questions about Aimee she was either evasive or didn't know.

Finally, he said pleasantly, "Well you've saved me a wasted journey, Fay. Let's forget business. Come and have a drink."

Her surprise was obvious, and he said, "You don't expect me to drink on my own, do you?"

She soon showed she wasn't a drinker, and Mark thought, this is going to be easy.

But even after several drinks Fay showed she was tougher than he had expected and was surprisingly loyal to Aimee.

He eventually said to her semi-seriously, "What's Aimee's big secret, Fay? She's been teasing me."

"Come on," he urged "I'll keep it to myself."

But she still kept mum. "Secret?" she repeated.

"Loosen up, Fay," Mark said. "You know what I'm talking about."

He took a shot in the dark. "I suppose you heard about Roger Harrison? HE knew."

She gave him a sharp look. "Why don't you guess?"

Mark knew she was laughing at him but he had no answers. "Guess?" he asked.

"You've had your hands on her body," she said.

Mark still couldn't work out the mystery, and his baffled look prompted Fay.

"Don't you think she's an exceptional figure?"

"Yes I do. I've often thought she could be a model."

Although far from sober, Fay said maddeningly, "Well, there you are."

"So she's had cosmetic surgery," Mark said. "So what?"

Infuriatingly, Fay only repeated what he'd said. "So what?"

Mark couldn't get anything more out of her and went home just as baffled, but he decided on a bold move to uncover Aimee's secret.

The next day he rang her. "I regret to tell you, Aimee," he said, "I got Fay a bit tight yesterday and wormed your surgical secret from her."

He heard her draw in her breath sharply. Then she dropped a bombshell. "So does it make a difference to you that I was born a boy?"

The enormous shock silenced Mark for a moment.

"Of course not," he said. "I'm interested in the person I've always known."

But he was lying.

Aimee'd had a sex change. She was part man, part woman. He couldn't stomach the idea, and suddenly everything about her fell into place and his desire for her vanished.

"You will keep mum, Mark?" she pleaded.

"My lips are sealed."

He put on an effort and managed a little chuckle. "Well, that's out of the way. See you soon, Aimee."

But his words meant nothing. The whole landscape had changed.

He sat reflecting and could foresee trouble.

He and Aimee were still partners and both party to Buckingham's murder. In addition, Maurice cutting Aimee out of the Palace bonanza was trouble waiting to happen.

Mark feared that sometime this would all blow up: Aimee versus Mark versus Maurice and he didn't want to think about the consequences.

He swung his thoughts to Leanne.

He was becoming more enamoured with her by the day. Her tawny locks danced in his mind, and he thought of her as his golden girl.

He thought with relish of the adventurous sex they'd enjoyed, and his mind ran riot as he thought of future pleasures.

But first another shock.

Olivia telephoned with an ultimatum. "I want my place back," she said. "The stables are my life."

"Sure," Mark said. "Buy me out."

"You know I can't."

"Well then?" He was becoming exasperated.

"There are other ways," she said.

Mark didn't like the way the conversation was going. "Come down and see me," he said.

Olivia turned up later in the week and sat in Mark's office.

"Your call, Olivia," he said.

"You know perfectly well what the stables mean to me, Mark," she said, "And I'm petrified my friends will find out I'm no longer the owner."

"You didn't let that interfere when you wanted my money," he replied, "and I've honoured my promise and not said a word."

"I know," she said. "But the pretence is killing me! I'm on edge all the time."

"So what do you propose?"

"I'm afraid I propose blackmail, but on a definite once only basis, because I only want one thing: my stables back."

Mark's face went grim.

"You'd better be specific, Olivia."

She swallowed. "The killing of Roger Buckingham. You were there that afternoon and helped with the cover up."

"But you did the killing."

"We know that, but suppose I told the police you did it. The gun was never found, was it? Maurice took care of that."

"I can't believe I'm hearing this, Olivia! From a friend I've leaned over backwards to help." Mark glared at her.

She said miserably, "I know it's despicable but I'm in a corner, Mark. I've no money to put on the table. This is all I have to trade, and I swear if you give me back my stables that is the end of the matter. I hate blackmail as much as you."

"I'm sure you wouldn't want to take a chance with the police, Olivia."

"I wouldn't. But, Mark, I have to have my stables back."

Mark could see this problem wasn't going to disappear and his mind worked quickly.

"All right, Olivia," he said, "I'll form a separate limited company to take over the stables. I'll make you a director. That makes you an owner."

Olivia was both ashamed and delighted; and also not far from tears.

"I still want to be your friend, Mark," she said.

"Well, bear in mind what you owe me," he said. "I may want to collect some day."

She got up and kissed him then left his office. When she was out of earshot Mark shut off his recorder and played the conversation back.

"An unprompted admission of the killing," he muttered. "What a piece of luck! Thanks, Olivia."

Mark was sitting in his office, contemplating an evening with Leanne, when Maurice came through on the phone. Mark thought he seemed a bit tense.

"I want you to do me a big favour, Mark," he said.

"I've got an American businessman coming over who wants to get out of the limelight for a few weeks. One of your villas would be just the job. That OK?"

"Unfortunately not," Mark said. "They're all occupied and we've a big waiting list; but we could put him in the hotel."

"No good," Maurice said. "It has to be detached and private."

Mark wondered what sort of person Maurice was referring to and guessed you could substitute the word 'crook' for 'businessman'.

But before he could answer Maurice took up the conversation again. "Mark, this is very important to me and t has to be next week." His voice rose, "Come on, you owe me."

Mark didn't like the veiled threat but he didn't want to battle with Maurice. "OK," he said, "I won't let you down, Maurice. But don't think it's easy. Millionaires don't like being kicked out. That's why they pay big money."

A smile struggled over Maurice's tight face. It had been easier than he'd anticipated.

"Appreciate it, Mark," he said.

"What's his name?"

"Call him Mr Wilson."

Mark wondered what his real name was. "Right, I'll make the reservation from Monday next," he said.

He sought out Barbara and explained somebody very important had to have a villa quickly, and he allowed her to think Mr Wilson was an American politician.

She said slowly, "There's only one couple I could really approach, Mr and Mrs Adams. Fortunately they're very nice people. They stay on and off, but I'll need a good excuse to make them leave at a moment's notice."

"I know," Mark said. "Any ideas?"

Barbara pursed her lips and was thoughtful.. "Suppose we say our maintenance crew report that the wiring should be exchanged. It could cause a fire, and it's a big job."

Mark blessed her inventive brain and gave her a kiss. "Brilliant, Barbara."

"I'll go and see them now," she said.

She was back in an hour. "No problem," she said. "I dressed it up a bit. Said our maintenance crew are very particular over fire hazards and would not subject our clients to the slightest risk."

She gave Mark a quizzical look. "So, it's 'Welcome, Mr Wilson'."

Mark thought she was inviting him to say more but he kept his mouth shut. "Well done, Barbara," he said. "I owe you one."

She said saucily, "Be careful I don't collect."

He gave her a gentle pat on the backside. And they both knew she WOULD collect and what it would be.

She was very interested when Monday came, and watched a long black Mercedes turn up to deposit Mr Wilson at his villa. He was quite a small person, wearing dark glasses, and he was accompanied by a big tough-looking man who hurried him into the place. Another big man stood at the car door sweeping the scene with his eyes.

The scene fitted Barbara's idea of an American politician. The long black limousine and the cop by his side, and she accepted the idea.

Mark picked up the phone to Maurice. "Mr Wilson is installed."

"Thanks, Mark," he said. "Knew I could rely on you. It's good to have friends you can trust."

Typical Maurice comment, Mark thought. Thanking and warning at the same time. "Don't forget, Maurice," he said, "that goes both ways."

Maurice surprised him. "Of course, Mark. Anything you want. From kissing to killing." He gave a light laugh, but Mark guessed that Maurice wouldn't be smiling.

He just hoped Mr Wilson wasn't going to bring trouble.

He allowed his mind to drift back to Leanne, and when the evening came he took a little trip to the Palace of Pleasure.

She was conspicuous in a slinky dress that clung to her superb figure as if it were an extra skin, and it was in a sensational green that matched her eyes and contrasted her flaming locks. She was the centre of attention and outshone everyone.

She greeted him with a dazzling smile. "You looking for a girl, Sir?"

Mark felt envious eyes following him. He was rather amused, but he had to admit it did his self-esteem no harm at all.

"I am," he said. "Any suggestions?"

"I know a girl in a green dress with green eyes who might be willing."

Mark grinned as he followed her to the penthouse. Leanne was a treasure.

She seemed to guess he was in a reflective mood and didn't hurry him. She sat close and leaned back against the cushions.

"You look as though you need cheering up," she said.

"And have I come to the right place?"

"Ask me later on," she said softly. Then she rose and fetched him a drink, returning in a dressing gown that opened as she moved.

She crossed her long legs, and Mark ran his hand up them until he reached her thighs and touched her reddish crop.

"Let's do the job properly," she breathed, and helped him off with his clothes.

Immediately they were both nude. She appeared to have risen from her gown without an effort.

Mark couldn't help comparing her to Aimee and remembered his admiration of her slim lines. Quite illogically, he now felt she'd cheated him, and he didn't regard his thinking as illogical at all.

Leanne was staring at him with a mischievous glint in her eyes. "You wondering what to reach for first?" she said.

Mark dissolved into laughter. Then he seized her and felt her stiff nipples. But it was her sensuous lips that beckoned, and when she opened them it was as though she was opening up herself, and she arched into him eagerly.

He let his hands wander and marvelled at the sensational touch of her firm skin. Just the touch of her body sent his senses soaring and he had to hold back.

But the warm centre between her legs was implanted in his mind like a raging signal and he felt for it gingerly, then more violently.

He realised she was ready, and he certainly was. The perfect moment! She drew back her legs and he drove into her, and it was as though the floods had come. They held each other tight and gloried as their bodies went wild. Mark could never get enough of Leanne and it was if their bodies knew it.

It was only afterwards they found they had pinched and clawed each other.

Leanne looked at her marks. "Honourable scars, darling," she said.

Mark fully agreed. "Small price for big music," he said.

Leanne liked that.

Two weeks later it was back to Barbara.

She glimpsed that long black limousine again and was amazed to find Mr Wilson quickly put aboard and, without a word to anyone, driven away. He had only been in the villa three weeks.

She got on the inter-com and told Mark, and he breathed a sigh of relief. He felt sure Mr Wilson had been hiding out. The only question was. Who from? The law, or the lawless?

He picked up the phone and rang Maurice. "Yeah?"

"So your little bird has flown the coop."

"What you talking about, Mark?"

"Mr Wilson. He left today without a murmur."

Maurice obviously didn't know and was caught off guard.

"What?" he said. "Who came for him?"

"The same limo that brought him."

Maurice's agitation was unmistakable. "You sure?"

"I'm sure."

Maurice persisted. "So it was quiet and orderly?"

"Like a funeral," Mark said.

There was silence for a moment. Then Maurice said, "That's OK then."

"Who was he running from?" Mark asked.

"Best you don't know."

But he didn't deny the running, and Mark realised he could have been perilously close to something very nasty.

"Well, don't forget I stuck my neck out for you, Maurice," he said. HE might want the next favour himself.

The next day Edward appeared in Mark's office. He didn't look happy as he sat down.

Mark guessed he couldn't be bringing good news. "What is it, Edward?"

He shifted in his chair uneasily. "Janet has asked me to do a monthly report on our finances."

Mark got a little cross. "Janet is an innocent with finance, you know that, Edward. Just generalise, and if she asks for details give her something by word of mouth."

Edward still looked unhappy.

"Something wrong with that?" Mark asked.

"Well, I might have to compromise myself."

"If you have to compromise yourself, bloody well do it!" Mark shouted. "I'm paying your salary. And I've already given you a generous upgrade."

"She could always bring in another accountant to check. Where would I be then?"

Mark strove hard to keep his temper. "If you do your job properly she won't think about anybody else." He gave Edward a venomous stare. "Convince her!"

As he spoke, the penny dropped and Mark realised what Edward was after, but was too frightened to ask.

He said brutally. "All right, Edward. How much?"

"Well, I do think my risk should be compensated."

"For Christ's sake!" Mark said. "How much?" His face was tight but composed.

"How about another five per cent?"

Less than Mark had anticipated. "You've got it," he growled. "But," and he stabbed a finger at him, "From now on you're MY man and my protector against Janet if necessary. Is that clear?"

"Crystal!"

He left, and Mark stared at his retreating back. If he let him down he'd kick his arse out quickly, a minute's notice, and replace him with someone more friendly. He also wouldn't hesitate to warn him what was good for his health. Maurices boys would see to that.

Mark sat back and drew a breath of relief, but the next day he had another problem brewing a real beauty.

He had a phone call from Alec Donovan, the private eye. "Could I come up and see you?" he asked.

"Come up when you like," Mark said. He wasn't very interested.

"Better I see you at home," Alec said.

Alarm bells started to ring in Mark's head; this had to be personal.

"Is it urgent?"

"At your convenience."

Alec knew very well Mark wouldn't delay. He'd want to know what he was up against. Or who'd caught up with him.

But he was wrong.

A further two weeks elapsed, and Alec rang again. "I'm still waiting to see you," he said.

"You said at my convenience," Mark said.

Jesus! He's cool, Alec thought. "Well how about this week?"

Mark grudgingly agreed on Thursday, around six, and Alec turned up almost on the dot. He was carrying a briefcase.

They sat in Mark's lounge. "So, what is it, Alec?" Mark asked.

"I'm afraid you won't like what I have to say," Alec said, "But hear me out. You will quickly see the reason."

Mark was mystified. "Go on."

"You will no doubt remember that when your father was killed your mother Helen was very dissatisfied with the outcome of the police investigation."

Mark interrupted. "It was understandable."

"Of course. But what you don't know is she engaged me to investigate the matter, expense and time no hindrance."

Mark was now tuned in but he still felt secure. The police had found nothing, and a lot of time had passed.

"But the police had an enquiry," he said.

"Not an enquiry," Alec said smoothly. "They accepted the evidence that was presented to them. But Helen was positive your father could not have been killed in the way it was described, that he was driving without lights. She said that was something he would never even consider."

Mark was getting impatient. "Human beings aren't always consistent, are they?"

"Your mother was absolutely adamant on this point."

Mark shrugged. "So?"

"I have been examining the matter and finding the people who were concerned in the accident. It took a long time, particularly with a very important witness. The lorry driver."

"You found him?" Mark was amazed.

"I found him, and I found a surprising answer."

"Yes?"

"His articulated vehicle was not carrying a load, nor was it headed back to its depot."

"What did the driver say?"

"Said he was going to another depot which was over two hundred miles away. It didn't make sense. His home depot was five miles away and he was headed away from it."

Alec looked at Mark and saw he had his full attention.

"I asked him about his itinerary for the day. He didn't have one. So here is the peculiar position: a large artic was on the road without a load or destination, going the wrong way, and without instructions from his office."

So what is your conclusion?"

"He was on a mission. Your father was his mission."

Mark was scathing. "That's a huge jump of imagination, Alec. A fairy tale. Where is the evidence?"

Alec gave Mark another shock.

"I investigated the office where the artic was housed and I spoke to an office girl who turned up her customers' file. It turns out the artic had been hired by a Vincent Adams for the precise time it left to meet your father's car."

Mark was now alarmed and on his guard. "Vincent Adams?" He pretended surprise. "I believe he was killed."

"Yes," Alec said, "And guess what? Another motor accident."

"One of thousands. You don't choose when you die."

Alec ignored Mark's comment. "I managed to track back on Vincent Adams quite easily. He seemed to be a sort of freelance, but at the time he was operating for a national building outfit who were very anxious to get their hands on your land."

Alec gave Mark a glance. "The directors confirmed he was acting for them in trying to obtain your land and that he was in negotiations with you personally."

Mark stared back at Alec. "I don't deny it. Business is business. Nothing wrong with that whatsoever. But the pictures you are painting are out of all reality."

"What we have is a series of coincidences that all lead to you and could be investigated much more fully," Alec argued. "I may say the police would love the obvious motive. To usurp your father and take over the multi-million business." His tone became ominous and he tapped his briefcase. "I have here all sorts of evidence and statements which back me up. Do you wish to examine them?"

He waited but Mark merely shook his head.

He continued accusingly, "I also feel certain that the directors who instructed Adams could provide a lot more detail, if pressed."

"No reason why not." Mark put on a coolness he didn't feel.

Then Alec delivered another broadside to Mark. "I happen to know he was in strong competition at the time with a David Summers who eventually got the contract. Wasn't that good timing?"

Mark now felt uneasy, and he'd heard enough. "Why have you come here?" he demanded. "If you are so confident of your allegations why don't you go the police?"

He sneered. "Perhaps they don't believe in fairy tales any more than I do."

Alec leaned a bit nearer and said with some menace, "Listen up, Mark! I have enough circumstantial evidence to merit a police enquiry, and I'm confident the CPS would run with it. Don't you forget circumstantial evidence often convicts people."

Mark became deliberately derisive. "So it's how much is it? As the yanks say, a shakedown." He waved a finger, "You won't get a penny out of me."

Alec bridled. "You're on the wrong track, Mark. I'm working for your mother, and she pays me plenty. If it wasn't for her my files would be on a police desk now."

He looked at Mark with scorn. "Do you think she could survive another shock worse than her husband's death? That her son had his father killed? She is the only reason I'm not presenting my findings to the police," he concluded.

Mark felt secure again. "You must do what you think best. So will I."

"I'll leave you with my main reason for coming here, which is to give you a warning," Alec said. "I am convinced you are responsible for two deaths and if anything should happen to anyone else who gets in your way, or your family, I will immediately go to the police."

Mark's voice shot up. "What!" he yelled, "Do you think I would kill my own mother?"

"Your father wasn't very safe, was he?"

"Get real, Alec!" Mark said callously, " Big business is littered with corpses."

Alec curled his lip. "YOUR business maybe. Not mine."

He threw in another shot. "From now on you'd better start walking on eggshells."

Mark didn't reply, and Alec said, "I shall report to your mother that I have no reason to think your father's death was not accidental." He glared at him. "But don't forget this is for now. It can change."

Mark said roughly, "Alec, let me remind you none of your allegations can be proved. They are suspicions." He challenged him, "Did the driver of the artic admit he deliberately killed my father?"

"Of course not. But don't forget, a jury could decide different."

"And the moon is made of green cheese," Mark mocked.

Alec was cross but not surprised with Mark's reactions.

"A last thought, Mark," he said. "I'm sure I could be disposed of quite easily, but be warned, then your problems would start, not end, because my records would go to the police."

He got up, collected his briefcase, and stalked out.

Mark didn't believe Alec had arranged for his records to go to the police if he became a casualty. He reckoned that was a bluff, and he had no intention of taking the slightest notice of his threat. But he certainly intended to protect himself.

For hours afterwards he turned things over in his mind and finally crystallised his thoughts.

Just let Alec try and start something! He'd soon find out how influence worked, and how money could alter the scene, twist people's tongues. Give them bad memories. Unable to find records.

And if that failed there was always Maurice to deliver the knockout blow. Perhaps another accident.

Mark gave a cynical grin. It was easier each time.

His confidence flowed back, and he cleared his mind.

Immediately, golden girl Leanne jumped into his thoughts. Yes, an evening with her would be just right.

He fished out his mobile.

FIN